The Gender Divide

by

David Boultbee

Shadowmere Publishing

Colonial Beach, VA

The Gender Divide

Shadowmere Publishing /by arrangement with the author
Paperback First Edition Printing/September 2007

Reviews

Chapter One

He sat there waiting patiently. Despite all the practice that he'd had it still wasn't easy. He swept the room with a practiced gaze, one calculated to take in the entire area. It was full of understated luxury. The largest single piece of blood-wood that he had ever seen fronted the receptionist's area. The blood-red color and silky smooth texture was fitting in the head office of Delphi Inc., the world's largest biotech company. The paintings on the wall looked real, but he had been here long enough to see them cycle through several images. Based on the high resolution and verisimilitude of the images, he knew the display was one of the latest organic LED panels or Olds. Flexible Olds wrapped the frame as well, allowing it to change to suit the image displayed. The customized frames and the high quality images were rare, a sign of Delphi's prestige. Overall, the whole room exuded a distinct yet subtle air of wealth and power.

Of course that wasn't what interested him. It was important to notice the general environment, but more important to him was the security layout, and he'd had more than enough time to analyze it. The standard security sensors were right where he expected them to be and that still puzzled him. The circumstances leading up to his interview pointed to problems, but this was bordering on the ridiculous. Although there was a possibility they had hidden the real security system, he doubted it. Admittedly, he hadn't had the opportunity to sweep the room as well as he would have liked, so he couldn't rule it out completely. However he had been working with bleeding edge security systems for most of his official life, which gave him an edge. Given Delphi's recent rumored security breach, it was unlikely they would have a system that he wouldn't be able to detect. If he had been able to bring his equipment with him, he would have been able to say so with complete certainty, but for this, his own internal scans were more than enough.

Based on the layout of the room and what he had been able to detect, he was able to narrow it down to only a few possible installations. He had passed close enough to two probable locations, narrowing the alternatives still further. There was only one real choice and it was surprising to say the least. He snorted mentally. If their security was this loose, then if the job didn't pan out, he could always break into the place to get what he wanted.

He sighed as he recognized the direction his thoughts were turning. It never failed with him. He'd had dozens of job interviews in his lifetime, and he always got more and more nervous the further the interview progressed. It didn't help that he had never had so much riding on an interview, and he was beginning to second and third guess himself. Of course, the main weakness against him was his gender. There was simply no way his experience could match any of the other candidates, all of whom were female. Not in years at least. What he did have to counter that was his experience with modern security systems.

He stopped cataloging all of his flaws and virtues and forced his thoughts in another direction. He checked the time, resisting the automatic urge to look at his watch. His neural feed provided instant access to Pubnets, but he had developed the habit of wearing a watch. It started as protective camouflage to avoid flaunting his neural linkage. Not that he needed to check the time to be aware that only five more minutes had passed. He had already been kept waiting for more than two hours. He knew that she was playing a little game with him by making him wait but that was okay—he was playing it right back at her. He had been sitting there patiently, not reading or fidgeting. He was so quiet and still that most people had come and gone without noticing him. The ones who did notice him would assume that he wasn't paying much attention to what was going on. In reality, he had been tracking every single detail and had been applying his well-honed intellect to make sense of it all.

As if that was the cue that she had been waiting for, Olivia Morgan, CEO of Delphi Inc., finally came out of her office. Despite being a true Californian, Olivia looked more like she belonged out east in New York. She was tall—six foot two—and leggy, with brunette hair so dark that it almost seemed black sometimes. His fondest memories were of that hair loose, cascading over her shoulders and framing her face. At the moment she had her hair piled high atop her head, held there in a tight bun by two dark sticks. If she recognized him there was no outward sign of it.

"Mr. Peters. Sorry to keep you waiting."

"Not at all," he answered, rising smoothly, "and please, call me Ryan."

She nodded, accepting the courtesy as her due. "Please, walk with me. I had intended to have a discussion with you first in my office, but I'm already running way behind schedule. I'm preparing for the board meeting later today, so we can chat on my way to the boardroom. It will also give me the opportunity to show you around the place."

She didn't give him any time to respond but immediately began walking away, assuming he would follow. For a moment he was tempted not to, but this was too critical a juncture for him to mess it up on a whim. He hurried to catch up, as her long strides outdistanced him and he finally caught up with her at the drop shaft. She glanced over at him as they arrived and somehow he knew that he had passed another test.

"Executive Level," she said, and after a moment the drop computer beeped, signaling that it had recognized the destination and verified that Olivia had access to that level. "So," she said as they began to rise, seemingly floating in midair, "tell me a little about yourself."

He started into the standard spiel about his job history and qualifications, but she cut him off. "I'm not interested in your curriculum vitae. You wouldn't have made it this far if you were not qualified. Tell me a little about your life. What interests you, do you have any hobbies, a family, that sort of thing."

He smiled humorlessly. "Well there's not that much to tell. The only family that I have is my aunt on my father's side. I'm not currently involved with anyone, partially from choice, and partially because I'm not 'hunky' enough to be someone's 'boy-toy'. Ditto for marriage—I don't have much to recommend me to women who could have their pick of any guy. At the moment, my job is everything to me. I need to spend all my time at it, otherwise I won't be able to keep up. Even at that, it's hard to prove that I'm as capable as a woman, particularly one that is two or three times my age."

"So prove it to me." They had reached the executive level by this time and she walked over to the nearest meeting room. Accessing the whiteboard, she pulled up a diagram of her office and the reception area.

"Talk to me about my security."

Ryan smiled briefly. It was all part of the game. He stepped up to the whiteboard without hesitation, and with quick taps of his index finger he marked the security points. He paused for a moment in concentration, as he used his neural feed to have the whiteboard show the probable make and model of the installation. Seconds later the info appeared.

Olivia studied the layout that he had diagrammed and then looked at him. "Are you guessing?"

Ryan smiled confidently and looked directly at her. "Am I right?" he countered boldly, and after a moment she nodded. "Then I'm not guessing, am I?" He thought that she suppressed a quick grin at his self-assurance, but he couldn't be sure.

"So, what do you think?" She gazed at him coolly, almost daring him to speak his mind.

"Frankly, your security system has several weaknesses. I don't know how much is real and how much you staged for my benefit, but regardless, I noticed several problems."

"Such as?"

She might have been discussing the weather and not the security layout for a multi-billion dollar company, and he had to admire her. He couldn't tell from her reaction whether she wasn't upset because she had already made up her mind about him or because she accepted his professionalism. After a moment, he decided that it didn't matter.

"Your security system is seriously out-of-date. Even at that, you could use it more effectively. A security system should free up time to allow security staff to focus on the exceptions and important areas. I'm not a fan of this system, especially since the units get out of tune easily. This doesn't affect their performance, per se, as it still provides the coverage needed. Unfortunately, the out-of-tune units emit an annoying high-pitched whine. That's how I was able to detect the units in your reception area. I was able to hear the whine for two of the units. As for the third, there are only a few possible layouts that would work for that system in that space. I made an educated guess by watching people as they entered your office."

Her raised eyebrow was the only acknowledgment that he was admitting he had been guessing when he diagrammed the layout earlier, but it was enough for him to continue.

"The whine is below the normal range of human hearing, but it is still detectable enough to irritate people without them understanding why. Visitors walked straight towards your office, but staff members detoured slightly to avoid the wall with the unit."

"Impressive."

"I'm only getting started. While I could have guessed who was a visitor and who was a staff member, I didn't have to. Each person who comes to see you checks in with the receptionist. I was able to hear their discussions, many of which were confidential, by the way. I don't know if your reception desk doesn't have a hush field or if your receptionist wasn't using it. Either way, it's a major oversight."

"That may be true, but most people who come to see me are not enhanced."

"True," he admitted, "but they don't have to be. A simple electronic device could easily pick up those sounds." He held up his left wrist, forestalling her objections. "I know that you scan all visitors, but something as small as a watch could easily hide such a device.

"The next point that struck me related to the drop computer. It took both of us to the executive level without querying who I was or needing additional authorization. Obviously, my badge wouldn't allow me to do that on my own, but it's possible that I could be forcing you to take me there. There should be a security code or check, before you permit unauthorized people into a secure area.

"That's just a sample of some of the problems that I detected. Given that I've only been here for a few hours, and seen a fraction of the grounds, it would surprise me if there weren't more." He stopped talking and she looked at him briefly, as if checking to see if he had finished.

"Very impressive," she repeated and this time he could tell that she meant it. "So it sounds like you have a negative view of marriage."

"Not really," he answered, adjusting to the non sequitur, "just realistic. Given that women live three or four times as long as men, it makes a successful marriage that much more difficult. Women are by nature more emotionally mature than men, a factor only increased by the experience and wisdom that comes with age. Therefore, the best time for men and women to marry is when they are similar in age or if the men are slightly older. There are very few women strong enough to be able to do that, knowing that they will outlive their spouse. It's a difficult concept to grapple with and the reality is even harder. As women get older, their remaining life expectancies converge with those of men. By that time, most women have lived two or three times as long as the man has. This gives women a completely different frame of reference, not to mention how living that long alters what they expect from a relationship, and what they are willing to put up with. Women are used to being in control and they won't tolerate the idiosyncrasies that most couples have to deal with on a daily basis."

He paused and shrugged. "It's not insurmountable. People in love have been overcoming even more difficult barriers since Adam and Eve. It does, however, make it more challenging."

He hesitated briefly again, wondering whether to risk mentioning his past with her, and then decided that it was better to do it now rather than later.

"It must have been different for my father. Back then, the artificial embryogenesis machine was relatively new. Only a few of the first generation of men born using the AEM had reached legal age yet and the ratio of women to eligible men was still almost five to one. It was easy for men to get their physical needs satisfied. Even marriage was a possibility. That's all changed now. Increased use of the AEM has swung the ratio the other way. Now men outnumber women two to one and women can afford to be picky. After all, they can take the time to be sure."

"I used to know your father, did you know that?"

He smiled mentally as she acknowledged the past they had once shared. It seemed like he wasn't the only one who remembered their relationship.

"No, I didn't." He looked at her curiously. "This must be confusing for you, my having the same name. My dad died shortly after I was born but he wanted me to take his name. His sister took me in and raised me. She didn't talk about my dad very much. I think she found it confusing, as well. She wasn't all that happy that he had used an AEM for me. She feels that it's degrading to force men to use this machine if they want a son. She also feels that it was unfair of him to bring me into the world."

"What do you think?" she asked softly and he shrugged again.

"Well, I'm here now and I happen to like it that way, so I have no complaints. And realistically it was the only way to address the demographic imbalance. After all, what woman wants to have a son only to know that she's going to outlive him? As a result, most women choose to have daughters, which given the difference in life expectancies, only aggravated the problem. The AEM gave men the chance to take control of their own reproduction and have a son. Mind you, there are many men who would still prefer a daughter. It's unfortunate the regulations surrounding AEMs only allow their use for male embryos."

She looked at him oddly, but just then the whiteboard cleared and the face of the receptionist appeared.

"Excuse me ma'am, but Brooke asked me to remind you of your meeting."

"Thank you, Charles. Would you mind asking someone in security to come and escort Mr. Peters out?" She turned to Ryan. "I have to go. Someone will be along shortly and I will be in touch with you, one way or another."

He nodded. "Thank you for the opportunity. It was a pleasure meeting you." He shook her hand and a moment later she was gone. He resisted the urge to wipe his brow, knowing that he was still under surveillance. He was certain that he had fooled her, but it had been tough. He hadn't expected all the old feelings to be so strong, but the sight of her brought them back in a rush. He forced his attention back to the present and a moment later a security guard appeared. The woman was surprisingly professional. She escorted him from the building, answering all his questions with the polite, but standard response of, 'I wouldn't know about that sir.' She also displayed a remarkable lack of curiosity about the man who could potentially be her boss' boss. He hoped that it was just self-control rather than indifference. Self-control he could work with. Indifference was a little harder. He thanked her once they reached the waiting limo. He noticed that she waited until the limo had lifted off the ground and was moving before leaving, and his hopes rose. Perhaps it was the self-control of professionalism and not the indifference of apathy. If that were the case, then at least he would have something to work with. Assuming he was hired that is. He sat back and activated the privacy shield.

Assured of his privacy at last, he buried his face in his hands and groaned. The momentum of the interview and the need to present a confident façade had kept his thoughts occupied. He dropped the façade and started to shake. He had known what he was getting into, but he thought that he could handle it. Now he wasn't so sure. Unfortunately, he didn't have a choice. This opportunity had come at an awkward time, but he couldn't afford to miss it. He had spent most of his second life developing the skills for this position, only the opening had occurred earlier than expected. He was almost too young for such a senior role, even for a male. The bitter corollary was that in less than a decade he would be too old for such a position.

In the end, it was determined that he had enough experience and his handlers had decided to risk it. They were aware of the relationship that Ryan had had with Olivia—it was why he was here after all—but they had reasoned that it had only been a brief six-month affair. Six months was nothing in the face of Olivia's eighty plus years of experience, not to mention that it had all happened over forty years ago. All of that made perfect sense, but since when did love have to make sense?

He had no idea what her feelings were, but for him it was like those forty years had never happened, and just being in her presence again was like a knife in his heart. That was why he had referred to his past. He had to know if she at least remembered him and plainly she had.

Unfortunately, he still had to figure out if that was a good thing or not.

* * *

Olivia collapsed in her chair and waited for Brooke, who had been monitoring the interview from the security center. Knowing it would take Brooke a few minutes to arrive, Olivia hoped she would be able to hold herself together for that long. She thought she had known what she was getting into, but she had been fooling herself. She had played the same waiting game with all the applicants, but with them it had all been part of the process. With Ryan, she suddenly felt like the tables had been turned and it had taken all of her willpower to make herself go out and meet him.

She had met with all the applicants in her office briefly, before putting them to the test, but she knew she wouldn't be able to do that with Ryan. Instinctively, she felt if she could just keep moving she would be able to retain control. She had managed for a while, and then to her horror, she heard herself asking him personal questions, about marriage, and about his father. She recognized Brooke's hand behind the interruption from the receptionist. She was glad that it was Brooke who had been monitoring them, and not one of the regular security personnel. She had barely managed to keep it together long enough to make it back to her office.

Just recalling the interview made her hands shake, and she held them up in front of her as a more detached part of her watched them tremble. Her office door hissed open and Brooke strolled in.

Brooke took in the sight of Olivia's trembling hands and shook her head. "That bad?" she asked sympathetically and Olivia nodded.

"Worse," Olivia said and Brooke grimaced. "I know that you warned me, but the physical resemblance caught me off guard. He looked exactly like the Ryan I knew forty years ago and it threw me for a loop. I mean, I expected a certain degree of resemblance, something generational, but he looked exactly like his father and I mean exactly."

She looked up at Brooke, as a silent tear ran down her cheek. She wiped her face angrily, ashamed somehow.

"Ryan, the Ryan that I knew, was the first and only man that I've ever loved. I know that's irrational, that it was just a brief affair that happened decades ago, but I was seriously considering marrying him. In the end, I just couldn't face the prospect of losing him. And so I left him. I thought that if I controlled the circumstances under which we parted that it would make me feel better." She laughed bitterly. "The truth is I was just lying to myself. I didn't even tell him why, I just couldn't. I knew if I told him why, he would make all of my fears disappear, and that scared me even more, that someone could exert that degree of control over me. And now here he is again, like a ghost from my past, looking exactly like he did forty years ago."

Olivia was grateful that Brooke knew enough to just listen quietly as she expressed herself, that Brooke could recognize her need for a cathartic release. Brooke already knew all of this. It was why they were such good friends. They were friends before the breakup, but afterwards, they became inseparable. She was also glad Brooke had the perspicacity not to bring up what she wasn't saying, about how Olivia's mother mishandled a similar predicament. While Olivia didn't exactly deny the impact of her mother's suicide, she also didn't like to talk about it.

"Listen to me. I'm eighty years old. I'm the CEO of the world's largest biotech company. I've got an admittedly intimidating vocabulary, and I've just said the word 'exactly' four times in less than a minute." Olivia pressed her hands to her head and groaned. "I've also got a headache that could kill a small animal." Her eyes watered and she fought to keep from crying again. "God, talk about irrational."

"Stop beating yourself up," Brooke said as she smiled at Olivia and handed her a Kleenex. "You can't help what you feel. You can use it sometimes, but that's about it."

Olivia dabbed at her eyes with the tissue as Brooke turned away to give her a moment of privacy. She folded the tissue and blew her nose, a large unladylike honk, and studied Brooke. In almost every way she and Brooke were complete opposites. She was unusually tall and Brooke was short. She was quiet and conservative where Brooke was outgoing and flamboyant. At the moment, she and Brooke had the same hair color, but given how often

Brooke changed hair color, that was only a temporary coincidence. It was hard to believe that someone so outrageous could be a Senior VP of Human Resources, but Brooke excelled at her job and was careful to keep her personal life just that.

She cleared her throat and Brooke turned back to her with a smile. She was holding a glass of water and two pain relief pills. Olivia eyed them hesitantly. It was ironic—and a private secret—that the head of the world's largest biotech company was reluctant to take her own products. The pounding in her head made the decision for her, and she gulped down the pills. Within seconds she began to feel better as the biological nanites swept through her bloodstream, multiplying as they scavenged waste products, and diminishing as they dispensed themselves in the form of relief to swollen pain nerves.

She closed her eyes as her headache disappeared and she began to relax. Even as she did, she had to admire the elegant design of the pills. They had a limited supply of reaction mass, and their success depended on being able to find waste products to allow the reaction to continue. The euphoric feeling that they produced made them highly addictive, or would have, but since they cleared out waste products so effectively, the feeling produced by subsequent doses was substantially lessened. Even at that she knew of people who took them daily. She supposed that she should be grateful, since it generated substantial profits, but the quasi-addictive nature of the pills made her uncomfortable.

A minute later she felt like a new person and she smiled gratefully at Brooke.

"Thanks."

"No problem. I did warn you that it would be weird. Of course, you would be a lot better prepared for this, in more ways than one, if you'd taken my advice and dated more often during the last forty years."

"I know you did, and for the first time I'm actually thinking that your advice in that regard had merit."

Brooke's eyebrows shot up in surprise. She blinked and then grinned at her friend.

"Wow, you must be really rattled to say that," she teased and her grin just broadened when Olivia glared at her. After a moment Olivia relented, grinning sheepishly back at her.

"Okay, I guess I deserved that."

"That you did. Mind you, I can understand your reluctance to date someone else. I didn't meet Ryan's dad when you guys were dating, but if Ryan looks like him then all I can say is wow. That killer body and tight buns

9

make quite a package, and even though he's serious, it's somehow appealing. There's also that military style brush cut that he's sporting. I usually prefer guys with long hair that I can run my fingers through, but this look works for him. Maybe it's how the dark brown color brings out the blue in his eyes."

"That's really helping me, thanks."

Brooke grinned again. "Hey, what are friends for?" After a moment she cleared her throat, wisely turning the conversation to business before she irritated Olivia. "So, what did you think?"

Olivia glanced at her and shook her head. "No, you tell me what you thought first. I'm afraid that I won't be objective."

Brooke gave her a penetrating stare. "Are you sure that you'd be okay with him working here? After all, there's no point to this if you won't be comfortable working with him."

Olivia thought about it for a moment. "Yes, I believe so," she finally responded. "I think that it was just the shock of seeing him for the first time. Besides, he's not his father, so it's my problem, not his." She grinned as Brooke started to frown at her. "I know, I know, that doesn't make it any less of a problem, but I honestly think I can deal with it."

Brooke leaned over and gave her a quick hug. It was the kind of hug that men usually misunderstood. There was a lot of talk of lesbianism, due to the constantly shifting demographic ratios, and Olivia had to admit there was a great deal of truth to it. Women turned to one another for emotional and spiritual comfort naturally, and this was even more true now given the age and experience differential that existed between men and women. From there, it was only a small step to physical intimacy. However, that did not mean that every woman was a lesbian, or that every little touch or gesture meant more than it did. Most men read too much into such small gestures; she suspected that Ryan wouldn't. The thought startled her and she missed what Brooke was saying.

"Sorry, I tuned out there for a moment. What were you saying?"

Brooke smiled and raised an eyebrow, causing Olivia to blush.

"Stop that. I was just thinking about—stuff," she finished weakly and Brooke nodded knowingly.

"I was just saying that you're not going to like what I have to say," she repeated, and now it was Olivia's turn to raise a questioning eyebrow.

"He's good, very good."

Olivia smiled. "Do I sense a bit of reluctance in that admission?"

"Maybe just a bit. I hadn't realized it until now, but I guess I am biased towards females." She paused and shook her head. "That's a terrible thing for a Senior VP of Human Resources to realize, and if nothing else I'm grateful to him for that. I guess it's just because females tend to be more thorough, not to mention more mature and self-assured. That's why it surprised me how confident and competent Ryan was. He behaved more like a man twice his age. Maybe it's his aunt's influence, but he's very observant and he carries himself well. Self-assured and confident but not cocky. He also knows what he's talking about. I've been doing an okay job filling in for you, but from what he said, we've been slipping badly and have been for years."

Olivia snorted in bitter amusement. "Well, if there were any doubts that a woman could be lazy and deceitful, Christina dispels them nicely."

"You can say that again. Maybe she could get a job as a poster girl for slothfulness." They both laughed and then Brooke sobered. "There's still a part of me that feels sorry for her. After all, she worked for Delphi her entire life, starting as a guard almost a century ago, and working her way up to VP of Security. This is all she knows and now there's no way she's going to get a job in security, not after you told our suppliers that we would stop dealing with them if they hired her, or knowingly worked with a company that did."

"Yes, well, her laxness cost us over a billion dollars, some of which I'm sure went to line her own pockets. Given the reaming I got from the Board of Directors, fully justifiable I might add, being charitable was not my first inclination."

Brooke cleared her throat cautiously and then continued. "Getting back to the topic at hand, he caught everything that most of the others did, and more. There is only one woman candidate who matched his performance and quite frankly she scared me a little."

Olivia frowned as she considered that. "Hmm," she said thoughtfully.

"Hmm, what?"

"I wonder if women are becoming so confident that they'll get the job that they aren't putting the same effort into it. Someone once said that if the Devil were to replace God, he'd have to assume the attributes of Divinity."

"What on earth are you talking about?" Brooke asked with a laugh.

"I just mean that women have replaced men as the top of the food chain. Now men are stuck under the glass ceiling and we're the ones with the lucrative careers and high-paying jobs."

"Whatever," Brooke replied. "You're the history buff, not me."

"Please, I'd hardly consider myself to be a history buff. It's actually very topical and a number of articles and opinion columns have been written about it. I used to dismiss them out of hand but now I wonder if they've struck on something." She looked thoughtful and Brooke waited patiently, comfortable with her idiosyncrasies.

Just then a soft chime sounded and the Monet painting hanging on the far wall shifted to reveal Charles.

"Sorry for the interruption, but the Board meeting starts in ten minutes, Ma'am."

"Thank you, Charles. Say Charles, what did you think of Ryan Peters?"

"Ma'am?"

"I'd like to know your thoughts and observations. You interacted with him, and technically, you spent more time with him than I did."

"I liked him. He seemed capable. You've played this waiting game on several candidates and he was the most patient of the lot. He didn't fuss or fidget, and he was polite but not distant." He shrugged. "I don't know if that's what you are looking for."

"That's perfect. Thank you, Charles. That's all."

The Monet reappeared and Olivia stared at it for a moment. The painting in her office was the same as those in the reception area. Like those, the image it displayed changed frequently, selecting from a number of different artists and their works. Olivia had always been partial to Monet, so his works appeared more often. This particular painting was entitled 'Nympheas Effet du Soir', and the flexible OLED fabric wrapped around the frame had changed color to frame it perfectly. It was simple and peaceful. It had been painted by a man at a time when men dominated the arts. Most women would see that as a reason to hire a woman rather than a man, as though someone somewhere was keeping score over the years. Olivia considered how it must have felt to be a female Renaissance artist, and how hard it must have been to succeed in a male-dominated world. Now women dominated most fields and it was the men that were struggling to succeed.

Olivia recalled how much she had hurt Ryan—her Ryan—years ago. She had been carrying that guilt around with her for a long time. Maybe this was finally the time to assuage it. She couldn't do anything for her Ryan, but she could give his son a chance.

"All right, get in touch with him and let him know the job is his if he wants it." Brooke's only comment was to arch an eyebrow. "Just do it. We'll talk later. I've got to run or I'll keep the entire Board waiting for me."

"Okay, see you at the fitness center later?"

"You bet." Olivia grinned as she left the office. She felt as if a weight had been lifted off her shoulders. Even the impending Board meeting couldn't dampen her spirits.

Chapter Two

A month later, Olivia yawned and rubbed her eyes as she left the office and headed over to the Medical building. She didn't need to worry about anyone catching her in the act—it was well after midnight, and anybody with even a shred of common sense had gone home long ago. Just because Olivia was still here didn't mean she lacked common sense. Unfortunately, prudence trumped common sense—at least it did for her. There was a shareholder's meeting tomorrow—make that today, she amended wryly—and she had long ago developed the habit of working late the night before to ensure that she was as well prepared as possible.

Despite her exhaustion, the mild night air and the walk refreshed her. She strolled along, enjoying the evening and the solitude. She turned a corner and corrected herself as she saw a security guard doing rounds. It seemed like not everyone had gone home. She smiled at the guard, who nodded at her respectfully. The new security measures that Ryan had implemented had eliminated the need for a guard doing rounds. Despite that, he still insisted on having the guards do a physical patrol. He maintained that security systems should help people do their jobs, not replace them. What he had changed was the method of doing patrols. Rather than following a fixed set of rounds, a program selected them randomly from a pre-designed group covering the entire grounds.

Thinking of Ryan made her smile as she recalled some of her direct reports meetings. Ryan was the only male in the entire group, but if that bothered him in the slightest he hadn't let it show. He also hadn't let their attitudes or behaviors affect him. Olivia wouldn't tolerate any visible discrimination from anyone in the company, let alone any of her direct reports. However, as Brooke was fond of saying, there's discrimination and then there's discrimination. Most of it was the traditional hazing that happens to anyone new, but Olivia knew there were more than a few comments about his looks, and what he must have done to get the job. Nobody was foolish enough to make those kinds of comments in front of her or Brooke, but Brooke had her own sources of gossip.

Olivia had no intention of interfering, and she hadn't had to. Most of her staff took their cues from her and Brooke, as it was common knowledge how close they were. The rest of them usually lined up behind one of the other two Senior VPs, either Gabriella Cole, the Senior VP for Research, or Nicole West, the Senior VP for Information Technology. There weren't many people who knew that Olivia, Brooke, and Nicole formed an unofficial triumvirate that Olivia relied upon to guide her when making major decisions. Nicole's experience and seniority outweighed Olivia's and Brooke's combined; despite that, Olivia had always felt comfortable around her. Olivia knew that she could rely on Nicole for support once Nicole had agreed to give it, and that meant a great deal to Olivia.

Gabriella didn't have the same degree of seniority, but aside from that she always made Olivia a touch nervous. However, Olivia couldn't fault her performance, and in an area like Research that was critical. There had been rumors of gender discrimination and sexual harassment throughout the department, but they were always just that—rumors. None of the rumors involved Gabriella directly, although Olivia was well aware of the 'tone from the top' principle. Admittedly, it was odd not to find one single male in the upper levels of Research, considering how many men worked in the smaller labs doing basic research, but with most of the senior researchers well over a century old, Olivia had to agree it made sense. Still, she had never felt comfortable around Gabriella. That unease kept them from interacting on anything other than a professional level.

Despite the rumors of gender discrimination, Gabriella was surprisingly neutral about Ryan's presence on the team. Lacking a rallying point, most of the harassment and discrimination died a natural death. Ryan's competence and maturity were no small factors either. Although there were reports of him being sexualized, he seemed to ignore it. It didn't offend or upset him, but more importantly, at least in Olivia's book, he didn't attempt to capitalize on it. All told he had settled in quickly.

That didn't mean that he wasn't making his presence felt though. On his first day he had come to Olivia with an ambitious plan. He wanted to revamp Delphi's entire security system and integrate it more thoroughly with other systems. Olivia had been pleased to see that he had obviously begun thinking about the job before he had even started working—it showed the dedication and hard work that she expected. She was also painfully aware of the sorry state of the current security system. She had been willing to support him, although his cost estimates had raised her eyebrows. More startling still were his time estimates, so much so that at first she had thought there was a typo in the proposal. Given the losses they had already suffered, she agreed to the funding without hesitation. She hadn't wanted to hold him to the time estimates, but he had insisted and so she relented. She had been afraid that he had bitten off more than he could chew, and at the time she wondered if he was trying to prove himself to her.

She still didn't know the answer to that question, but she had to admit that she had been wrong about him biting off more than he could chew. The project was on track and on budget, and Olivia wished that more of her direct reports were so diligent. Of course, he paid the price for it. Olivia had seen him around at all hours of the day and night, and she couldn't predict when or where she'd see him next. Even as she thought that, she wondered if he was still there. Without conscious volition, she turned around and found herself hurrying after the guard. Surely, the guard would know if Ryan was still at work or not.

* * *

Ryan looked around his office in Security Central with a sense of weary pride. It had taken him over a month to get his department up to his admittedly high standards. He had upset more than one person during that time, and had to fire three of the more senior members of the staff. Because of his gender he expected that few people would take him seriously. He knew that he would have to prove himself to them, something that he was more than willing to do. What he did have a problem with was insubordination.

The incident had happened on the second day, and the only good that had come out of it was that it had scared the rest of the staff enough for them to start listening to him. Admittedly, they were motivated by fear, but that hadn't lasted long. He had proven himself to them by working as hard as they did, usually harder, and by proving that he knew what he was talking about. Security was a twenty-four hour operation at Delphi, and he was around for almost all of them. He had an uncanny knack of showing up whenever an issue arose. He knew all the staff by name—not a difficult trick for someone with neural access—but more importantly he paid attention to what was going on in their lives. Ryan was realistic enough to know that no one left their personal life at home when they came to work, not really. Knowing what was going on in their lives allowed him to work with them more effectively.

It had taken a lot of time to get the cooperation and participation that he demanded, but in the end it was worth it. There had been more than one cynical remark about how much he cared, but in the end most of his staff appreciated his efforts, and as a result they respected him even more. They had seen that he was tough but fair, and consequently they were willing to work with him. Of course there was still room for improvement, but it was a major accomplishment, one made even more so because of his gender.

He looked down at the report on his desk. It was from an independent testing agency that many other firms used to test their security. He had run a baseline the first day that he had started, and had watched with mixed disbelief and amusement at the chaos that had followed. He had scheduled the agency to perform the tests randomly, once or twice a week, and present him with a report. Most of the time, he knew well enough what it would say. The results had been far from perfect, but it was encouraging to see that they were consistently improving.

This report was the result of their eleventh visit and he finally had something to be proud of. On the summary sheet, a box listed all the security breaches, classified by degree of penetration. Each previous report had mocked him with the total incidents. Never mind that they were getting better. Better wasn't best. That was what he expected and what he had gotten at last. There were no security breaches listed and that made all his hard work worthwhile. He attached it to the daily update that he was preparing for the next day. He hadn't shared any of the previous reports with the staff, but this one was different. After all, he hadn't done it all by himself, although at times it had felt that way as he struggled to get his staff involved. In the end, they had worked hard and they deserved to know just how well they had done. Not only that but they deserved a reward.

He thought about it for a moment and then grinned. He had expected this milestone and had already made his mind up about it weeks ago. He saw no reason to change it now. When he first started at Delphi, he had learned that each department had two bonus days, days he could grant to everyone in the department to reward work well done. He would have to explain each day to Olivia in person, but he didn't have a problem with that. Lord knows that his staff deserved it. They knew him well enough now to know that he wasn't trying to buy their loyalty. His total and utter disdain for anyone who had offered his or her loyalty in return for favors was common knowledge by now.

He finished the update and sent it off on a time delay for the next morning, sitting back with a sigh. He didn't have to check his internal clock to know that it was almost midnight. He had been there since six that morning, and his body was doing a fine job of letting him know how late it was. There were times when he felt his real age, and not the age he pretended to be. He knew it was all in his mind. Visibly he looked forty, but that was the result of subtle tricks of clothing and hairstyle. Physically his body was the body of a twenty-year-old, but mentally he was almost eighty, and the strangeness of it all still threw him occasionally.

He accessed his computer, purging the results of the weekly fitness reports from the personnel files of his staff. He had told them at the beginning that they would have this grace period, that he would only be using the information on their fitness reports to find out where potential weaknesses existed and to fix them. Whether that weakness resulted from a lack of training or someone working a shift that didn't suit them, he made whatever changes were necessary. Group training, restructured shifts, he addressed each weakness one by one. Now that he had achieved his goal he no longer needed that information. Everyone was starting with a clean slate now. What they did with it was up to them.

He continued to work away, dealing with all the necessary work spam that any high-level position produced. He also kept close tabs on the incoming feeds into Security Central, sampling them at random. As he did, his weariness fell away like water off a duck's back without his even noticing.

Half an hour later, an automatic alert interrupted him to let him know Olivia was on her way over to Security Central. A month earlier there would have been no way of knowing that, not with the archaic badges that Delphi had employed. Now the security system tracked people's movements automatically and monitored them for patterns. In reality, Security Central was anything but central, location wise at least. It quickly became obvious when anyone headed in that direction. All the tracking and analysis took place in the background, with the system flagging movements that met certain parameters.

The ability to do all that had been one of his first changes, and probably the only change that was visible to everyone in the organization. Nanitic bracelets had replaced the badges and the general response had been good. The bracelets were undetectable visually or tactilely once applied. There were various radio frequency ID tags in use that did the same task, but Ryan felt the nanitic bracelets were worth the price difference for the extra features they provided. They were irremovable and relied on a living person with specific biometric parameters to remain active. They were also easily scanned at a distance by special readers, which Ryan had installed throughout the company and linked into security. It made access much easier for the average employee, similar to RFID tags. Unlike the tags or badges, staff no longer had to worry about remembering them or needing to make sure that they were visible. Access was automatic—to buildings, to offices, even to computers.

He remembered the arguments that he'd built up to convince Nicole West, Delphi's Senior VP of Information Technology, of the benefits. He didn't need to have the computer network tied into the bracelets as it didn't impact security, but he'd seen real advantages from having the two systems merged. Despite the obvious benefits he had expected her to resist any changes, and since he didn't have the seniority to override her, he had been anticipating a real battle. After all he was male, well over two hundred years younger than she was, and had been at Delphi less than a month.

She was also intimidating. She looked like a typical Californian, but in reality she was a Canadian. She was tall, although not as tall as Olivia, with blond hair accented by her lightly tanned skin. Unlike Olivia, she wore her hair down but somehow that didn't make her any more approachable. Her beauty, experience, competence and age combined to make her seem aloof. Her staff adored her, but even they found her reserved. Still, with everything that he had been through, it would take more than that to keep him away.

He approached her with an open mind, clearly listing all the pros and cons of the project, as well as precedents within biotech and other high tech industries. She had made him jump through hoops, but he had gotten the strange feeling that she was playing with him more than anything. Not that he cared, if that was what it took to get the job done. In the end, she had agreed and he was a bit surprised at how well the two of them worked together.

After convincing her, it had been a straightforward implementation. There had initially been some quiet and unofficial grumbling by the employees, but not much. After all, Nicole was one of the most senior employees at Delphi and a Senior VP. It also helped that the incident that had led to his employment was still fresh in everyone's mind. Ryan had expected the unofficial grumbling to last longer than it had, but it hadn't taken long before the convenience of the bracelets had convinced everyone. It had been a real boost to his prestige and he had capitalized on it to the extent possible.

The new bracelets had also been a blessing to his overworked security staff. Security personnel could instantly identify who was a regular staff member and who was a visitor. It cut out a huge amount of administrative time previously spent tracking and issuing new badges every time someone lost one. He had made sure the timesavings had gone right back to enabling them to do the things that made a difference. It meant more time for patrols, more time for training and more bodies available. Overall, the changes and what it allowed them to do thrilled the security staff.

There was a significant temptation to rely on the system, but Ryan knew from experience that it usually wasn't the security system that was fooled—it was the people in charge. It all came down to the human element and he made sure that his staff knew that. That was one reason he insisted on regular patrols. He wanted his staff to be familiar with the grounds, and that wasn't going to happen sitting in an office watching screens.

He frowned mildly as he considered why Olivia would be visiting him so late at night. Apart from the direct reports meetings he had only met with her twice since he started, and he was beginning to wonder if she was avoiding him. He knew, anecdotally at least, that she met with her other direct reports more often. He had occasionally wondered about it, but he had been too busy to give it much thought. He banished the frown and looked up curiously as she entered, shutting his computer down as he did so.

He wondered if she were here to talk to him informally about how much money he had been spending. She had agreed to the program that he had outlined and he had been forthright about the costs involved. She had no problem with it at the time, but he was wondering if the reality of those costs was starting to sink in. Fortunately, he had front-loaded all of his costs just in case. He'd had his budget trimmed in the middle of a project once and he had gotten burned, at least initially, when there was a security breach. Nobody said that he wasn't a quick learner and since then he had ensured that it would never happen again. He still listed the company, a data storage company, on his CV. Massive lawsuits forced it to declare bankruptcy not long after he quit. He used it as an example whenever the issue of funding arose.

"You're working late tonight," Olivia said and as always the rich contralto of her voice sent shivers down his spine. God, how he had missed that voice.

"Just doing my job," he responded automatically and then cursed himself for such a banal response. "I work all hours of the day. It's good for morale and it helps give me a better feel for the place, seeing it at night when it's quiet and dark."

"I know what you mean," she said as she smiled at him. "Mind you, I'm more of a morning person. I find that I do more in the morning. My head is usually clearer, I'm less tired and stressed out, and it's just as quiet. I get in around six and those first two hours are usually my most productive. I jokingly refer to it as working 'undertime' as opposed to working overtime." She laughed at her own joke and then blushed as she realized that he probably knew that she came to work early. "But then I guess that you already knew that."

'Yes, I remember' was what he didn't say, although that was the thought that was running through his mind. "We don't monitor it at that level," was what he said. "That's the common misperception that most people have about security staff. They think that we are watching them night and day. The reality is there are way too many people for us to do that, even if we wanted to. We focus more on patterns and exceptions. Now being who you are, I am slightly more aware of your movements than anyone else's, but only slightly."

"I just wanted to stop by to tell you what a great job I think you are doing."

He couldn't keep his surprise from showing. "Really?"

"Don't sound so surprised," she chided him laughingly. "Not only are you new, but security is a big deal around here. I'd be a fool if I didn't pay attention to what you're doing."

"No, it's not that." He colored as he recalled his earlier uncharitable thoughts. It appeared that time and power hadn't changed the Olivia that he had once known and loved. "I thought you were coming down to speak to me about my budget," he confessed and her eyes twinkled.

"To be honest, my finance VP is a tad upset about how much money you've spent in such a short time." Olivia paused and looked at him seriously. "I told her to tell me when we reached a billion dollars and only then would I become seriously concerned."

Ryan nodded approvingly, pleased both by her praise and her acknowledgment of how important proper security was.

"Now don't go getting carried away. My only intention was to put it in perspective." Olivia looked serious, but his long ago experience with her told him where he should be looking, and all those signs suggested that she was joking with him.

"Don't worry," he laughed, "I've already done most of the damage."

She smiled at his laughter. "It's surprising how well you can read me. There are few people who can, and it usually takes them a while before they get good at it." She paused and cocked her head to look at him appraisingly and he felt a spurt of alarm. "It's strange just how comfortable I am with you."

He shrugged and grinned charmingly at her, caught off guard.

"Perhaps it's because I knew your father," she mused. "Maybe I'm mentally associating you with him and that's why I feel so comfortable."

He seized the opening that she had given him. "You mentioned that during the interview, but we never talked about it." His hope that she wouldn't want to talk about it with him backfired. Whatever had caused her to avoid him for the last month was absent, at least for the moment.

"No, we didn't." She gazed blankly over his shoulder for a moment and he could tell that she was accessing Delphi's Pubnet. "Listen, I know that it's late, but I haven't eaten anything since dinner and I dislike going to bed on an empty stomach. Would you care to join me for a quick bite to eat?"

He hesitated, torn about how to answer her—the No answer that he ought to give, or the Yes answer that he wanted to give. She noticed his momentary hesitation and offered him the out.

"Of course, if you're busy I completely understand." The light in her eyes dimmed as she spoke and he responded before he could think.

"No, that's not it at all," he said, cursing himself for his weakness as he hurried to come up with a believable reason for his delayed response. "I was just trying to figure out if I wanted dinner or breakfast." God, that's weak, he thought, but he sighed in relief as her face brightened again.

"If that's all, I know this great little place that makes a mean breakfast burrito. I've always associated burritos with dinner so for me this bridges the gap."

"Sounds good. Let's go." Now it was his turn to notice her momentary hesitation. "What is it?"

"It's a little embarrassing, but do you have a car? I let the limo service go. It's not fair for them to have to stay up late just for me. Besides, I have a shareholder's meeting this morning, so I was planning on crashing in one of the quiet rooms over in Medical. That's why I was working so late," she explained.

"Ah, well in that case I would be happy to oblige." He gestured for her to follow him as he headed towards the parking garage. As they walked, he thought for a moment and then decided to risk it. "Don't take this the wrong way, but the condo I'm renting is only five minutes away. I have a spare guestroom that you're welcome to use. Not only will you sleep better, but you can shower and freshen up in the morning."

She smiled at him wistfully. "That sounds great but I shouldn't. You're still new here and I wouldn't want to start any rumors. Something like that will wipe out all your hard won credibility."

"Well, the only people that I have to be credible for are you and my staff. And my staff knows me well enough by now so I don't have any concerns in that regard."

"I know. Still, I think it's better to avoid those kinds of situations where we can. Besides, the beds in Medical are actually pretty comfortable and they have showers, too." He smiled at her as she flushed, realizing she had revealed to him just how often she slept in the Medical building.

"Your call," he said, wondering why in hell he was pushing it. He hadn't received any specific instructions for dealing with Olivia, so he had opted to try to keep their relationship at a professional level. He was afraid that he would reveal too much if he got too close to her. All of which made him wonder just what he was doing. He didn't know what he wanted, other than to spend more time with her. And then it hit him. He missed her. He missed spending time with her. He had forgotten just how comfortable he was around her, how much he let his defenses down for her. There was a brief silence as he wrestled with that realization, and then fortunately for his peace of mind, they arrived at his car.

"Here we are." He gestured at the scruffy looking black two-seater about ten feet long. It was an old Mazda Miata and he knew that it didn't look like much. But he'd had the engine rebuilt and had replaced almost all the parts, including the gyroscope, with high performance racing parts. It was a lot smaller than most of the cars they were churning out these days, which was why he had chosen the Miata chassis. It was just big enough to accept the changes that he had made to it, yet still small enough to be highly maneuverable. The lightweight boron-carbon fiber frame would be worthless in a crash, but it allowed him to accelerate faster just about anything else out there. The way he figured it, it was an acceptable trade-off.

He kept his face impassive as Olivia looked at it rather doubtfully. "Oh why not," he heard her mutter and then he grinned as she climbed in awkwardly, trying to prevent her skirt from riding up. He averted his gaze as he slipped gracefully into the driver's seat, thanks to years of practice, and fired it up. The chassis rose gently off the ground and the HUD flashed to life in front of him. He ignored it, since he was also receiving the same information through his neural feed. The ducted propulsion vents swirled the air gently around them as the car moved forward. One of the perks of being a VP was underground parking, but since Ryan was the new kid on the block he got the parking space in the basement. Not that he complained. Hell, he would've preferred parking in one of the open-air covered lots or even the exposed surface lots. At least that way he could get some exercise and fresh air. Unfortunately, it wouldn't have sent the right message, or something like that. He didn't know since he had only asked once. He probably could have pushed it through, but if he had learned anything over the years, it was the value of fitting in. It didn't bother him and so there was no benefit in making it a point of difference.

After a few moments, the car reached the top level and Ryan paused, waiting for the all clear. There was a momentary delay before the guide lights changed to green, as the automated control tower spun up from standby. There wasn't much traffic at midnight and traffic control had powered down automatically. Out of habit Ryan checked his own feeds, before speeding down the rooftop runway and off the edge of the building into Delphi's main traffic lane. Within minutes he merged with a public lane as he followed Olivia's directions and a short while later they arrived.

Now it was Ryan's turn to look dubious. This didn't look like the kind of place where the CEO of the worlds' largest biotech company would eat. California sometimes seemed like one vast highway that ran parallel to the coast, crammed with cities and towns along the way. It was easy to forget there were places in the hills that were substantially less developed. This was one of those places. It was an ancient circa twenty-first century food stand and while it looked well maintained and clean, most people would associate old with dirty. The area was a small oasis of green grass surrounded by mudslide barriers and the brown scrub that dotted the hillside. There were a handful of incredibly well-preserved and brightly painted wooden picnic tables sprinkled around in what seemed like a random fashion. It obviously wasn't as there was something visually appealing about the arrangement. He continued to look around, his mind automatically cataloging security risks even as another part of him noticed the pleasing aesthetics.

Olivia looked over at Ryan as his gaze swept rapidly and appraisingly over the place. Not everyone that she brought here appreciated it and it was a litmus test for her. Normally, the lack of either facial or body expression would have made her nervous, but she was beginning to expect that tight control from him. In a way, she had started to depend on it, since it was something, no matter how small, that set this Ryan apart from his father, the Ryan that she had known. She wondered if that's why she was beginning to feel more comfortable around him because, finally, she had discovered something she could use to separate him from his father in her mind. It would have been easier if he were either older or younger. As fate would have it, he was almost the same age as his father had been when she had known him, and he looked exactly like his father. Not a family resemblance, but an almost identical match.

Part of why Olivia was having such a hard time with it was that she hadn't dated, and so she hadn't experienced this peculiarity firsthand before. The close resemblance was one of the quirks of the artificial embryogenesis machine. Not only was it expected, in fact it was quite common. Unlike sperm donors, there were few ova donors. A woman's ova were simply too precious for them to donate. Almost all women were on Menssation®, the drug that stopped menstrual cycles. It was the lack of a menstrual cycle that accounted for the increased life span of women over men, which made it difficult even finding an ovulating woman. Women only ovulated when they stopped taking Menssation®, something they did when they wanted to have children, and then for the time it took to become pregnant. The odds of finding one willing to give up even a single ovum ran to a whole lot of zeros. As a result artificial ova had been developed.

They were real enough to do the trick, but since they were artificial in nature, their DNA was basic and lacked any of the nucleotides that determined individual hereditary characteristics. That left only the male's DNA available to perform that function. The result was almost like cloning. Olivia suspected it was that feature that appealed to most of the men who used it. It allowed them to have a son who closely resembled them. In fact, the resemblance was often identical, as it was with Ryan. It was the male gender's grasp at an extended life and most women looked down on them for it, since it paled in comparison to a real extended life. Not Olivia. She found it sad that men and women were once again so divided.

The division was the result of an innocuous discovery that had fundamentally changed the world. It had also happened gradually, which was fortunate. Biologists had discovered a drug that appeared to control menstrual cycles in lab mice. After several years and clinical trials, they had been able to offer it to the public. Most women leaped at it—not so much from a concern about pregnancy, thanks to contraceptive implants for either men or women— but as a way to avoid the monthly 'curse'. It was decades later when the truth began to emerge and at first no one believed it. Slowly the demographic evidence grew more and more convincing, until it was an avalanche of data that no one could ignore. Women were living longer than men.

At the time no one knew how much longer or even why, although the speculation was that it had to do with the reduced demands on a woman's entire body. After all, menstruation is constantly occurring with only a limited visible impact. Still, for the first time there was concrete proof that there was a biological trigger for aging. A search for an equivalent for men began immediately, with the optimists wildly predicting immortality as just around the corner. Unfortunately, neither event came to pass, and it had only taken a couple of generations for the current situation to come about. It was almost unbelievable how much society had changed in that time, but historians pointed to the later half of the twentieth century as an era of similar social change in an even shorter period.

Olivia often wished that they had managed to come up with a way to increase a male's lifespan. She remembered when she had wept bitterly that they hadn't. That had been almost half a century ago, when she broke up with Ryan's father. She wasn't one for playing 'what if' with her life, but she couldn't help wondering if she'd make the same decision now.

Olivia's mother, Isabel, had married when she was only forty, the same age Olivia had been when she was dating Ryan's father. Isabel hadn't understood the full impact of an increased life span, despite the fact it was common knowledge. She'd had romantic visions of love and had run away with Richard, a man almost twice her age, when Olivia's grandmother refused to allow them to be together. Her grandmother had finally tracked Isabel down but not before Isabel had managed to get pregnant with Olivia. She had been furious, but Isabel had known what she was doing. Although abortions were still legal, in practice they almost never occurred anymore. Her grandmother finally relented and allowed Isabel to marry Richard. Sure enough her fears proved to be valid when Richard died when Olivia was only fifteen. Olivia lost both her mother and her father then, since after her father's death her mother was never the same. Withdrawn and quiet, she had only waited until Olivia was of legal age to inherit before committing suicide.

Happy twenty-fifth birthday to me, Olivia thought bitterly. Her grandmother had always resented Olivia, since she represented the physical incarnation of the disastrous mistake that Isabel had made. They had never been close and after her mother's death her relationship with her grandmother had fallen apart. Olivia had seen her maybe a dozen times in the sixty-odd years since then and not at all recently.

It was almost fifteen years after her mother's death when she had first met Ryan's father, the original Ryan. She still hadn't gotten over the loss of her entire family, and suffering through a series of disastrous relationships hadn't helped her self-esteem. She had been cold and cynical about the whole dating process, but somehow Ryan was able to get past all that. She had spent six wonderful months with him before she managed to mess it up for both of them. Ironically, it was the longest relationship that she'd had, then or since, and that was what had scared her. For the first time since the loss of her parents, she could see a future for herself with someone and it had terrified her. She had wanted to make it work, but the psychological scars from her parents' deaths were still too vivid for her to take that big of a risk. She had forced herself to break up with him and she thought that she had made the right decision. After all, she had only known him a short time and it already tore her apart to lose him. She couldn't imagine living with him for the next fifty or sixty years only to lose him then.

She brought herself back to the present as Ryan turned to face her. The smile that spread across his face reminded her of his father, more so than usual due to the direction her thoughts had been taking.

"I love it," he exclaimed. "It's like a little oasis of peace and history combined. Now just tell me that you don't come here only for the atmosphere and you'll have made my day."

Olivia glanced at her watch and laughed. "Given that we're only about an hour into the day those expectations may be a little high, but yes, the food here is equally good, if not better." His eyes lit up as she finished, but she couldn't help notice the questioning look he gave her when she had glanced at her watch.

"This is a blind spot in network coverage," she explained. "There are a few of them here due to all the valleys, but most of them have repeaters. This place doesn't. That's another reason why I come here—to get away. It's one of my guilty pleasures."

Ryan nodded in understanding and she watched in amusement as he eagerly turned to read the old-fashioned menu board. No interactive holographic displays here, that was for sure. She watched his delight grow as he dutifully rang the bell as directed by the hand-lettered instructions on the card in front of it. 'Please ring for service.' Olivia had been here at all hours of the day and night, and as far as she knew the place never closed. She looked around as Ryan waited at the counter. A crowd of late-night partygoers occupied a few of the picnic tables, but apart from that it was quiet. Moments later a real person showed up to take their order and they were soon sitting down, enjoying their burritos.

"So," she said, licking her lips as the last of her burrito disappeared between them, "were the burritos all that I promised?"

"Mmm, yeah," he replied, wiping his face with a napkin. "This place is a real treasure. Thank you for sharing it with me."

Olivia stared at him, caught off guard. It was uncanny how he knew how her thought patterns worked. Most people would have thanked her for letting them know about it, but Ryan understood that this was a special place for her and one that she didn't share with just anyone. She flushed as he frowned and for a moment she thought that it was because she had been staring at him. Then she noticed the unfocused look in his eyes, typical of someone accessing a neural feed. For a moment she wondered how he was able to get access when she couldn't, and then she remembered his car. It had enough power to boost a weak signal and it was what she had come to expect from him. His eyes cleared and a grim determined look replaced his frown.

"Let's go," he said without preamble and he matched action to words, getting up from the table in a quick but smooth motion.

Olivia scrambled after him but he was moving rapidly, and despite her longer stride she barely managed to catch up as they reached his car.

"What's up?" she asked as she slid into the passenger seat. It was rather graceless, akin to dumping a sack of potatoes, but it was fast and while she knew that he would wait for her, she didn't want to hold him from whatever was happening.

"Delphi's under attack," he replied.

Before she could comment, acceleration pressed Olivia into her seat as the little car took off with a speed that surprised her.

Chapter Three

Olivia stared at him, stunned, her mind refusing to process the words.

"Under attack?" she echoed. "What do you mean?" Her first thought was of armies with guns storming the grounds, but that didn't make any sense.

"We received an anonymous call from someone stating that they had planted explosives in the hydrogen processing building. Almost simultaneously, security detected an intruder breach at the north end of the complex."

Olivia's mind automatically edited in the word bomb instead of explosives, and she shuddered as she thought of what it would do to all the hydrogen stored there. The hydrogen processing building provided all the power for Delphi, as well as providing raw hydrogen for all the independently powered equipment. There was a massive amount of hydrogen stored there and while it was in an isolated location for safety, it was still critical and its loss would be catastrophic. Not to mention the PR disaster that it would represent. Then her mind caught up with the second half of Ryan's sentence.

"What do you mean they detected an intruder breach at the north end? That doesn't make any sense. That's nowhere near the hydrogen processing building. Besides, I think that they would want to be well away if there is a bomb in there."

"True, if that's what they're after," he said, glancing at her curiously and suddenly she put it all together.

"The lab. They're trying to destroy the lab."

"Possibly, but not likely. I think it's more likely they're after data. The bomb scare is just a tactic to draw our attention away, a feint if you will."

Olivia frowned as she considered that. "But that doesn't make any sense. Why would they call in a bomb threat just before they were planning on breaching the lab? It doesn't take a genius to put the two together."

"I don't think they expected us to detect them. Or at least not so early," he amended. "We replaced a lot of outdated equipment with newer equipment and beefed up some of the weaker spots at the same time. Coincidentally, the north end was one of those weak spots."

"That sounds a little suspicious to be a coincidence," she said darkly and to her surprise Ryan just smiled.

"Yes, it does, doesn't it?" It was more a statement than a question and Olivia looked over at him.

"You know something," she said accusingly and he shrugged as he guided the car to a landing directly in front of the security building. The building, so quiet when they had left less than an hour ago, was now a beehive of activity. Yet even to Olivia's untrained eye, there was something purposeful about it. It conveyed the impression that everything was under control and Olivia didn't doubt for a moment that it was true. She also knew that it would have been a different scene a month ago.

"I suspected something," he admitted, as she climbed out of the car and struggled to catch up to him. "The security here was so patchwork and the staff so poorly trained that it screamed either incredible incompetence or sabotage. My preference is to suspect sabotage until proven otherwise. That's why I've been busting my hump and the humps of my staff for the last month."

Ryan swept past the drop shaft and headed for the stairs, taking them two at a time. Olivia opted for the drop shaft, but as quick as it was, Ryan had already disappeared when she reached the top. Olivia let her gaze sweep the room and then she spotted him.

Almost all the senior staff were women and Olivia knew just how hostile they had been at having to work for a man. Now she watched as they looked up in relief as he stood in the center of a group of them, radiating confidence. It wasn't a panicked relief but more a welcome relief. She watched as he conferred quietly with them, listening intently as they brought him up to speed. After a moment, they all moved over to a large holo tank. Olivia drifted closer until she could see what the tank displayed.

She gasped and her eyes widened as she realized that she was looking at a perfect representation of the entire Delphi complex. As she watched, the tank twitched and rippled at a silent command to display two separate images. One of the images was a wire frame of a building. Olivia could see the details of the building layout, including transparent images representing various pieces of equipment and furnishings.

She suddenly realized that it was the hydrogen processing building. There were three colors overlaid on the image—green, orange and red. As she watched, one of the red sections changed to green and she realized that it was a real time representation of the security team's progress as they scanned the building. The red obviously represented the higher risk areas and the orange the less critical ones. Yet another red section shifted to green, leaving only a handful of red and orange left.

Olivia turned her attention to the other image. It was a smaller scale, but it was still clear enough for her to see that it was the buildings at the north end of the property. She gasped in silent surprise as she saw a trio of black suited figures appear in the image, heading towards the research labs. The computer tagged each figure with a red asterisk. A cluster of other figures wearing Delphi's security uniforms quietly closed up behind them while another group waited patiently in front of them, hidden around the corner of a building.

In less than thirty seconds it was all over.

Olivia watched in fascination as the trio of invaders came around the corner. They came to a ragged stop, and then collapsed to the ground as the security team stunned them before they could raise their weapons. It was like watching an adventure holo with the sound off. One of the security guards advanced cautiously while the others covered her. As they secured each intruder, the red asterisk changed to a small green lock. Once they had secured all the intruders, a security van pulled up and they loaded the prisoners aboard.

As if that were the cue that they were waiting for, everyone gathered around the holo tank relaxed in relief. Olivia flicked her eyes back towards the hydrogen processing building, long enough to determine that it was entirely green, before looking over at Ryan. Admittedly, he hadn't added anything to what had happened tonight. Most of it had already been in place when they arrived. Still, that clearly didn't stop the staff from congratulating him.

He shook his head, declining the honors, and she could tell from his gestures that he was praising them for all of their hard work. She smiled. Ryan hadn't just built up the security infrastructure in the last month—he had built himself a team, too. And while they didn't need him to be there, they didn't know that—not yet, not in their hearts. Or at least they hadn't. Tonight would go a long way to boosting their self-confidence. After a moment, Ryan turned away from the group and walked over to her.

"Sorry to drag you into all this," he apologized.

"Are you kidding?" she asked him. "I wouldn't have missed it for the world. It was incredibly exciting watching it happen. I can't believe how quickly it was over. I was still trying to process the fact that we were under attack. You've got a good team here."

His mouth twitched. "Well, we're getting there. I'd be happier with a little more experience behind us, but at least we had two things going for us. We have good equipment and we've been training constantly for the past few weeks on it. The staff still isn't fully comfortable with it, but the advantage of that is that they're not afraid to escalate issues for supervisor review."

He grinned at her. "That's how we managed to catch this so fast. The person monitoring the perimeter sensors noticed an anomaly and when she couldn't resolve it, she notified her supervisor. The supervisor had just taken the bomb threat call and she quickly put it together and called me. Total elapsed time, including the call, less than three minutes. When the supervisor contacted me, I gave her the authorization to activate the high-density scanners."

"Ah, I was wondering about those images in the holo tank. I assume this is the new technology that you've spent all our money on," Olivia teased him and he nodded.

"Yeah, the technology's still new, but the last place I worked was a beta site for testing them. I was pretty hands-on and it amazed me what they could do. I knew that I had to have them here and they cut us a deal, based on Delphi's reputation. I think they were hoping that we'd provide them with a product endorsement." His lips quirked again. "I assume that you'll have no problem recommending that to the Board?" he teased her back and she laughed and shook her head. Then her eyes widened.

"The shareholders' meeting," she exclaimed and he stared at her blankly for a moment before cursing.

"I should have thought of that. I've been expecting an incursion for some time now and I was almost beginning to doubt my instincts. But now it makes perfect sense."

He gazed at her and she looked back at him soberly. It made perfect sense all right, perfect sense if you were planning on striking Delphi a crippling blow. After the fiasco with Ryan's predecessor, she had been lucky to keep her job, and this would have been the death knell for her. And for Ryan, as well. Going beyond that, though, it would have been disastrous for Delphi from a public relations viewpoint, not to mention the lost research data. She shuddered as she realized how close the intruders had come and that sparked a thought.

"What happened to them? The intruders I mean. Where did you take them?" she asked.

"They are in a holding cell downstairs. We've called the police, who will be here shortly to take them into custody." Olivia twitched at that and Ryan laughed and smiled. "I know what you're thinking, but we've already found out that they don't know anything. All they know is that someone hired them to do a job, and I'd be willing to bet the trail stops cold at that point. I thought it best to hand them over to the police to try to build up some goodwill. Even at that, all the police will be able to do is hit them with a slew of charges, most of which will be reduced or dropped in return for their cooperation. I doubt they'll serve much time—in fact, I hope they don't."

She frowned at him. "You what? Why not?"

"I want them released, free to spread the message that Delphi is no longer an easy target. While I suspect that someone planned this long ago, it never hurts to get a little free PR."

"You have a perverse sense of humor," she said.

"I may have been told that once or twice," he admitted with a small smile and then frowned as she yawned. "Look, it's almost two a.m. I need to stay here, but take my car. I'll program it to take you to my place. You can rest there and then clean up." He held up a hand to forestall her protests. "I won't take no for an answer. I won't be there, so there's no longer any reason for you to decline. And you need to be fresh for the shareholders' meeting later this morning. I'm sure there will be a lot of questions."

Olivia opened her mouth to protest again, but she found herself yawning instead.

"Okay, okay," she laughed as he eyed her obliquely, "I'll go."

"Good. Now I know the meeting is at ten, but I've asked the shareholders who are also Board Members to arrive at nine, so they can receive their nanitic bracelets."

"God," Olivia groaned, doing the math in her head, "that only gives me a little over five hours sleep." She shook her head groggily and then felt instantly embarrassed as she realized that he wasn't going to be able to get even that much sleep.

"Sorry," she said contritely.

"It's okay. With my enhancement, I'm still good for a while, although I'll pay for it later."

"If you're sure," she said, only partially mollified. When he nodded, she gave him a brief wave good-bye and headed out to his car. She was so tired when she got there that she got in the passenger seat by mistake. She groaned at the thought of moving over and then decided there wasn't really any need to. She reached over to the driver's side and toggled the autopilot on. After a moment, it rose gently and headed towards the condo complex used by several of Delphi's employees.

* * *

Ryan stopped himself from rubbing his forehead. It didn't send the right message. No matter how tired he was, he didn't like to show it in front of his staff. Mind you, what he felt like doing was banging his head against the wall. The police had shown up to take the intruders into custody, but from the way that they were behaving, it was almost like they were interrogating him instead. His predecessor, Christina, was rumored to have had close connections with the local police. Evidently there was some truth to the rumor, since their behavior towards him went well beyond normal male-female prejudice.

He hadn't been the only one to notice it. His staff had picked up on it, and he'd had to spend almost as much time soothing them as he had dealing with the police. Their reaction warmed him, since it meant that they had finally accepted him as one of them. Even though the fallout from tonight's events and lack of sleep was giving him a massive headache that even his enhancement couldn't fully deal with, he wouldn't have changed anything. It made all his hard work and the veiled insults he'd dealt with over the past month worth it.

He knew it would only be a matter of time until he had the police on his side as well. Already the reactions of his staff to the police's treatment of him were sinking in with some of them. Meanwhile, though, he had to just deal with it and do his best to limit the contact between the two groups.

He was on his way to the control center when he received an urgent page from the supervisor on duty. Groaning, he quickened his pace. What now, he thought, and then he was there.

"What's up?" he asked her tersely, still worried, but put slightly at ease by the relaxed atmosphere in the control center. Obviously, it wasn't an emergency.

"We received a request for your immediate presence at the shareholders' meeting," she replied and then suppressed a grin as he winced.

"Ouch. That doesn't sound good." She just shrugged and he shook his head. "Thanks for the support," he said with mild sarcasm, knowing that she wouldn't take it the wrong way.

"We can't help you with whatever the Board wants, but we can make sure that you're presentable. After all, we wouldn't want to give security a bad name."

"We?" he echoed and she nodded.

"There's a security flitter ready and waiting downstairs and one of the off-duty guards has volunteered to drive you. There's also a small package containing some skin wipes, a shampoo brush and a clean shirt."

Ryan was taken aback by this display of support. He struggled to find the right words and finally settled on a simple "Thank you."

"No sweat boss. Now get going before you're both late and in trouble." She pushed him gently towards the door. "Good luck!" she called after him.

Ryan took the stairs four at a time, his hands gripping the railing and swinging his body forward with metronome-like precision, and was outside in seconds. As promised, the powered flitter was there waiting for him. He slipped into it, scooping the package off the seat before sitting down. He glanced over at the driver and she grinned at him.

"I'll have you there in a jiffy, sir. Clean yourself up and then hold on."

Ryan nodded and rummaged through the package. He ran the shampoo brush through his hair a couple of times until the light flashed green. The little brushes couldn't replace a proper cleaning, but they came close. He shoved the brush back in the bag and ran a skin wipe over his face. He quickly shucked off his shirt and ran a fresh wipe over his upper body. He noticed peripherally as the driver averted her eyes out of courtesy, and he smiled at the changes that had taken place over the last month.

He cracked the seal on the new shirt. It was the same crisp blue oxford that he usually wore, but this one was fresher than the one he had been wearing. He quickly buttoned it up and then braced himself against the doorframe and the dash.

"Ready," he said and almost immediately the acceleration pressed him back in his seat.

Flitters were small vehicles, slightly larger than an old-fashioned golf cart. They had minimal lift capacity and no inertial compensators. Despite their limits they were indispensable for short trips like this, especially given the weather that southern California was blessed with. Minutes later, the flitter reached the executive building.

For many years, buildings in this part of California were restricted in height because of the risk of earthquakes. By the time advanced materials made such restrictions unnecessary, it had become an architectural trend. As a result, the employees at Delphi occupied many smaller buildings spread across a vast space, rather than occupying a few larger and more imposing buildings. Ryan had to admit that he rather liked it. It gave the complex an open airy feel, and the many parks laced in and around the buildings only increased the effect.

The executive building was the only exception. It was more of a tower, at least compared to the other buildings. In just about any other city, it would have been a commonplace building. At Delphi, it towered over the other buildings being twelve stories high versus the standard six. Naturally, the boardroom was at the top.

Ryan rushed into the lobby and headed directly for the drop shaft, which whisked him straight up. Once there, he approached the security guards standing in front of the boardroom doors. One of them raised an eyebrow at him and he nodded. He could see her throat muscles move as she used the subvocal mike implanted in her throat to communicate with the guards inside. After a moment she nodded at him and opened the door.

Ryan had seen the boardroom before, but only when it was empty. He had thought that it had seemed imposing then, with the vast holo tank surrounded by a huge oval table that seated well over a hundred people. Those seats represented the top shareholders in Delphi, some of whom were also active Board members. Repeaters automatically rebroadcast the image in the holo tank to the smaller investors and news agencies over the world Net.

Now that shareholders filled the seats and the holo tank projected a huge image of the podium, it seemed even more imposing. He stepped up to the speaker's podium and his fifteen-foot tall image suddenly filled the display. He didn't normally have a problem speaking in public or to large groups, but he had to admit that having his image so hugely magnified made him a little self-conscious. He adjusted his enhancement to compensate for his nervousness. It would make him look less wary and more attentive, and he waited patiently for the Board to begin questioning him.

As he expected, it related to last night's assault. He shared with them his assessment of the security before his arrival and the conclusions that he had drawn from that. There were more than a few suspicious looks, but there were also several understanding nods. Most of the shareholders were fully aware of his predecessor's predilections. The suspicious looks he ignored. He knew that they suspected him of manufacturing the whole incident just to increase his profile, but he was confident he would be able to convince most of them of the truth.

Then he commented on the assault itself. He was forthright about where he was and whom he was with. To do otherwise would only look like he was trying to cover something up, and he was sure that Olivia would have provided them with the same details. He made the same comment about the response time and how that allowed them to get into position. He also made sure to give credit where credit was due, which in this case was the supervisor on duty as well as the staffer who detected the intrusion.

"I have holo images of the assault and our response to it that can provide you with a better feel for what happened." The chairwoman nodded and he inserted himself into the network and quickly brought up the recorded images from the night before. There was a collective gasp around the room as the holo tank shifted to display Delphi's complex. He focused first on the hydrogen building.

"This is the hydrogen processing building. As you can see, there are three colors overlaid on the image. The red areas are the areas of highest risk. We assigned the highest priority to these areas. The orange are either lower risk or more secured areas where penetration is less likely. The green sections are the ones the security staff have already searched.

"The search includes a detailed visual examination that is fed from each guard's optical nerve, through their neural implants, directly into the security computer. The computer runs a comparison of the images to standard images and sends any variations back into each guard's neural feed, flagged for follow up. As we clear each room, the section automatically turns green. This is a real time system, and although it was my belief the explosives threat was a hoax, security staff still managed to certify this large and complex building threat free in less than ten minutes."

He paused for a moment to let them recognize the scope of that accomplishment. He then turned to the images of the actual assault. The scale was a little different because of the wider area that it covered but the huge size of the tank made it almost irrelevant.

"As you can see, this shows a real time image of the complex as well as the people involved. We didn't need this for the hydrogen building, as security staff were the only ones on site. The intruders penetrated here, one of the areas that I had previously identified as a potential risk. We detected them immediately, but they crossed over to here before I was able to authorize the activation of the high-density scanners.

"These scanners are new to the security industry, and it is uncommon for a company as large as Delphi to have such complete coverage. Given how outdated Delphi's entire security system was, however, I knew we would replace it all. I contacted the manufacturer, who was more than willing to offer a significant discount on the system to acquire a client as prestigious as Delphi.

"Unfortunately, the scanners are expensive and they cover a tenth of the range that lower density scanners do. Despite the discount, the new system costs significantly more than most systems currently in use today, but the costs of a security breach would be far higher."

Ryan let the image run from its starting point, recounting the main points as the action unfolded. The shareholders watched in fascination and there was more than one disappointed mutter as the scene ended.

"We contacted the police at that point and the individuals in question are now in their custody." He paused and glanced around the boardroom. "Do you have any other questions that I might have missed?" he asked.

He waited for a moment and then nodded. "If there are any questions that arise later or that you would prefer to ask me in private, please contact me through the security office."

He waited until the Chairwoman dismissed him and then, nodding respectfully to the Board, he left the room. One of the guards winked at him on his way out so he guessed he had done okay, but at this point he was starting not to care. The fatigue was beginning to catch up with him, and he called his car while still in the drop shaft. It wasn't something that he normally did, but he was just too tired to trudge all the way over to the parking garage and the security flitter was long gone.

He propped himself up against the building sign while he waited for it to arrive and then he slid into it bonelessly, contrary to his usual graceful entrance. He dozed while the autopilot took him home, both facts a telling sign of just how tired he was. Normally, he didn't have a problem staying awake for days at a time. His enhancements kept him alert and prevented fatigue and toxins from building up in his bloodstream, but he had been pushing them to the limits as it was, trying to get Delphi's Security to the level he demanded.

The car swooped down in front of the condo complex and came to a smooth stop just inside his garage. He stumbled wearily from the garage and into his bedroom. He lay down on the bed, hoping that for once he could experience that old cliché about being asleep before his head hit the pillow. He lay there for five minutes before levering himself up with a groan. It never failed. No matter how tired he was, whenever he pushed his body like he had, it just couldn't believe the crisis was over.

He stripped off his clothes and jumped into the shower. He ran the water hot, and steam misted all around him soothingly. He quickly cleaned himself and then turned the spray to massage. He twisted and stretched while the jets pummeled him with pulses of hot water. As he got out of the shower, he had to admit that he felt a lot better. Still not sleepy but better. He wrapped a towel around his waist and padded out to the kitchen to fix himself a snack.

He was halfway across the living room when he heard a soft cough behind him. Startled, he whirled around to find Olivia standing there. She was smiling and looking discreetly to one side, and he flushed red as he realized the picture he must make. He darted back into the bedroom and pulled on some slacks and a lightweight turtleneck sweater before returning to the living room. She was sitting with her back to his bedroom, and for a crazy minute he wondered if it was to make him feel comfortable, or because she didn't trust herself not to peek. He shook his head at the weird direction his thoughts were taking and sat down across from her.

"Sorry about that," he said, "I wasn't expecting anyone."

"Don't worry about it, it's my fault. I should have called to let you know I was coming, but I wasn't sure if you'd be asleep by now. I did knock but there was no answer and the door was open." She arched an eyebrow at him and he accepted the gentle rebuke about his own security.

"Well, I was hoping to fall asleep," he remarked wryly, "but my mind didn't feel like cooperating. So did you come here to fire me in person?" he joked and she looked startled for a moment until she realized that he was kidding.

"No, nothing like that. In fact, it's just the opposite. As you know, I report to the Board, as do all my Senior VPs."

Ryan nodded. It was common practice these days, intended to ensure that the Board had all the necessary information. It was technically a dotted line reporting relationship, rather than a direct one. Despite that, while it was rare for a Board of Directors to overrule the CEO, it had happened. There were only a handful of Senior VPs at Delphi, and only for the most critical areas.

"Effective immediately, so do you. Report to the Board I mean." Ryan's eyebrows shot up in astonishment. She was letting him know that he was now a Senior VP. It was rare to find Senior VPs of Security in any company, and even more so to find a male holding that position. Olivia finally smiled and offered her congratulations.

"Obviously, you impressed them by what you've accomplished since you've been here. It also helped that we didn't lose any more valuable research data. Our one experience with that proved to be expensive, in a multitude of ways. As you know, we not only lost the data that we had spent hundreds of millions of dollars on—from prototype to preclinical, all the way to Phase II trials—but we also lost billions of dollars in future revenue. What was almost worse was the loss of face in the industry.

"When Avropax announced that they had 'independently developed' a similar compound in their patent application, it forced us to concede the market to them. Fortunately, we have a robust pipeline otherwise it could have shut us down, but it was still dicey. A second loss would have been catastrophic."

Ryan nodded again. He knew all this, but he was content to let her tell him the news in her own way. Besides, he loved listening to that voice of hers.

"Based on that, the Board decided that security was a mission critical function. They also voted to keep you on." She smiled again. "I know the Board too well to ever expect a unanimous decision from them on anything, but it was a strong majority, which surprised me."

He put a hurt look on his face and it was her turn to laugh.

"Oh, not like that. I already made my decision and it looks like I made the right one. But the Board is a little more conservative, and most of them have doubts about male competency. Those that don't, worry about investing so much in someone with such a short life span. As I said, you must have impressed them."

Ryan made a snorting noise. "I doubt it was me. It's more likely all the fancy new technology and the holo images."

"Perhaps," Olivia admitted. "I will allow that your innovations are impressive, but don't sell yourself short. I've seen you in action and I saw how you brought a collection of disparate, even hostile, individuals together to form one cohesive team. I said as much to the Board and they still rely on my judgment."

Ryan heard the bitterness in her voice in the last sentence. It was faint, so faint that it was possible that even she didn't realize that it was there. But he had developed the ability to sense things that other people might miss. Part of it was the security angle, but part of it was being male. Insight and perception used to be the sole domain of females. Funny how lifelong discrimination sharpened your perceptions.

He knew that she was still blaming herself for the security fiasco that she had mentioned earlier. Technically, she was blameless. His predecessor had duped everyone, not just Olivia. He also knew that as CEO, she took the heat for everything that went wrong. It was a thankless job, and the escrow rules around bonus payouts and stock options ensured that she wouldn't see any significant compensation for years. The Board could have fired her and taken a sizable portion of her escrow funds as penalty. That they hadn't, indicated their confidence in her—confidence clearly justified by solid Earnings per Share growth. And of course by her astuteness in hiring him.

He reminisced about how he had gotten to this point in his life. It was curious, he had never seen himself in security, but while inventing his new life, he and his handlers decided that he should enroll in the military. That didn't occur immediately, of course. As his 'son', he needed to wait until he was eighteen before he could do anything. It was, without a doubt, the most boring time of his life. Eighteen years of hiding, of waiting for something to happen. His handlers could have suggested he join a monastery and he would have jumped at it.

There were several benefits to joining the military. It gave him a good solid background story, for starters. His life officially began with his enlistment. For another, it provided him with solid training and exposure to security systems that civilian contractors could only drool over. And finally, it gave him his enhancement.

Neural feeds were common for females, but most males couldn't afford them. Physical enhancement, on the other hand, was still rare, regardless of gender. The military provided physical enhancement to anyone who signed up for a minimum term of service. This ensured that there was no shortage of volunteers, on the male side at least. It was also one of the few ways that men could get neural feeds. Only a small percentage made it past the initial screening, and the subsequent five and ten-year post-screening periods, to qualify for full physical enhancement.

At times, Ryan hadn't been sure that he would make it himself, even with all the experience from his previous life to draw on. In the end he had managed to pull through. During that time he had developed an interest in security, an interest that he had pursued with single-minded intensity. It helped that he had a talent for it, but he also had a degree of focus and concentration rarely seen in men his apparent age.

He realized with a start that he had been sitting there in silence, lost in his thoughts.

"I'm sorry," he said, shaking his head. "I guess my sleeplessness is starting to catch up with me."

"No, I'm sorry. I could have waited until later today or tomorrow to tell you this. I just thought it was good news and you'd want to know about it." She hesitated and Ryan raised an eyebrow inquisitively. "I also wanted to thank you again and to make sure you were okay." She looked embarrassed and he wisely didn't say anything. "Anyway, I should go now."

Ryan escorted her out to the waiting limo and then came back inside. There was so much going on inside his head that he couldn't sort it all out. He shook his head and made his way to the bedroom again. He stripped down to his boxers, lay down on the bed, and this time he finally managed to fall asleep.

Chapter Four

The suborbital landed at LAX and Ryan stumbled blearily out. His flight from Australia had only taken two hours, but his body still knew how many times zones he had crossed and it wasn't happy. His enhancements would normally have reduced the impact of crossing multiple time zones, but he had been going nonstop for two months now. Three, if you counted his first month at Delphi. Though Ryan knew that being a Senior VP would mean more work, he was surprised at just how much extra work there was. He thought that his military career and subsequent work experience had prepared him for this role, and it had, but barely.

Security was one of the more elite programs in the military. His maturity allowed Ryan to excel at it, and consequently he had his pick of industries that he could work at. Not surprisingly, he chose to focus mainly on the biotech and pharmaceutical industry. It wasn't one of the industry sectors that traditionally welcomed males. That meant fewer opportunities, but also less competition from other men. His focus and determination served him well and he'd had his choice of jobs.

He had taken ruthless advantage of this, and had acquired significant experience in a short time. Unfortunately, most of his experience had been with the smaller pharmaceutical companies or biotech startups. Those were the only companies who could afford to take a risk on somebody relatively unproven and with little experience. However, since they couldn't afford to hire more experienced individuals, everyone benefited.

Despite his extensive background, Ryan had never worked at a company the size of Delphi. The scale and scope of everything from R&D to Commercialization was dramatically different. As well, few of the other companies that Ryan had worked for had manufacturing facilities as large as Delphi's. Many didn't even have any manufacturing capability at all and just licensed their products to other companies. Fewer still had the worldwide exposure that Delphi had.

All of Delphi's manufacturing operations were located in Noram, the new nation formed when the United States, Canada, and Mexico combined. The name Noram was a derivative of the continent name that it occupied. The old United States had protested bitterly, but there was no denying the impact of adding Canada and Mexico. The new nation was more than double in land size and almost that much in terms of population.

The only non-Noram locations were Sales Offices, but there were still a large number of them scattered across the globe. Only countries with a population in excess of a hundred million had a Sales Office, but that still meant a dozen sites that he had to visit.

The Senior VP role was a new role in security and as a result it was still being defined. He'd had several discussions with Olivia about what he'd felt the role should be, and one of the areas that he was adamant about was centralizing security. Each of Delphi's affiliates and subsidiaries had been responsible for their own security, especially the Sales Offices. On the plus side, in most cases their security was better than it had been at the head office. Unfortunately, it also meant that their systems were not compatible with head office security, which made integration difficult.

Ryan adopted a 'sunset' approach to those varied security arrangements. He set up tighter linkages to the head office but apart from that, he didn't make any major changes. He also froze their capital budgets. They could do basic maintenance but when the time came for a major upgrade, they would have to upgrade to the new system. For the moment, that was enough. The security for most of the affiliates and subsidiaries didn't need to be as robust as at the head office. That was where all preclinical research and all the original documents were stored. Those were the lifeblood of the company and their safety was critical.

Although these changes were minor, Ryan spent the last two months traveling, learning about all the various security systems in use. He wanted to model out a workable upgrade schedule. His long-term plan was to have all the locations seamlessly linked with the head office within five years. Even as he developed this plan, he knew the odds that he would still be working at Delphi in five years were slim, but the professional side of him just wouldn't accept anything less.

Though he often faced the stereotypical resistance that a male in a high profile position did, his easygoing manner and extreme competence usually overcame that resistance. In the few cases where it didn't, they soon discovered that his easygoing manner only existed when he received the cooperation that he expected. He hated to throw his weight around, but he couldn't afford to look soft or get a reputation as a pushover. Fortunately, he didn't have to fire anyone. The turnover at the head office when he took over had given him a bit of a reputation and he didn't hesitate to use it.

He stopped woolgathering as he passed through customs, ignoring the appraising glances the customs agents gave him, and bypassed the baggage area. Despite being gone for almost a month, he had restricted himself to a carryon, preferring to use the hotels' laundry and dry cleaning facilities rather than have to wait for luggage. He knew from experience that in all likelihood he would have lost his luggage at least once.

He rounded the corner and stopped dead. Stifling a groan, he started moving forward again, approaching an apologetic looking Olivia.

"What's the matter?" she teased him, "aren't you glad to see me?"

Ryan felt his exhaustion lifting at the sight of her, although he knew that it would probably mean that his long awaited rest would have to wait a little longer.

"Yes and no," he replied grinning, and she arched an eyebrow questioningly. "I am pleased to see you, personally. I'm not so glad to see my boss since it probably means more work for me."

"You're in luck then, since only one of us is here." Ryan stared at her in confusion.

"What are you talking about?"

"Unfortunately, your boss couldn't make it, so it's just me."

Olivia watched the comprehension flow across Ryan's face and she smiled.

"I know you've been working hard and that you're looking forward to getting some rest." She looked at him sympathetically. "I haven't had to make that kind of whirlwind tour for years but I know how draining it can be. And I also know just how quickly one can get sick of eating in restaurants. So I thought that I would invite you over for dinner tonight. You probably don't feel like cooking, and I know the last thing that you feel like is yet another restaurant meal."

Olivia could feel her heart racing as he stared at her and she wondered, not for the first time, just what she was doing. She had been able to stay away from him when he reported directly to her. Anything else would have undermined his ability to do his job effectively. Now that he reported to the Board as well, it would be easier for them to see each other socially. It shouldn't have made a difference, but it did. Just knowing that she could see him made her want to. Or at least it made it harder to resist this indefinable urge that she had to see him.

She knew that part of it was that she saw more of him now than she did when he was just a VP. Regular VPs didn't report to the board and so it was up to Olivia to pass on any information that she found pertinent. Senior VPs did have to report to the Board, so Olivia had no choice but to meet with him regularly, just to ensure that she knew everything that the Board did. The first month when he had been visiting the Noram-based Delphi affiliates, she had met with him at least twice a week.

Even while he was in Australia and New Zealand, she had met with him over the holo at least that often. As a result, she had gotten a lot more comfortable with him. She had also missed him while he was gone. It seemed paradoxical, since she'd seen just as much of him over the holo, but it wasn't the same. Their holo conversations were primarily business driven, and it didn't leave much time for the informal chatting that Olivia had grown used to.

The wide smile on his face indicated his acceptance of her offer and Olivia found herself smiling back at him. She gestured for him to follow her and he adjusted his carryon into a more comfortable position and fell in beside her. Olivia resisted the urge to turn and look at him. She also resisted a brief insane urge to reach out and take his hand, and her thoughts raced.

When women had first taken the reigns of power in the corporate and political worlds, sexual harassment was not unheard of. It wasn't rampant, like it was in the early twentieth century when men had all the power, but it wasn't nonexistent. Like anything, it had changed and mellowed with time and nowadays it was almost unheard of given the number of available men. Since Olivia didn't have to worry about that becoming an issue that meant there was effectively nothing to stop her from seeing him socially or even having a relationship with him. Nothing, she thought, including my common sense, which had deserted her when she had caught sight of him in that towel almost two months ago.

She knew that it was common, given the differences in life spans, for older women to have 'dated' two or, more rarely, three 'versions' of the same person. It was like dating the father and then the son and then the grandson. Normally, the whole concept revolted Olivia. She couldn't imagine anything worse and that was why she was having a hard time reconciling her attraction for Ryan. She admitted that she was operating under a handicap.

Since she had broken up with his father, she had thrown herself into her work. It had taken her a long time to get over him, but now she had to face the prospect that she had been wrong, that she hadn't really gotten over him after all. If she had then she wouldn't be having these feelings for the new Ryan. And she had probably also been wrong in her decision to avoid any serious relationships. She hadn't even dated very often. Her intentions were good— she just wanted to avoid feeling the same pain she had felt when she lost Ryan—but it appeared the adage was true. Hell is paved with good intentions.

For a while it had looked like her strategy was working. She had made significant strides in her career. Becoming the CEO of a company like Delphi at the early age of eighty was an incredible accomplishment. But now it looked like she'd done herself a disservice. If she had dated more, she would have more experience under her belt and been more prepared to resist Ryan's charms. As it stood, her old feelings confused her and mixed with her attraction for the new Ryan.

They finally reached the street exit and almost immediately a sleek white limo glided up. Before the driver could get out to help them, Ryan had the door open. He smiled at her and gestured for her to enter the car. Olivia felt her face turn flaming red and she quickly ducked into the car and sat down. A moment later he sat down across from her, the carryon tossed carelessly on the seat beside him.

"So, what are we having?" he asked her and she smiled mysteriously at him.

"Wouldn't you like to know," she teased him good-naturedly and he grinned back at her.

"Well, not really. I'm sure that it will be good, but it's not about the food."

"It isn't?" she asked him, her heart racing. Surely, he wasn't going to say what she thought he was going to say. If so, she had completely misread him and that would make her decision a lot easier.

"No, it's about the company, about not eating alone my first night back. Having a friendly face to talk to, eating a real meal, being able to just relax and be myself. That's what it's all about."

Olivia felt herself relaxing, but she also felt a twinge of disappointment. She couldn't tell what disappointed her though. Was she disappointed because she wasn't wrong about him and that her decision was now in fact tougher to make? Or was she disappointed that he wasn't making a pass at her? She wondered if she was falling in love with him and she forced herself to examine her feelings for him during the trip to her house. Fortunately, she had the opportunity to do that, since Ryan closed his eyes for a brief nap.

Normally, something like that would have irritated her, but right now she was glad for the respite it gave her. She also realized that for some reason she wouldn't have minded it from him regardless of the situation. Did that tolerance mean that she was falling for him or was she reading more into it than was there? She thought back to her interactions with him over the past months, and analyzed them with the same professional detachment that she used for making all her most important decisions. She had to admit that part of her initial attraction was because he looked like his father, but there was more to it than that.

She had devoted her life to her career for the past forty years and, while she may have certain regrets and things that she wanted to change, she couldn't deny how important her career was to her. In the beginning, it had been a means to an end, a way to lose herself in her work and forget about

Ryan and what they could have had together. That was in the beginning. Now it had become an end in and of itself. She had worked hard to get where she was today. She had put in the time, but she had also put herself into her work. Her perfectionism, her integrity, her honor. All of those traits were what had allowed her to succeed.

She realized that Ryan had all those same traits and that was partly why she found herself so comfortable with him. She rarely had to ask him to elaborate or clarify anything when she was talking to him, and when she did, he immediately understood why she was asking. He never resented her need for details, her need to understand what was happening. The truth was that he shared those needs with her and so Olivia found herself doing something she would have never thought possible, particularly given the situation that existed before his arrival.

She was relinquishing control. She was beginning to rely on Ryan, something she did with few people, knowing that she could trust him to do his job properly and to her satisfaction, knowing that she could trust him to tell her what she needed to know. It was unusual for her, especially given his gender and the short time she had known him. There were women she had known decades whom she felt less comfortable with and she found it both liberating and unnerving at the same time.

She understood now why she didn't mind that he had closed his eyes for a quick nap. It wasn't a power play or a political move or any of the usual nonsense that she had to deal with most of the time. It was an indication of his trust in her and she felt herself relax as she successfully labeled her feelings for him.

Even if you discounted his resemblance to his father, there was no denying that his sheer maleness, combined with his competence, made for an attractive package. He was almost as tall as she was, which meant that her size didn't intimidate him. The Ryan she remembered had the same dark brown hair only it had been longer. Still, she had to admit that she had grown used to the short-cropped look. It highlighted his clean jaw line and twinkling blue eyes. And of course, he was incredibly fit.

She took the opportunity to study him in repose and then shook her head ruefully. In just about any other circumstance it would have tempted her. But even if she could get past who he looked like, she didn't want to risk what she had actually found, which was friendship. Given the intense competition between women for the good jobs, real friendship was rare. Real friendship between men and women sometimes seemed like it was nonexistent, even for gay men. There were too many differences these days and something that had already been rare became almost precious. No, there was no way that Olivia was going to risk her friendship with him for the sake of sex.

The limo glided to a stop in front of her house and Olivia reached over to nudge Ryan awake. She had just put her hand on his shoulder when his eyes opened and he leaned over to grab his carryon. It was on the other side of the shoulder that Olivia was touching, and as he leaned over she lost her balance and fell on top of him. She felt herself blushing crimson again and wished, not for the first time, that she had the enhancement that Ryan had. She tried to control her racing thoughts and she suddenly realized that Ryan had been speaking to her.

"I'm sorry," she said, flushing in fresh embarrassment, "what did you say?"

"I asked if you were all right," he repeated and she managed to pull a smile up from somewhere inside her.

"I'm fine, just a little startled, that's all. I guess I wasn't expecting you to move."

Now it was his turn to look embarrassed. "Sorry about that. My internal systems let me know that we had arrived. Besides which, it was rude of me to sleep. I hadn't expected to, but I closed my eyes for just a second and then suddenly we were here. I guess I was a little more worn out than I thought."

"Are you sure you're up for this?" she asked, studying him when he nodded.

"No really, I could use a good meal. Not to mention I wasn't looking forward to going home to an empty house. Just give me a glass of wine or Scotch, or something with alcohol in it, and I'll be fine."

"I don't think you should be drinking if you're this tired," she said cautiously and his sudden grin startled her.

"Trust me, it's exactly what I need when I'm this tired," he replied. Olivia raised an eyebrow inquisitively and he elaborated. "My nanites get their energy from what I eat and drink, just like I do. Alcohol is one of the easiest substances for them to convert. They are so efficient at this that it's almost impossible for me to become drunk."

"Oh," she replied and he gazed at her curiously.

"I'm a little surprised that you didn't know that. It's common knowledge on the dating scene." He elaborated at the puzzled look on her face. "Some guys have tried to use it to get a woman drunk. Stupid. If you're caught and convicted, the military removes your nanites and court-martials you. Unfortunately it still happens, although rarely."

"I had no idea. I don't date that much," she explained and then instantly regretted it. She covered her confusion by stepping out of the limo. She nodded her thanks to the driver and marched up the steps to her front door, wondering yet again if she were insane. The doors opened for her automatically and she walked through absentmindedly, her mind still struggling to label her relationship with Ryan. Just when she thought she had him fixed in her mind as a friend, she found herself attracted to him. Once again, she decided that he was just a friend.

She swept into the kitchen on a tide of resolve, trusting that he was right behind her. She reached out and pulled a bottle of expensive Chilean Merlot from the wine rack. Opening it, she automatically poured two glasses and handed one to Ryan before she realized that she had forgotten to ask him if he preferred red or white. Ryan's father had preferred red, and she came to the sudden realization about why she had so much trouble reconciling her feelings for him. Her mind kept mixing up her Ryan—Ryan's father—with the new Ryan. She viewed the new Ryan as a friend, but her mind kept trying to substitute him for his father, her one true love.

She opened her mouth to apologize for her presumption when she saw he was already sipping from the glass. It startled her, since white wine was all the rage right now, notably so in southern California. For a moment, she wondered if it was an echo of his father, that preference for red wine, and then she shook her head mentally. He had already told her his nanites converted it to energy. He probably didn't care what he was drinking at this point.

Chapter Five

Ryan cursed himself mentally for his slip, as he automatically accepted the red wine, but years of practice kept any sign of it from showing, unlike Olivia. She had clearly made the same mistake he had just made, but knowing that didn't comfort him. He knew this whole evening was a mistake, though he seemed incapable of doing anything about it. He took another sip of wine, waiting for his nanites to convert it and start boosting his energy levels. He shouldn't be here and he listed the reasons as he tried to convince himself to leave.

First, he couldn't afford distractions. Second, he didn't need the added visibility that being in Olivia's company would give him. For him to succeed, he needed to blend into the background. It was already bad enough that he was a Senior VP, the only male Senior VP in the entire company. In that case, he could make the argument that the increased authority and autonomy that came with it compensated for the added visibility. It was a weak argument, but given that he didn't have any choice in the matter, it was enough. Third, and perhaps most importantly, given where this was inevitably headed, he knew that it could only end one way—badly.

Olivia could only view what he was going to do, what he had to do, as a betrayal. It wasn't fair to either of them and he knew that if he wanted a long-term relationship with her he had to sacrifice being with her right now.

In the end, that convinced him and reluctantly he turned to face her, already framing the necessary excuse. The excuse miscarried in his mind before it was complete as he watched her putter in the kitchen. Despite not having been close to her for over forty years, he found that he could still read her and he felt conflicted as he read the happiness in her posture. A part of him rejoiced in the purity of the moment, but another part of him felt anguished at the underlying deception and the inevitable outcome looming like an iceberg just over the horizon.

He sighed mentally. He wasn't fooling himself. Despite all the reasons he had listed, he knew he wasn't going anywhere. He tried to rationalize it, and unbidden, a smile touched his lips as he recalled a comment Olivia had made decades before, in another lifetime. She had joked that the ability of humans to rationalize terrible decisions separated them from animals. He knew that was exactly what he was doing now, but it didn't stop him. He knew she would be furious with him, regardless of how close they became. He told himself it was only a matter of degree, and he ignored the more rational part of his mind that told him he wasn't fooling anyone.

He continued to sip his wine and watch her and even though neither of them was talking, it didn't matter. Soft classical music played in the background and he pulled himself up on a stool at the breakfast bar. He refilled his wine, content to just enjoy the moment. He frowned mentally, as the analytical part of his mind nagged at him, and then suddenly he figured out what was bothering him. The amount of food she was preparing was far more than the two of them could eat themselves, even as hungry as he was. He glanced over at the table and noticed that she had set it for four. He could have sworn there were only two place settings, but he had let himself relax in her company and so he couldn't be certain. He looked at her closely and noticed a certain tension in her posture that he hadn't noticed earlier.

Before he could say anything, he heard the sound of the front door opening and closing. Companionable chatter spilled out of the hallway and his enhancement automatically identified the voices. They were both Senior VPs at Delphi. One of them was Brooke Winters, the Senior VP of HR and the other was Nicole West, Senior VP of Information Technology. He had dealings with both of them, although only on a professional level, more so with Nicole as his implementation of the nanitic security bracelets had resulted in him working closely with her, if only for a short time.

He smiled a polite hello at them and turned back towards Olivia. He didn't know what she had in mind, but he just wasn't up for it right now. He should be angry that she had sprung this on him, except he was too tired to care. All he wanted was to go home and get some rest. He opened his mouth to say as much, only she beat him to it.

"I hope you don't mind, but this is the night that I usually have Brooke and Nicole over for dinner." The look on her face made him hesitate and just then Brooke and Nicole walked in. They seemed surprised to see him and he could tell that they weren't happy about it either. For a moment, he felt a perverse urge to stay just to tick them off, but he wasn't the type to play those games. He heard Olivia explaining why he was there and he started to interrupt, to tell them that he had to get going, but he couldn't. He knew he had the perfect excuse, but he also realized that they would both know that was all it was—just an excuse.

He hesitated and shot a quick look over at Brooke and Nicole and what he saw there decided him. Despite how unhappy they must have been at his presence at what was obviously a long-standing tradition of women only, they accepted that Olivia wanted him there. It didn't make it all right, but they accepted it out of the trust and respect they had for her. He couldn't do anything less—not and be the person he wanted to be.

"Not only do I not mind, but I'm honored," he replied seriously and Olivia smiled. It was only a small smile. Still it made him all the more glad he had decided to stay.

"Excellent. I'd hate for all this food to go to waste."

Nicole shook her head gravely. "I don't know about it going to waste. It would undoubtedly go to someone's waist and we know that Brooke eats like a bird."

"I most certainly do not," Brooke replied indignantly, the twinkle in her eyes belying the anger in her voice. "Perhaps in comparison to some," she sniffed disapprovingly and then laughed when Nicole stuck her tongue out at her. "Honestly, I don't know how you do it. You're at least twice my age and everyone knows that metabolisms slow down with age. I know that I can't eat as much as I did when I was younger, but even then I don't think that I ever ate as much as you do. And I know that I was never that skinny," she finished mournfully, and even Ryan had to laugh at the look she directed towards Nicole's slender frame.

"What can I say?" Nicole responded with a smile. "I guess I'm just blessed with good genes."

Ryan felt himself relaxing and beginning to enjoy their company. The friendly banter continued and they all made their way to the comfortable living room while dinner was cooking. He didn't know any of them well enough, except for Olivia, to contribute much in the way of witty repartee, but he was able to take part in the discussions that followed. He could tell that he surprised Brooke with the extent of his knowledge in areas outside his field of expertise, but he was used to that. What surprised him in turn was that Nicole wasn't. Perhaps he simply wasn't able to read her yet, but somehow he felt it was more than that, that somehow she had expected him to be knowledgeable.

The discussion continued over dinner, which Ryan had to admit was delicious. He ate more than his fair share, which wasn't surprising, given the demands that he'd been under. He was a little amazed by how much Nicole ate and he could see now why Brooke had felt so comfortable in teasing her. He made a mental note to check her file and see if she was enhanced. He had gone over all the personnel files once when he had first started, and he couldn't recall a history of military service, but it was possible he had missed it. Of course it was also possible that Nicole was one of those rare nonmilitary enhancements. Before the military took it over, it had been open for a brief time to anyone who could afford it and Nicole was old enough to qualify.

He looked around and had to admit that the four of them made a curious group. Besides being the only male, Ryan was the youngest, at least based on the age he was pretending to be. Even with his real age that was still true, although the margin dropped from a few decades to a few years. Olivia was only a few years older than he was, but given her rank and sheer presence, her age was almost irrelevant, at least in this setting.

Brooke was the next youngest, that being a relative term for someone who was almost one hundred and fifty years old. She, too, was a true Californian who didn't match the stereotype. She was short, topping out at slightly under five feet. She joked that was why she and Olivia got along so well, that together they were just two people—in height.

Which left Nicole as being the oldest by a comfortable margin, although she didn't look it. Approaching her third century, Nicole was perhaps the oldest person he had ever met and he was a little surprised to see someone so old still working. He knew there were many women as old as Nicole, but three hundred years allowed even the worst money manager to amass a comfortable fortune. After all, the magic of compound interest was working in their favor. As a result most women that age had long since retired. Nicole, on the other hand, showed no signs of stopping. Despite his misgivings, her energy, drive and competence impressed him, especially in a constantly changing field like Information Technology. He had almost chosen that field himself, so he knew how difficult it was to keep up with.

Though he enjoyed the IT side of his job, there were several reasons he decided against it so long ago. The first, of course, because it was just too obvious for what he was trying to do. Running a close second was the near impossibility of being able to succeed. Getting the job that he did have took a rare combination of a lot of hard work, the years of training that he had gotten in the military, some dumb luck, and perhaps some nostalgia. Getting the job that Nicole currently held, and in fact had held almost forty years ago, would have taken a miracle. Surprisingly enough, his handlers hadn't thought that Nicole would still have the job when the right time came. They just assumed that he would be competing against someone else, someone who would have just started.

Regardless of all that, the fact remained that Information Technology, at least at Nicole's level, was strictly a woman's field. In truth, although he had always had a knack for IT, he just didn't have the patience for it. People always seemed surprised by that comment, the few times that he had made it. After all, Security was a job that demanded patience as well, but for some reason, Ryan didn't mind it. Which, of course, made all the difference. He would never have thought of Security as a career choice, but looking back, he knew that he had made the right decision, even if it wasn't for the right reasons.

He stole a quick look at Olivia over the top of his wineglass as she elaborated on the current topic and smiled. She was the reason that he had accepted that proposal all those years ago. Not because he wanted to get back at her for dumping him or anything petty like that. No, he wanted to do this because he wanted to have a chance with her. He didn't need her to tell him why she had broken off with him; even then he was astute enough to figure it out. He was also astute enough to know that he couldn't change her mind and he wasn't even sure that he wanted to. After all, he loved her enough not to want to put her through that and so he had let her be.

When his handlers-to-be found him a few years later and finally convinced him that they were telling the truth, he jumped at the chance. He had never told them what the time he and Olivia had spent together meant to him—they had always assumed it was a brief fling—and at times he had almost regretted not telling them. He knew that they would take a dim view of it, not only the feelings that he still harbored for her, but also that he had kept it a secret all these years.

He understood where they were coming from. They had invested significant amounts of time and money, but they had more than enough of both. He had invested his entire life. Realistically, no one knew when or how this would end. When they first recruited him, they had presented his new life as a backup plan. At that time, they had still been hoping that they would be able to reverse engineer the polymerase. If they had managed to do that, then they wouldn't need him to access the formula hidden at Delphi. That was almost forty years ago, and he might have doubted the existence of the formula if it weren't for the obvious physical proof. With any luck, it would end here with him but even then there were no guarantees.

He turned his attention back to the conversation and realized that it had somehow migrated its way to work-related topics while he was busy woolgathering. He took a hefty sip of wine and forced himself to pay closer attention. He listened to the ebb and flow as they talked, partially to reorient himself with the discussion and partially out of curiosity. While he had gathered that this night was a regular event, he was coming to realize that it served as an informal executive team meeting as well. He had only attended two meetings so far in his tenure as a Senior VP, but he accessed his files on those meetings and went back over the votes. Sure enough he noticed that on any of the important issues, the three of them always voted together, or at least the same way.

He quickly replayed the conversation that he had missed in his mind. Due to his earlier inattention, before Brooke and Nicole's arrival, he had instructed his neural feed to record everything he saw or heard. Playing the conversation back, he noticed that it was Olivia who introduced the work-related discussions and that Brooke had seemed surprised. Interestingly enough, Nicole wasn't, and that was surprising. Nicole had hidden it well, but he was coming to expect that from her.

He finally put it all together and figured out Olivia wanted him to be part of these informal executive meetings. He found himself flattered, both personally and professionally. He resolved to pay more attention and to try to contribute more to the conversation. If she were going to do him the honor of including him, then he would damned well be sure he deserved it.

* * *

Olivia finished loading the dishwasher and looked around in satisfaction. Apart from two coffee cups, everything was clean. Both Nicole and Ryan had headed home, no big deal since the CEO and all the Senior VPs lived in the same gated community. Brooke had pulled her usual delaying tactic of going to the washroom as everyone was leaving. She never left with the others, but she also didn't want to rub it in.

As she waited, Olivia added cream to Brooke's coffee, wincing as she did so. How anyone could ruin good Columbian coffee like that was beyond her. It didn't even look like coffee anymore.

"Stop bitching about how I take my coffee," a voice said over her shoulder and Olivia smiled.

"What?" she protested, "I didn't say a word."

Brooke snorted. "You didn't have to. You always get that mixture of sadness and disgust on your face when you mix my coffee. What I'm never sure about is if you're sad that I don't drink 'proper' coffee or sad about the waste of good coffee."

"Oh, that's easy—it's the waste of good coffee," Olivia replied easily and then laughed as Brooke pretended to ignore her, sipping her coffee in bliss.

"So, do you think it worked?" Brooke asked after a moment and Olivia started.

Olivia took a sip of her own coffee to cover the involuntary movement as she stalled for time. "Do I think what worked?" she asked casually and Brooke just smiled and shook her head.

"Nice try but it won't wash. I know you too well."

"Oh really?" Olivia said in amusement "Do tell."

"For starters, I know this wasn't what you had planned for this evening, since you had canceled on Nicole and me earlier. My guess is that once you picked up Ryan at the airport, you realized that this was a little more than you were ready for. So you called Nicole and me and asked us to come on over as usual, neglecting to mention by the way, that he was still here. I know that I got the impression that he had gone home." She cocked her head and looked at Olivia. "How am I doing so far?" she asked brightly.

"Keep going," Olivia muttered darkly, but she couldn't help smiling as her friend grinned in triumph. Brooke was right. She does know me too well, Olivia thought.

"Then you waited to see how we would all get along together and once you had a handle on that, you decided to make him a part of our group. I think that just about sums it up, don't you?"

"Too well," Olivia admitted cheerfully, "so let me turn it back at you. How do you think it worked?"

Olivia watched Brooke as she considered her answer and reflected on what a good friend she was. No matter what happened, Brooke was always there for her and she knew that she could tell her anything.

"Despite getting off to a slow start I must admit that your buddy Mr. Peters contributed his fair share to the conversation. It did surprise me just how extensive his knowledge is, as did his maturity. There were times when I would have been uncomfortable or defensive with the grilling that we were giving him, but he just responded calmly to all our criticisms. He was also able to admit when he was wrong, something that I still have trouble with." She ignored the amused snort that Olivia couldn't contain and continued. "All told I think that he'll make a fine addition to our group."

"Yeah, I think so too. I think that he was more exhausted than I realized, which accounted for the slow start. Once he figured it out, though, he made up for lost time."

"What about Methuselah, what did she think?"

"Would you stop with that already?" Olivia glared at Brooke, who had the grace to look contrite.

"Sorry, I know I shouldn't do that. I mean I really like Nicole and we get along well, but there's just something about her that pops up now and then that jars me."

"I know what you mean but you're right about us all getting along. Besides which, I trust her. She's got an incredible wealth of experience that we can draw upon, she's almost scarily competent, and I know that once she agrees to do something, she'll do it, regardless of her personal feelings. It might take some work to get her to agree to it, but once that's done I know I can rest easy."

"You're right, you're right, I know you're right," Brooke responded and Olivia laughed. God, that movie was almost three hundred years old and it still made her laugh.

"There you go. There's another point in her favor. How else would we become exposed to stuff like that, if it wasn't for her?"

"All right already, I've already fessed up. But you still haven't told me what she thinks."

Olivia frowned thoughtfully. "To be honest, I'm not sure. She said that she was all right with it, but I was expecting a little more resistance. It just seemed too easy." An expression flickered briefly across Brookes face and Olivia pounced on it. "What?"

"You've mentioned her experience, you tell me."

Taken aback by her response Olivia frowned. "What does that mean?"

"It means that I can see how attracted you are to him and him to you. I'll admit that I can read this easier because we're so close, but I'm thinking that with almost three hundred years of life experience she should be able to see it, too."

Olivia stared at Brooke, horrified. "I'm not that obvious am I?"

"No of course not, it's just my experience with you in particular and Nicole's experience with life in general, that lets us read you that well."

Olivia was only slightly mollified by Brooke's response and then suddenly her brain caught up with her. "Wait a minute, what do you mean, he's attracted to me?"

Brooke smiled slyly at her. "Ah, you caught that?"

"I admit this isn't something I'm used to, but it doesn't mean I'm not paying attention."

"Unfortunately, I don't have the kind of insight into Ryan that I do with you," Brooke pointed out. "Normally, he's almost as hard to read as Nicole, but I think you were right about how tired he was tonight. There was a brief moment when he was looking at you and you could clearly see that he had feelings for you."

Olivia frowned as she considered this. "I'm not sure if I find that flattering or creepy. I mean, I know why I'm attracted to him and that bothers me enough as it is, but there's no reason for him to find me attractive."

"For Christ's sake Olivia, stop analyzing this so much. You are an attractive, successful, powerful, funny, wonderful woman. If I were a man, I'd find you attractive. Hell, I even know women who feel the same way. Stop analyzing," she repeated, "and start feeling."

"You don't think it's weird to think of going out with him?"

"No, I don't. I think that you're reading too much into that." Brooke paused and then continued gently. "You're going to have to deal with it eventually, you know. These days it's just a fact of life."

"I know," Olivia replied just a softly, "but that doesn't mean I have to like it."

Brooke just shrugged. They had been over this issue many times lately and there wasn't much more to say. Olivia sat back with a sigh and sipped her coffee. She wondered what she should do. She hadn't seen any signs that Ryan found her attractive—in fact, everything she'd seen had spoken to his just wanting to be friends, if men and women could be friends. She snorted in amusement as her mind somehow found its way back to that movie. She looked up to ask Brooke if she wanted to watch it with her and smiled as she saw that she'd fallen asleep. Typical Brooke, a few glasses of wine and she was down for the count. She rose and covered her gently with a blanket. She debated going to sleep herself but despite the late hour, she was too wound up. She decided to watch the movie after all and she instructed the holo to cue up 'When Harry Met Sally' as she grabbed another blanket for herself and curled up on the couch.

* * *

Nicole glanced over at Ryan as they left Olivia's. Since all the Senior VPs lived in the same gated executive community, they both lived within walking distance of Olivia's. The executive community held about a dozen houses nestled into eight acres on a hillside about an hour away from Delphi. At the current moment, there were only nine Senior VPs, including Ryan, which meant he'd had had a little more choice than usual when he selected his house. Of course, with so many vacant houses, the existing Senior VPs had picked the choice ones as they moved around.

Everyone thought that Nicole would have had the nicest house, since she had been around the longest, but that wasn't the case. Although her house wasn't the biggest, she had picked it carefully. It was one of the more isolated ones to start with, and although it was of average size, the houses bordering it were among the smallest. Given the fact that there were several other choices, no one had lived in those houses in over a century, which meant that she had a lot of privacy. All of that changed when Ryan showed up. She didn't know why, but for some reason he had selected one of these smaller homes, and so as it turned out, they were neighbors. As she thought about it, she decided to satisfy her curiosity.

"You know, I was wondering why you selected the house that you did."

Ryan looked embarrassed and he shifted his carryon bag on his shoulder. "Lots of reasons, actually. I liked the relative seclusion of it. I also don't need much space, which is why I selected one of the smaller houses."

"I'd imagine there's also an image component to that," Nicole said, hiding her amusement at the look of surprise on Ryan's face.

"You're right, there was an element of image management to it. I didn't want to pick the largest available house or the smallest. That still left me with some choices and like I said, I liked the relative solitude of this one." He paused and then looked over at her. "I didn't realize that I would be intruding on your privacy."

"Don't worry, you're not."

Ryan snorted. "That's not the message that I've gotten from some of the other Senior VPs."

Nicole laughed and shook her head. "It's true that nobody's lived there in over a century, but I always thought that was because the houses were small."

Ryan smiled in amusement. "Does that mean I don't have to move?"

"Heavens, no. I don't imagine you'll be throwing many wild parties and if you want to know the truth, I'm enjoying the thought of having someone nearby."

"Well, I'm glad. I don't think I've spent more than a week total there since I moved in, but despite that I've grown rather attached to it. Like yourself, I welcome the relative solitude and now that I know you a little better, I'm glad to have you as a neighbor."

Nicole smiled. "Me too." By this time they had reached the houses and Ryan inclined his head.

"Well, this is my stop."

"See you later," Nicole replied and a minute later she reached her own house. She went inside and changed into her pajamas and then wandered into the kitchen. She put on the kettle and thought about the evening while the water boiled. She didn't need her knowledge of the history between Olivia and Ryan to see the attraction between them, and she could understand what Olivia saw in Ryan. He was good-looking, quiet in a mature and confident way, competent and hardworking.

Nicole also knew what Olivia didn't—what Ryan had sacrificed to get to this point. She had been prepared to tolerate him because of that, but it surprised her how much she actually liked him. She also knew just how alone he was and as she thought about it, she decided to help him. She inserted herself into the network and scripted a monitoring routine for Ryan. The kettle started whistling and she absentmindedly poured a mug of water and added a tea bag as she finished the script. She wouldn't see any of his private correspondence, although she could if she wanted to, but she would see any general queries he sent to the network. With a little luck, she could find a way to 'accidentally' bump into him at a time and location where she could chat with him about his relationship with Olivia.

Chapter Six

Even though he had gone to bed a lot later than he planned, Ryan still forced himself to wake up early the next day. It was harder than he expected. The late night and the time zone differences took more out of him than he had realized. However, he had to get going. Not only did he have work to catch up on, he also knew from long experience that the best way to reset his body's internal clock was to force himself to follow the local time zone. At least he didn't have to go into the office today. He was all caught up with his paperwork, not to mention that it was Sunday. Given that he had effectively been off-site for the better part of the last two months, he felt he could spend his time better by randomly checking up on his staff.

He thought briefly about where to visit first and finally decided to head out to the field training building. This way, he would be able to kill two birds with one stone. He could get an update on how the training was going and get in some much needed practice at the firing range. It had surprised him to learn that Delphi had a small range, since all the guards, except the field-rated staff, only had stunners. Not that he disagreed with the need. After all, aiming and firing a stunner needed the same skills and reflexes as more lethal firearms did. He just hadn't expected it, considering the lax security measures that he had inherited from his predecessor. He had found out from one of the regulars at the range that she had been a real gun nut, which explained it.

Ryan entered the firing range and blinked in surprise. He quickly checked the network and relaxed as he found an entry stating that Delphi's field-rated security staff were having a field exercise today. That would account for the large group of people in close-fitting combat gear checking firearms out. Out of curiosity, he wandered closer. His movement caught the eye of the group's commander, Mia Reynolds, and she nodded respectfully to Ryan and then started to turn back. Abruptly, she checked herself and left the group to approach him.

"Hey Mia, how's it going?" he asked and she shook her head.

"Not so well, I'm afraid. The changes you made when you started shook everyone up enough that these goons started taking these field exercises seriously. The attempted data theft a month later reinforced it. Unfortunately, that was almost two months ago and they're already starting to get lax again. They were never good enough to be able to afford to do that, but I can't convince them of that."

Ryan frowned. If there was anything he despised, it was laziness and complacency. On the other hand, he didn't want to interfere. That was what the chain of command was for. If she needed help, she would work it through the proper channels. In fact, odds were that he would never have heard about this problem unless it had remained unresolved for longer than a month or unless the solution somehow needed his approval. Still, he was here now and he wanted to offer support if needed.

"Is there anything I can do?" he asked, careful to keep his voice calm and even. He didn't want her to think that he was trying to override her. To his surprise, she grinned at him.

"Actually, I was hoping you'd ask me that. I'd planned on taking these two squads out and having them play an advanced game of capture the flag. The problem is that they are both at the same level. It doesn't give them anything to work towards and it especially doesn't highlight their weaknesses."

Ryan nodded in understanding. Capture the flag sounded simple, but if played right it was a good field exercise. It needed stealth, discipline and teamwork. It also provided a much-needed element of competition. However, it sounded like the issues that Mia had mentioned would make the exercise effectively worthless. He got the impression that she had come up with a solution though, so he nodded for her to continue.

"Now that you're here, I just thought of an alternative. We'll give you a five-minute head start and then send both squads out after you. I think they need to know just how deficient they are."

Ryan nodded cautiously, hiding his surprise at her solution. Although it was slowly changing, his predecessor had been controlling, and as a result, most of his staff still had trouble taking initiative and thinking outside the box like that, particularly when it came to men and their abilities. "You do know that I haven't been active military in over ten years."

Mia snorted. "As if that matters." He looked at her inquiringly and she shrugged. "I've got a few friends in the military. When you started here, I checked up on you. What I heard impressed me and I haven't seen anything since that contradicts that impression. I also rather doubt that you're the type of person who would let their skills slip."

Ryan grinned despite himself as he thought about it. He really shouldn't, but it would give him an opportunity to showcase his skills. It would also send a clear message, not only to the squads taking part in the exercise, but to all of his security personnel. He would not tolerate laziness and complacency. "What load out are you using?" he asked and she grinned back at him.

"Just regular gunpowder. Nothing with a muzzle velocity higher than a mile per second." Ryan nodded—the field combat gear that they were using would be able to deal with that muzzle velocity easily, leaving the wearer with only a welt as a reminder. His enhancements would be able to deal with it as well, although not as efficiently as the field combat gear would. But then again, if he planned this right, there was no reason he should have to.

"Sounds good, let's do it."

"Great," Mia replied, her eyes lighting up. "Why don't you grab yourself a combat vest while I brief them?"

"No need," Ryan responded and he smiled wickedly as Mia's eyes widened. Then she grinned back at him.

"Ooh, I think I'm going to like this. In that case, I'd like to activate the high-density scanners. If we have a good record of this, it will go a long way towards keeping them on their toes." Ryan nodded and sent the request off to security central. He received the acknowledgment and inclined his head at Mia to let her know that they were now active.

"All right everyone, listen up!" Mia said loudly and the background murmurs died down as everyone turned to look at the two of them. "There's been a change of plans." That got everyone's attention and Mia quickly outlined the new exercise. Ryan had already shifted his enhancement to active combat mode, so he overheard a few uncomplimentary mutters, but he just ignored them. As soon as Mia finished, she nodded to him and he calmly left the firing range.

Once outside, he scanned the scrub covering the hillsides. At this time of year, dull brown scrub covered most of the hillsides. He wouldn't be able to spot what he was looking for visually, so he activated his thermal imaging and finally found what he was looking for. About a hundred feet away, a black-tailed jackrabbit sat frozen, waiting for him to move. He slowly reached down and felt around on the ground beside him until he found the right sized stone. Suddenly his armed blurred and the jackrabbit collapsed on the ground. He knew that he had just stunned it and he raced over to it before it could recover.

He grinned as he reached it. It was a male and so it was slightly smaller than a female, roughly a foot and a half in length. The fact that it was a male was somehow strangely fitting, and Ryan felt an odd sense of kinship as he quickly took off his crisp blue oxford shirt and tied it firmly around the jackrabbit's body. His pants were tan cotton khakis so they would blend in. His tan skin and brown, short cropped hair wouldn't give him away either.

He grinned as he helped the rabbit back to consciousness and then shooed it away. It leaped fifteen feet away from him in one huge jump and then started zigzagging. Its course took it almost directly away from him as well as the firing range and he grinned again as he wished it luck. He knew that it would only take it about ten minutes to squirm free of the shirt but that would be more than enough for his plan to work. He checked the time. He had two minutes left on his five-minute head start to find a suitable hiding spot, one that would provide protection from both visual detection as well as the standard thermal imaging gear used by the field-rated staff.

He had settled down when the doors to the firing range opened. He used his enhanced hearing to track the two squads as they fanned out and headed up the hill, barely pausing in their rush to catch up to him. He waited a few minutes and then followed them. As he expected, they were tracking the jackrabbit. Since the jackrabbit was the only moving heat source, they automatically assumed it was him. His blue oxford shirt and the jackrabbit's speed of thirty-five miles an hour only confirmed it for them. They naturally assumed that he was trying to use his speed to lose them.

He overtook one of the stragglers and quietly slipped up behind her with a chokehold. As soon as she slipped into unconsciousness, he eased her down and relieved her of her rifle. A few moments work overrode the built-in security designed to prevent anyone else from using the rifle. Then he triggered her emergency beacon and slipped quickly and quietly back into the scrub. As he expected, the rest of the squad realized he had fooled them and started heading back. He patiently scanned the scrub, using both thermal imaging as well as a pattern variance algorithm. It was similar to the algorithm used to clear the hydrogen building and it would highlight any movement instantly. He shook his head as he evaluated the squads. They barely gave concealment a token effort and so far both squads were reacting rather than pro-acting. Committing both squads to the same objective was a waste of effort. Worse yet, it was dangerous since it increased the risks without noticeably changing the odds.

He waited patiently until he had identified all the remaining squad members, and then he raised the rifle and fired off fifteen shots in less than five seconds. He grinned as he caught the distinctive buzz that meant the exercise was over emanating from every combat uniform. He stood up, slung the rifle over his shoulder, and headed back towards the security guard that he had knocked out. Out of all of them, she had gotten off the lightest, since she would only have a mild headache to deal with. All the others would have significant welts directly over their hearts. He picked her up effortlessly and slung her over his shoulder, fireman style, and then headed back to the firing range.

He managed to find another blue shirt for himself, and then began stripping and cleaning the rifle that he had used. As each person entered the building, they looked at him with a combination of embarrassment and grudging respect. He kept his expression calm, and acknowledged the occasional gesture of respect with a simple nod. Mia wasn't so restrained. She was practically gloating at having proved her point, and she barely waited for him to leave the building before launching into a scathing critique of their mistakes.

* * *

Ryan yawned and stretched, feeling the after effects of his trip. Although his participation in the field exercise that Mia had conducted had been gratifying, it hadn't done much to challenge him physically. He grinned as he recalled the reception that he had received throughout the day. It had surprised him how quickly the rumor mill worked. Within thirty minutes, word had spread to almost every guard on duty. In just a little over an hour, those who had access to security terminals had seen the recording of the event. He didn't know who was responsible for leaking it, but he had his suspicions. Apparently everyone who saw the video also knew that Mia had asked him to help out. Although some guards would still think that he had been showboating, as long as they did their jobs and didn't let their feelings interfere with their duties, he didn't care. On the whole, however, the positive responses had surprised and gratified him. Most of the guards already considered him 'one of the girls' and this only cemented it for them. He knew that his predecessor's laxness was as much responsible for that as his own attentiveness was, but it still pleased him.

He grimaced as he felt the tightness of his muscles and he checked the time, tagging the inquiry to the fitness center. As expected, the fitness center had closed for the night, at least for regular staff. There were several communal facilities that were available to the Senior VPs twenty-four-seven and the fitness center was one of them. In theory, he could meet one of the other Senior VPs there, but in reality that was far from likely. He considered it briefly and decided to head over anyway.

He had been to the fitness center before of course—there was no place on Delphi's grounds that he hadn't seen during his tenure—but he hadn't worked out there. He had been too busy during the first month getting the security force whipped into shape. As for the two months following that, he had been off-site more often than not. The center had something for almost everyone, but unfortunately it lacked the one piece of equipment that Ryan wanted to use—automated sparring equipment. The equipment was a poor substitute for a real sparring partner, but it was better than nothing.

Apart from that, Delphi's fitness center had it all. There was a wide variety of workout equipment, self-contained mini gyms, virtual treadmills and stair climbers, a rock wall, and even a few variable environment lap pools. He made a face at the thought of mindless reps, but it was better than nothing. As light a workout as it was, this morning's field exercise told him that he needed to work on his conditioning. It wasn't apparent to anyone else yet, but he could feel it.

Ryan arrived at the fitness center and changed quickly. He headed out into the central area and then paused in the doorway in surprise. The fitness center wasn't empty. Even more surprising was who he found there and what she was doing.

It was Nicole and she was lifting weights. Normally, he would have frowned on anyone lifting weights without using the automated spotting equipment, but given that she was bench-pressing almost seven hundred pounds, it was obvious that she didn't need one. The only way she could press that amount of weight was enhancement, which only confirmed his earlier suspicions. It also explained why she was here after hours, although he was a little annoyed that he hadn't checked to see if anyone was using the fitness center.

He shook off that first momentary pause, waved to her, and kept moving towards the bank of treadmills. He stepped into the booth and punched up one of the standard programs that he always used. The blank confines of the booth disappeared, replaced by a peaceful woodland trail. Ryan started running, slowly at first and gradually building up speed, but that was more for the benefit of the treadmill than for him. Even a high-end model like this one could only handle so much, and if he started all out he would have run into the wall before the machine had caught up with him. At least it had enough power to make him work a little, even if it didn't exactly tax his limits.

He ran for about an hour, feeling the stress drain out of him with each rhythmic thud as his feet hit the ground. He let the program shut down and then exited the booth. Despite the workout he wasn't even sweating, although he could feel his heart pounding. He moved on to the free weights next, noting in passing that Nicole had moved on to one of the treadmills. He completed a solid set of reps, pressing well over a thousand pounds himself. Then he hit the rock wall, barely giving his aching muscles time to relax. He set the difficulty to high and started climbing. As he approached the top of the rock wall, it started rotating beneath him, allowing him to keep climbing. He had climbed about a thousand virtual feet when he heard a voice below him. He looked down and saw Nicole standing there on the ground, thirty feet below him.

"Hey yourself," he responded, wedging himself into a more secure position.

"If you're done climbing to nowhere, how about sparring a little?"

Ryan felt himself grinning. "Sounds good," he replied and he let go of his holds, dropping the entire thirty feet before landing lightly beside her.

"Showoff," Nicole snorted and Ryan shrugged and grinned as he followed her to the mat.

"I was a little surprised to see you here," he said, and she looked back at him over her shoulder.

"I know you were. But you shouldn't have been, should you?"

"Ouch."

"Hey, the truth hurts. Deal with it."

"Yeah I know. It was a little sloppy of me, but I didn't expect anyone else to be here." He grinned and held up his hand. "I know that I could have checked. I just don't like doing that unless I feel I need to. People are twitchy enough about their privacy these days."

Nicole snorted again. "Privacy is an illusion," she retorted and Ryan nodded.

"True, but far be it from me to disillusion them. Besides, people are nervous enough around security personnel without my adding fuel to the fire."

Nicole grinned at him. "I know. I'm just pushing your buttons. I'm hoping that if I rile you up enough, you'll get sloppy and make mistakes."

"Ha," Ryan barked. "Not likely. Don't forget that I saw you bench-pressing almost seven hundred pounds. I checked up on you the other night and there's no record of you in any military database. That means you received your enhancement back when it was still open to the public. I'd be willing to bet you've been practicing martial arts almost that long."

"Busted," she admitted. "How did you know?" she asked curiously and he shrugged again.

"In the military, we start practicing martial arts as soon as we can once we're enhanced. It's one of the quickest ways to get control of our new reflexes and strength."

By that time, they had reached the mats and they each took their positions, circling each other cautiously. Ryan made the first move and found himself flying through the air. He twisted impossibly in mid-flight and landed on his feet with a wide grin.

"Damn, I've missed that," he said, and Nicole grinned at him again.

"Good, 'cause there's a lot more where that came from."

Ryan approached her again, lightning quick, and this time it was Nicole who hit the mat. She turned it into a somersault, but Ryan was on her before she could straighten up. For all the good that it did him. He found himself thrown over her shoulder, landing with a loud thud on the mat. Nicole tried to follow up with an elbow to the solar plexus, but Ryan was already rolling out of the way and her elbow landed with a lethal sounding bang on the mat. Ryan grinned again and sprang to his feet.

"That was incredible," Nicole said as they walked away from the mat and Ryan had to agree. "It's been too long since I've had a good workout like that."

Ryan snorted. "Well you could have fooled me."

Nicole grinned. "I've been keeping up with my katas and I spar against a training remote two or three times a month at one of the martial art clubs in town. It's hard to get more time than that since I always book the entire club. They don't lose out financially, but it's tough on their members."

"Youch! That sounds expensive. What on earth do you need the entire club for? Better still, why don't you just spar with the other members?"

Nicole looked a little embarrassed. "What can I say, I like my privacy. Besides, it's not like I can't afford it."

Ryan got the feeling there was more to it than that. After the other night, he had searched the employee files and then done a wider search on the Net with similar results. There was no record anywhere of Nicole being enhanced. Yet, here she was. For some reason she was willing to share this side of her life with him and it was oddly flattering. It also gave him a little insight into how lonely she must be and he shuddered mentally at the thought of being alone for so long. Hopefully, Nicole hadn't been so alone her entire life. The idea of close to three centuries of loneliness was horrifying. He wondered if she'd like to spar more often and decided to extend the offer.

"Now that I'm not traveling, I'm available. I wouldn't normally workout regularly since routine reps bore me, but if you'd like, we can set up a regular sparring schedule."

"Sounds good," she replied as they reached the executive changing room. When the fitness center had been built, for the regular users they had included separate changing rooms for men and women. However, there was only one executive changing room. Technically it was unisex but since there hadn't been any male executives before, it had effectively been a female changing room. As the first male executive, Ryan was uncertain about the protocol. That was partly why he timed his visit late, so that he wouldn't have to face this situation. He followed Nicole cautiously, watching for any signs that he was overstepping the boundaries.

Nicole palmed her locker and pulled her top over her head. "So why not every night?" she asked, her voice muffled behind her top. Ryan's eyes widened at the sight of her nude torso and he struggled to find a response. He was prepared for almost any reaction to his presence in what had been the exclusive domain of females but he hadn't expected this. Her casual approach to nudity threw him, but then again his experience with three-hundred-year-old women was limited. Actually, it was nonexistent. From almost anyone else, the casual nudity might have been a blatant invitation or a cruel tease. He knew that Nicole didn't play those games, and the rapport that they had found while sparring made it seem almost natural. Almost.

"What's the matter," she asked archly, "cat got your tongue? Besides, I thought you were interested in Olivia."

Ryan kept moving, but inside he felt a knot of coldness form. "What makes you say that?" he asked casually, pleased by his ability to keep control.

"Oh please, you may be able to fool everyone else, but I've had almost three centuries of experience in reading people. Usually your control is pretty good, like right now, but last night it slipped a little."

Ryan used the act of removing his track pants to buy some time. He hadn't expected to have to deal with this issue with anyone, especially not Nicole, and he sighed mentally. No matter how hard he tried, it seemed like there was no getting around the truth. Even after all this time his interest in Olivia hadn't waned. He just didn't know what to do about it.

"I think that you should go for it," Nicole said and Ryan almost fell over. He looked up at her, startled by how her comment seemed to be answering his thoughts.

"Why do you say that?" he asked, giving up on any pretense of not being interested in Olivia. It looked like the only person that he had been fooling so far was himself.

"I wouldn't normally be saying this, but I like to think of myself as a good judge of character and I know that you won't use this unethically." She paused and looked at him, hard. He nodded, recognizing the tacit warning that she had given him. "I've known Olivia for a long time and in all that time she's never expressed an interest in anyone, man or woman. However, I've noticed a change in her behavior in a couple of areas that suggests to me that she is interested in you."

Ryan had noticed that as well lately, but it was good to know that he hadn't been projecting his own wishes. However, it did raise the issue of why she was telling him this and he asked her as much.

"Like I said, I don't normally do this, but Olivia's been a good friend to me for many years. You're the first person that she's shown any interest in and I want this to work out for her."

"So you're going to be my Obi-Wan, eh?"

Nicole grinned. "Now there's a blast from the past. It's not often that I find anyone who can recall those movies. Can I take that to mean you're a movie buff?"

"Yes and no," Ryan replied. "The Star Wars movies are popular with the military. The outer space element plus the prominent role of men have a certain appeal. In fact, you'll find many men plugged into older movies."

"Why's that?"

Ryan smiled sadly. "Look at most movies made today. Although men make up over ninety percent of the military, most of the action movies today feature women in the starring roles. Men are relegated to supporting roles, often playing the buffoon or comedic foil."

Nicole nodded in understanding and there was a brief period of silence. Ryan knew that discussing the roles of men and women made most women either uncomfortable or confrontational, but he didn't get that impression from her. Perhaps it was because she could recall a time when men and women had been equal, a time when the genders had not been divided by life expectancy.

After a moment, he redirected the conversation back to the real topic, which was the relationship between him and Olivia or at least the potential for a relationship.

"So Obi-Wan, why you?"

Nicole shrugged. "Who else?" she asked simply and this time it was Ryan's turn to nod understandingly. Given Olivia's position, there were few people who could get away with doing what she was proposing. Brooke was one of them, but she was the one who Olivia turned to for advice. Ryan understood that Nicole was proposing to play the same role for him.

"So what's the first step?" he asked her as they headed towards the sauna and Nicole laughed.

"Start by asking her out."

Ryan frowned crossly at her. "I'd figured that much out myself thanks. I was wondering if you had any suggestions."

"Let's start with the basics. What do you know about her?"

"Well I know she likes coffee."

"Wrong."

"Wrong?" Ryan frowned. "What do you mean wrong, she loves coffee."

Nicole made a buzzing noise. "Sorry, wrong answer. The correct answer to that question is that she worships coffee."

Ryan laughed. "True, there is a degree of idolatry to her love of coffee."

"Okay, what else?"

Ryan thought for a moment and as he did so Nicole stretched, the motion arching her back and making her breasts bob. Ryan's experience with women was rare enough that despite his self-control he found himself distracted.

Nicole laughed at the expression on his face. "I'm sorry, am I distracting you?"

"Maybe just a little," he admitted sheepishly. "It's just a little weird to be discussing my relationship with Olivia while we're naked in the sauna together."

"So just think of me as a guy."

"Not likely," Ryan said as he pretended to leer at her.

"Lecher."

"Not hardly."

"So, what else have you noticed about Olivia?" Nicole asked, and Ryan forced himself to ignore her.

"She likes to get away," he said finally, and Nicole gave an approving nod.

"Very good," she replied, "not many people would have picked up on that. So, we've got at least two things that we know. Put them together and you should be able to come up with an idea for your first date. Now, enough about that. Let's talk about your little adventure today."

Ryan blushed despite himself. He should have expected Nicole to know what had happened today—the high-density scanners linked directly into the computer network—but oddly enough he had managed to forget about it for a little while. He didn't really want to talk about it, yet he felt he owed Nicole at least that. Despite the age difference, he really liked her. Part of it came from sparring with her but there was something more, something he couldn't put his finger on.

"What do you want to know?" he asked after a moment and she hesitated before answering.

"I was wondering why you didn't wear a combat vest. I mean, weren't you putting yourself at risk doing that?"

Ryan laughed. "Are you asking me if I'm bulletproof?" he said, and she blushed.

"Yeah, I guess so," she admitted sheepishly.

"Well, that's a loaded question, if you'll pardon the pun. The official answer from the manufacturer of our nanites is no. The real life answer is sometimes. I asked Mia, the group commander, what load out they were using. That, combined with some other factors, determines the muzzle velocity or how fast the ammunition is traveling. The figure that she gave me was relatively low, as expected for a training exercise. Based on my experience, I knew that my nanites would be able to stop everything except for a shot fired at point-blank range."

Nicole was listening to this with a combination of intense fascination and technical curiosity. "How is that possible?"

"You know that most interpersonal weapons are energy concentrating devices. That's why bullets are pointed and blades are sharp edged. They concentrate the force into a small area and this is what causes the damage. Armor, on the other hand, is an energy-diffusing device. The purpose of armor is to absorb the impact of that concentrated force and spread it out. The combat vests used in training work on this principle. They are soft and flexible when they aren't under stress, but the second they become stressed beyond a certain limit they stiffen up. This stiffening absorbs most of the concentrated force and spreads the rest out enough to leave the wearer with only a bruise or welt, as opposed to something more significant."

Nicole interrupted him impatiently. "Yeah, yeah, I know all that."

"Patience," Ryan counseled gently, "I'm getting there. I just wanted to ensure that you knew the basics. Anyway, if you know what you are doing, you can get your nanites to act like armor. The nanites form on the surface of the skin and absorb the damage. Obviously there is a lot of skin surface to cover, which limits the ability of the nanites to absorb damage since they are so spread out. You can increase the effective protection by only protecting selected areas. Most people elect for head and torso only, since limb damage is more survivable. That's what I did since that would match the protection offered by a standard combat vest and visor."

"I see. And I assume that you had a reason for doing this?" she asked and he grinned.

"You mean besides male bravado?" he teased her. "No, I did have a couple of reasons. One, it sent a stronger message to the individuals involved in the training exercise. Two, the combat vests used in training have no camouflage capabilities. My plan revolved around my being able to hide from the group until I thought it was the right time for me to reveal myself. My tan skin was significantly less visible than a black combat vest."

"So there is a method to your madness."

"Or a madness to my method," he countered and she smiled.

"You said the lower the skin surface protected, the higher the effective protection. How high could this get?"

"Good question. For most weapons available to civilians, the protection that I used is enough. With military grade weapons, the muzzle velocities are so much higher that you could concentrate all available nanites in one spot and it wouldn't even slow it down. Neither could a combat vest. That's why you always see soldiers wearing armor."

"What about a point-blank shot?"

"If it's a civilian weapon, then yes. Someone could be holding a gun to your neck and if you focused your nanites correctly, you could walk away with only a bruise. I wouldn't recommend it, though" he cautioned and Nicole smiled.

"Don't worry, I'm not planning on getting shot anytime soon. It's just that I don't know anyone else who is enhanced and so I never get a chance to 'talk shop'. One last question—is it difficult to do?"

"Not really. In fact, it's similar to what you do automatically when you're sparring. Your nanites form a basic body armor that absorbs the worst blows and falls. It's just a matter of developing conscious control over something that you already do automatically."

"Cool. I'll have to practice that. I'd better get going, I'll see you later."

With that, she got up and left the sauna. He sprayed a little water on the stones and took a deep breath as steam filled the room. He sat there, letting the heat relax his muscles, mulling over the ideas that he had discussed with Nicole and debating with himself whether he should go out with Olivia.

Chapter Seven

"I beg your pardon?" Olivia stared at Ryan, caught off guard.

He smiled at her confusion. "I was wondering if you wanted to go out for dinner tonight." She just stared at him and he elaborated. "You know, like a date. I had a good time last weekend, but when I got home I realized that I was a little disappointed in the evening."

"Disappointed?" Olivia echoed weakly and Ryan nodded.

"Yeah, it seemed odd to me, too, and it's been bugging me all week, but I finally figured out what it was. I realized that I had been hoping to spend the evening with you alone, getting to know you better. I don't know if there's anything to this or whether it's just me, but I figured that I'll never know if I don't ask. I just thought that if we approached it head on we could find out if there's any substance to this attraction that I think we both feel."

Olivia found herself nodding her agreement automatically as she struggled to regain her equilibrium, but she had to admit that he had a point. She had been struggling to define their relationship, and while she had to admit that her own hang-ups on the subject were part of the problem, the other part lay strictly with him. She had already begun to doubt Brooke's assessment of his attraction for her, mostly because of her issues with him and her unfamiliarity with the dating scene in general. It had been intensely frustrating and it didn't help when she pressed Brooke for confirmation that Brooke admitted she could have been wrong.

Normally, Olivia would have been delighted in an admission like that from Brooke, but this time she found that scarce consolation. In fact, the only thing she had found consoling was that she hadn't acted like a fool and actually asked Ryan out. That was thanks to her natural caution, augmented by the issues she had with him and dating to begin with. Instead, during the last week she had been subtly intimating that she was open to a relationship, and she had been wondering if it was so subtle that he had missed it. It seemed that wasn't the case.

"What's this 'we' stuff?" she teased him and it pleased her when he had the grace to blush.

"Busted," he admitted with a wry grin. "I'm the one who's been dancing around it and I apologize. I'm usually more forthright than this. Somehow this feels different to me and I've been a little hesitant about starting something."

"A little hesitant?" Olivia asked pointedly and Ryan grinned as she smiled to take the sting out of it.

"Okay, more than a little. I'd like to make it up to you, if you will allow me to do so."

"Well just what did you have in mind, good sir?" she asked coyly. "After all, I do have my virtue to think of."

"Just dinner, I promise. Excellent ambiance, equally good food and wine, outstanding coffee and satisfactory company."

"Sold," Olivia replied promptly and Ryan grinned at her.

"It was the coffee that did it, wasn't it?" he asked and now it was Olivia's turn to blush. "You see, I have been paying attention."

"Apparently," she replied dryly.

"Touché," he replied, awarding her the point. "So I'll arrange for a car to pick us up at eight tonight, if that's okay with you." Olivia nodded. "In that case, until then."

Olivia's thoughts raced as he left her office and she automatically called Brooke.

"You were right after all," she said when Brooke answered.

"Of course I was," Brooke replied with a cheeky grin, "I'm always right. I would like to know about what though." Olivia didn't say anything and after a minute Brooke squealed "I'll be right there," and disconnected.

A minute later she burst into Olivia's office and plunked herself down on the cushy sofa no one else used. Swinging her feet up onto the coffee table, she shifted until she was comfortable and then looked straight at Olivia. "Okay. I want to know what he said, word for word."

Olivia recounted the conversation. Brooke smiled at her and said, "God, I love living vicariously. It's almost as much fun as doing it yourself, but without the mess."

"So, what do you think?" Olivia asked impatiently.

Brooke shrugged. "It's all upside as far as I'm concerned. Not only did he admit that he was in the wrong, he hinted that he considers this to be serious. He has also been paying enough attention to you to know that he can never be your true love, at least not while coffee holds that place in your heart."

"Very funny," Olivia said and Brooke just grinned at her. "What do you mean he intimated that he considers this to be serious?"

"Christ Liv, why can't you just use normal words like hint? Intimate," she said with a fake upper class accent. "Who speaks like that?"

Now it was Olivia's turn to grin. "I can't help it if I love unusual words. It always fascinates me just how rich the English language is."

"Yeah, well, for the rest of us, hint will do just fine, thank you. Anyway, what I was referring to was when he said that this feels different."

"Yes, and your point is?"

"You need to get out more Liv. That's guy talk for serious. He realized that up front and that's a good sign. Most guys don't figure it out until they are in the middle of a relationship, usually after someone says those dreaded words."

Olivia look puzzled. "You're right, I do need to get out more. What words are you talking about?"

"I Love You. Forget about how rich the English language is. Those are the three most common and yet most powerful words in it. Those words can make or break a relationship, depending on when they're said, and who said them, and if you hear them back."

Olivia shook her head. "I feel like I'm in the Twilight Zone or something. I was under the impression that most modern relationships were short-term affairs. Why would someone say I love you in one of those?"

Brooke shrugged. "What can I say? Either we're creatures of hormones or we're all closet romantics, take your pick. Either way it usually comes at a bad time. That Ryan recognized that this could be serious up front is a good sign."

"But it isn't serious!" Olivia replied with exasperation.

"Isn't it?" Brooke asked quietly and Olivia opened her mouth to retort and then stopped as the realization struck her.

"You're right. What am I thinking? I can't go through with this. I've got to call him and cancel."

"Easy Tex. Take your hand off the panic button and step back into the sanity zone."

"But, I'm serious. I already screwed this up once forty years ago because I didn't think about it beforehand. I won't do that again. I know that I deserve better and I'm sure that Ryan deserves better."

"You're right, you do deserve better and that's why you need to do this," Brooke said firmly. "This isn't forty years ago. You've changed and grown since then and you need to realize that. This bugaboo of yours about Ryan has been holding you back and one way or another you need to deal with this. Now, I realize the Ryan that you knew is dead and buried, but that doesn't mean that you need to be there with him. Use this opportunity to free yourself."

Olivia stared at Brooke. "What are you talking about?" she asked weakly and Brooke snorted angrily.

"Don't play dumb with me, Olivia Grace Morgan. I've known you for too long. Who was there for you when you fell apart after breaking up with Ryan forty years ago? Who's been there for you since then? I've watched you develop as a businesswoman and an executive, but your personal life has been stagnating since then. Work and a career are all well and good, but you're missing the most important part about life—living! Get out there and put this behind you."

"I don't want to screw this up again. Besides, I don't think that I'm ready for anything serious."

"Don't worry about it, neither is he."

Olivia shook her head in confusion. "Wait a minute, I thought that you said that he was serious."

"Yeah, but he's a guy. Their version of serious and ours are different. Most guys max out in five to seven years. That's why it's called the seven-year itch. Seven years for us is nothing, so don't sweat it."

"You make it all sound so clichéd. Surely there's more to it than that?"

Brooke nodded soberly. "Indeed there is and if you're ever lucky enough to find it, hold on tight and don't let go."

"I was, once," Olivia replied softly. Brooke just smiled sadly since there was nothing else she could say.

* * *

Ryan went back to his office to ensure the security arrangements were in place for the evening. Despite Nicole's advice last weekend, he had delayed in asking Olivia out. He was honest enough with himself to admit part of that time was spent waffling. He had continued working out with Nicole and her silence on the matter was deafening. Still, Ryan had over eighty years of experience, and the last forty he felt like he had specialized in patience almost as much as he had in security. A few nights of deafening silence were almost inconsequential. He knew that she wasn't mad, that she was just trying to make a point. He knew that, but he also just needed a little time to sort out the ramifications that dating Olivia would bring to his mission.

Despite female opinions to the contrary, not all men thought with their loins. Ryan hadn't invested half his life just to piss it away. No matter what he felt for Olivia, what he was doing was bigger than that. He would even have been willing to sacrifice any chance of a relationship with Olivia if it was necessary, but after a few days of careful consideration, he came to the realization that it wasn't. In fact, as far as he could tell, there were no barriers that would prevent them from having a relationship.

He gave himself a few days to become comfortable with the decision, and a chance to second-guess himself. He spent the time doing some research on the various places they could go, and then deciding which ones would be suitable. He admitted that he was procrastinating and he finally got around to asking Olivia out.

In a sense, it was almost anticlimactic at that point. Between the subtle hints from Olivia and Nicole's silent support, he knew the odds were in his favor. It was a rare opportunity and one Ryan knew wouldn't repeat itself. That was why he had invested so much time up front.

Eventually, he had everything arranged. He called the limo service and reserved a car for the evening. Although all Senior VPs had access to the service, Ryan had never used it. He preferred to use his own car, trusting in it and himself to get him out of any trouble. He had expected it would be tedious to setup, but it surprised him how easy it was. He checked the time and although it was still early, he decided there was no point in returning to work, so he headed home to clean up for his date. Now that he had made all the arrangements, he found that he was able to relax and look forward to it.

* * *

At precisely eight o'clock Olivia stepped outside. She found herself smiling as the sleek white limo settled to the ground at that exact moment. Apparently Ryan's standards were as exacting as hers. The limo had barely touched down when the door opened and Ryan stepped out. She felt herself warming at the look he gave her, which she appreciated. It also concerned her a little—after all it was only a few days ago when she had almost given up thinking he was uninterested. She couldn't help wondering which represented the way he really felt. If it hadn't been for Brooke insisting she'd seen that same interest last week, Olivia would be wondering if he had an ulterior motive. Or would she have, she wondered idly as she walked down the steps to the limo door that Ryan was holding open. Perhaps not. Somehow she trusted him, which was unsettling.

"You obviously don't do this very often," she teased him. "The limo driver should be holding the door open." She smiled at him as she ducked into the limo and he settled down opposite her after closing the door.

"What can I say," Ryan replied with a smile and a shrug, "I'm a maverick. Besides, somehow I knew that you would be looking beautiful tonight and I couldn't wait another minute."

Olivia was wearing a simple white spaghetti strap dress that accented her warm tan, and a contrasting black pashmina that she had draped elegantly over her shoulders. Brooke had picked the outfit out and positively refused to let Olivia wear anything else. Personally, Olivia thought the outfit showed a little more leg than necessary, but Brooke disagreed vehemently, saying that if anything, it was on the conservative side. Olivia surreptitiously tugged down the skirt for about the tenth time in as many minutes and wondered just what kind of outfit made this seem conservative.

"Thank you," she replied graciously and then smiled mischievously at him. "I must say that you're looking handsome tonight, although I will admit that I'm partial to the khakis and no shirt look."

For a moment he just stared at her blankly and then he groaned. "How on earth do you know about that?" he asked after a moment and she grinned.

"What, you mean apart from Nicole calling me to complain that it was causing excessive processing demands as everyone tried to watch it?"

For a moment he looked completely horrified and then he realized that she was just kidding.

"Ha-ha, very funny," he said and she nodded.

"Actually it was. I just wish that I had a camera—you should have seen your face, it was priceless. I guess you're not after the fame." He scowled at her, but she could tell that he was trying hard not to smile and after a moment he relented.

"The thought terrifies me," he admitted. "Apart from that, though, it would be hard for the squads involved to live it down, and the intent was never to humiliate them, but to teach them a lesson."

Olivia nodded, impressed. Most people that she knew—men or women—wouldn't have been so concerned about the impact on their staff, or at least not immediately.

"So, you never did answer my question. How did you find out about it?"

"Actually, I wasn't that far off from the truth the first time. The high res images do take up a lot of space and consume processing power. Anytime there's unusual server activity, both Nicole and I receive an automatic notification. Most cases there is good reason for it, but occasionally, it's a hacker, or a Denial of Service Attack, or something similar. Once Nicole determined what it was, she notified me. It piqued my curiosity so I ran the image." She cocked her head and looked at him inquisitively. "I must admit that it was impressive. You've already implied that it was a lesson of some kind?"

Ryan shrugged and recounted the events of the afternoon to her as she sat back and listened. He had a presence about him when he spoke that forced people to pay attention, and he used his hands with a quiet economy that emphasized just the right points. Olivia found herself mesmerized with both him and the story. Consequently, the limo driver startled her when he announced their arrival. She noticed in amusement that Ryan restrained himself from jumping up and opening the door.

Once the driver opened the door, Ryan got out and then turned and offered her his hand. She laughed lightly and allowed herself to be helped out of the limo. She accepted the arm that Ryan presented to her and they walked into the restaurant arm in arm. They weren't exactly holding hands, but it had a certain elegant formality to it that tickled Olivia's fancy at the moment. The maitre d' escorted them to their table and Ryan waited until she took her seat before sitting down.

Once the usual restaurant formalities—ordering drinks, reviewing the menu, and listening to the specials—were out of the way, Olivia turned to Ryan and smiled.

"So you're getting along well with Brooke and Nicole," she said, half questioningly.

Ryan nodded. "I like Brooke—she's fresh and fun and friendly and you'd never in a million years guess that she's as old as she is. She's also a great HR person. Everyone that I've spoken to has nothing but good things to say about her."

"And?" Olivia prompted.

"And what?" Ryan asked, but the small smile on his lips betrayed that he knew what she was talking about.

"And what about Nicole?" Olivia asked.

He hesitated briefly before replying. "What can I say?" he said with a shrug. "She's incredibly competent and knowledgeable, not only in her area but across a wide variety of specialties."

Olivia just looked at him and he grinned lopsidedly. "Oh, all right, to be honest I find her a little intimidating. She's the oldest person I've ever met, not that you can tell that from looking at her. She's more restrained in her wardrobe choices than Brooke, but she has a classic beauty that more than compensates for that. But there's something in her eyes that throws me, usually just when I begin to think that I'm starting to understand her. I don't know if it's a reflection of the years of experience that she's had, or if it's something else, but it can be disconcerting." He paused and took a sip of his wine. "Anyway, enough of this. I didn't come here to talk about work with you. There are any number of forums for that already."

Ryan smiled as Olivia laughed.

"Well, what else is there to talk about?" she asked. "You admitted in the interview that your work is your life. At this stage of my career the same holds true for me."

"True, but I'm looking for more than just points of congruence." He grinned as she nodded in understanding.

He knew that with her love of language she would know what he meant, that he was looking for more than what they had in common. It also was a relief to shift the conversation away from talking about Brooke and Nicole. He had gotten the impression from Nicole that she didn't want anyone to know about her enhancement, and so he didn't tell anyone that he was working out with her every night. He struggled to keep Nicole's secret without lying to Olivia. If they kept talking about Brooke and Nicole, he would cross the line and start actively lying to her, and he didn't want to do that.

"What about politics, the economy, favorite books or movies, stuff like that?" he asked.

"Well not politics, there's not much to talk about there."

Long practice kept his expression unchanged, but Ryan felt a mental surge of disbelief. "What do you mean?" he asked cautiously.

She shrugged as she responded. "Well there's the situation in the Middle East. The only thing that's changed from the beginning of the millennium to now is that we no longer need them for their oil reserves. Apart from that, they still view us as the 'Great White Satan,' only now Satan's a woman. Our relationship with China went to hell in a hand basket at the same time, as did everyone else's. They still refuse to practice any form of birth control and so they are still abandoning female babies in the streets. The only problem is that now nobody wants them, because of the longevity impact of controlling menstrual cycles. Europe is more fragmented now that they have the EU than they were before." She shrugged again. "It's only here where everything is under control."

Ryan shook his head, staggered by the simplicity of her comments. That they were coming from the CEO of a major company both appalled and scared him. It also didn't help that they conflicted with his mental image of her.

"I'm not sure that I agree with your assessment, especially your statement that everything is under control here." She frowned at him quizzically and he continued. "Just because everything is stable doesn't mean that it is under control. And I will grant you that everything is stable at the current moment—just. Women hold most if not all positions of power with the rare exception of the military. This holds true even though men now outnumber women two to one. The only reason for this is that women have been able to use their economic influence to shape the political situation to suit their needs—buying votes is the crude term for it. But that can't last.

"There's a growing sentiment among men that we're getting shafted and when you strip away the rhetoric, it's true. Men make up sixty percent of the workforce, but only two percent at the executive level. At the same time men make up almost ninety percent of the active military and by active I mean troops out in the field, not support staff. When you put these two facts together it looks like men are just being used. Used as mules and cannon fodder. The situation's been building for a long time, but the use of the artificial embryogenesis machines has intensified it and it's approaching a crisis point."

Olivia just looked at him for a moment, as if he had turned into another person right in front of her and he knew how she felt—he felt the same way. "Is this how you feel about Delphi?" she asked quietly and Ryan waved his hand impatiently.

"Of course not," he replied, "but that's not the point. This impacts the entire country and it doesn't matter what kind of job you're doing here at Delphi, good or bad." He paused and looked at her. "As it stands, I think that you're doing a great job, both you and Brooke. It's why I'm here after all. First, since that is part of what attracted me to Delphi initially, and second, because without those policies there was no way that I would have the job that I do. In fact Delphi is one of the more enlightened companies out there. I guess that's why I was so surprised. I know that most women and even a lot of men share the same viewpoint that you expressed, but I thought that Delphi and, by extension, you were more aware than most. So don't get me wrong, this isn't a personal attack on you or on Delphi or even on women in general. I'm actually very fond of all of the above."

"Including me?" Olivia asked quietly, but with the beginnings of a small smile.

"Especially you," he replied and the smile grew wider, but it was still tentative. Just then the waiter approached them to take their orders and Ryan took advantage of the distraction to pull himself together. He had pushed too hard, and he knew it, and in reality he shouldn't have expected anything different. After all, he had been just as ignorant forty years ago until reality had grabbed him by the scruff of the neck and rubbed his nose in it. It was a little much to expect Olivia to be as aware of the political realities as he was, especially as they mostly affected men. On top of that, the way he had just hammered at her wasn't likely to increase her interest in it either.

He gave his order to the waiter and smiled at Olivia. "Sorry about that, it's just one of my hot spots. Now, I believe that you were mentioning favorite movies and books?"

Olivia accepted the change of topic gracefully and the rest of the evening passed uneventfully. Uneventfully and unevenly, although both Olivia and Ryan did their best to compensate for that. Ryan had known that it was bad, but when Olivia turned down a second cup of coffee, he knew that it was really bad.

The limo ride back seemed as long as the ride over had seemed short, as they struggled for something to talk about. He escorted her to the door and then returned to the limo. The limo rose and glided towards his house. Although it was only a five-minute walk, he just didn't feel like it.

He sighed and rubbed his eyes, unable to believe just how badly the evening had gone. It didn't turn out the way he had planned or even fantasized. He had been hoping for a romantic evening and all that that entailed, but they simply weren't able to get back to where they were earlier that evening. All that planning and preparation and he still managed to mess it up. He sighed again, suddenly feeling all of his eighty-odd years. He knew there was no way he was going to get any sleep tonight without burning off some serious frustration. He checked the time and knew that if he hurried, he could probably catch Nicole before she left the fitness center. He asked the limo to wait for him as he ran in and quickly grabbed his bag. Returning to the limo, he told the driver to head out to Delphi.

* * *

Olivia closed the door as Ryan left and then leaned her head against it. She felt like crying, and it was all she could do to retain control long enough for her to make an emergency call to Brooke. She changed into some pajamas and put on some coffee, but the moment Brooke walked through the door, Olivia just looked at her it and it all came apart. She cried for at least five minutes while Brooke held her and murmured comforting noises. At last she was able to sit up, blow her nose and wipe away her tears.

"It didn't go well, I take it?" Brooke asked dryly and Olivia started crying and laughing at the same time.

"God, it was terrible. I mean, it started out nicely, but it was a complete wreck before we even ordered dinner."

"Come on, it couldn't have been that bad," Brooke said.

Olivia just shook her head. "I didn't even have a second cup of coffee," she complained and then sniffled, "and it was really good coffee."

"Tell me what happened, and we'll see just how horrible it was and whether we can salvage anything from it."

Olivia recounted the brief conversation that had ruined the evening and Brooke just shook her head.

"Unfortunately, you're both to blame in this case, much as I'd like to take your side," Brooke said and Olivia stared at her incredulously. "Ryan should have known better than to mix romance and politics. That's been a recipe for disaster even before Clinton-gate. You, however, ought to know a little more about what's going on in the world. Ryan's analysis of the situation is bang on, and if you got out there a little more you'd know that."

Olivia stared at Brooke in confusion. "How on earth do you know all this?" she asked. "I didn't think you were political."

"I'm not," Brooke replied, "but unlike you I do have an active social life. While I will be the first to admit that this is not the topic du jour at most of the parties I go to, it does crop up occasionally, mostly among men." Brooke paused and coughed delicately. "I've also been conducting an informal survey of men that I meet, and it only confirms what I've heard discussed publicly."

"I see," Olivia said. "I'm not sure if I should be pleased that you've been doing something useful with your time, or dismayed at my own abysmal ignorance."

"That's not all," Brooke replied, not rising to the bait. "There is a reason I've been pushing you to ensure that we have a balanced workforce here at Delphi, a reason that extends beyond basic fairness." Brooke paused and looked at her, and there was something in Brooke's eyes that alarmed her. "There's a growing anger out there and I'm afraid that it's going to express itself sooner rather than later. I'm hoping to keep Delphi out of it altogether, or at least long enough for us to take the necessary steps to protect ourselves."

"What are we talking about here?" Olivia asked, suddenly concerned, and Brooke shrugged.

"I really don't know. It could be something as simple as job action or something more sinister like riots. Either way I want Delphi to be viewed favorably when the time comes. It shouldn't be too hard, given the behavior of some of the other big companies in the area. It also helps that Ryan works for us and in such a senior capacity. Delphi is one of the few companies to have a man in a Senior VP role and the response has been favorable. As well, Ryan has a solid reputation, which will help us in two ways. One is strengthening the positive PR that I already mentioned; the other is that people are aware of his skills in this area. They know that they're likely to get their asses kicked if they try something. Honestly, I don't think we could have a better person for the Senior VP of Security."

Olivia frowned. "You can say that again. From what I saw last week, I wouldn't want to take him on."

"What do you mean?" Brooke asked quizzically and Olivia shook her head.

"In a minute. Tell me why Ryan is so well-known and respected."

"Simple. He's worked in biotech or pharma all his life and has done well at it. You know as well as I do that this section of California has one of the highest numbers of those types of companies—that's why they call it the Pill Hills. Not only that but a lot of men are army reservists and it appears as if Ryan has a reputation there, too."

"I can believe that," Olivia mused and then gave in to the demanding look that Brooke was giving her. "Oh, all right, have a seat in the living room and I'll show you what I'm talking about." Olivia stopped in the kitchen to refresh her coffee, and then she sat down on the sofa beside Brooke, calling up the image of the training session that Ryan had participated in. Brooke was just as mesmerized as Olivia had been when she first watched it and even now it still amazed her. The image didn't take long to play—less than twenty-minutes all told—and Brooke whistled softly when it finished.

"Wow!"

"Amen to that," Olivia said and Brooke just looked at her.

"Oh man, I would love to get me some of that," Brooke groaned.

Olivia chuckled. "Hey now, hands off."

"Why, are you still interested?" Brooke teased.

Olivia glared at her and then relented with a bashful grin. "Okay, you got me. I admit it, I'm still interested. It was just disheartening to have such a bad first date."

"Don't worry about it. I know that as a general rule a bad first date only leads to a bad second date and so on, but in this case you should be okay. Just stay away from politics."

"I'd already figured that much out," Olivia retorted, but she had to admit that she was feeling a lot better. "Thanks," she said.

Brooke smiled. "Hey, that's what friends are for."

* * *

Ryan caught Nicole just before she left and they went right into a sparring session together. Ryan's distraction was obvious and Nicole took ruthless advantage of it. He knew that she would know that it was because of his date, and that she would want to talk about it. They finished and as they headed towards the change room, Nicole cocked her head and looked at him inquisitively. He knew that she was looking for info, and he debated with himself about discussing the details with her, but he decided against it. He wasn't about to make the same mistake twice. It had been a mistake to bring up politics with Olivia, and it would be even more of a mistake to bring it up with Nicole. After all, she had spent her entire life steeped in the existing structure and had reaped the benefits of it. He looked over at her and sighed.

"We had a disagreement just after we got to the restaurant and it didn't go well."

"How bad was it?"

"She didn't leave right away but she only had one cup of coffee."

"Mmm. Not good but not terrible. Is this 'disagreement' likely to come up again? I mean did you resolve it or is it still hanging out there?"

"We didn't exactly resolve it, but I think that maybe we can agree to disagree and move on."

"Okay then. Put it behind you and move on. Call her when you get home and apologize. Make another date before too much time passes."

"It's getting late, don't you think she'll be asleep?" Ryan asked, grateful that she was helping to put it into perspective.

Nicole snorted. "You're kidding, right? The first thing that she'll have done when she got home was to call Brooke. They'll have done a thorough postmortem on it, and assuming you're being honest with me, she should have calmed down by now. Trust me on this."

"Thanks," he smiled at her.

"No problem. So I don't need all the details, but I'd like to know general info, where you went, stuff like that."

They stripped down and went into the sauna. By this time, Ryan no longer thought anything about their nudity, and he filled her in on all the relevant details.

He left the fitness center feeling much better than he had when he had arrived, and he had a bounce in his step as he headed home.

He dropped his bag at the door and plopped down on the sofa to give Olivia a call. He could have used his link to call her whenever he wanted but he wanted to be able to give the conversation his full attention. Sure enough when he called her she answered immediately. He had barely finished apologizing to her when she apologized to him. They both laughed and Ryan felt the knot inside his stomach ease. He cautiously suggested another date and to his relief she agreed. He felt himself relax, and he chatted with her for another half hour before they reluctantly decided that it was getting late. He changed into clean boxers and got into bed. He fell asleep almost immediately, dreaming of a strange woman who was part Olivia, part Nicole, and part Brooke.

Chapter Eight

Ryan felt torn. He wasn't making much progress in terms of retrieving the formula but his personal life couldn't be going any better. He and Olivia had been taking it slowly. It appeared to be a mutual decision, albeit an unspoken one. They had gotten into a comfortable routine of having one date a week, exploring the lesser-known restaurants in the area and getting to know each other better.

So far it was working. Both of them had been cautious, wary about setting off any more land mines, but everything had gone well up to this point. So well, in fact, that Ryan was thinking about taking the next step and becoming intimate with her. It was funny—he saw Nicole naked almost every day in the sauna after they sparred. And he'd had more physical contact with her than he'd had with Olivia, although he would be the first to admit that it wasn't the physical contact that he preferred. He was also more comfortable talking with Nicole. Much of what he talked about with her was his relationship with Olivia. He still wasn't sure why she was giving him advice, but he had to admit it was invaluable.

For a while, he felt slightly guilty about that, but he rationalized that Olivia had Brooke to talk to. Still, he knew that Olivia was receiving advice from Brooke, whereas neither of them knew that he was getting help from Nicole. He didn't know why, but for some reason Nicole didn't want anyone knowing about her enhancement. Ryan had figured that out quickly and although she hadn't said anything, he knew his understanding in that regard pleased her. Apart from that mild guilt, his personal life was in great shape. His work life was ticking along smoothly, as well, and if that were all there was, he would have been content. As it was, he wasn't. And that was due solely to the real reason he was here at Delphi.

The coded messages that he'd been receiving from his handlers had been developing an increasingly irate undertone, and he didn't blame them. Unfortunately, he couldn't do anything about it and they knew it, which was why the irritation was still an undertone and not directed specifically at him.

His whole purpose for being here at Delphi was to try to recover the formula for the DNA polymerase, hidden by its creator somewhere in the R&D database. The only people who could access it were the few men who had already been treated with the formula and as a result had an extended lifespan. An artificial DNA polymerase added a codon to existing DNA that extended the life of men by fourfold. The codon was easily detectable using existing technology and was the only way to access the formula.

Unfortunately no one knew how to add the codon to existing DNA. The polymerase broke down within the body after adding the codon, having fulfilled its sole purpose, so there was no trace of it. Ryan knew that while he had been busy creating a new life for himself, the group that supported him had been unsuccessfully trying to either reverse engineer the formula or recreate the polymerase. Unsurprisingly they'd had little luck with the task. Research into male longevity still occurred, although it commanded a fraction of the attention and funding it had right after Menssation® was discovered. If two hundred years of research hadn't found the answer, it obviously wasn't simple. It was one of the rare spark of genius moments that was impossible to recreate.

The task of finding the formula now lay squarely on Ryan's shoulders. In a sense, he was almost grateful that it had come to this. After all, he had spent the last forty years creating a new life for himself, a big part of which was developing a career in security.

At first glance, it would have been easy to assume that a career in R&D would have been a better choice than security, but that wasn't the case. It was rare to find men working in R&D these days, especially at the senior levels. There was no more senior level than those who worked at a small, highly secure lab at Delphi. Almost all the significant R&D came out of that lab. A company the size of Delphi obviously had more than one lab, but all the other labs only had a number to identify them. There was only one lab that didn't need any further identification and this was it. The Lab.

You could almost hear the capitalization when people spoke of it. It was the lifeblood of a company like Delphi, and you had to have serious R&D experience under your belt to work in the lab. Since serious R&D experience only came with age, the lab was the sole domain of women. Automated equipment performed the janitorial tasks, so the building was a virtual bastion of impenetrability if you were a man. Security was the one chink in the armor, which is why Ryan made that career choice long ago.

As the Senior VP of Security, it was self-evident that Ryan had complete access to any building anywhere on Delphi. This state of affairs did not make Gabriella, the Senior VP of R&D, happy and she had insisted on physically accompanying him anytime he visited the lab for security reasons. Ryan had agreed to this control for the simple reason that it didn't matter.

The security system that he had installed at Delphi was bleeding edge. The advantage to that was that Delphi had one of the most secure corporate headquarters in Noram. The drawback was that such bleeding edge systems usually suffered from small glitches or quirks. Although the system technically only allowed one security profile per user, the preproduction version of the software allowed for multiple profiles for testing purposes. Ryan had two profiles. One was his profile as the VP of Security and this one included the access control for the lab. The other was a superuser profile, nominally only used for testing, that had no limits. Better still, shutting down his official profile wouldn't impact his superuser profile. It was the perfect backdoor and one that Ryan was more than willing to use.

Access wasn't the problem. Not getting caught was. Most of the R&D people who had access to the lab had been working on R&D for at least a hundred years. They focused on their work, often at the expense of their social lives. In fact, after security, working in the lab was the closest thing to a twenty-four-hour-a-day operation.

Of course, at the end of the day, the people who worked at the lab were people, first and foremost. Like anyone else, they had their little routines that they followed. Fortunately, Ryan had almost three months worth of data to work with by the time he could even consider accessing the lab. It had taken him a couple more weeks after he had returned from his visit of Delphi's other sites to gain access, but he had finally done it. He let his mind wander for a moment as he recalled that night.

Ryan approached the lab nervously. All of the models he had run indicated that the lab should be empty and it was. That part was easy enough to verify. The tricky part was ensuring that he wasn't caught, which unfortunately was impossible. The models indicated it was statistically unlikely for anyone to visit the lab at this time, but he remembered a saying made popular by Mark Twain—There are three kinds of lies: lies, damned lies, and statistics. Still, he didn't really have much choice.

He paused and switched to his superuser profile, disabling his official profile. Although it was disabled, his official profile was still active on the system, so if someone attempted to locate him, they could. However it bypassed the restrictions that Gabriella had insisted on and it also removed him from the security logs. As far as the logs were concerned, he had disappeared. It was a necessary risk, but it concerned him. If someone ever ran a trace on his activity, it would stand out like a sore thumb.

He entered the lab, overriding the automatic lights and accessing a map of the building with his neural feed. It automatically mapped his movements, showing him exactly where he was. He could have navigated the building blindfolded if he had to, but the map and infrared imaging provided more than enough detail for him to 'see' exactly where he was.

He made his way over to the nearest DNA reader. Taking a deep breath, he sat down in the cockpit-like seat. He settled in and the hood closed down over him, cutting him off from access to external systems. He put his arms on the armrests, with his hands palm down. He felt a tingle as it scanned his palms and gazed obediently at the spot on the inside wall when directed to. He stated his name, and then felt the small pressor beams playing over his body as the chamber determined that he was the only occupant. Moments later he felt several simultaneous pricks all along his arms as the reader took multiple DNA samples from random spots. After a moment, a message flashed on the screen in front of him.

USER PROFILE NOT ON SYSTEM. NEW USER?

He indicated his assent, as his stomach knotted. Despite his enhancements, he felt nauseous. There was little outward sign of his nervousness but inside he was a mess.

STATE YOUR NAME AND NETWORK ID. AN EMAIL WILL BE SENT ONCE YOUR DNA SAMPLE HAS BEEN PROCESSED.

His mind froze. He hadn't expected this. For a moment panic threatened to overwhelm him, but years of control took over. It was an incredible risk, yet he had no choice. He had to give his real name and network ID. He didn't know what would happen if he submitted a false ID, but he didn't want to take the chance. It was possible that giving a fake ID would just mean repeating the process all over again. On the other hand, it could trigger an error message that would require human intervention.

Submitting his real ID increased the risk of getting caught, but odds were that it would all be processed automatically, without anyone ever finding out. At least he hoped that no one would find out. He didn't know enough about Gabriella to know if she was the type of person to read all the system-generated emails she received.

Crossing mental fingers, he provided his information and waited.

THANK YOU. YOUR SAMPLE HAS BEEN SENT FOR PROCESSING.

The hood opened and fresh air wafted in. Despite the efforts of his enhancements, the air in the reader had become acrid. He took a deep breath and then belatedly glanced around even as he accessed the security system. He relaxed as he confirmed that no one had entered the lab after him.

He swung his legs over the side and stood up as confusion warred with apprehension. That was it? He didn't know what he had been expecting, but it wasn't this. Unfortunately, no one knew exactly what was supposed to happen. The only directions he had were sketchy and he had followed them to the letter.

He waited for a moment longer, and then the system pinged him. One of the researchers had just returned. She was currently in the parking garage, but it would only take her a minute to get close enough to the lab to spot Ryan. He quickly left the lab, fading into the darkness moments before the researcher came into sight. He gave the building one final look, and then reactivated his official profile.

That was almost a month ago. Given that he had been working at Delphi for four and a half months, it didn't seem like he had done much. Still, it was more than anyone else had managed to do in the last forty years. Ryan knew all of this and he knew that his handlers knew it as well, but their messages were beginning to irritate him. He had taken a big risk in accessing the machines and although the possibility of discovery grew smaller everyday, it was still there, like the sword of Damocles. With every day that passed, he worried that Gabriella would somehow find his sample or see him in the user database and confront him or Olivia or worse, go straight to the Board.

He was fortunate that he'd had a lifetime of practice with partitioning the different parts of himself or he would have gone quickly insane. As it was, he sometimes wasn't sure how much longer he could last.

He made an effort to shake the morose tone of his thoughts as he glided to a stop at Olivia's front steps. He was going to take her on a picnic today and since the place he planned to visit was private, he elected not to use the limo service. He was just about to hop out when Olivia came out the front door and skipped lightly down the steps. He noted that she was wearing sensible clothes, comfortable blue jeans, a light T-shirt and a sweatshirt wrapped around her waist. She climbed into the passenger side of his vehicle with that same combination of elegance and awkwardness that always reminded him of the first time they had gone out before he had become a Senior VP.

"Ready?" he asked her with a grin and she grinned back at him.

"Ready," she echoed and he glided carefully out of the gated community, rising to cruising height as soon as he could. He could see Olivia look around curiously as they headed towards the desert.

* * *

"You never did mention where we're going," she said and Ryan just smiled secretively.

"You'll just have to wait and see," he teased her and she pouted playfully.

"Aw, you're no fun," she started to say, but he leaned over and kissed her gently, with a hint of passion.

"You were saying?" he asked dryly.

She smiled at him. "I was saying something, but you must have stolen the words while you were kissing me."

Ryan frowned. "I know that line," he said and she giggled. "Where do I know that line from?"

"If you figure it out, I'll let you kiss me again."

"Now that's a worthwhile endeavor." Ryan made faces as if racking his brain and spouted nonsense answers she was sure were designed to make her laugh. He had just rhymed off his tenth guess when the car speakers crackled to life.

"WARNING. ENTERING RESTRICTED AIRSPACE. IF YOU HAVE NOT FILED A VALID FLIGHT PLAN LAND IMMEDIATELY."

Olivia straightened up sharply, but Ryan just smiled and patted her reassuringly. The message repeated twice and then silence settled over the car again.

"What was that," Olivia asked slowly, "and just where are we going?"

Ryan sighed theatrically. "So much for surprises. Darn military."

Olivia's lips twitched into a smile, but she forced them to be still again. "Ryan, I'm serious."

"Well, if you must know, we're currently cruising along a designated flight path over Edwards Air Force Base."

"And why are we flying over an air force base," Olivia asked with forced patience.

"Well, because that's where we're going. Don't worry about that message. I have a valid flight plan filed and I've already received clearance from Edwards GC."

"GC?" Olivia echoed.

"Sorry, Ground Control."

"I still don't understand why we are going to an air force base for a picnic," Olivia pressed, but he ignored her. It seemed like an odd spot for a picnic, but she knew from looking at Ryan that she wouldn't be getting anymore out of him. She also trusted him, strangely enough, and so she held her tongue. They cruised in silence for about another ten minutes when Ryan suddenly spoke up.

"Meatloaf," he said cryptically and Olivia blinked.

"What?"

"Meatloaf. That's the name of the singer. 'And then you took the words right out of my mouth, Oh—it must have been while you were kissing me'," he crooned and Olivia giggled.

"God, that's terrible. Don't give up your day job," she teased him and he pretended to look hurt. He started to sing the rest of it, but then the car began descending and he had to take control. Olivia sighed gratefully, not because his voice was bad—he was a decent singer—but because of the next words in the song. 'You took the words right out of my mouth, And I swear it's true, I was just about to say I love you.' So far neither of them had mentioned the L-word and she wasn't ready to hear it yet, even in jest.

She turned her attention outwards as they continued to descend, surprised to see they were in the mountains. She hadn't realized that Edwards Air Force Base extended so far. Oh, she'd heard something about it expanding decades ago, but she hadn't paid any attention to it. The craggy, snow covered peaks looked menacing, and she felt a chill despite the fact the force screen kept the car comfortably warm. She couldn't imagine a less likely place for a picnic if she tried, and she was starting to wonder what Ryan was doing. She realized the little car was working hard to remain stable as high winds gusted around them, and she started to turn towards Ryan to ask him to take her home. Just then they rounded a towering spire of rock that loomed over them like a giant needle, and below them Olivia saw the most unlikely site.

She blinked, unable to believe her eyes, but the sight didn't change. It was a small meadow, bordered by bushy evergreens. As they got closer Olivia could see the wildflowers that dotted it, and there was a small stream that flowed along one edge of the meadow. She clapped happily and turned to Ryan as he raised one eyebrow questioningly. Olivia blushed as she recalled her earlier uncharitable thoughts and she leaned over to kiss him in apology. The car settled down gracefully at one edge of the meadow and Ryan hopped out, going around to help her. She accepted his assistance gratefully. The trip over had been just long enough for her to become settled in her seat, which made it more difficult to get out. If Ryan noticed a lack of grace in her exit he didn't say anything.

"So, what do you think?" he asked, beaming proudly.

"It's incredible," she said simply, looking around her in wonder. She thought she'd have to untie her sweatshirt and put it on, but the temperature was pleasantly comfortable. "Just what is this place and how did you hear about it?"

"This plateau has always existed, but a quake about a hundred years ago caused some of the surrounding landscape to shift, creating a wind block. The existing trees and shrubs flourished under the new protection, creating this little oasis. When Edwards expanded thirty years ago, one of the survey teams found this site. Its location is an open secret among the senior officers at Edwards, who use it as a picnic spot."

"Interesting. Still, given the public appetite for places like this, I would have expected some developer to snap it up."

"Well, it's isolated and only accessible by aircar, and a powerful one at that."

Olivia shrugged. "Powerful aircars are not that uncommon."

"True, but you're forgetting that this is only accessible via restricted airspace. Although this is near the edge of Edwards, it is still within their jurisdiction. Not to mention that it's only known to senior officers."

"So how it is it that you know about this? And how were you able to get access to it?"

"Well I was stationed here for several years before I started working in industry. The biotech and pharma industry has always interested me and Edwards is a good location. It's close to Pill Hill, which allowed me to develop some contacts, and it's not as flashy as Vandenburg or the Presidio."

"True," Olivia granted him, "but I don't recall you achieving senior officer rank. At least, it's not on your curriculum vitae."

"No, but I was the Base Security Officer. As SO, I was responsible for perimeter security. Although most of the officers who use this spot work at Edwards, retired officers use it on occasion. Since they needed to file a flight plan, I needed to know about it. As for how I'm able to use it, let's just say that I have friends in high places."

"Mmm, well that's good to know." She reached up and wrapped her hands around Ryan's neck, pulling him close for another kiss. As she did, she could feel her heart start to race. They continued kissing and Ryan wrapped his arms around her waist. She could feel his erection pressing against her and she felt her nipples stiffening in reaction underneath her shirt. They were both flushed when they finally separated. He grinned nervously at her and then stepped back to spread a large blanket on the ground, gesturing for her to sit down.

As he dashed back to the car, Olivia took the time to try to pull her chaotic thoughts together, but she failed miserably. Her mind kept returning to the feel of his body against hers and she looked up at him as he returned with a large wicker basket. He managed to distract her as he proceeded to extract a bottle of wine and all manner of appetizers from the basket. He laid out bread, vegetables and dip, chips, pate and more in front of Olivia as her eyes widened.

"My goodness, I hope you don't expect us to eat all of that."

Ryan eyed the spread with a grin and shrugged. "No, at least not all at once. We have this little oasis all to ourselves for the next six hours so we have plenty of time. I thought we'd just nibble for while, sip on some wine, and just drink in the natural beauty around us."

"Six hours?" Olivia repeated, her earlier thoughts returning. The brief distraction had been like the eye of a hurricane, and somehow the sudden resumption of the onslaught of feelings made them harder to resist.

"Yeah, some of the senior officers who come here like to have their privacy and don't want any interruptions."

"Hmm," Olivia murmured, "I wonder why they don't want any interruptions."

"Yeah, I wonder," Ryan chuckled and then his eyes widened as Olivia gave into temptation. She stood up and untied her sweatshirt and pulled her T-shirt over her head. His eyes drank her in as she shimmied out of her jeans. She did a little wiggle for his benefit and then reached behind her and unfastened her bra. She coyly held the loose cups to her breasts, teasing him, before she tossed it to the ground beside her jeans. She slipped out of her panties and stood before him naked. She smiled at the look on his face and then pirouetted gracefully, letting the sun warm her skin.

"I thought that maybe we could work up an appetite, given that we've got all this food to eat," she said suggestively and he grinned appreciatively.

"Sounds like a plan to me," he said as he stood up and removed his own clothes. Olivia had seen him with his shirt off before, but that paled in comparison to how glorious he looked nude. His body was firm and muscled, and his tanned skin looked perfect. He looked like a Greek Adonis or Michelangelo's David, and she felt the perfection of this moment deep inside her. They came together slowly and kissed each other gently, exploring one another's bodies with their hands. After a while, they sank down onto the blanket and continued their journey of discovery.

Olivia took a bite from the bruschetta and grimaced as a piece of cold tomato dropped onto her naked breast. Before she could wipe it away with her napkin, Ryan leaned over and gently licked it off.

"You're awfully handy to have around," she laughed and then moaned softly as his mouth moved down across her breast to her nipple.

"Stop that," she groaned, "or we'll never get anything to eat."

"Speak for yourself," he teased. But, to her relief and disappointment, he sat back up. They were both still naked and Olivia had never felt more satisfied or free in her entire life. Though, it wasn't the way she had pictured the afternoon, it felt so right. Even the food was perfect. Ryan hadn't removed most of the appetizers from their thermal containers. Although the containers had been sitting out in the sun for over two hours, they were still the right temperature, as evidenced by the cold bruschetta. Olivia couldn't say the same for either her or Ryan. A light sheen of perspiration covered both of them and Olivia eyed the stream thoughtfully.

"Is that swimmable?" she asked, and Ryan looked over at it.

"Technically, yes. However it's fed from runoff from the surrounding mountains so it's ice-cold." She looked at him speculatively and he shook his head. "No way, Jose."

"Aw, come on, don't be such a wimp. And don't tell me you're not just as hot as I am."

"Well, actually I think that you're hotter, if you'll pardon the pun," but he levered himself to his feet and then came over and picked her up.

"Hey," she squealed, "what are you doing?"

"You did say that you were hot." He jumped into the stream with her still in his arms.

Olivia gasped from the shock of it. "Oh my God, you weren't kidding, this is freezing," she exclaimed and Ryan splashed her as he swam gracefully around her.

"Start moving, it's not so bad once you get used to it."

"Easy for you to say," she managed to get out through chattering teeth, but she took his advice and started swimming. He splashed her again and then swam out of reach as she tried to splash him back. They spent the next few minutes playing around in the stream before Ryan swam to the bank. He heaved himself out of the stream so quickly and gracefully that it almost looked like he'd leaped out. He turned and offered a hand to Olivia who accepted it gratefully. He pulled her out of the water with ease and set her down on the bank beside him. For a moment the air felt cold on Olivia's skin but then the sun started to penetrate through to where she could feel it. She arched her back and twisted in the sunlight, soaking up the welcome warmth. She opened her eyes to find Ryan looking hungrily at her.

"You have recovered nicely from the cold," she teased him, "or at least parts of you have."

He looked down and grinned. "What can I say, you do have that effect on me."

"Am I correct in assuming that you have more than just appetizers in that basket of yours," she asked and he blinked at the apparent non sequitur but nodded. "Good. I'm still full, but perhaps a little afternoon workout might be able to restore my appetite. After all, I'd hate for it to go to waste."

He smiled as he figured out the direction that she was going with this, and she smiled back as she walked up to him and led him back to the picnic basket and the waiting blanket.

The rest of the afternoon passed all too quickly for both of them and it was only that it was getting dark that finally forced them to leave. Ryan was adamant on that point, that it was too dangerous to fly out of there when it was dark, and Olivia didn't press the issue, remembering the winds that had buffeted the car on the way in. She kissed him good-bye when he dropped her off at her place. For a moment, she almost gave into the temptation to invite him up but if she did, she knew that he probably wouldn't leave again, at least until morning. It was a little too soon in their relationship for him to spend the night, at least for her. To her relief he didn't press the issue. Then for an insane moment she felt as if he didn't want her to invite him up and she almost did, just to prove herself wrong. She successfully resisted that crazy impulse, smiling as he drove away. She was still smiling when she opened the door.

She heard sounds coming from the living room and for a moment she'd thought she'd left the holo on, but then she realized that it was probably Brooke. She smiled to herself, wishing that she had invited Ryan up, just to see the look on Brooke's face. She contented herself with the knowledge that she would finally manage to stun Brooke when she told her the events of the afternoon. However, as soon as she walked into the living room, Brooke took one look at her.

"Finally. Thank God, I was beginning to crack from the pressure and I already have a healthy sex life."

Olivia gaped at her. "How did you know?" she asked and Brooke snorted derisively.

"Are you kidding? There's only one thing that makes a woman look like that and that's good sex. It was good, wasn't it?" Brooke asked and now Olivia held the upper hand.

"It was okay," she replied nonchalantly and Brooke reached behind her and grabbed a pillow.

"Okay, okay," Olivia laughed, holding her hands up in mock defense. "It was wonderful."

"That's better," Brooke replied approvingly, "now come here and tell me all about it."

Olivia made her way to Brooke's side and she could feel her body start to tingle again as she thought back to the afternoon. She sat beside Brooke and pulled a pillow up against her chest, as she sat back and regaled Brooke with the events of the afternoon.

Ryan watched in the mirror as Olivia made her way up the steps. He had mixed feelings about leaving her. Part of him longed to continue what they had started that afternoon, but another part of him was leery about moving too fast. That was what had done them in so many years ago, and while he knew in his head just how different their relationship was here and now, his heart didn't.

Besides, another part of him didn't want to miss his nightly workout with Nicole. He had become used to their daily ritual and it was surprising at times just how much he looked forward to it. It was his chance to relieve the stress of the day, and he knew that most days he needed that. Not just the sparring, but sparring with Nicole. They sparred like they had known each other for years, and at times it almost seemed as though they were dancing. He looked forward to Nicole's no-nonsense approach to whatever issue they happened to be discussing. He would have expected someone so old to have a jaundiced view of the world, but there was none of that in Nicole. Just a straightforward 'this is how I see it.' She was always willing to listen to him when he disagreed with her, but she always cut straight to the heart of the issue. Talking with her was like the verbal equivalent of the sparring that they did— smooth, fluid, effortless. He grinned in anticipation and rushed home to shower before heading over to the fitness center.

Chapter Nine

"It's about time," Nicole grunted as she completed her last set of reps and Ryan shrugged.

"Sorry, I was out with Olivia and we got back late."

"Later. Get your butt on the mat so I can start kicking it."

Ryan grinned. Although his years of training couldn't begin to match Nicole's, they were almost evenly matched. He stretched quickly and then took up his position opposite her on the mat. To his surprise and chagrin he found that she was kicking his butt. The first three falls were hers and that had taken less than five minutes. He knew that nothing material could have changed in their skills from the previous night so the only difference was mental. Although he still had a lot on his plate, he had to admit that he was a lot more relaxed than usual. Determined not to let that affect his performance, he forced himself to concentrate.

He reached for his center, difficult to do while flying through the air, but once he found it his performance picked up. Nicole adapted to his change in performance flawlessly, not that he would have expected otherwise. Many of his past partners would have allowed themselves to become complacent based on his earlier performance, and the change would have caught them off guard. Not Nicole. He didn't know if it was her perfectionism or her years of experience or both, but she was always ready for anything.

Despite his late start, he managed to acquit himself and they both finished with an even number of falls.

"Nicely done," Nicole panted as she mopped her face with a towel.

"Thanks."

"What happened there, at the beginning? You were a little weak."

"Just not focusing enough," he said, but she just cocked her head and looked at him. "All right, I was a little more relaxed than usual."

"Oh?" she replied, and Ryan thought that he detected a faint chill in her tone, which puzzled him. "I take it your date went well."

"Yeah it did. Very well."

Nicole sighed. "Stop beating around the bush. I don't know if it's because you're a man or if it's because you're young, but don't do it."

"Sorry," Ryan replied, as his puzzlement turned to confusion. She clearly had an edge to her tonight and he wondered if it was because he was late.

"I take it that you consummated your relationship with Olivia," she said and Ryan just nodded. Nicole paused for a moment and then shook her head.

"I can't do this anymore."

"What?" Ryan exclaimed. "What can't you do anymore?"

"This. Working out together, sparring together, all of it."

"Have you gone mad? What on earth are you talking about? Nothing's changed."

She looked at him in annoyance. "Don't give me that. You know just as well as I do that this changes everything."

"Why?" Ryan pressed, still not getting it, and she pursed her lips and looked at him.

"Look, before you and Olivia were just dating, but now you're intimate with each other. That's a big step in a relationship, any real relationship. I won't get in the way of that."

Ryan stared at her as she turned and walked into the changing room. He started to follow her and then stopped as she came back out with her bag. She brushed past him and left the fitness center without bothering to change. He called after her, but she just ignored him and he was too confused to run after her.

He walked into the changing room slowly and stripped off his clothes as his mind raced. He took a long shower as he tried to sort everything out, but in the end he had to admit that he was just as confused as he was when she left. This should have been the best day of his life. His relationship with Olivia was getting back to where it was forty years ago, he had just had the best sex that he had probably had in forty years, and he knew that was what he should be thinking about. Strangely enough, all he could think about was Nicole and why she was acting so oddly. All of his previous joy was gone and he made his way home depressed and confused, hoping that maybe he would understand more in the morning.

* * *

The next week was pure hell for him. He became obsessed with trying to find Nicole so he could talk to her and straighten things out. Unfortunately, the only time he saw her was in a business setting and there she behaved normally. There was nothing at all that would suggest that she was avoiding him and yet he knew she was. It was frustrating since he couldn't talk openly with her. After all, no one knew that they were good friends, who worked out every night. She was careful not to be alone with him and Ryan knew he couldn't push it.

The day following his date with Olivia was a Sunday and so he wouldn't normally expect to see Nicole except during their workout. He had spent the day fretting, and he had half hoped that she would change her mind, but when he went to the fitness center the following night she wasn't there. He stayed almost the entire night just on the off chance that she would pick a different time, but she never showed. He did that for the rest of the week and then he got an idea. It made him cringe but he was desperate to talk to her.

He arranged for a date that weekend with Olivia and made sure that Nicole knew about it. Then, at the last minute, he called up and canceled on Olivia. He hated to do it, but he hadn't seen Nicole all week except in a business setting. His guilt almost caused him to change his mind when he called Olivia to cancel. He could hear the disappointment and frustration in her voice and he promised that he would make it up to her. As he disconnected, he knew that he didn't really have a choice. He had been so wrapped up in trying to figure out what was going on with Nicole that he had been neglecting everything else. His relationship with Olivia was suffering and so was his work, and neither of them deserved it. This was the only thing that he could think of to try to solve the problem before it got even worse. He shook his head and headed towards the fitness center, hoping that Nicole had taken the bait.

* * *

Nicole walked into the fitness center. She knew her workout tonight was going to hurt. She hadn't been to the fitness center all week, not since her blowup with Ryan. She had to find a solution and not for the first time she cursed the restrictions of living in the executive community. The thinking behind it was logical. It provided all the Senior Executives with safe and comfortable living quarters. The safety issue had waxed and waned over the years, but as a long-term solution it made sense, especially since the houses were already there. It also worked to constrain any excessive or inappropriate spending, which was why she couldn't just pay to get an automated sparring machine installed. Of course, that would have been hard to hide and would have revealed her enhancements.

By ensuring that all the Senior Executives lived in a similar, but luxurious manner, it removed some of the temptations that led to excessive spending. Living beyond one's means was effectively impossible in the executive community. Before the Earnings Escrow Act, it had kept Delphi from following the lead of many other companies, companies that had been subject to SEC investigations, bankruptcy or management fraud. Of course, the Earnings Escrow Act had done a lot to close the door on those issues, especially given the long-term view that most Senior Executives took, being women.

The concept was simple—any earnings above a certain threshold were held in escrow for a varying number of years. The tricky part had been deciding the earnings threshold and number of years in escrow, as well as tightening what defined earnings. It had been a little rocky at the start, but it had been running smoothly for well over a hundred years with no significant business scandals, in sharp contrast to the years leading up to it. Unfortunately, the executive community had predated the Earnings Escrow Act and try as she might, there was nothing that Nicole could do to change it.

She walked into the changing room without looking and had just put her bag down on the bench when she heard a voice from behind her.

"Fancy meeting you here."

She felt her heart leap at the same time that her stomach sank, and she didn't know whether to laugh or cry.

"That's not very nice Ryan."

"What, sneaking up on you?"

"That, too, but that's not what I'm talking about. You set me up and you used Olivia to do it. Somehow, I thought you were better than that." She tried to convey her disapproval in her tone of voice, but it was difficult, since she was obscurely pleased by his efforts to sort this out.

"Yeah, me too. But I also thought that you were my friend."

Nicole heard the pain in his voice and she almost closed her eyes, but she knew that she couldn't let him see how this hurt her.

"I am your friend," she replied quietly.

"Then help me understand. Because right now I don't. I don't understand why you refuse to see me, why you won't work out with me anymore. All that's left is work and that's not friendship, that's business."

I can't help you understand because if I did then we'd both know just how I feel about you, she thought. But she couldn't say that and so she fell back on the one thing that did make sense—sort of.

"Have you told anybody about us?" she asked and he shook his head.

"No, how could I? I got the impression that you don't want anyone knowing about your enhancement. Am I at least right about that?" he asked and she nodded.

You shouldn't even know about it, she thought.

"I can understand where you're coming from and I respect that. However, that leaves me with the little problem of explaining how we can be friends when I never see you."

"You haven't even told Olivia?" she clarified and Ryan shook his head.

"I told you, no one," he repeated and Nicole smiled sadly at him.

"Do you really think that you should be keeping secrets from Olivia, now that your relationship is serious?" she asked softly and he opened his mouth and then closed it again slowly.

"Think about it. How would Olivia react to finding out that you've been keeping secrets from her? Not only that but we've been discussing your relationship. While she does the same thing with Brooke, at least you are aware that it's happening. If you don't want Brooke to know something you can ask Olivia not to tell her. Olivia doesn't have the same choice. When she finds out about it, she'll feel betrayed and rightly so."

"I'm willing to take that risk," Ryan responded after a moment.

Nicole smiled to herself. Of course you are, she thought. After all, what's this compared to your real secret.

"Maybe you are, but I'm not," she said firmly. "Olivia is my friend, too, and she depends on me. More than that, my ability to do my job depends on her being able to trust me. There's just too much at stake here."

He was quiet for a moment and then he nodded.

"Well, I got what I asked for, if not what I came for," he said raggedly and Nicole wanted to reach out and comfort him.

In the end she just stood there and he finally left. She wanted to break down and cry, but it had been years since she had allowed herself to do that. Instead she forced herself to straighten up, her manner crisp and firm, without a hint of the feelings that raged inside her. Then, she went to work out her despair and loneliness in that age-old fashion of exercising.

* * *

Olivia groaned as the doorbell chimed. She had no idea what time it was, but since sunlight streamed in the window, it must be sometime during the day. She reached out and checked the clock and groaned again. It was only nine, less than four hours after she and Brooke had finally gone to bed. She had called Brooke over after Ryan stood her up, and they had gotten gloriously drunk. Except now she was paying the price for it.

She wondered if Brooke was still in the guestroom and a sudden loud snore answered the question for her. The doorbell chimed again, and Olivia winced as the sound reverberated inside her brain. She forced herself to stand up and realized that she was still a little tipsy. The thought made her giggle as she pulled on a robe and made her way to the front door.

She was just about to open the door when it occurred to her that she wasn't expecting anyone and that she probably could have just ignored it. It was too late now, of course. Whoever was outside would be able to see her silhouette. She opened the door, blinking in the bright morning sunlight. She put her hand up to shade her eyes, and her hangover-inspired irritability got a fresh boost as she saw that it was Ryan standing there.

She opened her mouth, to say what she wasn't sure, but he beat her to the punch.

"I wanted to come by and apologize in person," he said and then he brought his arms from behind his back. "I come bearing gifts. Coffee and breakfast."

The thought of food made Olivia nauseous and she almost told him to go away when she smelled the aroma of fresh coffee. She relented and invited him in. She followed him as he made his way to the kitchen and poured her a cup of coffee from the thermal carafe.

He handed it to her. "Here you go."

Olivia mumbled a vague thank you as she gratefully took a sip. She could feel life returning slowly and she continued to sip her coffee as Ryan bustled about the kitchen, unpacking the breakfast that he'd brought. He carefully arranged it on Olivia's plates and laid it out before her on the breakfast bar. By the time he had finished, the coffee had worked its magic and she was actually starting to feel hungry instead of nauseous. He topped up her coffee and Olivia took a closer look at what he had laid out. There was a wide variety of bagels, an assortment of jams, and her favorite cream cheese spread. There were also fresh blintzes and a mouthwatering selection of fresh fruit.

"Wow, this looks delicious."

He laughed. "You sound surprised."

"I am," she admitted. "No offense, but most men think that breakfast consists of nothing more than bacon and eggs."

"Don't forget the sausages," he teased her and she blushed.

"There's something else that I'm not forgetting," she said, annoyed that he had managed to make her do just that for a few moments.

"I know," he replied and now it was his turn to blush. "I'm sorry about that. There was an issue with a friend of mine last night. I know the timing was bad, but there was nothing I could do about it. Also, just so you know, that's why I was so distracted last week. It had been building up all week and last night it finally came to a head."

"What was it?" Olivia mumbled around a mouthful of blintz, her curiosity peaked despite her original anger.

He hesitated. "It's not my place to say anything. She asked me to keep it confidential and I have to respect her wishes."

Her. Olivia felt a stab of jealousy at his use of the feminine pronoun.

While it wasn't unheard of for men and women to be friends, the age differences usually precluded it. Which meant that whoever it was, she was likely close to him in age. Or younger.

"How old is she?" she asked, horrified that she was asking.

To her relief Ryan didn't laugh when he answered her. "Much older than you, that's all I can say. Don't worry, there's nothing romantic going on."

"It's not that, I was wondering if there was anything I can do to help." Olivia was quite proud of herself for managing to come up with such a reasonable response, particularly in her less than lucid condition.

"Don't worry about it. Like I said, it came to a head last night and I think that we pretty much resolved it."

"Well the offer stands, just in case."

"Thank you," he replied seriously and then he cocked his head at her. "Does this mean that I'm forgiven?"

Olivia tried to glare at him, but she just couldn't put her heart into it. "I suppose so," she said grudgingly and then Ryan leaned over and kissed her gently on the lips.

"Thanks for understanding," he said and then he sat back.

"That's it? That's the best you can do?" Ryan looked at her, his confusion evident and she laughed. "I thought that I recalled you being a better kisser than that. However, maybe I'm mistaken, it has been a while after all."

She had barely finished when he leaned over and kissed her again. Then his mouth left hers and moved behind her ear. He began planting soft, gentle and incredibly warm kisses behind her ear and down her neck and Olivia moaned softly.

"Is that coffee I smell?" a voice mumbled sleepily behind her and Olivia felt herself blush bright red. She had completely forgotten that Brooke was still here and she thanked God that Brooke had come in now and not five minutes later. "Whoops, sorry. I didn't mean to interrupt."

Ryan sat back and flashed her a quick grin. "Not at all."

"Yes, come on in. There's still some coffee left for you to massacre and there's plenty of food."

Brooke hesitated in the doorway. "Are you sure?"

"Yes, come on in." Olivia repeated.

Brooke walked over and plopped herself down next to Olivia. "Thank goodness. I didn't know how much longer I was going to last without coffee."

Olivia feigned surprise. "And this from the person who is always teasing me about my addiction? Could this be a case of the pot calling the kettle black?"

"Nonsense. There is a difference between a clearly proven medicinal application of a substance and the gross abuse of that same substance."

"Ah, is that what this is?"

"Of course," Brooke replied with stiff dignity as she finished doctoring her coffee. She carefully raised the cup to her lips and took a deep gulp. "See, I'm feeling better already."

Ryan had been watching this byplay with amusement and now he looked at them curiously. "What happened, did you two go out and party last night?"

Brooke stared into her coffee as Olivia answered him. "Something like that."

Olivia didn't want Ryan to know that they had stayed in and gotten drunk while male bashing, especially not after this morning. He'd had enough respect for her to come over and explain and apologize in person.

"Well, at least someone had a good time," he replied and Brooke looked up from her mug in curiosity. Olivia waited until Ryan wasn't looking at her and then mouthed 'Later.' Brooke nodded and went back to gazing at her coffee.

The three of them sat around chatting and drinking coffee and constantly nibbling at the food for another half-hour or so. Then Brooke yawned and stretched. "I should go wash up."

"I should probably leave," Ryan said. "I've intruded long enough."

Olivia tried to tell him that it was all right, but he insisted on leaving. He repackaged the salvageable leftovers, put them in the fridge and then swept the rest into the garbage. He gave Olivia a quick kiss on the cheek and then left. A silence settled over the house after he left, a silence finally broken by Brooke.

"I'm sorry," she said meekly and Olivia just waved her apology away.

"Don't be," she said as her brow furrowed in thought. "I don't know why, but somehow I got the feeling that he wanted to leave and was just looking for an excuse."

Brooke looked puzzled and Olivia didn't blame her. "But I thought that everything was okay between you."

"Yes, so did I. But he's been a little off all morning and I'm not sure, but I think he was relieved when you interrupted us this morning. Maybe not relieved, that might be too strong, but he didn't seem to mind."

"Sorry about that, too," Brooke said, looking more and more miserable and Olivia smiled at her.

"Don't worry about it."

Brooke stared at her. "Who are you and what have you done with my friend?"

"What?"

"Look at you. Last night you were miserable because he stood you up. We spent the entire night trashing him and every other male that we know and getting completely smashed in the process. Now you're back together again or maybe not and you're happy about it?"

"I wouldn't say that I was happy about it, but I'm done with being miserable," Olivia said.

"Okay, that I get. No guy should be able to make you feel miserable. But you're smiling!"

"Well, part of it is that I'm finished wallowing in my own misery and am taking control of my life. The other part of it is that there's a mystery going on here."

"Ah, light dawns on marble head."

"Exactly. You know how I feel about mysteries."

"Yup. Love them in fiction, hate them in real life."

"That's right. It may be nothing, but whatever it is, I'm going to figure it out."

Brooke took another sip of her coffee as Olivia looked absently across the room, her thoughts clearly elsewhere.

* * *

Nicole walked up the steps to her doorway and paused in surprise. Propped up against the doorway was an archaic envelope with her name handwritten across the front. She looked around to see if there was anyone watching her, but if there was, she couldn't see the person. She reached down and turned the envelope over and her eyebrows rose in astonishment. It was sealed with what appeared to be wax of all things. She studied the initials pressed into the wax and frowned. RP. There was only one person she knew who had those initials and she debated whether to open the letter. In the end, her curiosity won out over her good sense. She took the letter inside, slit it open with a knife in the kitchen, and then made her way to the living room. She settled down into her favorite chair and then, after taking a deep breath, she slipped the paper from the envelope.

Dear Nicole

I'd like to apologize for lying to you. It was wrong of me to trick you that way, and wrong to involve Olivia. I hurt both of you. I understand why we can no longer spar together and I respect you for that.

Please continue to use the fitness center whenever you want. I will not intrude on you again.

Your friend
Ryan Peters

It took Nicole two tries to read the entire note, since her eyes immediately teared up. She hadn't expected this from him. Despite what he said, she knew that he didn't really understand what was going on. That would have driven a lesser man away, but not Ryan. She wished she could have told him why she couldn't see him anymore—that she couldn't bear the thought of talking about his relationship with Olivia. It had become harder and harder for her to do it, but she had forced herself to keep at it. A part of her was angry with him for sleeping with Olivia, but only a small part. After all, she had been instrumental in getting him that far.

And, it wasn't like he knew that she had fallen in love with him.

She had never expected it to happen.

When Olivia finally fired Christina, Ryan's predecessor, she knew the time had finally come. She had been waiting for this for forty years, since the day she learned Justin had died. She had so desperately wanted to go to the funeral home and cry and weep and hold him in her arms for one last time but she hadn't. He had warned her of the possibility of his death, although neither of them had expected it so soon. She was his hidden ace, the card up his sleeve that no one knew about.

Fulfilling his dream was more important to him than anything else and so it became important to her. She had bided her time, waiting, knowing that one day the time would come. She knew why Ryan was at Delphi and what he was after, and for her to succeed, he had to succeed first. She had come to terms with that a long time ago, and it galled her that she had to wait for a mere man to fulfill Justin's dream. But Justin had been a mere man, too, and she had fallen in love with him and he with her. She had thought that stage of her life was over, but Justin had proved her wrong. She had been sure that she would never get over Justin—only the second man she had fallen in love with in her life and the only one worthy of it—but she had.

And now somehow she had fallen in love with Ryan. That he was instrumental in helping her to achieve Justin's dream only made him more special to her.

Ryan had impressed her with the passion and talent he brought to the mess that had been the existing state of affairs at Delphi. As the Senior VP of Information Technology, she was more aware than most of how important security was. She was also more aware of just how difficult a task it was and how much time and money it took to make it seem effortless. Personally, she had expected Ryan to fail, not that it would have mattered. The forces that had manipulated the current situation would have ensured that he stayed long enough to do what he needed to do. But he hadn't failed. That was impressive, and the man behind the job even more so.

She had only been advising Ryan on his relationship with Olivia out of friendship at first. Slowly, that had changed over the last few weeks, as she gradually fell in love with him. Once she realized that, it had become more and more difficult for her to keep up the pretense of only being his friend. When she found out Ryan had become intimate with Olivia, she decided she couldn't do it any longer. She admitted that she had reacted badly when she found out, but she hadn't understood the depth of her feelings until then.

Unfortunately, her poor handling of the situation had unforeseen consequences. Ryan had put his relationship with Olivia in jeopardy, but he obviously cared about Nicole enough to try and understand what had changed. He also wanted her to be happy, hence the note. It was just like him, and Nicole wished that she could just end this pretense and tell him how she felt, but she couldn't. She couldn't do that to Ryan or Olivia. She carried the note into the kitchen and made herself a cup of tea. She sipped the tea, as she absentmindedly stroked the note with her fingers.

Chapter Ten

"Take a look at this," Olivia said, as Brooke walked into her office. Brooke plopped herself down in her usual chair and studied the wall screen.

"What is it?" she asked curiously.

Olivia looked at her briefly. "Remember when I told you that I was going to solve this little mystery with Ryan?"

"Yeah, so?"

"This is a log of his activity since he's been here. I started by filtering out any activities that involved one or more of the Senior VPs, but that still left me with a lot of time. Further analysis of the remainder indicates that for almost ninety five percent of it, he is with his staff or in his office. I hesitated about cutting out so much data all at once, but I decided to analyze the remaining five percent first."

"Again, so? That looks like it accounts for almost all of his time."

"Almost all being the key. He also takes random strolls around the campus at all hours, nothing unusual in that. But I did find one event that struck me as odd."

Brooke raised an eyebrow inquiringly and Olivia continued.

"When I was digging in the records, I found that he had applied for a user account in the lab. Interestingly enough, the security logs don't have any records of that visit."

"Why was he in the lab?" Brooke asked, as she sat up straight in alarm. All the key research data was in the lab, protected by the DNA readers. If he were trying to access the data, the first step would be applying for a user account.

Olivia frowned. "That's just it. As far as I can tell, he only set himself up as a user. There has been no activity associated with that profile since then. In fact, it's due to be rotated into inactive storage."

"Does Gabriella know about this?"

"You'd think so, but apparently not. Otherwise, I'd have heard chapter and verse about it from her a long time ago."

"That's odd. She usually knows everything that happens in the lab." Brooke shook her head dismissively as she returned to the main issue.

"Are you sure he didn't add anything to the system or pull anything up?"

"Positive. I've crosschecked all the usage logs and there's nothing there. I called up Nicole and asked her if there was anyway for anyone to access the system without leaving any traces, and she assured me that it was impossible.

I even asked her if it was possible to encode a virus in a DNA sample and use it to corrupt data and she just looked at me like I'd been reading too much science fiction."

"You didn't tell her that it was Ryan you were investigating, did you?"

Olivia looked over at Brooke and shook her head. "No, if it were official I might have gone further with it, but I'm pushing the limits on this as it is."

"You could say that. Because of your relationship with him, your motives are questionable. As the CEO, you are in a slightly stronger position than most people. We could argue that you detected a change in his behavior on a personal level and were concerned about it affecting his job performance, or worse still, that it suggested a security breach. Which is what you have, in effect, found."

"Yes, but I seriously doubt that he's trying to steal our data. I don't know what's going on here, but it's not industrial espionage."

"Are you sure? You can't afford to be wrong on this one, not after that fiasco with Christina."

"Yes, I know. Look at it objectively. His performance has been exemplary and he's been working well beyond standard business hours. Not to mention how much he's tightened security since we hired him. In fact, this data search that I just did wouldn't have been possible, at least not in the detail that I've gone to, without the changes in security that he made. In all the months that he's been working here I've found one incident that seems slightly odd. One incident in which nothing illegal or unethical occurred."

Brooke started to interrupt and Olivia shook her head and continued, "I know, technically he's not supposed to be in the lab without Gabriella, and he's definitely not supposed to be using the DNA reader, but those are minor infractions and are more a matter of company policy. If push came to shove I'd be willing to terminate his employment contract and let the lawyers fight it out, but I think that there's more to be gained by waiting and watching."

Brooke grimaced. "That's a pretty slim rope to hang everything you've worked for on."

"I know, but I just get the feeling that there's more going on than we can see. Don't think for a minute that I won't be keeping a close eye on him."

"Why don't you just confront him, see what he has to say?"

"I don't want to tip my hand. As it stands now, he thinks that he's gotten away with this, whatever it is. If I confront him, it puts the ball back into his court. If he is up to something, he'll be more careful in the future."

"So how are you going to handle your relationship?"

"That's the million dollar question, isn't it?" Olivia thought for a moment and then sighed. "I'll keep seeing him, but I don't think that I can be intimate with him."

"Are you sure you're okay with that? You sound a little odd."

Olivia blushed. "I was just thinking back to our picnic," she confessed and Brooke laughed.

"Ah, I see. The sex was that good, eh?"

Olivia laughed. "Stop that. You sound like Nicole when you do that."

Brooke grinned an apology at her and then tilted her head inquiringly.

Olivia sighed. "To tell you the truth, I really don't know."

"How can you not know, it either was or it wasn't. Besides, I thought you told me it was wonderful."

"It was, but I don't know if it was just that one time. After all, I haven't had that much sex in the last forty years."

"So?"

"So, maybe it was just the release of pent up desire that made it so good."

"Maybe, but I doubt it. Good sex is good sex, period."

"Great, that makes me feel a whole lot better." Olivia glared at Brooke, who shrugged.

"Sorry," Brooke said.

"No wonder I haven't done this in forty years," Olivia complained. "It's too hard."

"It can be, but that's usually the hallmark of something worthwhile. After all, did someone just walk up to you and say, hey there, we're looking for a CEO? Are you busy?"

Olivia laughed despite her frustration. "No, that's not exactly how it happened. Still it didn't seem this hard."

"Of course not. Relationships are the hardest thing in the world to manage and make work. And at the end of the day, that's what it all comes down to as far as I'm concerned. If you don't have a good relationship with someone then you don't have anyone to share all that other good stuff with either."

"I have a relationship with you," she teased and Brooke grinned at her.

"Sorry, I don't walk on that side of the street. Seriously, as close as we are, it's completely different when you find a good relationship with someone who you can be intimate with, someone who is part of your life rather than just in it."

"So far I don't have a very good track record."

"Don't worry," Brooke said cheerfully. "You still have lots of time to screw up more relationships."

"Thanks," Olivia replied sarcastically and Brooke smiled sadly.

"I mean that in the best way. Since we're both unfortunate enough to be heterosexual, it's almost certain that we will love and lose, probably more than once. If you and Ryan stay together, you've got another forty or fifty years together max. Realistically, you can expect to live at least another three hundred years. Doing the math, you'll probably have another three to six serious relationships, or dozens of less serious ones. Now I know that's scary, but to me what's even scarier is denying yourself the richness of those relationships out of fear."

"Like I did with Ryan, forty years ago," Olivia said quietly.

Brooke reached out and held her hand. "Just don't make the same mistake again. You're smarter than that."

"Sometimes I doubt it," Olivia forced a grin and then looked at Brooke. "All right, enough of this. Let's go somewhere sunny and have something good to eat."

"Sounds good, let's go."

* * *

Ryan draped the towel around his neck as he finished his workout. He had been pushing himself hard. It allowed him time to clear his mind and lately there had been a lot going on. He had started going out with Olivia again, at her initiative surprisingly enough. They had also taken the unusual step of having midweek dates. On the surface everything appeared okay, but there was a subtle wariness on both their parts. Perhaps because of that wariness they hadn't been intimate again, something Ryan found that he didn't have a problem with. He half wondered if it was a déjà vu moment for her. After all, it had been at roughly the same stage in their relationship forty years ago that she had broken it off with him.

Back then, they had been going out several times a week for months before they had finally made love. It had given them time to get to know each other, and Ryan had always wondered if that was the trigger. Physical intimacy was common—too common. When they finally made love, there was an emotional connection that made it special and rare. Perhaps too special, and that could have been what frightened Olivia so much.

Although the relationship that they had now had progressed differently, he wondered if the physical act of loving each other had triggered that association in Olivia's mind. It was certainly possible. It could also have been triggered by his odd behavior during the week after they made love. He had to admit that he had behaved badly that week, as he tried to talk to Nicole.

He had been doing a lot of thinking about it recently, and he realized that he had been relying on his forty year old memories of Olivia. They hadn't spent the same amount of time together yet, and Ryan had let himself believe that they didn't need to, that there was a connection that still existed after forty years. He understood now just how naïve that was, and so in a sense, it was a relief that they hadn't been intimate again. It gave him the time to get to know her better, as a person rather than as a lover. Not only were the two parts of Olivia different, but he knew that if sex entered the picture, he would never see Olivia for who she was. For some reason, that had become very important to him.

He had been taking it slowly on their dates, remembering the fiasco from their first one. So far, he hadn't found any surprises, not that he had expected to. He had been shying away from controversial subjects up until now, but that had to change. Eventually, this would break wide open and he needed to know where Olivia stood. After all, in a sense he was doing this for her, for them. He knew how important it was. Whether he had a relationship with Olivia wouldn't change anything at this point, but for some reason he needed to know if there was still a 'they' out there waiting for him.

He looked around the empty fitness center as he headed for the executive changing room, and his mind automatically thought of Nicole. He had been monitoring the access logs for the fitness center, so he knew that she had started working out regularly again. It pleased him that she felt comfortable enough to do that, but he still missed working out with her. He also missed not being able to talk to her about his relationship with Olivia.

He wondered idly how she would react to some of the sensitive issues that he wanted to bring up with Olivia, and then he grinned suddenly as he had a wicked thought. He would kill two birds with one stone, and bring some of the issues up at the weekly meetings they all had at Olivia's. Even as he thought of it, he realized that it would work even better than discussing it with Olivia alone. It would be less threatening, for one thing. Not only would it not be just the two of them discussing it, but it wouldn't be occurring during the charged atmosphere of a date. He would also get a good sample of the views of different women on the topic. Between the three of them, Olivia, Brooke and Nicole, they represented a wide cross section of women. It was Friday night, so he only had to wait another day before the next meeting.

He smiled as he stripped down for the shower and realized just how ironic the situation was. Nicole had refused to see him once he became intimate with Olivia, only now he was no longer intimate with her. He whistled cheerfully, not once suspecting that perhaps the two situations were more closely linked than he realized.

* * *

Nicole arrived at Olivia's with an unusual sense of anticipation. Tension had filled the atmosphere between her and Ryan all week. Or almost all week. Yesterday he seemed positively cheery and Nicole wasn't sure why. He'd had another date with Olivia the night before so perhaps it had gone well. That had been Nicole's original theory, one that she was oddly unhappy with. She knew that she couldn't complain since it was an unhappiness of her own making. She would just have to live with it.

Since then, she'd seen Olivia and decided she was wrong. It wasn't that Olivia didn't seem happy, she just didn't seem happy enough. She had hung out around Olivia and Brooke long enough for her enhanced hearing to confirm that Ryan and Olivia hadn't in fact slept together. Nor did they have a date for the weekend. So there must be something else that accounted for Ryan's cheerfulness and there were only three major things in his life at the moment. One was the reason he was here in the first place, and Nicole would have known if something had changed on that front. The second was his relationship with Olivia, and from what she could gather, nothing had changed there either.

Which only left work. Given that it was the weekend, the only work related item on his agenda was this regular Saturday informal executive team meeting. For some reason Ryan was looking forward to this meeting, and in an odd sense Nicole was, too. She supposed that it was partially relief that his happiness didn't stem from being intimate with Olivia, but he had also managed to peak her curiosity without even talking to her.

She forced herself to be patient as the first half hour passed uneventfully, but then Ryan started talking about disastrous first dates. Some of his stories had been hilarious, but Nicole knew that it was leading somewhere. He was surprisingly subtle about it, managing to draw all of them into telling bad first date stories. And then he got the ball rolling.

"You should have seen the first date that Olivia and I had. Man, talk about bad."

For a moment, Nicole felt tempted to let him hang, since she knew that he was counting on her to ask the necessary next question. She was too curious to see where this was going, so she followed his lead.

"It couldn't have been that bad," Nicole teased them both. "After all, you're still going out."

"No, it was that bad," Brooke countered with a wry smile. "Olivia didn't even have a second cup of coffee. And apparently it was really good coffee."

Nicole winced visibly and everyone laughed. "So what happened?" she asked.

"Well I had to open my big fat mouth and bring politics into the mix," Ryan admitted with chagrin.

"Ouch. Why not just mix up some oil and water while you're at it?"

"Admittedly, some of it was my fault," Olivia interjected. "I'm afraid that when it comes to politics, I'm pretty naïve."

Nicole started to get a glimmer of just where Ryan was going with this and she had to admire his shrewdness. It was a neutral way to discuss a controversial topic, and one that gave him insight into various viewpoints. She also admired the way he had drawn her into the conversation. He knew that she had to pretend ignorance on the topic or risk having Olivia find out that she and Ryan were friends. Mind you, technically she was ignorant, at least about the details and so she decided to run with it.

"Politics covers a wide range of topics. Just what were you discussing?" Nicole asked.

"I asserted that I thought that the political situation here was stable and Ryan disagreed with me, specifically regarding the roles of men and women in society."

"And Kaboom!" Nicole shook her head. "Now I can see why the date went south. Talk about a hot topic. The 'Gender Divide' is perhaps the single most important social issue facing us today. Although I must admit that I'm not surprised at your assertion about the stability of the situation. You're a businesswomen and as such you look at the economics first. Viewed from a solely economic vantage, then yes, I'd have to agree with you. However, when you look at it socially, then I'd have to disagree vehemently."

"Perhaps that's where Ryan and I conflicted. But you've got me curious now. Would you mind elaborating?" Olivia asked.

"Hmm, where to start? Let's see. There have always been differences between the genders, in the areas of intellectual and emotional intelligence, as well as the gross physical differences. In fact, at various points in time, seemingly otherwise intelligent so-called scientists actually advanced theories that men and women were really two different species. That's an exaggeration but there have always been differences between the two."

Nicole paused for a moment, gathering her thoughts. "I can still remember what it was like when I was young. In the twenty-first century, we had finally arrived at the point where we celebrated these differences and recognized what each could bring to the mix. That was an after-the-fact realization of the value of family, since a good marriage recognizes, accepts and values these differences." There was a sad, almost wistful, tone to her voice and it had a sobering effect on everyone.

"That was before Menssation®," Ryan said quietly.

Nicole nodded in agreement. "Yes it was. Once women started turning their menstrual cycles off, this delicate balance burst like a soap bubble. The geopolitical consequences have obviously been enormous, and that's what everyone focuses on, to the detriment of social trends. It's a natural tendency, given the major geopolitical and economic issues that resulted from this change, but the social issues are very real and are becoming increasingly important.

"Once women began turning off their menstrual cycles, these gender differences became a gender divide. Instead of minor differences that we could bridge, we now have a massive chasm dividing the two genders. The first place this chasm was noticed was in demographic data, as our birth rates began to plummet. Unfortunately, this was only a symptom of the underlying problem, but like many doctors, the politicians chose to address the symptom and not the problem. The use of the artificial embryogenesis machine helped to correct the demographic imbalance, but it only postponed the social crisis. In fact there are some who argue that it made it worse."

Brooke was nodding in agreement but Olivia looked puzzled.

"Think about the balance of power," Ryan said with a sad smile. "Remember what I talked about that night, about the disparity between the number of men in the workforce versus the military?"

Nicole shot Ryan a warning glance. He was on the verge of getting worked up about Olivia's ignorance in this area, and she could understand why. However, it was likely that he would need Olivia's support at some point in the future, and he couldn't afford to alienate her. Unfortunately, that's exactly what would happen if he tried to explain it to her. There was an unconscious assumption that he was exaggerating the issue, just because he was a man. Olivia would be more likely to listen to the facts, and less likely to discount the seriousness of them, if Nicole presented them.

"Ryan's right. There are many men in the workforce today, but almost all of them have blue-collar jobs or basic entry-level white-collar jobs. They rarely go any further than that. Most men don't even bother to go to college or university after high school. After all, what's the point in wasting another five years of your life for something that likely won't bring you any benefits? There are more advantages to be had by starting work right away, or even better enlisting in the military with its built-in advantages. Free housing, on-the-job training, respect, perhaps the best benefits package in the world, just to name a few."

"Tell me about it," Brooke retorted. "Do you have any idea how hard it is to offer a competitive package? Despite the extra cost, I think it's worth the effort to ensure a balanced workforce. Mind you, I'm a little on my own in that regard. Most other companies don't even bother to try.

"That only adds to the problem," Nicole confirmed. "The existing structure makes it difficult for normal businesses to compete and as a result, few do. It's a self-perpetuating problem. For every year that passes, the military attracts more men and businesses, fewer. Despite the predominance of men in the military, they take their orders from the elected political power. Since women control the economic and political power in this country, this effectively neutralizes the military as a group.

"However, the artificial embryogenesis machine has changed the power structure, or at least created the possibility for it. Currently men outnumber women two to one. If they wanted to, they could effectively assume political power in this country." Despite herself, Nicole smiled at Olivia's expression of surprise and she elaborated. "The only reason that hasn't happened yet is that men as a group are relatively content. Female politicians have been effectively buying their votes, offering better military benefits and other perks designed to keep them happy. A constantly expanding tax base has allowed them to pay for all of these promises. Unfortunately, that's all about to change. The promises are growing faster than the tax base. As well, the demographic shift, from women outnumbering men, to men outnumbering women, has changed too dramatically, and there are a growing number of politicians concerned enough about this to want to curb it."

"How are they proposing to do that?" Olivia asked.

Nicole could tell that she was dreading the answer. "There's been talk of tightening the licensing requirements for artificial ova, minimum and maximum age limits, even limiting the number of licenses to the death rate."

"That doesn't sound good." Olivia winced.

Nicole smiled bitterly. "It gets worse. No offense Ryan, but men naturally lean towards force as a way of solving problems. Given that men outnumber women two to one, that most of them have little education, and that they have effective control of the military, you can see why this has started to make people nervous."

"Nervous? Is that all?" Olivia shuddered. "Brooke mentioned something like this to me a while ago, but I discounted it. Not anymore. I'm officially scared."

Nicole smiled. "Yeah, me too. And believe me, there are many people who are just as scared. The problem with that is that fear often brings out the worst in people. It blinds them to solutions and they reach for simplistic answers to complex problems. And then, of course, there is the one thing that most people, men and women, overlook."

"The Xerox effect," Ryan pointed out softly.

Nicole glanced at Ryan and nodded. It wasn't surprising that he had done as much thinking on this as he had, given why he was here at Delphi, but the depth and breadth of his knowledge pleased her.

"That's right," Nicole agreed, "The Xerox effect."

"What's the Xerox effect?" Brooke asked.

Nicole shot another warning glance at Ryan as she responded. "It refers to the old days before all correspondence was digital. Nowadays we can make perfect copies of almost anything, simply by copying the digital pattern underlying it. In the old days, people made copies of documents by taking a picture of the document and then printing that picture. If you kept on copying the copy, eventually you'd get a document that bore no visible relation to the original."

Nicole looked at Brooke and Olivia as she continued. "The same effect is beginning to happen with the AEMs. It worked fine for the first generation of men to use it, but now you have men who represent the second, third and even fourth generations, and the problems are growing worse. The first AEMs had a horrendous number of defects. Thousands of ova were aborted since they weren't viable or else they just didn't survive. The success rate was somewhere between twenty and thirty percent. With time the technology improved and the success rate climbed to well over ninety percent.

"Now it's starting to plummet again." She glanced at Ryan. "The ova are still good, but the DNA used is second or third generation and flaws are starting to show up. These flaws increase the number of ova aborted, driving down the success rate. It's hard to know how much of the decrease is related to flawed DNA, but the overall success rate is now in the low seventies. The net result is a decrease in the birth rate for men, the first in decades. Put the lower birthrates for men together with their shorter lifespan and you have a very disturbing trend."

Nicole took a deep breath. "The long and short is that there is an extremely volatile situation building up. Once men realize what is happening, there's a strong possibility they may attempt to seize power. It will be bad enough if they do it in a controlled fashion, using the existing political structure, but I don't think they will. My guess is that they'll use the military first. Either way, the situation has the makings for a civil war of an unheard-of scale."

Nicole finished and silence reigned. She glanced at Ryan and knew that he had mixed feelings. On one hand, Brooke and Olivia were finally aware of the seriousness of the situation, but on the other hand it was a serious situation with no solution in sight. No solution except for what he was trying to do. To her surprise he looked up at her.

"Well, there's nothing we can do about it right now, and my intent was not to bring this up again and depress us all." Ryan smiled oddly at her as he spoke. "The situation wasn't created overnight and it won't be solved overnight. The important thing is that we understand the seriousness of it, think about it, and do what we can when we can."

"True," Olivia seconded, clearly relieved at the thought of moving on to a less disturbing topic. Brooke came in with a bad date anecdote of her own and the mood gradually lightened. Nicole joined in as she always did, but she found herself thinking about the strange smile that Ryan gave her all night long.

Chapter Eleven

Ryan was still thinking about Nicole on Monday morning when he went into work. His idea had worked better than expected. Much better in fact, and he owed it all to Nicole. She had surprised him with how well-informed she was on the 'Gender Divide,' as she had so aptly called it. The depth of understanding that she displayed on the issue had rivaled his. It shouldn't have been surprising, especially given her age and experience, but in a sense those were the reasons it was so surprising.

Of course, that didn't mean that she supported him. It could mean the opposite, that she was so knowledgeable because she in fact supported the existing social order, but he didn't get that feeling from her. He had been thinking about it almost constantly since then. His handlers had never suggested that they had an inside source, but they knew too much about how Delphi worked not to. Perhaps Nicole was that source. For some reason he found that prospect appealing.

With a sudden burst of insight he realized he was falling in love with her.

He sat back in his chair, dismayed and confused. He was in love with Olivia, wasn't he? He marshaled his thoughts and tried to recall everything about Olivia he loved. To his dismay he found himself struggling. He continued to wrestle with his thoughts, sure that he was letting his feelings for Nicole blind him to what it was he found attractive about Olivia.

After about half an hour of going through his memories of Olivia, he realized that everything he loved about her was forty years old. He had naïvely assumed he would be able to pick up their relationship where they had left off. He realized that when he had agreed to undertake this mission forty years ago, he had gone into it with her on his mind, and that had ensured that she had stayed in his thoughts and memories all that time. The reality was that he had changed dramatically during that time.

He suddenly understood just why it was women had been able to dominate the worlds of politics and business so quickly. The knowledge and life experiences he had garnered during his first forty years paled in comparison to what he had done since then. That was what had given him the edge he needed to succeed in the military and in his related business experiences.

He had never felt the same bitterness that other men had about women holding the reins of power. Part of it had been his early experience with Olivia and his feelings for her, but part of it had been his knowledge that he was working to change all of that. Nevertheless, he would have had to have been a saint not to feel resentment as all the choice jobs went to women first, and if there was anything he was sure of, it was that he wasn't a saint.

Now that resentment vanished, washed away by understanding. There was a reason women got the choice jobs. It was the same reason he now had this job. Their experience gave them an edge, an edge that only grew with time. That he now understood the reasons for it better didn't change his resolve to see his mission through, though. In fact, if anything, it only strengthened it. After all, he was a poster boy for what this could do for men everywhere, if his mission were successful.

He understood he really wasn't in love with Olivia anymore. Now all he had to do was figure out what to do about it. One part of him wanted to break up with Olivia and ask Nicole out on a date. It might be pointless, but there was no denying his attraction to her and a proper date would allow them both the chance to get to know each other. On the other hand, given why he was here, a smidgen of prudence might be a better choice.

He didn't know whether he would need Olivia for him to be able to succeed in his mission. He also didn't know if he would be risking his role or Nicole's role, by being open about his feelings. Most of all, though, he knew he shouldn't rock the boat, at least not until the reason he was really here came out into the open. He reluctantly decided to keep seeing Olivia, but try to keep it casual. He didn't want to lead her on or risk hurting her, but realistically he had no other choice. That neatly took care of his decision about Nicole as well, although he wasn't happy about that either.

Now that he had his personal life sorted out, it was time to do some work. He pulled up all the messages that had piled up over the weekend, checking priority messages first. There was a message from Olivia and given who she was, his filters had automatically bumped it to the top of his message queue. He scanned it quickly and noted that it was another Thursday date invitation. Given all the thought that he had just given their relationship, he accepted it automatically. He continued to work his way through the rest of the messages, finally working his way down to the end of the queue.

He stared at the last message in disbelief. It was a simple message, but if he was right, it meant that he was about to succeed. It was an automatic message from the lab, telling him the sample he had submitted was ready. The only sample he had submitted had been the blood sample for the DNA reader. He tried the link embedded in the message, knowing that it probably wouldn't work. Sure enough, it told him to confirm his identity at the source first. He sat there and stared at the message, trying to wrap his mind around it. This little e-mail had been the focus of his life for the last forty years. It had consumed half of his life so far, shaped who and what he was, had even shaped his love life. It was hard to accept that it was almost over, hard to believe that he had almost succeeded. Now all he needed to do was to get access to the DNA reader so it could confirm his identity.

That thought shook him out of the fog he was in, and with a wry smile he started to search for a time when he would be able to get into the lab without getting caught. He still had all of his data from earlier, plus another month or so of data he had collected since then, so it didn't take long for the results to come back. Thursday. He stared at the screen, suddenly certain there was a God. Either that, or the universe had a very twisted sense of humor.

He double-checked the date just in case and immediately saw why the lab was free that night. Both Friday and the following Monday were holidays, so many of the researchers were away for an extra long weekend. The pattern analysis had shown that on the first night of a long weekend, even the hardcore researchers took the night off. The weekend itself was harder to predict, at least to the degree of statistical significance required. He sighed and knew he had no choice. He would have to go to the lab after his date with Olivia. He debated canceling it, but having just analyzed all the reasons he needed to stay on her good side, he couldn't do that.

A new thought hit him suddenly and he paled. He and Olivia had only been intimate that one afternoon. Since then, all of their dates had been during the week, when the excuse of work made it acceptable for each of them to go their separate ways at the end of the date. Given that Friday was a holiday, Thursday now counted as one of those major date nights they had been avoiding. He wondered if Olivia had realized this when she set up the date and almost immediately he knew that she did. If she hadn't, she would have made a date for both Tuesday and Thursday, the two nights they had been dating during the week. Since she had only picked Thursday, it was obvious she was ready for them to be intimate again.

The only problem was he wasn't. Not only that, but he didn't have the time. Besides, even if he had all the time in the world, what he and Olivia had once had was over, at least for him. It wasn't fair to her or to him to pretend otherwise, and if it weren't for the overriding importance of his mission, he would have ended it. Be that as it may, there were lines he wouldn't cross, and this was one of them. It may be foolish, but he had to be able to look at himself in the mirror every day for the rest of his life, and be comfortable with what he did and how he behaved.

He knew he would have to manage their relationship carefully, otherwise he could wind up increasing Olivia's suspicions or, worse still, hurting her. He grimaced as he amended that to 'hurting her more than he already would.'

His earlier prediction about how this could backfire on him was coming back to haunt him, although in a different fashion then he had originally thought. He sighed as he began figuring out how to make it all work.

* * *

"Hey there, what's up?"

"Hi Brooke." Olivia looked up and smiled.

"Okay, what gives?" Brooke eyed her with suspicion.

"Pardon me?" Olivia asked innocently.

Brooke snorted. "Don't give me that. You're up to something, I can tell. I know you too well. That smile means something."

"As it turns out, you're right. I've asked Ryan for a date this Thursday."

Brooke's eyes widened. "This Thursday? You do realize that Friday is a holiday, don't you?" When Olivia nodded, she continued. "Then you also realize that Thursday is no longer a safe night." She paused and looked at Olivia. "Ohh," she said slowly, "right, of course you do. That's why you're smiling. I thought that you were going to take it slow with him, try to find out what he was up to before you got intimate again."

Olivia shrugged. "I was and I did, take it slow I mean. It's been almost a month now. I haven't found anything else to be suspicious of, and the dates that we've gone on have all gone well."

"Did you ask him about why he had been in the lab?" Brooke asked quietly.

Olivia shook her head with a small blush on her cheeks. "I couldn't think of an easy way to work it into the conversation. I was beginning to think that I overreacted. Or it could have been both of us. Maybe it was just too soon."

"Or maybe he wanted to get a handle for how you felt about this 'Gender Divide' that Nicole mentioned."

"You caught that too? I was wondering where he was going with that, given that three out of the four of us knew what had happened on our first date." Olivia frowned as she recalled her naivety. "After everyone went home that night I started thinking, trying to figure out why he had brought it up. The only reason I can think of that makes sense is that he wanted me to understand the situation out there, something that I refused to do that first date. Obviously this is important to him for some reason that I can't see, since it hasn't impacted him. Maybe he wondered what kind of relationship we'd have if we couldn't even talk about it."

"Wow, you certainly did do a lot of thinking."

"That was when I decided it was time for us to be intimate again. I think the timing is right. I'm no longer suspicious of him, and after last week, I hope that he feels more comfortable with me."

"Well as long as you're comfortable. I don't want you doing anything you don't want to."

"Whoa, where did this come from?" Olivia asked in surprise. "Weren't you the one telling me that I need to live a little more?"

"Yeah, but that was before you started checking up on him."

"Do you think that I still have something to worry about?" Olivia asked frowning and Brooke pursed her lips hesitantly.

"No, not really. Definitely not about your physical safety, that's for sure. I don't think I've ever met someone who I got such a strong 'I'll keep you safe' vibe from. It adds to his overall maleness and I know that's a tough package to resist. It's more the emotional side that I'm worried about. He may or may not have a secret that he's keeping from you, but either way I'm worried about you getting hurt."

"Especially by him. That's the part you didn't say," Olivia chided.

Brooke grinned. "Busted. However that doesn't detract from the validity of my concern."

"No and believe you me I've thought about it myself. But I honestly think that I'm okay with it now. In retrospect, this little 'break' that we've been on has been good for me. It allowed me to figure this out at my own pace, and without the crushing heartbreak of a failed relationship to cloud my thinking. I realized that I've held myself back for too long, and in fact I think that it's good that my first real foray into dating once more is with Ryan. It made me realize that what's past is past, and that I can't let it hold me back. It was my parents' past that held me back with Ryan the first time, and it was our past that's held me back since then. I need to let go of it all and start living in the here and now."

"Wow, that's healthy of you."

Olivia colored.

Brooke shook her head. "No, I'm serious. I've got friends my age who still haven't grasped that fact. They're still dealing with all the baggage from their past, real and imagined. At least all of your issues were real."

Brooke paused and looked hard at Olivia. "Whatever happens with this relationship with Ryan, you can finally move ahead. I just wish that you had asked him about why he was in the lab. I would feel better if we had a good answer for that."

Olivia shrugged. She wished now that she had never mentioned it to Brooke. It was one minor infraction, one that he likely had a valid reason for. The truth was, she couldn't figure out how to ask him without revealing that she had checked up on him, and that would be too embarrassing. Brooke took the hint and changed the topic to a personality conflict she was trying to resolve.

* * *

Ryan approached the restaurant with anxiety. He had sent a limo to pick Olivia up with an apology about why he couldn't pick her up personally. He had subtly maneuvered one of his subordinates into calling a last minute meeting, supposedly to discuss security issues before the long weekend. The reality was that he had also prepared an excuse to allow him to return to Delphi straight from the restaurant. It would be easier for him to use his own car to return to Delphi and let the limo service take Olivia home. These unusually deceitful practices and his nervousness about what he would or would not find in the lab that night combined to make him uncommonly edgy. His nanites were working overtime to keep him from looking and acting like the nervous wreck he was.

He arrived at the front door and hopped out of the car. He gave his name to the maitre d' and then followed him to the table. As they approached, Ryan felt his spirits sink. Olivia looked stunning. She was wearing a slinky long halter-neck, black dress that showed off her shoulders and her entire back. As he walked around the table to take his seat, he noticed that although the dress was floor-length, a slit ran almost up to her thigh. The dress left her back bare, except for a provocative series of bands around her lower back. The front was a tiny triangle-shaped scrap of fabric, with the top of the triangle pointing enticingly at her bare throat. The bottoms of the triangle ran into the bands around her lower back, subtly but surely revealing the soft curves of her breasts as it did so. It was sexy and sultry and he let out a low whistle as he bent over to give her a kiss and then sat down.

"Do you like it?" she asked preening and he smiled.

"What's not to like?" he exclaimed. "You look spectacular. I feel like a complete jerk. Not only did I not pick you up, but I was running late and I didn't have time to get ready properly."

"I think you look presentable enough, although I'm still mad at you." He arched an eyebrow quizzically and she elaborated. "I had thought that we could recreate our picnic in a more comfortable environment. I was going to suggest that we just skip dinner altogether, but I couldn't get in touch with you." She looked at him coyly. "It's not too late, you know."

Ryan suppressed a gulp as he realized how close he had come to getting in too deep. If he hadn't developed this plan to leave on time, he wouldn't have been avoiding her messages, which meant that it would have been a lot harder to turn her down gracefully.

"What, and miss seeing you look like this? You must be kidding," he said and she blushed at the compliment. "Seriously, you look sensational. And even though I've seen you in less, somehow this is sexier."

"Well you can still admire it on the way home," she pressed and he grinned at her.

"Everything in its time," he said calmly. "Just think of how much better it will be with all this anticipation."

"I've already got weeks worth of anticipation," she pouted and he looked at her pointedly. "Oh, all right," she groused good-naturedly, "I suppose I can wait a couple of hours longer."

"Good, because I've been looking forward to this all week long. They serve a mean ostrich filet here, drizzled with a port wine sauce, with a side of fresh baby vegetables."

"I can't believe it," she teased him. "Did I just hear you put a bird so dumb that it puts its head in the sand over me?"

"First, that's just a myth. Ostriches don't actually put their heads in the sand. They just stretch out their necks and lay their heads on the ground to keep predators from seeing them. And second, let's say I expect this meal to be the first step on a pathway of perfection, with you being the last and best stop."

"That's a little better," she replied mollified and he grinned.

"I hear that they have world-class coffee here, too," he teased her and she sat up straight.

"Why didn't you say so earlier?"

They spent the rest of the evening chatting and flirting, and all the while Ryan cursed the efficiency of their waiter. The man couldn't take his eyes off Olivia, and he hovered around them constantly, checking her out. It would have irritated Ryan at the best of times, but given how dramatically it improved the service they got, it really ticked him off. For a moment he considered not leaving a tip, but the poor guy didn't deserve that. Olivia would make a blind man look twice. As it went, the waiter was fairly subtle about it, and Ryan had to admit that it was perhaps the best service he had ever received.

He did his best to stretch the time out, lingering over his appetizer, and even going so far as to send his ostrich back, complaining it was undercooked. He also consumed vast quantities of wine, which his nanites converted almost immediately to energy. Fortunately, Olivia knew better than to keep up with him or she would have gotten drunk enough to want to start on the rest of their evening early. He had just settled the bill when the alert he had been expecting came. He suppressed his sigh of relief as he pretended to focus on the details.

Olivia suddenly got a sinking sensation in her stomach. Ryan had just gotten a vague look on his face, and Olivia somehow knew that it was bad news. Just when she thought the evening was finally going well, this had to happen. His eyes refocused and he turned to her with an apologetic look on his face.

"Sorry, I've got to run."

"What is it?"

He shrugged. "It could be nothing. There have been a couple of near breaches at random spots along the perimeter. It's probably just some college kids blowing off steam, but standard operating procedures dictate that I have to go check it out."

"Do you want me to come with you?"

He shook his head. "No, that's okay. Given the number of breaches and the randomness of the locations, it's probably going to take some time to resolve it. I've got my car so I'll head straight there and you can take the limo home."

She tried to suppress her disappointment, but she failed.

"I know that this is the furthest from what you planned for tonight and I'm sorry. If I didn't have to go, I wouldn't." He smiled warmly at her. "You really do look stunning."

She grinned at him, cheered up despite her disappointment and frustration. "That's a little presumptuous, assuming there will be a next time."

"Well if not, then it will be my loss." He stood and kissed her softly on the mouth. "I'd better go."

Olivia sat back and sipped at her coffee as she watched him walk away. He turned the corner out of sight and she sighed regretfully. She had been working herself up to this all week, and it frustrated her immensely to have their evening cut short like this. She put down her coffee cup and smiled as their waiter instantly refilled it. Now she finally understood all those stories that Brooke had told her. She had found it hard to believe that young men could be so easily manipulated, but this one had been hovering around them all night long. She was a little surprised at his reaction—after all, her dress was relatively conservative. Still, Brooke had told her that she filled it nicely and wore it well, and sometimes that counted more than showing skin would have. Apparently Brooke was right. Olivia snorted in amusement. Of course her friend was right. When it came to men, Brooke was never wrong. Olivia sipped at the fresh coffee appreciatively, but it just added to her frustration. She sighed and ordered some of their homemade ice cream, hoping to drown her frustration in its calorie rich embrace.

She made it halfway through the bowl and realized it wasn't working. She drummed her fingers on the table, irritated. Suddenly she had a thought. Although Ryan hadn't said how long he would be, there was no reason he couldn't come over to her place as soon as he was free. He could let himself in and wake her with soft kisses. She smiled in anticipation and pushed her chair back as she headed for the limo. She knew she wouldn't be able to reach him while he was busy and this was another one of those messages she didn't want to leave. Therefore, she needed to tell him in person. Olivia smiled brightly as the limo pulled up and she told the driver to take her to the security complex.

Chapter Twelve

Ryan strolled through the door into the control center.

"Hey Anita, what's up?" he asked, as the tall young woman looked up at his entrance. She was only recently promoted and normally he wouldn't have allowed her to work such an important shift. However, there hadn't been any real security concerns at Delphi for months, not since that first attempt after Ryan had started. Given that Ryan wasn't going away for the long weekend and so many others were, he had decided to allow her this opportunity, but with fixed guidelines in place. Ordinarily, Ryan would have been a little more cautious, but since it worked in his favor, he hadn't raised any objections to the proposal.

"Hello sir," she replied formally as she flushed with embarrassment. "I'm sorry that I had to call you."

Ryan felt slightly guilty for putting her in this position, by arranging the events that had forced her to call him, but he'd had no choice in the matter. He tried to compensate by reassuring her that she had done the right thing, which she had and then some.

"Nonsense. That's what the protocols are for. You followed them exactly by calling me when you did."

"Thank you sir, but I still feel badly. It looks like I pulled you away from your dinner for nothing. About five minutes after I called you, the incidents stopped and they haven't started again." Of course they did, he thought. He'd arranged for some of his buddies to 'test' his security for him and they had stopped their 'testing' after he called them, which he had done as soon as he left the restaurant.

"You did the right thing," he reassured her, trying to ignore this addition to the enormous burden of guilt that he was already carrying. "And it wasn't nothing. The incidents may or may not have any substance to them, but I sure hope the SOPs do. That's where you were taking your cue from and you did it perfectly." He smiled at her and she managed to smile back at him, albeit tentatively.

"Now, let's take a look at those records and see what we've got."

He spent the next ten minutes reviewing everything they had, which wasn't much.

"It looks like your assessment was bang on," he concluded and she smiled again, more firmly this time. "College kids." He grinned and shook his head reprovingly. "Well, it looks like we're good to go for now. If anything else crops up, you know how to reach me. And once again, good job."

He clapped her on the shoulder, nodded to the rest of the staff, and then left the control tower. He sent his car home and started strolling casually around the campus, working his way towards the lab.

Once he reached the lab, he used his clearance to gain access. He made his way over to the DNA reader and the sense of deja-vu was overwhelming. He got into the reader and the canopy closed, blocking his access to other systems. He went through the same process as last time, as the reader took multiple DNA samples. He waited impatiently while the reader processed the samples and compared them to one another before finally linking to the network. It then matched his DNA to the sample he had previously submitted and validated his other biometrics—palm prints, retinal and iris scans, and radioactive dating. The red light changed to green as it confirmed his identity. It displayed the email that he had received earlier that week, only now he could access the enclosed link.

He accessed the link and a warning flashed on the screen.

WARNING. THE OUTPUT OF THIS JOB CANNOT BE DISPLAYED ON THIS MACHINE. WOULD YOU LIKE TO SEND A COPY TO THE MS WRITER?

Ryan frowned. That was strange. He couldn't access the data without jumping through hoops to confirm his identity, and now it was just going to spit the data out to a molecular stick writer? He studied the message, puzzled for a moment, but he couldn't see any alternative so he indicated his consent. After a few moments, another message appeared and he tensed.

WARNING. COPYING THE DATA TO THE MS WRITER WILL PURGE IT FROM THE SYSTEM. DO YOU WANT TO CONTINUE?

He held his breath as he considered his choices. All of this was new to him. True, no one had known what to expect, but they had modeled countless scenarios, based on the small amount of data that they did have. He wished he could ask someone for advice, and for a moment he considered leaving without the data and doing just that. However, it had taken over forty years to get this far and who knew if the opportunity would arise again. He finally indicated his consent again, and he heard the MS Writer spin up as it began to assemble the pure carbon strands that would hold the data.

Memory sticks could contain an incredible amount of data and were almost indestructible. The smallest memory stick, or M-Stick, was the size of a drinking straw, and could hold hundreds of petabytes of data. Large memory sticks were literally the size of a small stick and could hold up to a zettabyte of storage, or a million petabytes. They were also read-only once created, so they were the storage medium of choice for data archival. He was just about to get up to take the M-Stick from the reader when another message flashed on the screen.

TWO SUNS, TOGETHER IN HARMONY, WILL LEAD TO THE DAWN OF A NEW DAY.

He stared at this message in puzzlement. It made no sense, but after a moment the message blinked out of existence, and the canopy of the DNA reader began to retract.

* * *

Olivia walked into the security center and smiled at the guard on duty as she headed for the dropshaft.

"Control Room," she said, but to her surprise the computer buzzed its denial.

"Please see the guard on duty," it said melodically and Olivia frowned. She turned back to face the guard on duty, but she was already calling the control room. After a moment she nodded politely to Olivia.

"Sorry, Ma'am, it's standard operating procedures. I've told them you're coming and you have clearance now."

Olivia nodded a curt acknowledgment and turned back to the dropshaft. Her initial surprise was quickly turning to anger. It was unconscionable that she didn't have immediate access to any building or room at Delphi. She entered the dropshaft and rose quickly to the control room. She stepped out and looked around for Ryan, intending to discuss the matter with him.

"Excuse me, Ma'am, can I help you?" Olivia turned and looked at the young woman who addressed her.

"And who might you be?" she asked curtly, still angry about being denied access, and the woman flushed.

"Sorry, Ma'am, I'm Anita Bush and I'm the security officer on duty tonight."

"You are?" Olivia asked in surprise. "I thought that Ryan was here."

"He was here, but he left maybe ten or fifteen minutes ago." Anita hesitated briefly as Olivia frowned. "Is there something that I can help you with?"

"Well for starters you can tell me why I was denied access to this facility."

"It's just standard operating procedure, Ma'am. Unless there is a senior security officer on site, any non-security personnel need clearance before being admitted to the control room."

"Even the CEO?" Olivia asked challengingly, but Anita just nodded.

"Even the CEO," she replied firmly and Olivia shook her head. She shouldn't be getting into this with a junior officer, she should be taking it up with Ryan. Her frustration was starting to get the better of her. This whole evening hadn't gone the way she had planned from the beginning. First, she couldn't get in touch with Ryan to invite him over to her place, then once she had gotten over that disappointment, he had to leave, and now this.

"Where is he?" she asked abruptly and Anita turned to one of the security technicians.

"See if you can find Mr. Peters," she said firmly and the technician nodded. A moment later the holo tank filled with a flat image of the entire complex. It shifted rapidly and then stabilized on one location and Olivia's heart stopped.

"He's in the lab," Anita said unnecessarily and Olivia struggled to kick start her frozen brain. Why would he be in the lab again? What was he doing? She gazed at the image for a moment longer before turning decisively to Anita.

"Is there a field team available?" she asked and Anita's eyes widened.

"Actually there is, Ma'am. The same SOPs that required me to call Ryan also required me to activate a field team. They are currently patrolling the perimeter."

"Get them here. I want them to escort me to the lab." Anita hesitated and Olivia turned to look directly at her. "Do you have a problem with that?" she asked coldly and Anita straightened up.

"No, Ma'am." She nodded and turned away and Olivia began to pace the room impatiently as she waited for the field team to arrive. She was pleasantly surprised for the first time that evening when the dropshaft deposited a woman in lightweight body armor less than five minutes later.

"Mia Reynolds, Commander, Field Team One," she said briskly and Olivia nodded in satisfaction.

"Excellent response time, Commander. I'd like for you and your team to escort me to the lab." She gestured at the holo tank. "Mr. Peters is in the lab. Although he does have access rights, those access rights require him to be accompanied by Gabriella Cole. I want to know why he is there and how he is able to enter the lab without Gabriella present. As well, I think that he is accessing a DNA reader, and there is nothing that I am aware of that should require him to do that. I want to learn what he is doing and why. There may well be a reasonable explanation for it, but I'd like you and your team along just in case I'm wrong."

"Yes, Ma'am. We've got a group of flitters outside and we can be there in two minutes."

"Excellent. Let's go then."

* * *

The canopy finished sliding open and Ryan started across the room towards the MS Writer.

"I assume that you have an explanation for this." The familiar voice was the temperature of liquid helium and Ryan froze. He turned towards the entrance of the lab and saw Olivia there with Mia and the rest of Field Team One. Mia was standing beside Olivia, but the others had spread out to cover him. Ryan gulped as he looked at Olivia and Mia. Olivia's face was expressionless, but he could read the signs of anger in her posture, not to mention her voice. Mia was more open in her disapproval and her face clearly reflected her disappointment in him.

"I guess I could start by saying that this isn't what it looks like, but then it never is. I know that it looks like I'm removing data from the lab and I will freely admit to that. However, the data that I am removing has never shown up in Delphi's pipeline, or research prospectus or any of Delphi's press releases. In fact, the researchers here at Delphi are unaware that this data even exists.

"My intent in removing the data is only to ensure its security. I suspect the group I represent would be willing to allow Delphi to manufacture, distribute and market this compound as long as you make it available to anyone who wants it at a reasonable cost."

"And this 'group' you represent would do this out of the goodness of their hearts I presume, without anything as distasteful as monetary compensation."

Ryan smiled despite the tenseness of the situation. The emphasis Olivia gave to the word group made it sound like a curse. "Actually, that's correct."

Olivia shook her head in disbelief. "They wouldn't want anything from Delphi?"

"Only your assurance the product would be available at a reasonable cost."

"Is there a market for this compound?"

Ryan smiled tightly. "Oh, of that I have no doubt. I would estimate there are billions of potential customers for this worldwide."

Olivia shook her head and allowed her disbelief to show. "So let me get this straight. This is a compound on one of our servers that no one at Delphi knows anything about, but has a potential market of billions of customers worldwide?" She shook her head. "Nice try. Got anything else?"

"There is nothing else. That's the truth."

"So far, all I've heard is nonsense," Olivia snapped. "Vague bits of information about a mysterious product with unbelievable market potential. You've got one minute to tell me what's really going on before Mia takes you into custody to await a visit from the police."

Ryan sighed. "Everything I've told you is true. I'll tell you the details around it, but you won't believe me. All I ask is that you give me the time to convince you that I'm telling the truth."

"One minute," Olivia repeated, ignoring his plea.

"All right, the compound is an artificial DNA polymerase. It adds a codon to existing DNA that extends the life of the subject by fourfold. It only works on men, but it would allow men to compete with women as equals for the first time in almost three hundred years."

Olivia stared at him, shaking her head in disbelief. "That's impossible."

"No, it's quite possible."

"How is it that you know about it?"

Ryan hesitated. He knew that his answer, while true, would be hard to believe. If fact, he knew just what Olivia and the others would think when he told them. However, he also knew that he had no choice.

"I know about it because I was an unknowing recipient of the compound."

Sure enough, before he had finished speaking, Olivia's expression changed from disbelief to barely disguised pity. One of the guards wasn't as charitable and her face twisted in disgust.

"I know what you're thinking. You think that I'm suffering from PDID."

PDID, or Parental Dissociative Identity Disorder, was a new psychiatric affliction resulting from the use of the artificial embryogenesis machines. The close physical likeness of male children to the father, combined with the lack of any other significant family influence, affected their mental development. Often, the son assumed the identity of the father on his death. In a few rare and grisly cases, PDID had resulted in patricide, as the son became unable to deal with watching 'himself' grow old.

PDID differed from normal Dissociative Identity Disorders in that it wasn't the effect of severe trauma in early childhood, or repeated physical, sexual, or emotional abuse. In fact, many PDID patients had normal and healthy childhoods. This lack of a contributing cause combined with the uniqueness of the groups in which PDID occurred challenged the accepted dictum, which stated that people only had one personality.

Of course all of that was irrelevant to Ryan. His son had only ever existed as part of the cover story that had allowed him to get to this point in his life.

"It's all right," Olivia said hesitantly. "I admit that I don't know much about it, but I do know there are many therapists who can help you. I can speak with Brooke and see if she can recommend someone for you. We'll pay for your treatment and maybe you'll be able to return to work, albeit not in the same capacity."

"I'm not nuts, Olivia," he said patiently. "Think about it for a moment. PDID is the result of long-term association between a father and his son. My cover story has my 'father' dying shortly after I was born. That would make it impossible for me to be suffering from PDID. I'll admit there are rare forms of PDID that don't require this association, but in that case the son is lacking the necessary details about the father's life needed to support the disorder. They know the bare bones, but they don't know all the details.

"I know both the facts and the details because I lived them. I was with you forty years ago when we began dating for the first time. I know how each and every date went, when we first made love, what we talked about. I know why you broke up with me and I also know that I couldn't do anything about it. That fact came close to making me bitter, but it didn't."

"Why not?" Olivia asked, drawn into the conversation despite herself.

"Because I loved you too much. I loved you enough to respect why you couldn't be with me. Yes, I knew what you were feeling and why—it was something that occurred to me also, and while I wanted to grow old with you, I didn't want to grow old on you. So I left you alone and did my best to move on with my life. A few years later, I was approached by a group who claimed that I had been an unwilling participant in an experiment on male aging. Like you, I was skeptical. In fact, your initial reaction was more generous than mine. However, they persisted and eventually provided me with proof."

"What kind of proof?"

"They took a sample of my cells, cultured them, and then subjected them to a chemical process designed to simulate the effects of aging. My cells didn't age as fast. That still wasn't enough for me. I demanded to repeat the test, only this time I collected random samples from dozens of strangers. I performed all the tests myself and sure enough my cells survived four times as long." He shrugged. "It was about as conclusive as I was going to get without actually living that long, and so I agreed to work with them." He glanced down at himself for a moment and then grinned. "I guess the proof is a little clearer now."

Olivia shook her head as she tried to shake off her confusion. "I don't understand. If you knew about this forty years ago, then why didn't you say something? Why didn't you come to Delphi and get us to help you?"

"That was my first question too when they contacted me. The researcher who had developed this artificial DNA polymerase had worked at Delphi. Rather than going through the normal process of in-house approval followed by FDA approval, he had arranged for a clandestine and highly irregular clinical trial. I was one of several unwitting participants in this trial." He paused and laughed. "Ironically, it was because of my association with you that I am here today, as I ingested the oral solution in one of Delphi's cafeterias while I was visiting you. Like most of the subjects of that bizarre clinical trial, I had no idea it had happened until they contacted me years later."

"You said this researcher worked at Delphi. Where does he work now?"

Ryan smiled grimly. "His instincts to keep this secret were correct. Unfortunately, someone found out what he was doing and he died under mysterious circumstances a few months later.

"His sister had been one of the few people he had trusted with this secret. She enlisted the aid of some of her friends, and after years of cautious research, they determined who had received the codon and managed to track them down. All told, there were less than a dozen of them in total, at least that's what they told me. For security, none of us knows any details about any of the others."

He paused and flicked his eyes around the room, encouraged by what he saw. Despite what they perceived as his betrayal, Mia and the other guards wanted to believe him.

"His sister knew the original research still existed at Delphi, hidden away in their network. Given that someone had killed her brother to suppress his research, they decided the only way to get the data was to try to recover it secretly. That is why they contacted me."

"But why you?" Olivia pressed insistently. "Why not one of our existing researchers? Or if they wanted to keep it secret, we've had dozens of network breaches over the years. Surely they could have gotten the data they needed without needing to get you involved. It's been forty years after all."

"Actually that's not true. For some reason, the creator of the formula hid it in a time-coded program. Although the data was on the network, no one knew where it was or even what to look for. The only way to retrieve the data was to get one of the test subjects access to the lab."

He gestured at the machine behind him. "That's why I used the DNA reader. The baseline sample that I submitted contains my DNA, which has a codon that only exists in the men who have been treated with the formula. It was this unique DNA profile that unlocked the data and allowed me to retrieve it."

"That seems unnecessarily complicated," Olivia said confrontationally.

Ryan nodded. "True, it does seem a bit unwieldy but it served its purpose. It prevented anyone who wasn't working with one of the test subjects from accessing the data. And it plainly has kept the data safe and secure all these years."

He watched as Olivia paused and tried to sort out all the information he had given her. He knew it was a lot to take in all at once. It had taken him years to figure it out. Mind you, he'd had years. For their plan to work, he'd had to begin his life anew, all of it focused on penetrating Delphi and wrestling away the secrets locked deep inside it. After a moment, she cocked her head and looked over at him.

"You do realize this all sounds like a paranoid fantasy, don't you?" She didn't wait for him to answer as she continued. "Just how much of what we had is real and how much is because of this?"

He sighed and ran a hand through his hair. "Sometimes I don't know. My whole life changed forty years ago. I basically threw away the life I had back then and began a new one, all of it focused on this day. There were only two things I took from my old life. One was my relationship with my sister. She supported me and provided a cover story for me by agreeing to raise 'my' baby. The other thing was my feelings for you. I was still in love with you and thought perhaps this was what we needed to be together. I carried those thoughts with me for forty years, and when I first started here it tore me apart. I wanted to tell you the truth, but I also needed to access the data and I didn't know if you would believe me. I finally decided I couldn't be selfish enough to risk losing access to the data and so I didn't tell you the truth. I even hesitated about starting up a relationship with you again, afraid it would compromise my objectivity."

"But you did," Olivia said softly.

Ryan nodded. "Yes I did. I really wanted to and while I could list dozens of reasons why I shouldn't, I was able to rationalize every single one of them away." He paused and laughed. "I still remember that comment you made years ago, that the ability to rationalize terrible decisions was what really separated humans from animals."

"Does that mean you think it was a terrible decision?"

He shook his head. "No, not at all. For a few weeks I thought I was in heaven. I had the perfect job, excellent staff and was with the woman I loved."

He hesitated, suddenly conscious they had an audience. He glanced around at the guards, who were watching them with open curiosity. This wasn't how he had wanted to tell Olivia he wasn't in love with her anymore, but she had forced his hand. Taking a deep breath, he continued. "But then all that changed."

"After we made love."

It wasn't exactly a question but he answered it anyway. "Yes, after we made love. Something happened then that made me realize I wasn't in love with you anymore. I didn't realize it at the time, but that's what happened. I realized I was in love with the you from forty years ago, and that too much had changed since then. You had changed, my entire life had changed, the world had changed. That's part of the reason I played all those games tonight. I knew you were ready for us to be intimate again, and I couldn't do that now knowing I wasn't in love with you anymore. It wouldn't have been fair to you or to me, and there are some lines I am just not willing to cross."

"So the ends don't justify the means after all," Olivia said softly.

Ryan nodded sadly. "I'm sorry. I wanted to tell you, but I decided that I couldn't risk it."

"So what happened? You just woke up one day and realized that you didn't love me anymore, is that it?"

"No, nothing like that." He hesitated, not wanting to hurt her, especially in front of everyone else, but he had to be completely honest. "I had fallen in love with someone else without realizing it."

"Who is it? Do I know her?" Before Ryan could respond Olivia shook her head angrily. "God, listen to me. Repeating the same pathetic lines that dumped women always say. None of that matters. This all sounds like some insane story you invented. I still don't have any proof you are telling the truth."

"Ah, but he is."

Everyone jerked as the voice rang out from behind Olivia. A moment later the owner of the voice appeared.

"You!" exclaimed Olivia and Ryan simultaneously.

Chapter Thirteen

"Yes, me," said Gabriella Cole. She sauntered past Olivia and Mia and before anyone could recover from the surprise, she plucked the Molecular Stick from the DNA reader. She tossed it from hand to hand as she looked over at Ryan and grinned. He grinned back uncertainly, as he struggled to regain his equilibrium.

First, Olivia had walked in on him, catching him in the act. Now Gabriella Cole suddenly appeared, claiming to know what was going on. He wondered if she was his handler, even as he hoped she wasn't. The grin she gave him seemed mean and cruel, rather than celebratory. He was well aware of her reputation, even though he had never been subject to her biting sarcasm.

"You know about this preposterous story Ryan's just told me?" Olivia asked Gabriella challengingly.

"Know about it?" Gabriella grinned. "I was instrumental in creating it."

Ryan knew he should feel victorious at this confirmation that Gabriella was his handler. She would be able to convince Olivia he was telling the truth and this whole charade would finally be over. Yet despite that, a part of him felt faintly troubled. Something didn't feel right, and years of subtle innuendos suddenly came together into a pattern of behavior at odds with their stated goals.

"So he really is the same Ryan I knew from forty years ago?" Olivia asked faintly and Gabriella nodded.

"One and the same. Of course he's a little more experienced now. Tell me, what was it like when you finally had sex?"

Ryan felt his face go numb with shock. He noticed peripherally that Olivia seemed just as shocked, but all of his attention was focused on Gabriella.

"I've always wondered what it would be like to have sex with a man with all that experience, but the stamina and staying power of a young man. I'll bet it was pretty good. Of course you probably just thought it was 'magical' because you were in love." She snorted. "What nonsense. I'm telling you, the best thing that ever happened to society was when we finally reversed the roles of men and women. It finally freed us from the shackles that men have bonded women with for untold millenniums. The worst of these was love. Love doesn't exist. It's a fantasy created by men to give them more control over women."

She looked over at Ryan, taking in his shock, and laughed cruelly.

"Poor Ryan, he's a little shocked by my behavior. It doesn't jibe with the idealistic bullshit we've been feeding him for the past forty years. You know, I've been thinking about this moment for years, trying to figure out what would be more satisfying. I'd thought of leaving him to take the fall for this, hoping that he would be diagnosed as having PDID. Unfortunately, there are too many parts of this story he could prove, even if we killed his sister. It's too bad. It would have been such a pleasant way to finish this up. However, in some ways, this is better."

"What are you talking about?" Ryan stammered, stunned to hear her talking like this.

"Come on," she sneered, "Aren't you supposed to be the smart one here? Don't tell me you haven't figured it out yet."

Gabriella sighed theatrically and looked over at Olivia and Mia. "Men. Always having to spell it out for them."

She turned back to Ryan and smiled viciously.

"You've been played, player. All this time you thought you were working to safeguard this little secret, to make it available to men everywhere. Guess what? You've been working for the wrong side. I'm the one who killed the little weasel who developed this abomination."

She paused and her mouth twisted angrily.

"Unfortunately I didn't realize until it was too late that he had already hidden his nasty little secret away, or that he had actually used it. It took me a while to find all the men he had infected with this plague of his. I wasted two years of my life, tracking down every single male visitor to Delphi during the last six months of the nasty little worm's life. Two years to track them down and get cell samples for testing."

She paused to give Ryan an appraising look.

"Of course, like any job, there are always a few perks that make it bearable. Most of the samples I got by having sex with the men in question, but there were a few who were resistant to that particular form of enticement. I've always regretted you were one of them."

Ryan felt his skin crawl. He'd been objectified more times then he could remember, but he'd never been this repelled. Despite his enhancements, his revulsion must have shown and Gabriella's face tightened.

"Yeah, you thought you were too good for me back then, too," she said, and suddenly Ryan had a flashback to forty years ago. It was in a club, one of the few times he had gone out, and this woman had come on to him constantly the entire evening. His friends had elbowed him in the ribs, making crude jokes, but it didn't interest him. One-night stands had never appealed to him and he was still getting over Olivia. Besides which, the woman's behavior had bordered on the far edge of weirdness and Ryan knew better than to get involved, however slightly, with someone like that. He suddenly realized that it had been Gabriella. She had seemed familiar, but he had chalked it up to her having worked at Delphi even longer than Olivia. Now he knew the truth.

Gabriella laughed fiercely. "Oh, I just might have to change my mind. I'm so glad I decided to tell you the truth. It's even better than I thought it would be. I bet I know what you're thinking now. What about the sister?"

Ryan worked hard to keep his face straight, but it was tough. She was one step ahead of him so far, which didn't bode well for his struggle to find a way out of this. And she was right about the direction of his thoughts. He had thought that he'd been working for the inventor's sister, who was striving to keep his secret alive.

"It was his sister who had me kill him."

Despite his best efforts, Ryan couldn't keep the shock off his face.

"Yeah, who'd have guessed? It was the perfect cover, and it lent just the right air of legitimacy to the whole thing to keep you or any of the others from guessing the truth."

"But why?" Ryan asked and Gabriella looked at him pityingly.

"God, men really are stupid. Why do you think? She spent her entire life raising him, protecting him, getting him into the best schools and the best jobs, and this is how he repays her? By destroying her life? By returning us to the dark ages, when women weren't in control, when men dominated and manipulated them? By inventing this abomination?" she said, shaking the M-Stick angrily. "It's like thanking your mother for giving birth to you by giving her a hysterectomy. It showed an appalling lack of common sense, let alone gratitude and respect. She knew that despite her best efforts, there was something fundamentally wrong with him. Besides being a man of course. She had no choice but to kill him."

Ryan stared at her, appalled. She was certifiable. He slowly readied himself, waiting for the right moment.

"In fact," she continued, as he watched her for his opening, "he forced her to do just that, yet one more example of just how badly he messed up. And now we've spent the last forty years trying to clean up the mess that he left. So typical. Men make the messes and we women spend all our time cleaning them up." She grinned triumphantly then and lifted the M-Stick high above her head. "No longer. With any luck we'll be able to figure out a counteragent to stop this abomination in its tracks, just in case anyone manages to recreate it. Failing that, we'll just destroy the formula and take our chances with the future."

"You won't get away with this," a voice said quietly and Gabriella spun around to sneer at Olivia.

"Oh yeah, just watch me," she said and she suddenly reached into the pocket of her lab coat and tossed a small object on the floor. Ryan tensed as he recognized the familiar shape of a neural grenade. Even as he started to move he knew it was too late, and he braced himself as a tidal wave of disorientation swept over him. His enhancements kept him from blacking out, but he felt like he was in a fog and his whole body was numb. With an effort he forced his eyes to focus, and noticed Olivia and Mia slumped on the floor, unconscious. He had to assume the rest of Field Team One was down for the count as well, since he couldn't even move his head enough to check. That left only Ryan and Gabriella still standing, and he stared at Gabriella as she stuck the M-Stick into her lab coat. She looked around and then reached into her lab coat again, this time emerging with the familiar shape of a handgun.

"And now for you. I'm sorry to have to do this, mostly because I was hoping that I'd finally be able to try you out, but as you can see I've gone to some effort to setup the proper tableau. That neural grenade has conveniently destroyed their short-term memory so the only person who I have to worry about is you. Which isn't a worry, since I've been planning this for years. In fact, the neural grenade has your fingerprints on it, and anyone who tries to track it down will find out that you were responsible for the facility that stored it years ago. Fortunately, no one tracks neural patterns, so no one will be able to tell the grenade was keyed to me and not you."

Gabriella grinned as she walked over to him and Ryan felt his horror grow as she ran her hands over his body. Most of his body was still numb so he couldn't feel much. The little bit that he could feel, combined with the lecherous look she was giving him, scared him more than anything else in his life ever had. She noticed his look and laughed.

"Don't worry, your virtue is safe. As much as I'd like to, I don't have any time for entertainment. Pity though. I've always been fond of domination. Unfortunately, I just can't take the risk of you regaining control."

She leaned forward and forced her tongue into his mouth, and he could feel her hands cupping his butt possessively. Horror warred with revulsion, but then a cold anger overwhelmed everything. After a brief, seemingly endless moment, she pulled back.

"Duty calls. Now, who do you think I should give the honor of disposing of the great Ryan Peters to, Mia or Olivia?"

She sauntered casually over towards the unconscious pair and Ryan struggled to be able to move. He used his anger to try to get his body to react, but try as he might, he just couldn't. His brain felt like it was wrapped in cotton batting and his body felt like an unresponsive lead weight. It was all he could do just to keep standing. Despite his lack of progress, his anger left no room for despair, so he kept struggling. He began to notice small improvements, finally regaining enough control that he managed to turn his head to keep her in his vision. He knew that if he had just a few more moments, he might be able to move enough to keep Gabriella from killing him right away. It was a small improvement, but every extra second helped. And then he looked over at Gabriella and knew he had run out of time. She was standing behind Mia and her hand manipulated Mia's, pointing the gun at him. She smiled evilly as she looked over at him.

"Good-bye, Ryan," she said and then suddenly the gun flew out of her hand as something hit her forearm with a loud crack.

Ryan blinked in surprise, and then realized that it was an M-Stick, probably one of the many archival M-Sticks used in Research. He continued to work his muscles as his mind cleared and he saw Gabriella look around wildly. She cursed violently, and then awkwardly tried to grab the gun with her left hand but it was out of reach. She hissed in pain as she straightened and he noticed with a grin that her right forearm bent at an unnatural angle.

The pure carbon structure of M-Sticks made them perfect for high-density storage, but it also made them heavy as hell. Whoever had thrown it had to have been incredibly strong to be able to throw it that hard and that precisely. It could have just been luck. Somehow Ryan knew it wasn't.

Gabriella noticed his grin and she looked at him venomously. She looked over at the handgun that she had dropped and then glanced nervously back at the main entrance. Whoever had thrown the M-Stick wasn't visible to either Gabriella or Ryan, but that didn't mean the person couldn't see them. With a snarled curse, she hurried away towards the emergency exit and disappeared. Ryan felt relieved he was still alive, but he was also bitterly disappointed. He had been duped for the last forty years and now the formula was gone for good. Thinking back, he realized he hadn't told anyone about the system erasing the formula after copying it to the M-Stick, and he struggled to think of how he might leverage that information.

Just then a black suited figure walked into the room. Ryan must have been more out of it than he had realized. He had forgotten about the thrown M-Stick that had saved his life. Still unable to move, he looked expressionlessly at the figure as it paused and surveyed the room.

He thought it was female, but the black suit covered the body entirely. The nano weave of the fabric blurred and shifted constantly, making it almost impossible for him to even focus on the figure, let alone discover its gender.

He tensed as the individual reached down and picked up the handgun Gabriella had dropped, and then fired it half a dozen times, seemingly randomly, at the walls. Then the person dropped the gun and one arm reached up to pull the hood off its head. Long blond hair spilled out over the figure's shoulders.

"You!" Ryan blurted as Nicole hurried over to him. She pulled something from her pouch and unwrapped it. Ryan recognized it as a high-energy nutrient patch, and he smiled at her gratefully as she slapped it against his arm. Seconds later he could feel his nanites greedily absorbing the energy. His body started to feel less like a lead weight and his thoughts began to clear. He suddenly realized what she had been doing. Each of the seemingly random shots had taken out the high-density scanners and cameras and he felt a sudden chill. She wouldn't have taken them out on a whim; therefore she must have known that they were active. They must have recorded every second of his confrontation with Gabriella. He remembered how quickly his field exercise with Mia's team had circulated. It would be impossible to keep something like this under wraps.

"Come on," Nicole urged, interrupting his train of thought, "we have to get going. The Second Field Team will be here any minute."

"What's the use?" Ryan muttered tiredly. "Gabriella has the only copy of the data. The system purged it automatically and now the whole secret is out anyway."

"Gabriella has less than either of you think she has. You need to trust me on this. Now let's go," she urged.

Ryan looked over at her. He gave her a wan smile as he struggled to keep up with her. He let his body automatically follow her, even as he inserted himself into the security system long enough to execute a routine he had buried there. That brief mental effort taxed him more than he realized and he stumbled as he lost track of where he was going. Nicole reached out and grabbed him before he could fall. He looked up at her in gratitude.

"I love you, you know that," he blurted out.

She gave him a look that mingled amusement with mild disapproval. "Yes, I'd heard something like that earlier. However, this is neither the time nor the place to get into this."

"I disagree," Ryan said. Between the nutrient patch and the exercise, his body was finally beginning to feel normal. "I think you should tell someone the moment it occurs to you, and I've already been sitting on this since the beginning of the week. It's unconscionable to wait a single second longer."

She looked back and shot him an unreadable glance. "We've got to hurry. We're almost at the perimeter, but they can still track you until then."

"What about you?" he asked. He suspected the answer, but he wanted to see how she would answer it, and she held up her arm.

"I used my own nanites to burn the bracelet off. I didn't want the system to know where I was. We don't have time to do yours now, so we need to get out of Delphi's tracking range."

"If you don't have your bracelet then how did you get access to the lab?" he asked curiously and she grinned.

"You're forgetting that I have almost three hundred years of IT experience."

Ryan snorted in amused disbelief. "You hacked the system?"

Nicole shrugged. "Better. I built in a backdoor when I helped you install it. I've been waiting forty years for this moment to come. I spent that entire time honing my skills and thinking about what I'd need."

Ryan opened his mouth to ask her just how she fit into all of this, but she motioned for him to be quiet and dragged him into some bushes.

"Damn," she muttered, "it looks like there's another security team patrolling the grounds." She moved forward a little and cursed under her breath. "Shit, they've found the flitter I had stashed." She wriggled backwards while Ryan watched admiringly. "How are you feeling? Are you fully recovered yet?"

"Almost. Why?"

"Because it looks like we're going to have to make a run for it before they find us. I'm a little surprised that they haven't yet."

He grinned mischievously at her. "You're not the only one who's been planning for this for forty years now. I've disabled the tracking portion of my bracelet, which effectively cancels my security profile. However, I have a secondary superuser profile normally used for testing that is still active. They can't see it to track me, but I still have the clearance and access."

Nicole whistled softly. "Does anyone else know about this?" Ryan shook his head. "Good. At least you have a little bit of self-preservation instinct. I was beginning to think Gabriella had you completely fooled."

"I was completely fooled," he said bitterly "but I'm not a complete fool. That's the one thing about living longer—you begin to realize just how few people you can really trust. I've never had any doubts about what I was doing, but believe it or not, I did have doubts about who I was working with. I just never expected it to turn out like this."

"Well, we still have a chance, but only if we get out of here. Are you up to running?"

"Yeah but why don't I just call my aircar?" He smiled at the look she gave him. "Trust me on this. The car is clean of any bugs or trackers. The only way they can track it is visually or via radar. If you watch my back, I can pilot it remotely. That way I can tell if someone is following it and if I can't lose them, then I'll get the aircar to lead them on a wild-goose chase while we run for it."

"Okay, but make it fast. They might not be able to track us on the system, but if we stay here too long, they'll be able to find us using other methods."

Ryan shook his head. "We should be okay for a little while. We're outside the range of the high-density scanners and standard search tools are IR-based. It's still warm enough out that our body heat won't give us away, not if we stay here in the bushes. They hold in the heat, so they are hotter than the surrounding air, effectively masking our IR profile. Mia's team is trained well enough that they might search the bushes on principle, but they're down for the count at the moment."

She nodded impatiently, her eyes sweeping the grounds. Ryan propped himself up against a root and closed his eyes. He maintained a constant link to his aircar—that was how he knew no one had tampered with it—but it was a light link. To pilot it remotely, he needed a deeper link, and that meant he had to be able to focus on it fully. He navigated the additional security protocols needed for a deeper link, and then he had full access to the aircar's systems.

He scanned the immediate area, coming up clean. He knew this window of opportunity wouldn't last long, so he activated the fans and gently guided the car out of his garage. He overrode the automatic running lights and transponder as the car lifted into the night sky like a black phantom. He wished he had been able to equip it with stealth gear, but just being able to turn off the running lights and transponder would have gotten him into enough trouble if anyone ever inspected it. Still, keeping it low to the ground kept it off most tracking systems and the flat black paint job made it difficult to spot visually. He restricted himself to passive scanners all the way over to Delphi, and sooner than he thought possible, he landed the car gently less than a few hundred feet away, hidden by a copse of trees.

"All right, let's go," he whispered and Nicole smiled in relief. After one last scan of the area, using all their senses—natural and enhanced—they cautiously left the relative safety of the bushes and made their way towards the car. Five minutes later, they were both strapped in and airborne.

"Okay, now what?" he asked.

Nicole glanced at him. "I have a safe house that's not far from here. Why don't we head over there and talk about what to do next."

"Does that include an explanation for all of this? Because, I have to say that I'm more than a little confused."

She looked at him seriously and nodded. "I don't blame you and I wish that I'd been able to talk to you about it earlier."

"But?"

"Drive now, talk later," she chided gently and he grinned as he focused on following the directions she gave him.

Half an hour later he slipped the aircar into the garage of a nondescript house on a quiet street. The location was normally only ten to fifteen minutes from Delphi, but given they were traveling without running lights and trying to avoid detection, it took significantly longer. Ryan felt a tension in his neck that his sorely abused nanites hadn't been able to deal with and he rubbed it wryly.

"It's been a long time since I've had to do anything like that," he commented.

Nicole cast him an appraising look. "I don't know if you're fishing for compliments or not, but either way you could have fooled me."

"Maybe," he chuckled, "and thanks." He followed Nicole into the house and looked around curiously. The place was small, but neatly furnished. It didn't have that lived-in feel, but it was clean and tidy and well organized. He followed Nicole around as she gave him a quick tour. The room they had entered doubled as a living and dining room. Beyond, there was a small bathroom and a small bedroom.

Ryan eyed the double bed wistfully. There was a part of him that longed to sleep, but he knew that as tired as he was, he'd never be able to sleep until he got some answers. He gave the bed a last longing look and then followed Nicole out to the kitchen. Idly, he checked the fridge. It was empty of course, but it had a water dispenser and an icemaker. As he closed the fridge, Nicole opened the cupboards and showed him the canned goods and emergency rations. He made a face at the sight of the rations and Nicole grinned in sympathy.

"I know what you mean," she said. "They're just barely edible, but that's the price you pay for a shelf life of a hundred years."

"When was the last time you were here?" he asked curiously.

Nicole frowned in thought. "Forty years ago. It was just after Justin's death. I quietly set about buying safe houses and stocking them with supplies. I must have a couple of dozen throughout Noram, mostly major cities, but a few rural locations, as well. I have about three in the local vicinity."

Ryan whistled appreciatively. "Wow, that must have set you back a pretty penny."

"Tell me about it," Nicole responded wryly. "It wasn't just the cost of the house. About half of them also have used, but powerful, aircars, and they are all well stocked with consumables. There are also basic emergency medical supplies, as well as a supply of cash, negotiable bearer bonds and an assortment of precious stones."

Ryan just looked at her, stunned by the extent of her preparations, and she flushed and shifted in embarrassment.

"It's not as bad as it sounds," she said. "After all, I'd been working for over two and a half centuries when I started this. The hardest part was finding a way to liquidate my investments without raising any red flags—that and keeping the assets out of my name, but under my control. This was the first house that I bought and the only one in my name."

Ryan shook his head admiringly. "Still, that's a huge accomplishment."

She shrugged depreciatingly and then suddenly grinned at him. "The good news is that all of them have appreciated substantially in value. I've probably made more doing this then investing in the stock market. Not that this is how I'd choose to invest my money, but still."

"So you mentioned that you started this forty years ago after Justin's death. I take it that Justin's the person I have to thank for being here today?"

Now it was Nicole's turn to stare at him in astonishment. "You mean you don't know the name of the person whose discovery you've spent half your life trying to find?"

Ryan shook his head. "No. I asked, but they told me it was better I didn't know. Their rationale was that I might slip up and betray myself by reacting if I heard his name. I always chalked it up to massive paranoia, but now I see that it was an issue of control."

"Wow, we really do have a lot to talk about." She grinned again and reached into another cupboard, pulling out a bottle of wine. "I think that perhaps this has aged enough." She fished about in one of the drawers, emerging with an old fashioned corkscrew. With well-practiced motions, she opened the bottle. She poured a couple of large glasses, handed one to him, and then took an appreciative sniff from her own.

"Mmm, smells okay." She took a cautious sip and then another, drawing in some air as she did so. "It looks like I've found another advantage to equipping all these safe houses. It's a wonderful way to ensure a supply of well-aged wine."

Ryan took a grateful sip of his own wine, feeling the welcome warmth as it hit his belly. Wine wasn't something one normally stocked in a safe house, but given Nicole's enhancement, it made sense. Alcohol was a quick and easy source of energy for anyone with enhancements and Ryan finished his glass in less than a minute. Nicole obviously knew that he needed it and she poured him another glass wordlessly. She then made her way to the living room and settled down in one of the armchairs, placing the wine bottle within easy reach of both of them on the coffee table. Ryan settled into the other armchair and took another sip of his wine as he waited patiently for Nicole to begin.

"Oh, where to start?" she began and then grinned at Ryan. "I know, don't say it, I should start at the beginning and I will. Just bear with me, okay?"

Ryan nodded his agreement and Nicole tilted her head back in thought.

"I met Justin at Delphi. He was one of the few male junior researchers, and the only one allowed in the lab. I think it was Gabriella's way of keeping an eye on him for his sister, Stephanie.

"Anyway, one day I noticed the power consumption for the lab had increased almost exponentially. When I dug into it further, I found he was using all the computing cycles available from every computer in the lab. It's common in most systems, but the computers in the lab weren't designed for it. None of those prima donnas wanted to share with anyone else, so they all had their own computers. Somehow Justin had written a crude program to link them together. It may have been crude, but it was effective, and he had even managed to keep anyone from finding out. In fact, if it weren't for the increased power use I never would have noticed. Technically, I should have reported it to Gabriella, but I knew that she didn't support men in research. I once overheard her say that it was like letting monkeys into the lab.

"So I didn't tell her. It was only happenstance that I stumbled across it in the first place. I figured I had plausible deniability. Even if they fired me, I didn't care. I was beginning to approach that stage in life where most women my age finally retired. Justin intrigued me, and despite myself I was curious about what he was using all those computing cycles for, and why it was worth defying Gabriella. So one day I finally introduced myself to him."

She smiled at the memory. "He saw right through me. He realized why I was there and what I was doing and he called me on it. I was unused to that kind of directness from anyone, and I found it refreshing. We hit it off and began hanging out together. It wasn't too long until we realized that we were dating each other. We kept it low-key, which wasn't hard. We were both private and independent people, and we were a little self-conscious about the age difference. At least I was—I knew he didn't care. I thought it was just the innocence of youth." Nicole paused for a moment, lost in her memories and Ryan waited patiently for her to continue.

"We didn't intend to keep it a secret from his sister, but she was very controlling, and I gathered she wouldn't approve, that she would be one of those 'no one is good enough for my brother' types. She had raised him on her own after their parents had died, and she had mapped out his whole life

148

for him. It never bothered him, since he had always been able to do what he loved, which was genetic research, but suddenly the restrictions she placed on him began to matter. Despite being very sheltered, he wasn't naïve. He knew she wouldn't approve and even why, which is a lot more than most men would have known. And so what began as a little white lie turned into active deception. We both knew it would come back to bite us in the end, but at the time we couldn't think of anything else to do, and we didn't want to risk what we had.

"We'd been dating for a few months. I guess we finally got close enough for him to tell me what he had discovered. I was the first person he had shared this with and it blew me away, both the extent of what he had found as well as the trust he had in me."

Nicole looked up at Ryan and he could read the sympathy in her gaze. "He also told me what he had done to you and the others. Initially, I was furious with him, but then he outlined just why he had done it. I couldn't believe my ignorance. Even though I had lived over five times as long as he had, I had no idea of the reality of political and economic power. I was just as bad as Olivia was on your first date, worse probably. He walked me through it carefully and I realized what an idiot I had been. I also realized how much danger he was in, so I offered to create a program that would hide a copy of his data and keep it safe. He agreed, but for some reason, he wanted it hidden for forty years." She shook her head ruefully. "I wrote it so well even I couldn't crack it, and I've spent the last forty years trying. That's why I was so glad when you arrived at Delphi."

She took a deep breath and continued. "As I mentioned earlier, I knew all the men who Justin had 'administered' his formula to, and I'd been keeping an eye on them. There were only a dozen to start with, partially for secrecy, and partially because Justin wanted to ensure he was giving this gift to the right person. Most of them were Delphi employees—you were the one exception, so you must have made an impression on him. Five of them left Delphi to join the military." She looked up at him again. "You know better than most the casualty rates we deal with."

Ryan nodded grimly. It was one reason for the underlying current of anger in the male community. It wasn't that the casualties were all that bad, it was just that they were consistent, and it was always the men on the frontline who paid the price.

"Anyway, they were all killed in action within the first ten years. Of the remaining seven, one had cancer and the formula sent it raging out of control. I've always been grateful that Justin didn't live long enough to see that. It was horribly painful and the only saving grace, if you can call it that, was that it was relatively quick. Two more died in accidents, one racing aircars and the other while scuba diving in the tropics."

Ryan had been keeping track of the number in his head and he looked at Nicole quietly. He sensed he wasn't going to like what she was about to say.

"And the other four?"

Nicole looked uncomfortable. "Stephanie—Justin's sister—and Gabriella found all four of them. My guess is they thought they would be able to reverse engineer Justin's work by looking at the changes in their DNA. Their immediate focus was on figuring out how to block the formula from working, like an antibody to it. They were brutal about testing and they ignored every basic safety rule. I found one of the four dead in a morgue and the other is in a vegetative state in a mental ward. That just leaves you and one other. As far as I can tell, the other person disappeared without a trace. I suspect that they are keeping him under wraps in case you don't pan out and they have to try again later."

Ryan just shook his head grimly as he tried to take it all in. It was a lot to handle, and he grinned briefly as he felt a momentary burst of sympathy for Olivia. No wonder she'd had a hard time believing him. He knew it would be difficult for her, but he had forgotten just how hard it was. He had been living with it for so long he just took it for granted. Now he was on the receiving end, as he tried to process all the new information. And a part of Nicole's story still didn't make sense. As he looked over at her, Ryan let his mind try to pinpoint what was bothering him.

Chapter Fourteen

Nicole waited patiently as Ryan sat back and absorbed it all. She knew that it was a lot to take in, to learn that the last forty years of your life had been a lie.

After a moment he cocked his head and looked at Nicole. "Correct me if I'm wrong, but there were only twelve men who Justin treated with the formula. Gabriella seemed pretty confident she had managed to find them all and you've confirmed that. They also knew about the formula hidden in the Research Lab, unavailable to anyone except these same twelve men. Is that correct?"

Nicole nodded and he frowned.

"In that case, why did they take the risk of having me recover the formula? I know they wanted to create an antibody to it, but if they killed off all twelve of us, then the formula would be inaccessible forever. Why keep any of us alive? It just seems like an unnecessary risk. Admittedly, they would be taking a risk if someone else developed the formula independently, but that's a more manageable risk. After all, there's no guarantee that even if someone rediscovered the formula, it would be the same or at least similar enough for the antibodies you said Gabriella was trying to develop to work."

Nicole's brow furled as she thought about it. "You know, you're right, it doesn't make much sense."

"The only way that it makes sense was if they knew someone else knew about the formula." He looked straight at her and she met his eyes unflinchingly.

"Me."

"You," he confirmed. "They must have known about you. Now the question is did they know that it was you, or did they just know there was someone in his life who he shared this with?"

Nicole felt the hairs on the back of her neck rise as she looked at Ryan. She had spent the last forty years feeling safe in her anonymity, even though she had never completely relied on it. She suddenly got a glimpse into how Ryan must be feeling as she thought about her anonymity being an illusion.

"If they know it's me, then this is the one safe house they know about for sure. I wasn't thinking about security when I suggested we come here. I just picked it because it was the closest."

"We should leave," Ryan said, rising from the sofa. As if on cue, both the front and the back door crashed in.

Instantly Ryan launched himself forward, grabbing her and crashing through the large picture window behind her. The glass gave way with a crash and they were airborne for a few seconds. Nicole braced herself for the landing, but Ryan twisted in midair and as they landed they rolled, using their momentum to get away from the house and into the open.

Nicole felt an instant of panic as the curtains tangled around them, blocking her vision and hindering her movement, but it passed as the curtains parted like wet paper towel under their combined efforts. She dropped the tattered remnants and looked around in surprise. They were still alone on the front lawn and she looked at Ryan breathlessly.

"What was that about?"

"I don't know how many of them there are, but I'm sure they'll outnumber us. The only way we can make it out of this is if we fight as a team. We can't do that effectively in the cramped confines of the house so…" He shrugged as he scanned the grounds visually and then his eyes glazed over as he linked into something, likely his aircar. A few moments later his eyes cleared as her guess was confirmed.

"I just linked to the scanner in my aircar and it looks like there's an even dozen of them. From what I can tell, only two of them have enhancements, probably the team leaders."

Nicole felt panic wash over her again as she considered the odds. Ryan must have sensed it since he turned to her and grinned tightly.

"It's not as bad as it sounds. Most people, enhanced or not, aren't as trained as we are. We faced this all the time in the military. This is a typical example of a team that looks good on paper, but it takes more than numbers or enhancement to make it work. It takes training and teamwork. It's not going to be easy, but we can do it."

"But?"

Ryan laughed, a short, bitter bark.

"Well I started jamming communications, but they might have called for reinforcements earlier. I put in a call for some reinforcements myself but I don't know if they'll get here in time."

Nicole bit her lip as she considered this. Even as she did, figures began emerging from around the sides of the house. "Would it do any good to call the police?" she asked as she instinctively assumed a combat stance, her back to Ryan's.

"No offense, but most of the police are females. Not only that, but technically we are in the wrong here."

Nicole sensed he was about to say something else, but their assailants had finished gathering, and they headed towards Ryan and Nicole in a headlong rush. Nicole swallowed nervously. Despite all her training she had never been in a real life combat situation before. The first assailant was on her before she could even think, but she found she didn't need to. Her mind remembered her training and she reacted automatically. The next ten minutes were a blur of action, as she and Ryan worked flawlessly together as a team. It was almost like they were fighting as one, and she felt a surge of exhilaration, unlike anything she'd ever felt before. She tossed her last assailant away effortlessly and turned to Ryan.

"Oh my God, that was incredible!" she panted and a brief smile flickered across his face before disappearing. Her exhilaration vanished and exhaustion took its place. "There's more coming, aren't there?"

It wasn't really a question, but he started to answer her anyway. Before he could even open his mouth the ground lit up, as a large aircar swept the area with a powerful floodlight. Her enhancement automatically protected her vision, as the aircar settled ponderously on the ground about forty feet away. The full-sized door opened and police in riot gear spread out in front of it. A moment later Gabriella stepped out, looking smug.

"We meet again," she smirked at Ryan

"Indeed we do," Ryan responded calmly, and Nicole shot him a glance as she detected an undercurrent of confidence in his voice.

"I take it that I have you to thank for this," Gabriella said to Nicole, lifting her right arm up, encased in a quick heal wrap. Nicole saw it and she smiled broadly.

"Anytime," she said and Gabriella's face twisted and then cleared.

"Yeah, well enjoy it while you can," she threatened. "In a couple hours the bone will have knitted enough for me to return the favor. As soon as that happens, I'll make sure you'll regret every second of enjoyment and then some."

"I don't think so," Ryan interjected and Gabriella shifted her focus to him.

"I wouldn't be so quick to talk, Ryan. I've outsmarted you for forty years, what makes you think this time is any different?"

"No, you've tricked me all that time. That's not the same at all. As for why this time is different, well I'll let my friends explain it to you."

"What friends?" Gabriella sneered and Ryan waved his hand casually. Suddenly the air beside Ryan and Nicole wavered and shifted, and then cleared to reveal a full platoon of marines. They weren't wearing any combat gear, but they outnumbered the police. It also didn't hurt that the troop transport loomed behind them. One of the auto-cannons traversed silently, and the police commander turned pale. The expression on Gabriella's face was pure evil as she stared at them in frustration.

"Do you have any idea what you've done?" she spat and Ryan nodded.

"I've only kick-started the inevitable. You know as well as I do that this is exactly the sort of confrontation we've been headed towards as a nation for decades now. You just thought you could keep it a secret and that you could control it. Well, I have serious doubts you would have been able to control it, but now that the secret is out, I can guarantee that's not going to happen."

"What do you mean, the secret is out?" she asked, suddenly unsure.

Ryan lifted his eyebrows in mock surprise. "I'm surprised you don't know. It's been all over the news. Olivia activated the high-density scanners before coming to confront me. The whole sordid incident, my revelation to Olivia, your confirmation of it and your role in all of it, your confession of Justin's murder, everything. It was all recorded."

Gabriella's face paled as Ryan continued speaking.

"I was a little surprised at how readily the marine commander at Edwards agreed to support me, but I didn't look a gift horse in the mouth. It did get me to wondering though, and it didn't take me long to find the recording. It's been sweeping the airwaves and all the major newsnets are picking it up."

"You didn't." The words came out quietly, but the menace beneath them was quite clear. It didn't affect Ryan or his response.

"No, I didn't," he replied. "I don't know who did, but regardless, the secret is out now."

For a long moment, Gabriella just stared at him bitterly, and then unexpectedly she tilted her head back and laughed.

"Congratulations Ryan, you've won this battle." She laughed again and smiled cruelly at him. "That's once in forty years, so I guess I can let you have the victory. Especially since I've won the war."

Ryan felt a chill and he hoped that she was talking about something else.

"There's a reason I haven't been watching the news. I linked into the computers at the lab and was busy reviewing the records of your unauthorized incursion. I was hoping to find out where the data you had recovered was stored so I could erase it. As it turns out, I didn't need to worry about that since it had already been erased—by you."

Ryan's face muscles tightened as she made it seem like carelessness on his part.

"So the way I look at it, you've lost. I've got the only copy of the formula in existence and you've got nothing. Even if you try to reverse engineer it, that will take time and by then we'll have figured out how to stop you. So enjoy your moment of victory. It's all you have."

With that she turned and entered the aircar. The police trooped in behind her, casting occasional nervous glances towards the platoon of marines arrayed around Ryan and Nicole. Seconds later the floodlights shut off as the aircar lifted and darkness fell again. Ryan felt like the darkness had invaded his soul as well as shattered his last hope. He'd been praying Gabriella wouldn't find out about the data erasure and that he could force her to negotiate. Now he had nothing and he felt empty.

The disappointed faces of the Marines only made it worse as they boarded the troop transport. Moments later it rose into the air and headed back to Edwards. He was all alone and he sank to his knees in despair. He bent over and buried his face in his hands and then started as he felt a hand on his shoulder. He knew it was Nicole—there was no one else it could be—but he couldn't bear to face her. This had been her dream, too, and he had failed her.

He had failed them all.

"You haven't failed us and you haven't failed me." He hadn't realized he'd said the words aloud, but he must have.

"Yes I have. Gabriella is right. She's got everything and we've got nothing."

"You don't listen very well, do you?" Nicole responded and the wry humor in her voice penetrated his despair.

He lifted his head out of his hands and looked at her, and suddenly he remembered the comment she had made to him when they left the lab. 'Gabriella has less than either of you think she has, you need to trust me on this.' He echoed the words out loud and she nodded.

"That's right. Now we need to get ourselves to another safe house before she realizes just how little she has." She laughed bitterly. "That is, if any of my safe houses are actually safe anymore."

Not surprisingly, something inside him responded to her bitterness, and he found himself smiling gently at her as his despair lightened.

"Now, now, enough of that. Tell you what, I'll promise not to beat myself up if you promise to do the same. I don't think they'll be able to find us again but just in case, we'll take a few precautions this time, like using the long-range scanners in the aircar to give us more warning."

"Yeah, and not going to a safe house in my name," Nicole quipped, but she was smiling this time, and Ryan smiled back at her. Then he leaned forward and kissed her gently on the lips. She didn't resist him at first, though she pulled back soon after with a confused look on her face. They stood there looking at each other until Nicole shook her head.

"Later," she said firmly.

Ryan nodded in understanding. There were too many other things going on that needed their attention, and as much as he wanted to, he knew now wasn't the time to figure out if they could make this work.

He turned away from her and headed towards the aircar. His eyes lit with satisfaction as he saw the familiar oval shape of a stealth field generator sitting beside it. He figured he was so far on the wrong side of the law at the current moment that possession of illegal military equipment would be the least of his worries. He couldn't come right out and ask the commander at Edwards for one, but he had hinted that it would be useful. He had worried that either they wouldn't be able to give him one, or they had taken it back with them after Gabriella's comments. It looked like he had been fretting for nothing. He spent a few moments securing it to the aircar and tying it into the aircar's systems. He justified the time as well spent, since once it was operational it greatly increased their ability to move undetected.

Nicole watched as Ryan fussed with the aircar. She was impatient to get going, but she knew he was, as well. If he was willing to spend time doing whatever he was doing, then it must be worth it. She welcomed the brief break since it gave her time to think about their relationship. She hadn't expected him to be attracted to her and she needed the time to adjust.

Despite having lived as long as she had, she had only loved two men. She hadn't expected to fall in love this late in her life, and that was part of her indecision. She also didn't know if it was fair to Ryan for her to be in love with him. Thanks to Justin's formula, he had well over three quarters of his life ahead of him, whereas she had almost three quarters of her life behind her. She had gone through the anguish of losing the people who mattered most to her too many times in her life. She didn't want to inflict that pain on anyone. As she remembered the people that she had outlived, she felt her resolve firming up. She knew the decision she had to make, and she almost decided to tell Ryan right away, but at the last minute she changed her mind. The comment she had made to him earlier still held. There would be time for this later, and in the meantime they had to focus on what they had to do. As if on cue, Ryan looked up and smiled at her again.

"Ready to go."

Nicole looked at the oval shape he had fastened to the top of the aircar and raised an eyebrow as she climbed in.

"Stealth field generator," he explained and she nodded in understanding. No wonder he had taken the time to get it hooked up. She settled in and he looked over at her.

"Brace yourself," he said and then they shot forward with a surprising burst of acceleration. This was only the second time Nicole had been in his car and she hadn't expected it to be this powerful. She watched as he made several random course changes, and then the outside view became distorted as the gentle hum of the stealth field filled the car. Ryan made a few more random course changes and sat back in the seat.

"Okay, we should be good now. If anyone was following us, they have no idea where we're going. Of course, neither do I," he said, grinning and Nicole laughed.

"Well let's hope that it stays that way. I have two more safe houses in this area. One is more centrally located and the other is rural."

"Rural," Ryan said firmly. "Our presence will be more easily noticed, but that applies to them as well and frankly I'd rather be able to see them coming. Besides, with the stealth field, we should be able to arrive unnoticed."

"Doesn't that apply to them too? I mean, if we can get a stealth field, what's to stop them from using one?"

"Nothing," Ryan admitted. "The technology is tightly controlled, but I'd have to be naïve to assume they couldn't get a unit if they wanted to. However unless they know about all your safe houses, we should be okay."

"And if they do?"

He shrugged. "I've got a list of a few places we could hide out in for a while, but they are nowhere near as well equipped as yours. Unless we know for sure that your list has been compromised, I'd rather use one of your safe houses. Just in case though, the first thing I'm going to do once we arrive is to load some supplies into the aircar, just in case we need to make another quick exit. If we do, then at least we'll have some supplies and a source of currency. If push comes to shove, we can live out of the aircar for a few weeks using public freshers. It won't be comfortable but …"

Nicole nodded. "True but I'll bet that it beats the hell out of being in Gabriella's hands." She shuddered at the thought and Ryan nodded.

"That's for sure," he said somberly. "That woman is crazy. I don't think I've ever met anyone as outright insane as she is. I've seen a lot of things in my days, especially in the military, but she takes top prize."

They were both silent for a moment as they thought about being in Gabriella's hands and then Ryan shook his head. "Enough of that. So, where are we going?"

Nicole provided him with the GPS coordinates and they headed off. She watched him out of the corner of her eye as he skillfully plotted a course that gently arced towards her rural safe house. Even as he did, he was busy accessing military satellites, scanning for any suspicious activity in that vicinity in the last few years.

Nicole watched him as he manipulated the data screens with ease. She could have done the same job much faster of course, but he was doing a competent job considering that this wasn't his area of expertise. As if he had heard her thoughts, he looked up suddenly with an embarrassed look on his face.

"It just occurred to me that you could probably do this better and faster than I could." He blushed furiously, as Nicole smiled in confirmation. "Sorry, I'm just not used to working with someone else, let alone someone as competent as you."

"That's okay, neither am I. I think that we both have our strengths and it's going to take each of us time to understand where those lie. It took me off guard when you jumped out the window earlier, but it didn't take me long to understand why you had done that. So far we've managed to muddle through together, and it can only get better as we become more comfortable with each other, so I wouldn't worry about it too much."

"All right then, but I still think you should do this. I'll concentrate on getting us there safely, while you concentrate on making sure it is safe for us to do so."

He concentrated briefly and Nicole's implants were suddenly able to access the aircar's systems. She ran a brief scan to find out what she had access to and what level of access she had. The scan ended and Nicole raised a mental eyebrow in surprise. Ryan had given her full access to the aircar. Not only that, but he had given her access to all his data files, which included information for dozens of other systems, such as the military satellites he had linked to earlier. She wondered why he hadn't linked to any other satellites, but when she tried to do that, she couldn't get a signal. The only sources she could find were all military. She puzzled over that silently for a moment before she realized it was the effect of the stealth field. Since the stealth field generator had come from Edwards, it knew the available military data sources and was letting them in. The shield deflected anything else.

She had never dealt with military data sources and she felt a little uneasy, what with being a civilian and all. She wondered why Ryan had given her such complete access. Was it because he was so tired he didn't realize what he had done? Somehow she didn't think that was likely, so she ruled out that possibility. Was it because he trusted her or because he had nothing left to lose? Or was it because he loved her?

Her mind flinched at that thought, especially given the decision that she had made. She hadn't thought that it would be so hard and she realized that when he had said that he loved her, that he had really meant it. They weren't just words for him either.

She also considered his background. He had been in love with Olivia for the last forty years, and for him to reject her meant that he had given this serious thought. In many respects, going with Olivia would have been the easier decision for him, and the decision that most men in his position would have made. He already had a relationship with her, it appeared she was in love with him, and her position as CEO of Delphi was a huge advantage. But his integrity wouldn't let him do that.

It was a tough decision to make and she respected him for it. It also reinforced the rightness of her decision. She owed him the same integrity and respect that he had shown her. As much as she wanted to spend the rest of her life with him, she knew it wasn't fair, that he deserved more. She knew what losing someone did to a person and she had spent a large portion of her life alone because of that. The kind of love she'd had wasn't easy to replace and she wasn't willing to settle for less. Instinctively, she knew Ryan felt the same way and she refused to inflict that on him.

"We're here." The soft words intruded on her thoughts and Nicole realized how tired she was. For her to become so absorbed in her own thoughts that she hadn't noticed their arrival was unheard of. She gave her head a shake to clear it.

Ryan laughed at her. "Stop struggling to stay awake. We've been through a lot tonight and a fight like the one that we had takes a lot out of a person. Why don't you go and crash for a while? I'll set up a perimeter scan and then load up the aircar."

"What about you?" Nicole protested wearily, even as her body screamed at her to follow his advice. "You've been through even more than I have tonight, not to mention the mental shocks."

"True, but between the nutrient patch you gave me and the wine, I'm in decent shape. I wouldn't say no to a bed right now, especially one that had you in it, but I can hold out for a while longer. Besides, one of us should always be awake. Normally, that wouldn't be a problem, thanks to our enhancements, but they need time to recover."

Nicole blushed at his comment about sharing her bed, and even as tired as she was, she felt a rush of desire as well. She frowned at her body's betrayal.

"Sorry," Ryan apologized. "I shouldn't have pushed. I know we agreed to table that for later."

Nicole stared at him confused, and then she realized he thought that she'd been upset by his comment about sharing a bed with her.

"No, it's not that," she said automatically and then bit her tongue. She would have been better off to leave him with that mistaken impression. It would have made it easier in the end when she told him she couldn't be with him. First her body and then her mind, both of them betraying her, both of them denying the decision she had made. She shook her head again and then smiled tiredly at Ryan.

"I think you're right, I'm more tired than I realized," she admitted before heading towards the house. She paused and turned back to Ryan. "Don't let me sleep too long," she warned him and he grinned at her.

"I won't," he promised. She looked suspiciously at his grin and then yawned suddenly.

"Okay then," she said slowly and headed into the house to crash.

Chapter Fifteen

Olivia woke with a groan. Someone was shaking her, but she had a monstrous headache. Each gentle shake of her shoulder went straight to her brain, somehow multiplying in strength along the way. She managed to reach up and put a restraining hand on whoever it was. The movement stopped and Olivia used the respite to regain her equilibrium. When she felt like she could open her eyes without being sick, she did so. She squinted at the strange brunette woman in the Delphi security uniform.

"Who are you and what's going on?" she rasped.

"I'm Mia Reynolds. I command one of the field teams here at Delphi. They didn't want me to disturb you, but after I saw the recordings, I knew that you would want to be woken up."

Olivia groaned and closed her eyes. She couldn't imagine anything that would make her want to feel like this. Then the rest of the sentence caught up with her. She opened her eyes and looked around. She was lying on one of the beds in Medical, and there were about a dozen other people unconscious in the beds around her. There were a couple of doctors hovering over Mia's shoulder and armed guards in full combat gear at the entrances. Her eyes widened as she saw the guards were armed with rifles and not the stunners they usually carried.

"Just what is going on here?" she exclaimed.

"Follow me and I'll show you." Mia got up and strode away and with an effort Olivia forced herself out of the bed. One of the doctors started to say something, but Olivia looked at her scathingly and the woman hastily stopped talking. The first few steps were painful, but Olivia persisted, and she caught up with Mia at the wide-screen communications console in the admin section of the medical building. As soon as she came into view, Mia looked at the console and Olivia followed her gaze. She stiffened as a recording began to play and she realized that she was seeing herself doing something she had no memory of. Even as she thought that, she could feel the memories coming back to her. It was an eerie experience and she almost didn't notice her headache fading as the scene played out in front of her.

"How long ago was that?" Olivia asked more briskly than she felt.

"Three and a half hours," Mia said. "Neural grenades normally knock you out for twelve to eighteen hours, but Anita had the doctors wake me earlier since I'm the highest ranking person in security onsite. I took one look at this and then had them wake you up, too."

Olivia nodded approvingly. "Good call, both of you." Absently she checked the time. It was ten to three in the morning and she tried to reconstruct the sequence of events, just to make sure she wasn't missing anything. Let's see, dinner at eight, Ryan left just before ten, she arrived at Delphi at ten thirty and confronted him in the lab at quarter to eleven. Gabriella showed up at eleven, and then the last clear memory she had was watching the neural grenade spinning slowly on the floor in front of her. She shook her head at how close Gabriella had come to getting away clean. If she hadn't ordered Anita to activate the high-density scanners, no one would have known what had happened. She hadn't remembered anything until Mia had shown her the video, and although she had only viewed the tail end of the evening, it completely reversed the effects of the neural grenade. She shook her head again and glanced up at Mia.

"Anything else?" she inquired and Mia nodded.

"Anita also had the foresight to order the grounds sealed. No one has come in or out since they found us."

"Excellent." She smiled at Mia, only to frown as she thought for a moment. She glanced back at the bed she had so recently vacated and she noticed the other members of Field Team One. She inclined her head in their direction. "Have the doctors wake up the others. We might need them. Tell the doctors to have them watch this video when they wake up. It will take care of their headaches and allow them to orient themselves quicker."

Mia's eyes widened as she realized what Olivia was saying and then she nodded. She stepped away and Olivia took the time to think about what had just occurred. If this had happened six months ago, she would have been woefully ignorant of the ramifications. She hated to admit it, but she had Ryan and Nicole to thank for opening her eyes. She had barely finished that thought when another occurred to her, concerning the identity of the mysterious stranger who had rescued Ryan. She didn't know for sure who that figure was, but she would have bet a significant portion of her escrow account that it was Nicole. She would have been willing to bet an even larger portion that it was Nicole that Ryan had fallen in love with. Suddenly it all made sense.

Mia returned and nodded to her. "Ready."

"Good, let's go," Olivia said, then paused. "Is there a flitter here we can use?"

Mia nodded again, before turning and striding out of the building, Olivia following close behind her. There was something familiar about the security commander, and Olivia continued to study her even as they got in the flitter and headed towards Security Central. She was competent, intelligent, and decisive. Whatever his faults might be and despite his hidden agenda, Ryan had succeeded in building a first-class security team. And then it hit her.

"You're the one who asked for Ryan's help on a training exercise, aren't you?"

"Guilty as charged," Mia admitted with a grin.

Olivia's smiled briefly in return. She was beginning to like this woman. "You've obviously worked closely with Ryan, what's your opinion on this?"

Mia paused for a moment to ground the flitter in front of Security Central before replying. Then she turned to face Olivia. "Security is one of those fields that has more exposure to men, more than almost any other profession. Not only that, but most of the men that we interact with are competent, because of their military training and experience."

Olivia nodded in understanding. The incompetent ones didn't last long.

"Because of that exposure, I am more sympathetic to, and understanding of, the issues they are facing. There are many women who know what the issues are, but they don't understand them, not fully."

"But you do."

Mia nodded. "I think this issue has the potential to be a time bomb if it becomes public. The fact we were able to view the recording in the Medical building, instead of Security, makes me think it might have happened already."

Olivia winced and then nodded for Mia to continue.

"I think Anita made the right call in sealing the grounds. I think we have to take it to the next level and get all Delphi personnel here where they can be safe. We should also contact the affiliates and tell them to do the same. Once all of that is done, we should determine our position on the issue and how much of that we want to go public with."

"And what do you think our position should be?" Olivia asked curiously.

Mia shook her head. "That's not my call."

"Pretend it is. There are only three people whose opinion I value more at the moment, and I'm pretty sure that two of them are already deeply involved in this mess."

Mia took a deep breath. "In that case, I think Delphi should support this effort to bridge the gender divide. I think we should do whatever we can to bring this formula to production and make it available to anyone who wants it."

Olivia concealed her start at the term gender divide and then raised her eyebrows speculatively at Mia's aggressive solution.

"You don't think that we should take a more cautious approach to this?"

"No, I don't. There has been a powder keg of resentment building in the male population. This information will be like putting a match to it. There's no way to control the explosion, you just have to ride it out. At least, within Noram. In other countries, we can adopt a more gradual approach, allowing men access to the formula, provided that the women have access to Menssation®."

Olivia considered that for a moment. She hadn't had the time to think about it properly, but her instincts told her that Mia's were correct. Ryan was lucky to have this woman on his team. That thought reminded her of something else and she asked Mia another question.

"What about Ryan? Do you still trust him?"

Mia had already been looking at Olivia, but she squared her shoulders and looked Olivia straight in the eyes. "Yes I do. If you weren't here and he was, I would still be willing to follow his orders, even knowing what I know now. I will admit I was disappointed in his behavior when we caught him in the lab, but given what we're dealing with, I can understand why he did it."

Olivia nodded thoughtfully. There was no faulting Mia's honesty and for a moment Olivia wondered if she were making the wrong decision, leaving Mia in control. Yet, Mia had proved her competence and intelligence and it also appeared as if her instincts were sound. Mia fidgeted impatiently and Olivia smiled.

"Go," she said and Mia hopped out of the flitter and strode into the security building. Olivia followed her a moment later, lost in thought as she ascended to the control room. When she arrived, she saw that Mia was busy conferring with Anita and a bunch of others, and she guessed that Mia was following her own advice about protecting Delphi's employees. Suddenly Olivia thought of Brooke. She beckoned to a guard.

"Please locate Brooke Winters and arrange to have her brought here immediately. If she is off-site and there are other Delphi employees nearby, bring them here as well. You have my authorization to stun anyone who resists."

The guard looked at her wide-eyed and then snapped off a salute and rushed off. Olivia spotted a vacant terminal and sat down in front of it. She began to compose a press release incorporating the elements Mia had suggested. She was deep in thought when she heard a voice behind her.

"Boy, you don't do anything by half measures, do you?"

Olivia stood with a smile and embraced her.

"Thank God you're here. I need someone I can trust."

"I gathered that from the rather abrupt way I was brought here." Brooke gestured at the press release on the screen. "What in the hell is going on?" she asked and Olivia detected an undercurrent of fear in her voice, not that she blamed her. If Olivia had the time to think about it, she would probably be scared about now, too.

"Take a look at this." Olivia banked the press release to memory and pulled up the video of her confrontation with Ryan and Gabriella. Brooke watched in silence and then looked at Olivia once it finished, stunned.

"So that's what he was up to. I had wondered about that press release, but it makes perfect sense now. Is that your idea?"

Olivia shook her head. "The basic concept belongs to the commander of the field team that was with me. She's shown incredible initiative tonight and from what I can tell, her instincts are sound. However, I wanted you for a sanity check before I send it out."

"Well in that case, wait no longer."

"Are you sure?" Olivia looked at her friend seriously. "It's an aggressive stance. It could backfire on us if all of this fizzles out."

Brooke looked grim. "My guess is that this isn't going to fizzle out. If it's true, if there is a formula that extends the life expectancy of men, this approach will help Delphi emerge from this stronger than ever. If it turns out there is no formula then at least we'll emerge intact, which is more than I can say for some other companies."

"What are you talking about?"

"Remember the discussion we had after your first date with Ryan?"

Olivia blushed to remember how ignorant she had been, but she nodded.

"Well," Brooke continued, "if this becomes public, it is going to set off a chain reaction of events. If the formula doesn't exist, I'm afraid that those events will result in violence. I know for a fact there are many companies whose policies will make them attractive targets. I'm also sure that none of those companies have prepared for it, at least in terms of security. Not that you can really prepare for something like this, but you can make sure that your people are highly trained."

"Like Ryan did."

Brooke just nodded and then looked at Olivia in concern. "So are you okay?"

Olivia shrugged. "I've still got a slight headache, but other than that, I'm fine."

"Not that, I meant are you okay about Ryan being in love with someone else?"

"Oh, that."

"Oh, that?" Brooke echoed disbelievingly.

"Yes, I'm okay with it. I think he and Nicole make a good couple. I can't say that I'm not disappointed, but strangely enough, I'm not devastated." She laughed harshly. "I guess having your world turned upside down does that to you."

"Whoa, wait a minute. Ryan and Nicole? When did this happen? Did I miss something? Is there another video I should see?"

Olivia grinned. "Well, I'm just guessing, but I think the person who rescued Ryan is Nicole. I don't have any way to prove it, but it feels right." She noticed Mia out of the corner of her eye and turned to face her.

"What's up?" Olivia asked.

"Nothing good. The recording has indeed become public and riots are breaking out all over the country. There's a report of a showdown between the police and a platoon of marines at a house about fifteen minutes from here, although both groups are officially denying they were present. Since it was unofficial and since neither group was willing to start something, it resulted in your basic standoff situation, thank God."

"What do you mean, 'thank God'?" Olivia asked with a frown. She was no fan of violence, but Mia's reaction went beyond that.

"Riots are bad enough. I shudder to think of the casualties and property damages from those, but if the police and the military start mixing it up, it's a whole different ball game."

"Civil war," Brooke said weakly, her face pale, and Mia nodded.

"Exactly. And if it comes to that, we're all in big trouble. The police have the edge in numbers, but the military is better trained and better equipped. It will be a complete disaster and no matter who wins, we'll all lose. This is the type of internal conflict that just about anybody who opposes Noram salivates over."

Olivia sensed that Mia had more to say on the topic, but she didn't want to hear it. The current situation concerned her enough without getting all worked up about possible future events that she couldn't control.

"What else do we know?" she interrupted. Mia favored her with an appraising look and nodded.

Olivia appreciated the commander's understanding since she was looking to move forward with something she could affect. Given who the players were, it was possible that whatever decision she made could tip the balance either way.

"As I said," Mia continued, "nothing happened. Public records show the house where the confrontation occurred belongs to Nicole West. There's also a rumor floating around that Gabriella has the only copy of the data and that Ryan purged the data from Delphi's network."

"Whoa!"

Olivia grinned despite herself at the exclamation from Brooke.

"Sorry," Brooke said, "I'd just like the world to hold still long enough for me to figure out what the hell is going on."

"That's okay, I feel the same myself." Olivia squeezed Brooke's shoulder as she turned her attention to Mia. "Comments?"

"I think you're right," Mia said. "The figure who rescued Ryan was Nicole West."

Olivia looked at Brooke expressively, who just nodded. Obviously Mia had been paying attention to what they had been saying earlier, another sign of her competence.

"Security records show that until a few weeks ago Ryan and Nicole were sparring regularly at the fitness center," Mia offered expressionlessly.

Olivia blinked in astonishment at this news and then chuckled quietly as she realized why she had missed this key fact. When she had investigated Ryan's activities, she had filtered out anything involving Senior VPs, figuring that if a Senior VP was present then it was work related. She shook her head ruefully and focused on what Mia was saying.

"If she is the person in the recording who rescued Ryan, it is obvious that she's enhanced, although we have no record of it. Besides the confrontation between the police and the marines, there are also reports of a brief skirmish on the front lawn, before the police and the marines arrived. My guess is that Gabriella mobilized a small field team to try to take out Ryan and Nicole before the police arrived. Or maybe the police were called as reinforcements. Either way, it obviously failed, which isn't surprising. A good team of two enhanced individuals is hard to beat, even by a larger group. Ryan's training is top-notch and if this Nicole person was sparring with him, she's got to be at least in the same league."

"What about the rumor that Gabriella has the only copy of the data and that Ryan purged it from the system." Olivia had her own thoughts about that, but she wanted to hear Mia's view.

"I don't believe any of it. First, although I'm not in IT, I do know there are always multiple copies of data floating around. The problem is usually ensuring that all copies of something get deleted rather than deleting something vital in error."

"So you think it was an error?"

Mia shrugged. "Either that or an automated security program. After all, this data has managed to remain hidden for forty years. But if you're asking me if I think Ryan purged it purposely, the answer is no. Any info to the contrary is likely just Gabriella putting her own evil spin on it."

Olivia looked over at Brooke, who just raised her eyebrows expressively. Obviously, somewhere along the way, Gabriella had made an enemy of Mia. Olivia grinned at the thought. Gabriella's loss was their gain.

"Excellent. Keep me posted of anything else you find out. And if either Nicole or Ryan calls, put them through to me immediately. If you can't find me, you know what to do."

Mia nodded and then turned and strode away.

"What was that about?" Brooke asked curiously.

"Oh, when I asked Mia if she trusted Ryan, she said that she would follow his orders if I wasn't here, even knowing everything that she knows."

"Smart woman."

Olivia looked at Brooke in surprise. "You agree? I'd have expected a little more caution from you."

"Well, given who and what we are dealing with, I don't think we can afford caution. Besides, we've only just found out about this. It's obvious that Nicole and Ryan have known about it for years."

"Yeah, who'd have thought," Olivia commented.

"I wonder what they're doing now," Brooke mused and Olivia just shrugged.

* * *

Ryan woke up feeling refreshed. Automatically he checked the time and learned that he had been asleep for just over two hours. He grinned as he imagined Nicole's reaction. He had let her sleep until she woke up naturally, and she was infuriated to find out she had slept for almost six hours. She had complained that he had promised not to let her sleep too long, and he had told her that he hadn't, that she had slept just long enough. She had glared at him, and then relented in the face of his amusement, conceding she hadn't said what 'too long' was.

He knew she had been hoping to do the same to him. That he had only slept for slightly more than two hours would irritate her, even though it didn't mean anything other than he had deeper reserves, a result of his military training. In truth, while both of them could have used more sleep, even as little as an hour worked wonders, especially if they kept their nanites supplied with nutrients. Both he and Nicole had slapped on a couple of the high-energy nutrient patches like the one she had used on him earlier before hitting the sack. Their nanites had used the downtime to rebuild their reserves as well as sweeping their systems for any buildup of waste products.

He knew that it worried Nicole that he had been pushing himself too hard while she was asleep. He supposed that in a sense he had, but only because he knew he would have this opportunity to catch up. Even then, he didn't push himself as hard as he could have, since they didn't know for sure that this safe house was safe. To that end, he needed to ensure he would be able to respond properly to any crises that might arise. His priority had been to load the aircar with supplies. It still amazed him how well Nicole had managed to stock her safe houses. He couldn't get over the huge resource commitment that it implied. He had loaded the aircar full of supplies, barely leaving room enough for the two of them. Admittedly, his aircar didn't have that much storage space, but it was still able to hold an impressive amount. Despite that, it had barely made a dent on the household supplies.

Once he had finished that, he had checked on Nicole. She had stripped off the black nano weave suit and lay sprawled on the bed. Like most enhanced individuals, she avoided the use of covers since their enhancement provided better temperature regulation that way.

He had only meant to check on her but he found himself lingering, watching her sleep. Part of it was physical, an admiration of her body, clad as it was in only a bra and panties, but it was mostly mental. Despite the past few centuries, men still had a powerful instinct to protect women and Ryan was no different. In fact, given his unique circumstances, he was more qualified than most men to be able to provide that protection. Yet, out of all the women he knew, Nicole was undoubtedly the most capable, able to protect herself, and he knew it. Despite that, he felt the urge to protect her more strongly than ever. It was almost like the urge to protect a teammate and he suddenly understood that it was a reflection of his love for her, the desire to make life easier for her and to help her.

He realized he had never felt anything like that for anyone before, and he knew he was committed to her like he hadn't been committed to anyone ever. He had never thought of marriage, not really, not even with Olivia, although that was mainly because of the life expectancy difference, but he was ready and willing, even eager, to marry Nicole. He felt a little sense of irony that the life expectancy difference that he had experienced with Olivia, also existed between him and Nicole, only in reverse, but he didn't share the same reservations that Olivia had.

As he looked at her, he hoped she had lived long enough not to be subject to the mental doubts that had assailed him when he had first thought about the differences in life spans forty years ago. Somehow he suspected that wasn't true. As one of his military trainers had said to him, objectivity only occurs when it's happening to the other guy. Things that were self-evident when they were happing to someone else became a whole lot less clear when you experienced them personally.

He stayed and watched her for a few moments, until the urge to snuggle up next to her became almost irresistible, and then he forced himself to leave.

He explored the house thoroughly, getting a good handle on all the ways into and out of the building, and all the possible makeshift weapons scattered throughout. After that, he borrowed Nicole's nano weave suit and went exploring. He got a good feel for the area and using his link to the aircar, he was able to find a few blind spots the sensors couldn't cover. He returned a little later with some small net repeaters that allowed the aircar to detect movement in those areas. He also confirmed that no one had been in the area in years or perhaps even decades. Nicole's data searches had all pointed to that fact, but somehow it was more convincing knowing it on a more intimate or visceral level.

He had returned, only to find Nicole still asleep, and so he did a few 'housekeeping' issues. He ducked into the shower for a quick rinse, keeping close contact with the aircar so he wouldn't miss anything, followed by a quick lunch. The emergency rations, while tasteless, did provide him with needed energy. Fortunately, liberal applications of wine made them a lot more palatable. All of which meant that by the time Nicole woke up, he had gone a long way to addressing his energy deficiencies. That, combined with his existing reserves, was what had allowed him to recover quicker.

He stretched and looked around the room, noticing that Nicole had cleaned and folded his clothes, leaving them on the dresser for him. He hadn't had to do the same for her, since she had stocked each safe house with extra clothes. He stripped off his dirty boxers, automatically checking the aircar's systems even as he did so. Assured that all was well, he jumped into the shower. He took more time on this one, luxuriating in the spray of hot water. He twisted and turned under the showerhead, letting the spray massage his aching muscles. Then he dressed quickly and went out to find Nicole, feeling better than he had in hours. He didn't know whether he was being unrealistically optimistic or not, but for the moment he didn't care.

He strolled into the living room to find Nicole waiting there with a glass of wine for him and he laughed.

"I guess I should trust an IT person to have a monitoring program in place," he chuckled as he accepted the glass of wine from her.

"As truth would have it, I didn't really need one."

"Oh?"

"Indeed. You don't live as long as I have without realizing that people are creatures of habit. I'll admit that I don't know a lot about your personal habits yet, but your chosen profession, combined with your military training, tells me a lot. I know that you had already explored the surrounding area, but I thought that it would be wise for me to get a feel for the property myself. I was linked into the aircar and so…" She shrugged and Ryan laughed.

"So of course the first thing that I did when I woke up was check the system," he finished for her wryly and she smiled at him.

"Truthfully, I will admit that I was monitoring you. This house isn't very smart, especially compared to modern houses, but it's still smart enough to let me know when you woke up, and then that you were in the shower. I guess the other thing I've learned in all my years is not to rely on just one system."

"Good point," he answered soberly, as he thought of the system that Justin had used to secure the formula. It didn't surprise him when Nicole brought that up, since he was already beginning to appreciate how in tune with each other they were.

"So speaking of systems, I guess we should talk about the data in the lab." Ryan nodded and she gestured for him to take a seat. He looked melodramatically at the doors as she did, as if expecting Gabriella's agents to come storming in, eliciting a giggle from her. He paused to refill his wineglass before sitting down opposite her.

"Now, first things first," Nicole began. "I told you that I'd written the program so well I couldn't crack it and that's only partly true. There were several elements to the program, a few more obvious ones and a subtler hidden one. Additionally, I designed the program to hide itself. In a sense, it was a benign virus that I inflicted on Delphi's network.

"There is a concept in Information Technology called Data Lifecycle Management or DLM. Most data is only relevant to the user for a short time, but there are various legal statutes that require companies to store data for varying periods of time. There are too many statutes to manage and many of them overlap so the simplest approach is to pick the longest storage requirement and apply it to all the data. This is simple to implement, but it needs a lot of storage capacity. We use molecular disk drives for current data. These are similar to their precursor, magnetic disk drives, but they are exponentially faster and larger. They are expensive to buy and run so we try to limit their use. Then we have M-Sticks. They are slower but much cheaper. They are good for archival purposes, but they are not fast enough to be a live data source, not to mention that they are read-only. There is also a significant amount of data stored on storage mediums somewhere between these two extremes.

"The program that I wrote 'lives' in this space. It constantly monitors the activity of data around it and ensures that several copies of itself are accessible. It doesn't overwrite any existing data to do this, and except for the space and CPU cycles used, both of which are negligible, it doesn't impact the network. Also the amount of data stored there is huge and is constantly changing. Even with the advances in computing power, it is still impossible for me to find the data without freezing the system and there is no way I could do that."

"So that's why Gabriella couldn't find the program. She was looking in the wrong places for it."

"That's right. That was the first layer of protection. The second layer of protection were all the warnings that you got, the warnings that forced you to write the data to an M-Stick, and then the erasure warning." She paused and looked straight at him. "None of those warnings are completely true. The program and that data that it contained still exist on the storage mediums used for DLM. It does erase that data from the Local Network Storage."

"Ah, verbal semantics. Gotta love 'em."

"Is that sarcasm I detect?" Nicole asked archly.

Ryan flushed. "A little, I guess. I mean, I know that I should be glad the data's not gone, and I am. But I'm also a little ticked about being tricked like that."

"Oh, then you'll love this. The data on the M-Stick? Garbage. It looks good and it would take a brilliant researcher days to determine that it's worthless. As much as I dislike her, I do have to admit that Gabriella is brilliant. Sick and twisted, but brilliant. We also have to consider that they have a head start. After all, they've been working on this for the last forty years. So the odds are that if they don't already know the data is worthless, it won't take them much longer. Regardless of all the trickery, you really did need to get the data. Now we can sit down and proceed with the next step."

"Which is what?" he blurted, astonished by her revelation.

"Getting the real formula, of course."

"But if it's not on the M-Stick, then where is it? Is it still on Delphi's Network? If so, that's going to take a little doing. If it wasn't for my role as VP of Security, there's no way that I would have been able to penetrate the lab."

"Easy Tex, don't get your knickers in a twist. To answer your question, I don't know where the formula is, you do."

Ryan just stared at her, stunned. "I do?" he echoed in surprise after a moment and she nodded.

"At least I hope you do," she amended, suddenly anxious. "Did anything happen after you approved the erasure of the data to the M-Stick?"

"Not really," he answered in confusion as he tried to recall the events of last night. Although it was only about eight hours ago, it seemed longer than that.

"Nothing, not even a message?" Nicole pressed nervously and Ryan frowned.

"There was a message," he admitted, "but it sounded like nonsense to me."

"Do you remember it?" she asked eagerly, her relief obvious, and he nodded.

"Sure. 'Two suns, together in harmony, will lead to the dawn of a new day,'" he recited and it was Nicole's turn to frown as she sat back.

"Two suns, two suns," she muttered to herself and Ryan nodded.

"See, it sounds like nonsense," he started to say and then stopped at the look on Nicole's face.

"Oh Justin," she murmured, "you've been dead for forty years, but you still keep pushing me." Ryan stared at her in confusion, which changed quickly to shock as she began to cry. In seconds, he was kneeling at her side, with his arms wrapped around her. He didn't know what had upset her so much, but he desperately wanted to comfort her. He didn't know what to say, but at least he could hold her and let her know she wasn't alone. After a moment, she sat back and wiped her eyes.

"I'm sorry about that," she said, "it just caught me off guard. Although I think about him every day, it's more of a background thought. Being reminded like this threw me for a loop."

"Who, Justin?" Ryan asked.

Nicole shook her head.

"No. My son, Michael."

Ryan stared at her, stunned yet again. He couldn't recall a time when he had been more confused, or had suffered more mental shocks in such a short time. He'd had basic bios on all the Senior VPs at Delphi before he even started there, and he used his position as Senior VP of Security to add to them. As well he had done a little basic research on Nicole once he realized that he was in love with her. None of the material or background information he had gathered had even hinted at a son. As far as he knew, she'd never even married.

Nicole interpreted his confusion correctly and she smiled gently at him. "What a shocker, eh? I'll bet you're having a hard time picturing me as a mommy. You can rest easy on that score, since I wasn't much of one. It's the only part of my life that I've ever regretted."

Ryan leaned over and gently hugged her again, and then sat beside her on the love seat, holding her hand.

"Tell me about it," he said softly and she smiled at him gratefully.

"It happened a long, long, time ago, when I was just starting my career. At that time no one knew or even guessed about the impact of shutting off the menstrual cycles. If they had, I would have handled it a lot differently. As it was, Michael's father and I broke up, badly, a few months before I found out I was pregnant. I was in shock after the breakup, so I didn't pay much attention to my cycles. I didn't realize I was pregnant until it was too late to do anything about it. I'm not sure that I would have changed anything anyway, but I didn't even have the choice. In a panic, I turned to my older sister. She had been married for almost seven years. They had already had one child and had been trying, unsuccessfully, to have another. I asked her if she would be willing to 'adopt' Michael and raise him as her own. There were some misgivings on everyone's part at first, but it really was the perfect solution. They would get the second child they so desperately wanted and I would be able to keep my career and still be able to see Michael whenever I wanted. I would also know that he would be raised by someone who would love him and take care of him the way I would if I was doing it.

"Once we decided, we had to figure out how to pull it off. Fortunately, there were no medical records of my pregnancy anywhere. The size of my belly and a pregnancy test meant that I didn't need to get a doctor to confirm that I was pregnant. So my sister Alexis and I both went into seclusion for a while. We were the same blood type so we didn't have to worry about compatibility or any of those kinds of issues. I took some time off work, for 'stress management,' and Alexis' husband, Mark, took midwife training. I had the baby in their home. They filed for a birth certificate for Michael in their name and shortly afterwards I went back to work, but as an aunt rather than a mother. A few years later, Alexis and Mark found out that Alexis had ovarian cancer and that it had spread. It amazed her OB that she'd been able to have Michael, but of course she hadn't. She had her ovaries removed as well as having a hysterectomy, and between those two radical procedures and some advances in cancer treatment, she was able to survive, cancer free.

"As a result, she never took Menssation® but I did, almost religiously. I didn't want to take any risks. It was years later when the impact of it finally became known and by that time it was too late to do anything about it. I watched as I lost my family bit by bit. Our parents were the first to go, but Alexis wasn't far behind them. Mark survived her by a few decades but he never remarried. Finally, it was just Michael left. His older brother, Robert, had died a few years earlier. I willingly put my career on hold to take care of them, but it didn't even come close to relieving my sense of guilt. I also debated viciously with myself about whether to tell Michael the truth. I didn't want him to die not knowing who his real mother was, but I also didn't want to risk losing what little time I had left with him.

"It was after Robert died when the stark reality of it hit me and that was when I told him." She smiled sadly. "His reaction was exactly like I had feared. He felt betrayed by me, felt like he'd been living a lie his whole life. I told him that I had wanted to tell him earlier, but that it just wasn't fair to Alexis or Mark. He shouted and accused me of abandoning him, and I tried to explain myself. I didn't try that hard since I agreed with everything he said.

"We spent a few uncomfortable years apart, and as much as I wanted to regret my decision, I couldn't. I knew that it was the right decision and if I could have changed anything, it would have been to tell him sooner. My only fear was that my son would die with anger in his heart. I didn't care about me, I knew that I deserved that and more, but I didn't want him to die angry and alone. As it turned out, he was smarter than I gave him credit for, and we reconciled a few years before he died."

She paused to wipe at her eyes again and Ryan smiled at her and gave her hand a gentle squeeze as she continued.

"After Michael passed away, I ended up with a lot of money, the result of being the only surviving family member. In addition, I inherited a plot of land that had been in Mark's family for years. It wasn't much to look at, but it had meant a lot to him, since his entire family was buried there. It was also where Alexis, Mark, Robert and of course Michael, were buried. There's even a headstone for Justin there. Oh, I know that he's not buried there, but it helps to keep his memory alive. I'm not sure if I would have done it myself, but as it turns out, I didn't have to. Justin had arranged for it and so every year on Michael and Justin's birthdays, I make a trip out there to see them. Apart from that I don't go there much. I have a service that is responsible for security and maintenance, so there's no real need to me to go more often than that."

Nicole finished and looked up at him. "So now you know everything about me. Most of my life is a matter of public record. This, though, is the one piece that I've managed to keep to myself."

Ryan shook his head slowly and exhaled. "Wow, I can't even imagine going through something like that."

"It's tough," she admitted, "more than I thought it would be. Even now it still gets to me, but at least I'm able to deal with it. For a long time after Michael's death I focused solely on my career. It was a bitter irony that the one thing that had mattered so much to me at the beginning, now meant so little. But I had nothing else to fall back on and so I buried myself in my work. Justin was the first man I allowed myself to love after Michael's death. In fact, given the poor relationship that I had with Michael's father, you could almost say Justin was the first man I had ever really loved. He was also the only other person who I shared this part of my life with."

Even though he was focused on Nicole and the incredibly painful life story she had shared with him, a part of him hung onto the last few sentences.

He had been open about the way he felt for her, but she hadn't done the same for him. He didn't know if it was because she was focused on achieving Justin's dream, or whether she didn't love him and didn't want to hurt him. But, the information she had just shared with him, she had only ever shared with Justin. Given that she had also loved Justin, he took it as a hopeful sign that she could possibly love him.

Granted, it was a little thing, but it was the first sign that it was even possible, and he latched onto it gratefully.

Chapter Sixteen

"So, what does all this have to do with the formula?" Ryan asked gently.

Nicole looked at him oddly before responding. She detected some change in his manner, something subtle but real, triggered by whatever she had just said. She frowned mentally and then let it go, at least for now. "Well the piece you're missing is how Justin viewed you."

Ryan nodded to show that he understood from the emphasis she placed on 'you' that she meant all the men who had received the formula.

"You see," she continued, "he had taken the formula himself first, so in a sense this was something that all of you shared. He saw you as his hope for the future."

"His sons," Ryan exclaimed and Nicole nodded. "But he said 'two suns'. Doesn't that mean that he needs two of us?"

"I don't think so," she replied slowly. "Obviously he didn't discuss this with me, but he did tell me that this message would lead us to the formula and that I needed to be there. Given that, I think that he means my son and his son."

"But what does the working together in harmony mean?"

"I think that he means that we need to work together. Justin was adamant about the union of male and female. He felt it was critical to maintain a balance between men and women, and felt that any disruptions of that balance would be corrected, one way or another. Despite his science background, he had a strange belief in fate or destiny. He always argued that discovering this formula and bringing balance back into the world was the reason he'd been born. He also felt that, if for whatever reason he was unsuccessful, nature would correct the balance in its own way. In fact, that was the only thing that he ever admitted frightened him. Even when we discussed the very real possibility of his death by murder, it didn't frighten him."

She paused for a moment, obviously lost in memory, and then continued. "Anyway, my guess is that if we, you and I, female and male, can't work together to solve this riddle, then we don't deserve to find the formula."

"And if we do, then that will lead do the dawn of a new day, a restoration of balance."

"Exactly. At least I think so." Nicole frowned as she considered other alternatives.

"Well, given that there's only one place that involves Michael, it sounds like we need to take a trip."

"Yeah," agreed Nicole unhappily and Ryan cocked his head at her.

"What is it?" he asked, "you don't sound very happy. Is it the prospect of visiting Michael's gravesite?"

Nicole felt warmed by his concern, but she shook her head. "Not really, although that's part of it. I'll admit that I don't like to be reminded of it, and I'm a little ticked at Justin for bringing Michael into this, but all that's pretty minor."

"Then what is it?"

"Apart from the safe house, that's the only piece of land registered in my name. There's a real possibility that Gabriella has it staked out, just in case."

"Good point. I guess it will make it a little hard to try to solve a riddle in the middle of a fight." He grimaced as he considered it.

"Let's not assume the worse," she said. "I've avoided accessing the Net, even through the aircar, so first I should find out what's going on in the rest of the world. I'll do a few data searches, see what I can find. If it looks clean, then we'll go in."

"Do you think that we should split up, maybe have one of us do a brief reconnaissance?"

Nicole grinned. "By one of us, I assume you mean you," she said and he blushed.

"Well," he protested, "I have trained for exactly that."

"Yes, and Gabriella knows that. Besides, I don't think that it matters which of us goes in, so it might was well be both of us."

Ryan looked at her curiously. "I'd love to hear your logic on this," he said and she knew that he wasn't challenging her. He was just trying to see where she was going with it.

"From what we've determined, it's going to take both of us to solve this riddle," she pointed out. "That rules out the divide and conquer approach."

"True," he admitted, "but the other person could always stage a rescue."

"Only if they knew where the other one was," Nicole said as she arched an eyebrow and Ryan's brow furled in thought.

"Hmm, good point. I take it that you haven't been successful at gathering intelligence about Stephanie and Gabriella."

"No, and believe me, I've tried. But Stephanie has a dozen properties she owns outright in this state alone, and who knows how many more she has hidden or can access if needed."

"Damn."

"And my second point is, that if it is a trap, we have a better chance of getting out of it together than we do alone."

Ryan grinned at her. "That's right, we do make a good team, don't we?"

and she grinned back at him, warmed by his praise.

"Okay then," he said, "you do your data searches and I'll get the aircar ready." He paused for a moment and she looked at him.

"What?"

"Well, I was just thinking of someone else who we could ask for help." He squirmed uncomfortably and Nicole sighed.

"Spit it out."

"Olivia," he said simply and Nicole's brow furrowed in puzzlement.

"I don't get it, how could Olivia help us? Apart from providing us with manpower, and I doubt she'd be all that happy about getting Delphi more involved in this than it is already. And that's if she wants to help us, which I doubt given how upset she was the last time we saw her."

Ryan grinned at her use of the term manpower. Years of political correctness and years of women dominating the workforce hadn't been able to remove the term from common use.

"True," he admitted readily, "but I wasn't thinking about manpower. I've probably got a good couple of dozen friends I could call on if needed, but if it comes down to that, then we're really in trouble. No, I was thinking of something a little more subtle, like using Olivia to help us with some misdirection."

The puzzled look cleared and Nicole grinned. "Of course. Gabriella probably has dozens of people planted at Delphi who feed her information. If we can come up with a plausible reason to make her believe that we can still access the data, she'll have no choice but to shift her resources around. We can take advantage of that brief window of opportunity to visit the cemetery and solve Justin's riddle."

Ryan nodded. "I figure that Olivia is our best bet. Now that she knows the truth, I'm willing to bet that she'll do everything she can to support us, within reason."

"But what about the neural grenade? It destroyed her short-term memory. She won't remember anything."

"Not true. The high-density scanners recorded the entire confrontation. The first thing that Olivia will do once she regains consciousness is to review those records. If she does, it will remap her memory and she'll be able to remember everything."

Nicole blinked in surprise. "I didn't know that."

Ryan's smile broadened. "Not many people do. There's a long technical explanation for it, but the long and short of it is that it isn't memories that are wiped by the neural grenade, but the connections to them. By viewing the scene, you can reestablish those connections. If you don't reestablish the connections within twenty-four hours, the memories are lost for good, but given what's going on and who she is, it would surprise me if she hasn't seen the records already."

"Very interesting. I'll do my data searches and you prep the aircar. I should know by then if we need to call Olivia, okay?"

"Okay," he echoed.

"All right then, let's get to it." Impulsively, she leaned over and kissed him on the lips. She pulled back in surprise, dismayed by her impulse, and hurried from the room.

Ryan watched in surprise as Nicole hurried away and then he grinned. Obviously, there was something going on between them, and he felt a sudden rush of relief to know that he wasn't the only one struggling to define their relationship.

He headed out towards the aircar, but there was nothing to check there. He had already done all that he could earlier, but he forced himself to spend a few moments going over everything yet again. It was possible that he had missed something minor earlier, and long experience told him that little things had a way of becoming big things. As he suspected, he had indeed covered all the bases, but it was good to have the confirmation. It was like that adage about woodworking—measure twice, cut once.

He had just clambered out of the aircar and started back towards the house when he heard Nicole calling him. He didn't detect any panic in her voice, but he braced himself just in case.

He edged cautiously around the corner into the living room and then stopped dead. Whoever had owned the house before Nicole had invested in a full wall console. Even though it was split into half a dozen different news feeds, each of them was large enough for Ryan to understand what he was seeing. Of course the serious looks on the commentators, the shots of huge crowds of men surging against hastily erected riot barricades, left little room for any errors of interpretation. The frequent appearance of the word 'riot' in the closed captioning was almost an afterthought.

"Good Lord." The words slipped out without any conscious choice on his part. He had known from talking to the commander at Edwards that the news was public, but he hadn't expected such a quick reaction.

"Those feeds are from the six largest cities across Noram. I've also checked the news for dozens of other cities and it's all the same."

"What about the police and the military? Has there been any violence there yet?" Ryan asked with a sick feeling in his gut, but Nicole shook her head.

"Nothing significant. A few isolated incidents here and there, but no major outbreaks."

"Thank God for small favors," he said and Nicole quirked her lips.

"You might just want to take that back," she said and Ryan looked at her quizzically. "All the major newsnets alternate between coverage of the riots and commentary and discussion of this." She pulled up a document on one of the sextants of the screen. "This is the original document that I found posted on Delphi's website."

Ryan quickly read through the press release and then whistled. "Wow, that's a quick reaction. Someone must have woken her up early for Delphi to have gotten that posted so quickly."

"You're not surprised by the position she's taken?"

"Surprised, no, gratified, yes." Nicole gestured for him to explain. "I never doubted that Olivia is a good person who always tries to do the right thing. That's why she has done so well at Delphi and why Delphi's done as well as it has. Delphi already had a pretty good reputation in the male community, a reputation that only got better when she hired me for such a senior position. I will admit that her ignorance on the subject concerned me, but between you, Brooke, and I, we obviously convinced her of the seriousness of the situation in the last few weeks." He paused and looked at her. "Why, were you surprised?"

Nicole frowned for a moment. "No, I guess my reaction is the same as yours. I'm not surprised by her decision, but I will admit that if you'd asked me, I would have honestly said that it could have gone either way."

"True," Ryan admitted, "and I think we have Gabriella to thank for that. If she hadn't shot her big mouth off and then tried to cover it up, it might have gone differently."

Nicole laughed. "I'd never thought that I'd be thanking Gabriella for anything. I guess it also answers the question of whether Olivia will support us."

Ryan started to reply, but just then the screen showing the press release flickered and refreshed. Ryan looked at it and felt a familiar eagerness as his mind started to race.

"Olivia's agreed to be interviewed live in about an hour," he replied in response to Nicole's inquiring look. "I think that this might be the opportunity we've been looking for."

"You mean get Olivia to drop false hints to get Gabriella off our trail?"

"That's one possibility. I was thinking of something a little more devious than that. I'm sure that Olivia will support us in whatever we do, but there's no reason for us to lay all our cards on the table just yet."

"So far I agree with you," Nicole prompted him and Ryan flashed her a big grin.

"Then again, there's no reason not to."

Nicole frowned in puzzlement and then she smiled suddenly as she got what he was driving at.

"Oh, that's not very nice," she said appreciatively. "I can't think of anyone who deserves it more."

* * *

Olivia frowned down at the outfit Brooke had picked out for her. It had been a relief to get out of the revealing dress she had worn on her date. She had also hoped that she was finally going to like one of the outfits Brooke picked out for her. After all, she was about to do a national press conference, perhaps the most important press conference in Delphi's history. Certainly it was the most important press conference Olivia would ever do. So perhaps she could be excused for thinking that for once she would be able to wear something respectable, like a pantsuit for Heaven's sake. Instead, she was in yet another dress. She had to admit that this one wasn't as bad as the others that Brooke had pressed her into in the past, but still, what she wouldn't give for a decent pantsuit.

"Stop grumbling," Brooke chided.

Olivia smiled despite herself. "What?" she protested. "I didn't say anything."

"You didn't have to," Brooke replied as she shot Olivia a look that was both a stern rebuke as well as a last minute appraisal. "Besides, nobody's making you wear anything you don't want to."

"Well, I'm not likely to override my two experts. I agreed with the arguments you and Mia presented, but that doesn't mean I have to like them."

"True, but it would make it easier if you would. You need to feel comfortable in it. We have to convince the male community you are serious about what you said in the press release. That means you have to dress like a woman, and not just that, but a woman who knows she's a woman. At the same time, you can't come across too sexy, or the men will be too busy ogling you to listen to what you're saying, and the women will dismiss you as promiscuous. You need a dress that says you are strong and successful and confident and above all a woman."

Olivia blinked and looked down at herself again. That seemed like an awful lot for one little dress to convey, especially this one. It was a simple light beige one-piece, completely unadorned except for slight ruffles at the top and bottom. The bottom ended slightly below her knees and the ruffles swished gently as she moved. She had to admit that it had a subtle elegance to it, especially when combined with her long tan legs. She turned and looked in the mirror again. There was a small amount of cleavage showing, enough to leave no doubt that she was a woman. The ruffles came down from her shoulders and met in a V in the middle of her cleavage. The ruffles continued down below her left breast, disappearing into the fabric of the dress, muting the impact of the V. Her arms were bare below her shoulders and her loose hair completed the picture.

"You know, I had thought that this would be better if you were blonde, like most Californians, but it actually works for what we're trying to accomplish."

Olivia stuck out her tongue. "You're one to talk. We can't all dye our hair whatever color suits us. Besides, my natural color is brown and not black."

"True, but most of the time it looks black. I'd forgotten how brown it really is and this dress brings it out beautifully."

Olivia looked at herself in the mirror again and spotted Mia approaching them. Given the crisis, Olivia hadn't wanted to leave Security Central and so she was getting dressed in the changing room. It was a far cry from how she normally prepared for press conferences that she'd seen but it was fitting to the circumstances.

Mia stopped in front of her. "I got a message from Ryan," she said. "It was just a plain text message, but he said that he's going to be calling in a few minutes and wants to talk to you."

Olivia raised her eyebrows and looked over at Brooke. His timing was impeccable. Hopefully, he and Nicole would be able to shed a little light on the status of the formula, information they could use in the impending press conference.

"Great, is there a secure office we can use?"

Mia hesitated and Olivia looked at her inquiringly. "What is it?"

"He didn't say so, but I got the impression that he wanted you to take the call in the control room."

Olivia shook her head. "That doesn't seem very secure."

Mia looked uncomfortable. "No, it doesn't, but like I said, that's the impression I got."

Olivia looked at her carefully. "There's more that you want to tell me, isn't there?"

Mia nodded, her discomfort clearly evident. "I don't have any proof, but I suspect that at least one of the console operators up in the control room may be sympathetic to Gabriella's position."

"There's a difference between sympathetic to her position and willing to support it and her. That's what you're alluding to, isn't it?"

Mia nodded. "I can't say for sure and if I share my suspicions with anyone, it becomes a self-fulfilling prediction because then none of the other personnel will trust the woman and it may even get violent."

"Is Ryan aware of this guard's views?"

"Yes, but I doubt that he'll know that she's on duty. All the schedules are totally useless and we're kind of winging it right now."

"I see," Olivia said quietly as she pondered for a moment. "I agree with you that Ryan probably doesn't know that this person is on duty, but I think that he's hoping that her or someone like her is."

Mia looked puzzled for a moment and then shook her head angrily.

"I can't believe that I didn't think of that."

"Easy, you can't do everything. We're all in this together and we'll all get through it together. If you want to, look at the corollary of it."

"The what?"

"It's a fancy word that means consequence or result," Brooke piped up helpfully. "If you continue to hang out with us, you'll find that your vocabulary will grow exponentially, exposed to this word-loving fiend. The only way to shut her up is to satisfy her other addiction, coffee."

"Enough," Olivia said good-naturedly. "What I mean is that if you didn't see it, odds are that no one else will. The trouble will be trying to read between the lines, to figure out what Ryan and Nicole really want us to do."

"I wouldn't worry about it," Brooke said breezily, "I'm sure they've already considered all these angles."

"Oh, really?" Olivia replied with amusement. "And what makes you so sure about that?"

"Just my HR instincts. That and I know how they operate—Ryan to a lesser extent than Nicole." Olivia gestured for Brooke to continue. "It's simple. Neither of them are the kind to leave anything to chance, especially something like this."

"That's true," Mia replied as she nodded in agreement. "That's something that I've always admired about Ryan, his ability to define and control complex situations."

"All right, I'm convinced. I won't try to read more into what he is saying. But just in case I want you," Olivia looked at Brooke, "to be there with me. The two of us are a common enough sight that it shouldn't raise any suspicions, and I'd like to have your input if needed."

"The four musketeers, reunited, if only virtually."

Olivia grinned despite the tension she was feeling. It was true, the four of them had proved to be an effective team.

"As for you Mia, as much as I would like you with us, Ryan won't expect you to be there, and I'd rather have you watching our backs."

"Got it." Mia nodded firmly and Olivia smiled again as she sensed the commander's relief. Despite all Mia's confidence, when it came to areas outside her scope of expertise, she knew she wasn't as competent and it showed.

Olivia and Brooke headed towards the control room just in time to take Ryan's call. The huge holo tank cleared and then Ryan appeared. Olivia could see from the background details that he was calling from his aircar.

"Well Mr. Peters, you do have a knack for stirring things up," she stated and he grinned at her.

"Guilty as charged," he admitted ruefully. "It's certainly not what I had in mind when I went to recover the data last night, but it's funny how life doesn't always go the way you want it to."

"Isn't it just," Olivia replied softly and he looked at her sadly.

"I'm really sorry about everything. I never would have gotten involved with you if I had known that it was going to turn out this way."

"When? Six months ago or forty years ago?" she teased him. "Seriously, I'm glad you did. I think we've both been stuck in the past for the last forty years, and even though it didn't work out the way we wanted it to, we can both finally get on with our lives." He nodded in understanding and it surprised Olivia to realize just how true it was. Beside her, she felt Brooke take her hand and squeeze it gently.

"Anyway, I'm fairly sure that's not why you called," she remarked dryly and he laughed.

"No, it's not. I read the press release on Delphi's web site and I think that it's perfect. It makes me proud to know you and to work for Delphi." Olivia acknowledged the compliments with a nod and he continued.

"I also saw that you were planning on doing a press release and I just wanted to caution you on how much to reveal." He hesitated and looked embarrassed. "From what I've been able to garner from all the coverage, it looks like Gabriella's parting shot about me destroying the data was successful. Depending on the coverage, I'm either a huge hero, or the worst villain in history, or both."

Olivia laughed despite her tension. She knew that he was leading up to something and she had to admire the indirect way he was going about it.

"I believe I did hear something about it, but knowing you as I do, I immediately discounted it."

"Well, it is true, after a fashion. It wasn't malicious or anything but it was part of the security that Justin, the inventor of the formula, put in place."

"So the data's gone?" Olivia asked incredulously and Ryan immediately shook his head.

"Yes and no. I'm fortunate enough to have Delphi's resident computer expert with me, and she thinks that we might be able to find an old archival copy at one of Delphi's off-site backup storage facilities. As you know, all of Delphi's data is stored locally, but there are also several secondary data storage locations off-site for redundancy."

"So that's where you're headed now," Olivia mused and he nodded.

"That's right. I'm glad you are on our side. Mind you, there are usually guards at those sites, but that isn't currently the case."

Olivia's eyes widened as she recalled the steps that Mia and Anita had taken to consolidate all of Delphi's staff on-site. "That's right," she agreed slowly. "In terms of access, that isn't an issue since only you or Nicole can access the site but it does mean that we are…"

Olivia frowned as his holo image disappeared and she glanced around the control room.

"What happened?" she asked. "Can you get him back?"

The security personnel were scrambling with their consoles and then suddenly one of them froze and looked up in horror.

"What is it?" Olivia asked and the woman just looked at her and then shook her head in disbelief. Olivia was about to ask again when she spoke in a wooden tone.

"I just picked up an air force signal about an aircar shot down by a surface-to-air missile. The coordinates put it about fifty miles from here and according to the vector data, it looks like the aircar was traveling towards San Bernardino."

Olivia felt a chill as she responded to the unspoken question.

"One of our off-site data storage facilities is just outside San Bernardino." She tried to shake it off, hoping against hope that this was the trick that he had been planning to play on Gabriella, but she somehow knew in her heart that it wasn't. She looked over at Brooke, and she knew that her own face must look as pale and stunned as Brooke's.

Just then Mia burst in with a grim look on her face and rushed over to one of the console operators, a pair of armed guards following her. There was a brief scuffle and then the two guards were dragging away the console operator, who was unconscious and had a bloody gash across her forehead. Mia turned to face her and Olivia recoiled despite herself. She had never seen such a mix of anger and sorrow together in the same expression. A moment later she understood why Mia looked that way.

"I accessed the logs of each console. She had used her console to run a trace on the signal and then she broadcast the coordinates to someone outside Delphi. I caught her just in time—another minute and she would have managed to erase the log showing what she had done."

Olivia felt numb. So it was true. Even her anger at what the console operator had done couldn't penetrate what she was feeling. Ryan was gone. He had been such a big part of her life for so long, even when he wasn't there. After she had learned that Ryan was actually her Ryan from so long ago, she had realized just how much he had influenced the direction her life had taken. She had never planned to become the CEO of Delphi, but after she broke off with Ryan forty years ago, she had thrown herself into her work. It had become her life, and it took his reappearance for her to let go of the fear that had been holding her back. And now he was gone.

Mia gently guided Olivia and Brooke into Ryan's old office and Olivia felt a fresh stab of pain as she realized where they were. She pushed it away numbly, in a haze. Everything had a bizarre, surreal quality to it.

"Are you okay," Brooke asked her and Olivia shook her head, not in negation but in puzzlement.

"I don't know," she replied slowly.

"The press conference starts in ten minutes. Should I cancel it?"

Olivia grabbed at the question desperately. The one advantage to having spent the last forty years focused on work to the detriment of her personal life was that it was easy to fall back into that pattern if needed. And she really needed it now. She couldn't afford any distractions. There was just too much going on, and there was no way that she was going to drop the ball now and let Gabriella win. She looked at Brooke and shook her head firmly.

"No, we're not going to cancel the press conference. That would just play into Gabriella's hands and it would likely do more damage than good."

"What are you going to say? Do we risk breaking the news about Ryan and Nicole?"

"I think we have to. Our credibility is all that we have going for us. If we look like we're trying to hide anything, no matter how small, it will blow up in our face and do more damage than good. Certainly, Gabriella won't be expecting it."

Brooke laughed weakly. "I guess that's as good an indicator of what we should be doing as anything. But what about the formula? We still don't have it and nor do we have any idea about how to get it."

"Part of that comes from the press conference. I'm going to tell them the truth, let them know what Ryan and Nicole were trying to do."

"Are you crazy?" Brooke blurted out. "You'll start a riot."

Mia nodded. "Brooke's right. Those data storage facilities will become the spark points that will setup off a conflict that will spread across the state and then throughout Noram."

"We have to do something," Olivia snapped in frustration. "We can't just leave them completely unsecured. We have to assume that Gabriella knows about them. She doesn't even have to get access to them, all she has to do is destroy them and it's game over."

Mia frowned thoughtfully. "I think I've got a solution for that. We already know that Ryan's got contacts at Edwards and we know they're willing to help. After all, they've done it once already by all accounts."

Olivia's eyes lit up. "That's a great idea. You see what you can do about working that end of it, while I'll hold the press conference as scheduled and let everyone know what happened to Ryan and Nicole. I will tell them that we have a lead on copies of the formula and that we're arranging to secure it. Once we've secured it, we'll do whatever's necessary to get it into production." Olivia frowned and cocked her head to look at Brooke, who had a strange expression on her face. "What?"

"Well," Brooke began hesitantly, "I was just wondering if this is part of what Ryan and Nicole were hoping to do."

Olivia shook her head sadly. "I wish it was. There's a part of me that's thinking the same thing, wishing and hoping that it is all a ruse. But I know that's not true. Whatever Ryan hoped to accomplish, destroying his aircar could not have been part of it. I still think that he was going to provide some information that would misdirect Gabriella's efforts to get her hands on them. I don't think that he ever imagined that she would be so desperate as to blow up his aircar." She paused and her mouth twisted into a bitter grimace. "Obviously we've got Gabriella running scared if she's willing to go to that extreme. I just wish we had realized it in time."

She looked up at Brooke, fighting back tears, and she gave an angry shake of her head.

"Enough. We've got work to do. There'll be time enough once we finally settled this for all of us to mourn them properly. For now we've got to do what we can to salvage everything that they've worked the last forty years for. That's what they would want and that's what we're going to do!"

Chapter Seventeen

"Holy shit!" Ryan hissed in pain.

His body folded itself into the fetal position as the neural feedback from the explosion wracked his internal systems. He realized he was lying on the ground and he staggered to his feet. His eyes watered, his head pounded and his sense of balance was off. He felt Nicole reach out to give him a hand, but he couldn't open his eyes to see her, and likely couldn't focus enough to do that even if he could see. Although his eyes were closed, sparks of light danced in his vision, each one sending pain stabbing directly into his brain. He knew it was the result of his linkage to the aircar when it was blown out of the sky, but that didn't make it any easier to bear.

After a few minutes, his internal systems finally stabilized and his vision cleared. He still had a pounding headache, but that was the only lasting side effect. Well, that and the decline in his reserves. He estimated the last few minutes had consumed almost half of his reserves, between nanites destroyed by the feedback, and the frantic efforts of the remaining nanites to compensate for their loss and protect him from any damage. If it weren't for his enhancements, the neural feedback from the explosion would have fried his brain.

He opened his eyes to find Nicole looking at him with a mixture of worry and frustration. He could tell she was worried about him, but was doing her best to keep herself under control. She obviously had no idea what had just happened. Relief spread across her face and she threw her arms around him.

"Thank God you're all right. You really scared me."

Ryan blinked in surprise. This was the first time that they had embraced. Apart from their sparring sessions, Nicole had never even touched him casually. He had found it a little odd, but he watched her carefully and it wasn't just him, she was the same with everyone. He finally decided she was one of those people who just weren't into casual contact. That was why he was so surprised by the hug. His own arms went out in an automatic response and he closed his eyes again as he savored the experience. Finally, he felt her pull away and reluctantly he let go of her.

"I hope I don't have to go through that again," Ryan said, "but if I'll get another hug out of it, I will."

She scowled at him for a moment and then to his surprise she not only gave him another hug but a passionate kiss as well.

"Does this mean what I think it means?" he asked cautiously and she laughed at him.

"Men, you are all the same. You have this need to define what everything means. Just accept it for what it is and don't read too much into it."

Ryan mentally translated the unspoken, but clearly conveyed message—don't push it—and he nodded. They still had to figure out how to find the formula and that had to be the focus.

"So what happened?"

"Gabriella shot down the aircar with a SAM." He saw her eyebrows raise inquisitively and he clarified. "Sorry, Surface-to-Air Missile. Given how deep my linkage was, the neural feedback overwhelmed me for a while."

Nicole shivered and whistled softly. "Good thing we decided to use it as a decoy."

Ryan nodded fervently. "Yeah, although having it blown up is not exactly what we had in mind." The original plan was for them to let everyone think that they were going to one of Delphi's off-site data storage facilities. They had expected that someone at Delphi would track the aircar, extrapolate which data storage facility they were going to and let Gabriella know. The hope was that she would redeploy the guards she had assigned to Nicole's private cemetery. They had used the aircar to land them as close as they dared to the cemetery. Once they had offloaded a few supplies and a high-powered semi-portable scanner, Ryan had linked into the aircar and sent it on its way.

Nicole nodded and then smiled. "I think that Gabriella's finally outsmarted herself. Everyone has to assume we died in the aircar explosion. Hopefully, she'll do the same and pull out the guards currently at the cemetery."

Ryan nodded cautiously as he thought it through. "You're right, it should work. The only possible snag is the lack of any biological matter in the crash debris. It won't take the investigators long to figure that out."

"True, but since the car was shot with a missile, the military will handle the investigation. I doubt they'll be willing to share the data with Gabriella. I couldn't say the same about the police, but I think that we've seen firsthand there is no love lost between the two groups."

Ryan snorted. "That's for sure. The police have always resented that they don't have jurisdictional rights for any active member of the military." He paused and then shrugged. "Even if she does find out, we should still have a window of opportunity. Either way, it's likely to be our best chance. How about breaking open a bottle of wine while I check the scanner?"

Nicole nodded and absently squeezed his shoulder as she headed over to the supplies they had kept with them.

Ryan got up and moved towards the scanner, distracted by that simple touch and its implications. He forced himself to concentrate as he reviewed the display, although he had already done most of the work earlier. Given that Nicole hadn't used anything like it before, he had set up a couple of preprogrammed routines before he linked into the aircar. This scanner was a low-density scanner and it couldn't provide the breathtaking resolution the new high-density scanners could. It compensated for that by having a much greater range. The range of the high-density scanners was roughly a third of a square mile, which would have been useless for Ryan and Nicole, as they were about half a mile away from the cemetery. That was as close as they had dared to get and Ryan would have preferred to be a little further away. Although the low-density scanners had a greater range compared to the newer models, it wasn't that large—only slightly less than a mile. They had carefully scouted out possible hiding places, and it was either this spot or one right at the edge of the effective range. Ryan had reluctantly picked this spot over the further one. He didn't want to push the limits of the scanner too much.

Once they had it up and running, it had confirmed their suspicions. There were an even dozen guards scattered across the property. It would have been easy enough for him and Nicole to handle that number themselves, but all it took was one call for backup. They had debated using the aircar to jam any outgoing transmissions, but had decided that doing so would effectively let any backup teams know they were there.

Ryan watched the scanner carefully. So far there weren't any signs of movement, but it was too early for that. He had already known there would be no change, since he had programmed the scanner to alert them of any significant changes, including a proximity alert, but it was human nature to want to confirm that. A moment later Nicole touched his arm gently and handed him a glass of wine.

"Thanks."

"Any change?"

"Nothing yet, but it's still early. I'm guessing it will be at least a couple of hours before we see anything."

"Looks like we've got a lot of time to kill, eh? Any ideas?" she asked coyly.

Normally Ryan liked to tease her about the Canadian 'eh' that she still added to the end of her sentences, but he was floored by what she was implying. He shook his head mentally, convinced he must be misreading her, but then he noticed that she was toying with one of the buttons on her blouse.

He watched, suddenly dry mouthed, as she slowly unbuttoned her blouse. He had seen her naked dozens of times in the sauna after a workout, but this was different. The way that she was doing it, combined with a glimpse of her bra and the smooth unblemished skin of her stomach, suddenly gave him a painful erection. Despite the raging intensity of his emotions, he couldn't move. He was afraid to move, scared he'd break the spell. Nicole sensed this in that strange intuitive way women did and she smiled gently at him as she finished unbuttoning her blouse, revealing her bra completely.

He suddenly remembered he had seen her in bra and panties just last night, but that seemed like a different life. She moved closer to him, reaching for his hands, lifting them to the bare skin just above her hips. Ryan closed his eyes momentarily and then opened them again, looking at her. He felt frozen in place, but as he made eye contact with her, he could feel himself beginning to thaw.

She smiled again and he smiled back, his eyes full of the love he felt for her as she reached out and began to undo the buttons on his shirt. He slowly moved his hands up her side, delighting in the feel of her, and then he reached around behind her and ran his fingers gently up and down the small of her back. She let out a low moan and the sound echoed inside him, places he'd never felt before, physically or emotionally. She finished unbuttoning his shirt and her hands moved back to her bra, as she unsnapped the clips that held it closed at the front. Her breasts spilled out and she moved closer to him, rubbing them gently against his chest. Her nipples were tight and his hands slid inside the waistband of her panties, gently cupping her buttocks, without him even realizing it.

For the first time in his life, Ryan wasn't consciously aware of what he was doing. He was reacting to the moment and letting it guide him. It wasn't exactly a loss of control, more like a loss of the inhibitions and self-conscious fear he usually felt. Despite how important this moment was, he had never felt more comfortable or natural in his life.

That feeling vanished as her hand dipped into his pants. His breath hissed out of him as she wrapped her hand around his erection and he grabbed her buttocks harder, pulling her into him. Their mouths met, completing the circuit, and Ryan could feel the excitement circulating between them. After a moment she extracted her hand and unzipped his pants. The sound was unnaturally loud and incredibly erotic, and he felt his control slipping away. But that was okay because she had lost her control as well. Passion swept over them as they moved in sync, more like one person than two.

Nicole rolled off Ryan and lay beside him, slick with sweat, her chest heaving. She had never felt anything more perfect in her life and she knew that she had made the right choice. She told herself she couldn't let Ryan know that she was in love with him, but her resolve had taken a big hit when she had heard him proclaim his love for her in front of Olivia. It would have been easier for him to lie to Olivia—after all, she didn't know the truth and it wasn't like he knew that Nicole was there to hear it—but that wasn't the person Ryan was. He had proudly announced his love for her despite what it cost him. Being there and hearing it made it difficult for her to stick to her resolve, but she had.

Then the aircar was shot down and Ryan had collapsed in front of her, like a puppet whose strings had just been cut. She'd barely had time to react before he started convulsing, and she knew real fear for the first time since Justin's death. Despite her dedication to fulfilling Justin's dream, she was almost about to risk it all and call for help, but then she heard him hiss in pain as he stopped convulsing and watched him curl into a fetal position. A moment later he tried to get up, staggering about drunkenly, and she had reached out to help him up. His eyes were closed and his face was screwed in pain, but he seemed like he was going to recover.

She managed to pull herself together, but her resolve had been shaken. She had wasted so much time, first with Michael and then Justin, before she lost them, and each time she told herself that it would be different the next time. Yet, here she was making the same mistake with Ryan. Her reaction to his near death experience showed her that with brutal clarity. She had been willing to risk it all to help him and that instinctive reaction brought her feelings into stark relief.

When he had opened his eyes, her sense of relief had been so overwhelming she had embraced him. She didn't know which was greater, his shock or hers. He had called her on it and she had responded automatically, as she grappled with the implications, but it was just a delaying tactic to allow her to become comfortable with the decision. When she did, she made her move and she had known all along what that move would be.

It wasn't all that surprising—Nicole had lived long enough to know how powerful the human urge to deny death was, and there was nothing more intrinsically life affirming than making love. Still, she knew that if her embrace had shocked him, this would blow his mind, and sure enough it had. It always amazed her just how much power a female could exert over a male when it came to making love. She had almost giggled at the expression on Ryan's face when she was toying with her buttons, but fortunately she hadn't. He would have had countless opportunities to pay her back in spades as she writhed helplessly beneath him, lost in passion and arousal.

"That was amazing," she said softly and Ryan propped himself up on one elbow and gazed down at her.

"I'm afraid that I have to disagree," he said seriously and she gasped in mock outrage and rolled over on top of him again, pinning his hands as she gazed at him fiercely.

"You'd better rethink that answer, Mister," she growled.

He grinned at her. "You didn't let me finish."

"Then finish. And it had better be good."

"To say that something is amazing is to imply that it is so remarkable as to elicit disbelief. When something is this perfect, there's no room for disbelief. It's so life altering that you just have to accept it for what it is."

"You make it sound like a religious experience."

Ryan raised an eyebrow quizzically. "I distinctly recall someone screaming 'Oh God' several times."

"I think that was you," she replied with a grin.

He grinned back at her. "Oh, yeah, it was. Well then, I guess it makes it a religious experience for one of us anyway."

Nicole smiled, filled with happiness at such unabashed sentiment and leaned over to kiss him.

"I love you, you know that," she found herself saying and for a moment she cursed herself for her weakness, but then the smile on his face erased any such concerns. She leaned forward to kiss him and his hands wrapped around behind her and cupped her buttocks. She could feel him growing beneath her and she felt herself becoming aroused in response. Her nipples stiffened and she let out a low moan of desire. Suddenly a soft buzz from the scanner sounded. It was like being doused with cold water, and they both groaned in unison, and then laughed as they realized just how in sync they were.

"Well, it looks like it's show time," Ryan commented unnecessarily, but Nicole didn't bother teasing him. They quickly and quietly dressed, and moved over to the scanner together. By the time they got there, the display was clear. Ryan's fingers tapped expertly on the control panel and the events of the last five minutes repeated themselves in double time. Two new icons appeared and even as unfamiliar as she was with the scanner, Nicole didn't need Ryan's murmured comment to know that they were large aircars. The icons Ryan had used to mark Gabriella's guards merged with the two new icons, and then the whole group moved quickly out of range.

She looked at Ryan questioningly and he nodded. Taking a deep breath, she turned and started heading towards the cemetery. Seconds later, Ryan caught up with her and reached out to take her hand. Smiling gratefully, she glanced over at him as he squeezed it reassuringly. A moment later the narrow trail forced him to let go, but it had already had its intended effect. Although she was nowhere near calm, her nerves were much steadier now and she knew she was ready to face whatever they were about to find.

Ryan looked around the cemetery curiously. He had never seen such a small private cemetery before and it looked more like a park than anything else. He looked over at Nicole, but it was obvious why she only came here twice a year. She seemed like she was in shock, and all the changes that had been happening in her life recently certainly didn't help.

He decided to give her a little time and quietly walked away along one of the many immaculately maintained gravel pathways. The grounds were beautiful and although the plot of land was slightly less than a hectare in size, it felt much larger. The landscaping made effective use of the natural contours of the land, combining them with a wide variety of plants and trees. The effect was peaceful and soothing.

After wandering around for about ten minutes he came around a corner and spotted Nicole again. She was standing in front of a headstone and he walked up to her and stood silently beside her. He read the inscription on the headstone and saw that it was Michael's. He looked over at Nicole and judging that she wasn't ready yet, he looked around.

One gravestone caught his eye. It was slightly apart from the others and much newer looking, and instinctively Ryan knew that this was Justin's. He walked towards it, leaving Nicole to pay her respects to Michael. They still had no idea what they were looking for, but maybe Justin's headstone would give them a clue. He had discussed this theory with Nicole, and while she didn't disagree with the need to examine it, she doubted that it would be so obvious. He knew where she was coming from—after all, she had been coming here for forty years. It was unlikely she would have been unaware of anything so obvious, but Ryan knew the human brain relied on memory when viewing familiar scenes. It was possible the answer was here, but not obvious unless you were looking for something, something that Nicole hadn't been looking for all that time.

He stepped around in front of it and as soon as he saw the symbol on the headstone he stiffened in excitement. He hadn't meant to be so obvious, but then again he hadn't expected the answer to be so obvious. His reaction pulled Nicole out of her reverie and she hurried over.

"What is it?" she asked excitedly and Ryan pointed to the headstone.

"Tell me what you see," he commanded and Nicole looked at the headstone and shrugged.

"I see a palm cross, representing Palm Sunday."

"Are you sure?"

"Of course I'm sure," she said slowly. "Look at the inscription. 'Hosanna. Blessed are they who come in his name.' It's almost a direct quote from the Bible—John chapter twelve, verse thirteen—describing Christ's arrival in Jerusalem on Palm Sunday. I know the carving doesn't look like a traditional cross but that's because it is a stylized representation of a palm cross. The loop at the top and the slightly flared arms are exaggerations showing that the cross is made from a palm frond. Why, what do you think it is?"

"An ankh."

"An ankh," Nicole echoed skeptically.

"Yes. An ankh is basically a cross with a loop at the top."

"I know what an ankh is," she replied crossly.

"Okay, but do you know some of the meanings behind an ankh? It's the Egyptian hieroglyphic symbol for life, sometimes everlasting life. It represents the unity of the male and the female, again the basis for everlasting or eternal life, and it's also a sign of fertility. They all tie back to the formula. The formula extends the male lifespan, it bridges the gender divide and unites men and women once again. There's no need to have to resort to artificial sources for male fertility. Reproduction can resume its normal course. The ankh is also symbolic of the sunrise, which ties back to the message."

Nicole frowned as she considered it. It was obvious to him, but he knew she was dealing with over forty years of seeing it in a certain way. It was going to take her a little time to adjust to it.

"But what about the inscription?" she asked weakly after a few moments.

"At first I thought that it was camouflage, but I've been thinking about it and now I'm not sure. The actual phrasing in the Bible is 'Hosanna! Blessed is he who comes in the name of the Lord.' This sounds similar, but if you look at it, there are key differences. 'Blessed are they who come in his name.' I think the 'they' refers to us and 'his name' refers to Michael. If you do those substitutions, it ties back to the message Justin left us that led us here. It all ties together and it makes sense."

Nicole shook her head, not in negation, but in halfhearted disbelief.

"I don't know. It just seems too easy. I guess I'm also just used to seeing it as a palm cross because that's how I've been thinking about it for the last forty years."

"Was Justin a religious person?"

"No and neither am I. In fact, I can remember having to look up what the inscription was and what it meant. When I learned that it was representative of Palm Sunday, I guess I just assumed the carving was a palm cross. After forty years it's hard to see anything else."

"I guess seeing it with a fresh eye, knowing that we're looking for something, made me examine it more closely."

"Yeah, I can see it now and I think you're right. But if that's the case, where's the formula?"

"Hmm, good question." Ryan looked at the headstone carefully. "Do you have any idea what this is made of?" he asked.

Nicole shook her head. "I told you, I didn't have anything to do with it. I just showed up one day and it was here. I had a security company scan it, just in case, but they were only looking for any explosives or anything else dangerous."

"Well, I think that it's high time we corrected that lack." He shrugged the backpack off his shoulders and knelt down to rummage around in it. Before they had sent the aircar off, they had pulled out a few tools and supplies they might need and he knew just what he was looking for. It was a hand scanner, the type used by security guards everywhere. It was quick and efficient and impossible to fool. Ryan pulled it out and aimed it at the headstone. It didn't take long for preliminary results to flash up on the display.

"I thought so," he said triumphantly. "Pure carbon." Nicole gaped at him.

"But that's impossible. I thought only M-Sticks were made of pure carbon."

"Not really. You only think about M-Sticks because that's what you're familiar with. The diamond form of carbon has always been used in many industrial settings and since we learned how to create it, that's only become more true."

"But if this was created in an industrial setting, how did he write the data to it?"

"He didn't. I'll bet the data's hidden somewhere inside it." The scanner beeped and he looked down at it. "See, the preliminary scan only picked up the major elements, all of which were carbon. The full scan can pick up discrepancies and irregularities in those elements. Although the headstone looks like one piece, it appears as if the carving was done separately and then added to the headstone later. The fit looks flush, but you can see the lines between the pieces clearly on the scan. You can also see a large tubular piece buried in the center of the headstone."

Ryan waited for Nicole to fill in the obvious blank, but when she didn't he glanced up at her and froze.

Chapter Eighteen

Gabriella stood there with one arm wrapped around Nicole's neck and the other holding a gun.

"Very clever," Gabriella said. "I can't believe how many times I've been out here and I never noticed. Of course you're not the only clever one. Justin was too clever by half as well, or at least he was after he started hanging out with this bitch." She pressed the muzzle of her gun harder into Nicole's neck, making Nicole wince.

Gabriella noticed the look of surprise on Ryan's face and laughed bitterly. "Oh, I'll bet you're wondering why I'm here. After all, everyone thinks you're dead, right? I never bought it. I even argued with Stephanie about shooting down your stupid aircar, but she just wanted this finished, once and for all. Stupid cow. She even argued with me about pulling the guards off this place. I tried to convince her I knew what I was talking about, but she wouldn't listen to me."

"So did you kill her off, too?" Ryan asked sarcastically and then his face twisted in shock as Gabriella just looked at him.

"Yeah, I did. And do you know why? Because this whole mess was never about the formula or at least not entirely."

"Then what was it about?" Nicole asked only to wince when Gabriella rapped her sharply on the head with the gun.

"Shut up, bitch," Gabriella growled. "Do you really want to know what it's all about?" Nicole didn't answer and Gabriella laughed cruelly. "It looks like old dogs can learn new tricks. Not that it will do you any good in the long run. You know why? Because you're what it's all about."

"What are you talking about?" Ryan asked, trying to ignore the fear in his gut. He had already thought that Gabriella was crazy, but finding out that she had killed her partner told him she had really lost it. He wasn't sure what had pushed her over the edge. It could have been seeing all her plans fall apart after forty years, or it could have been that she had been that crazy all along and this just brought it out into the open—but the reasons didn't matter. All that mattered now was that she felt she had nothing to lose, which made her desperate and unpredictable.

He kept all his movements smooth and slow and stayed down on his knees. He knew Gabriella would find it less threatening, which was fine with him. It wasn't as weak a position as it looked and he knew he needed every advantage he could get.

"Do you want to know what really happened forty years ago?" Gabriella gloated. "When Stephanie found out what Justin had been up to, she wanted me to kill him and destroy the formula. She had no idea what she was asking of me. She didn't know I loved him. I didn't know what to do. Oh, there were no doubts about destroying the formula, but I didn't want to kill Justin. The two of us confronted him and he admitted to creating the formula. When Stephanie left me alone with him, I told him we could run away, that we could hide from Stephanie and have our own quiet little life together."

Her mouth curled and to Ryan's horror it looked like she was about to cry. He felt like he was trapped in some warped surreal version of reality.

"He turned me down. At first I thought that it was about the formula, but then I suddenly realized there was someone else." Gabriella glared at Nicole and Ryan saw her finger tighten on the trigger. He tensed, getting ready to move, but then she relaxed a little. "As soon as I knew there was someone else, I knew who it was. I wanted to use Nicole as a bargaining chip, threatening to kill her unless he came with me, but I knew he wouldn't budge. He told me that he had hidden two copies of the formula away."

"Two copies?" Ryan echoed stupidly and Gabriella laughed harshly.

"Yeah, two copies. He said that one copy was life insurance for Nicole, that if she died, then that copy would be released and sent to all major media outlets."

Gabriella twisted her gun cruelly behind Nicole's ear.

"We couldn't let that happen, as much as we wanted to kill you. It's funny—Stephanie always assumed I wanted you dead for the same reason she did—corrupting her brother. My reason was just as personal, but I knew that men are born corrupted—it's in their nature, they can't help it. No, I wanted to kill you for stealing Justin from me.

"But both of us agreed on one thing and that was preventing the formula from becoming available. That was where the second copy came into play. Justin told us it was hidden on the servers at Delphi, but that we would need the help of the men that he had tested the formula on. He also said the formula wouldn't be accessible for another forty years. He had this bullshit line about giving Stephanie time to change her mind, but I think he just hoped we would spare the lives of the men he had treated with the formula. It almost worked, too. Stephanie wanted us to just track them, but I disagreed. I told her we only needed one of you, and we should kill the others before they spread this disease any further. And that's where you came in Ryan."

"Why me? Why not one of the others?"

"Because of your relationship with Olivia. Given what had happened to me I was in the mood to hurt someone and I'd never liked Olivia. I can't believe the Board was stupid enough to make her CEO, but even before that, the prospect of messing with her mind tickled me."

She laughed at Ryan's shock. "Yes, we knew all about your affair with Olivia and from your reaction when I propositioned you, I was certain it was more serious than it appeared. Once we had identified all the men who had received treatment, we used them as guinea pigs. We tried to figure out how to reverse engineer the formula but everyone we tested our formula on ended up dead. Since that didn't work, we tried to reverse the effects of it. We were more successful in that regard but there was one unfortunate little side effect—it killed the guy we tried it on." She shook her head sadly. "It's unfortunate, really. I was this close to getting it right, but I ran out of men to test it on. Anyway, thanks to your intransigence, you were one of two men we hadn't used as guinea pigs. You were my first choice, as I mentioned, and once you agreed, we kidnapped the other guy and stuck him into cryogenic storage, kind of as a backup."

"But why all this sneaking around?" Ryan asked. "I mean, once the forty years had passed, you could have smuggled me into the lab, particularly with the security as loose as it was."

"Oh, security wasn't the issue," Gabriella said cryptically and Ryan stared at her for a moment and then suddenly the light went off in his head as he realized she was talking about his predecessor, the previous VP of Security.

"Christina!" he exclaimed and Gabriella nodded.

"That's right. Christina worked for us. That's why we steered you into security as a career choice all those years ago. We knew that we could create an opening for you whenever you were ready. That's part of why I wanted you over the other guy. I was hoping it would influence Olivia's choice for a replacement."

"But why," he repeated. "If you could get me into the lab whenever you wanted then why all this subterfuge?"

Gabriella shrugged. "Why not? I was bored and the thought of toying with you and Olivia amused me."

Ryan reeled as his thoughts raced. The sheer scope of how much Gabriella had manipulated his life staggered him. He couldn't believe it was all because of boredom. He had known how much he was giving up for this and he had been okay with it, but now he found it was completely unnecessary. He had spent the last forty years building his life around this, sacrificing friends and any semblance of a normal life, only to find out that it was all false.

He shook his head and looked at Nicole despairingly. She had closed her eyes, but just seeing her gave him new strength. No matter what had happened in his life, his relationship with Nicole was real and that was something that they couldn't have planned on. That they were here, the three of them, at Nicole's private cemetery hadn't been planned. Those wild cards were the only chance he and Nicole had and he had to figure out how to play them.

"Looks like you had it all planned out," he said quietly and Gabriella smirked at him. "Was killing Stephanie part of your plan, too?" he asked and Gabriella snarled at him.

"Shut up, just shut up."

"I guess even the best laid plans can go wrong from time to time," Ryan chuckled and Gabriella screamed in frustration as she pointed the gun in his direction and pulled the trigger. Ryan flinched as the bullet whistled past his ear and ricocheted off the headstone behind him. Before Nicole could take advantage of the situation, Gabriella had the gun pointed at her neck again.

"Shut up or she gets the next one," Gabriella growled as she pressed the gun viciously into Nicole's neck. The barrel was still hot from the discharge and Nicole flinched involuntarily. Ryan tried to think of what else he could do. He had hoped that he could get Gabriella to take her attention off Nicole long enough for her to break free, but she had moved faster than he had thought she could. His mind raced for another idea as he waited for Gabriella to calm down, but he couldn't stop thinking about Nicole. He knew the pain was minor and her nanites would be able to—

He broke off as a new idea formed in his mind. It was incredibly risky, but they were running out of options.

"Yes," Gabriella continued, "everything was going as planned, right until this bitch rescued you. We had always known about her, but we didn't know about her enhancement and so we discounted her." She pressed the gun into the burn behind Nicole's ear, twisting it hard as she addressed Nicole. "Don't worry, I won't make that mistake again. Anyway, that's when it all started going downhill. I still wanted to kill you and Nicole, but thanks to your cowardly trick with the marines, I had to let you go. Then I discovered that the data on the M-Stick was bogus. It didn't take long—we had amassed a large amount of data during our experimental phase, which helped us figure it out. Once we knew the data was false, I knew you and Nicole were key.

"That's where Stephanie and I differed. She wanted to cut our losses and just get rid of you. After all, we were close to finding a way to reverse the effect of the formula and with a larger pool of men to experiment on, we would finally be able to figure it out. She's always been a 'behind-the-scenes' person and she didn't like the publicity. But that wasn't enough for me. I wanted to see the two of you suffer. I thought that it would be enough to let you find the formula and take it away from you, but then I spotted you getting busy and I knew that you were more than friends. I was tempted to pull the guards earlier, just to frustrate you with coitus interruptus, but I kind of got off on watching you."

Ryan felt physically sick as he thought about Gabriella watching them make love, but he forced himself to concentrate, to wait for the right moment.

"I must say, your stamina is impressive, the both of you. I just wish that I could have gotten the chance to try you myself, but I'll settle for killing your lover right in front of you."

"Do it and you're dead," Ryan said flatly. "I know you're armed but unless your gun is a military model it won't stop me from killing you." Ryan looked hard at Nicole as he said this, risking a slight emphasis on the word military, and he felt his tension grow as her eyes widened as she realized what he wanted her to do.

"No, the gun's an ordinary gun. But I'm not. You see, you and Nicole are not the only ones who are enhanced."

She laughed at Ryan's shock. "Oh, it's black market stuff and as such it's not quite as powerful as yours, but I figure the gun gives me the edge." With a cruel smile she pulled the trigger and Nicole dropped to the ground beside her.

Ryan was already moving as she turned the gun towards him and fired. He felt the bullet graze the top of his head as he fell forward. He turned the fall into a somersault and then sprang up to tackle Gabriella. They landed hard and before she could recover, he wrenched the gun away from her and crushed it. He dropped the remains on the ground as she recovered from her surprise and lunged at him. It was obvious that she hadn't taken any martial arts training but despite that, the strength her nanites gave her made her dangerous, as did the unpredictability of her madness. He knew he had to disable her quickly before she managed to hurt him. Although he desperately wanted to check on Nicole, he forced himself to concentrate.

He ducked beneath the wild punch she threw at him and then grabbed her outstretched arm, turning and using it as a lever as he threw her over his shoulder. She landed in a graceless heap with a loud 'oof' as the fall drove the wind out of her.

Ryan grinned viciously. The first thing that you learned in martial arts was how to take a fall.

Before she could recover, he spun on one foot and kicked her outstretched arm with the other. It was the arm Nicole had broken the other evening. Although the bone had knitted enough for her to use it, it wasn't completely healed. It broke with a cruel snap and Gabriella staggered in pain.

He used his momentum to spin around and launch a second kick at her other arm. He heard a crack as it broke as well and for a moment he gazed down at her as his hate and disgust got the better of him. As soon as he determined she wasn't a threat anymore, he hurried over to where Nicole had fallen.

Fearfully, he knelt down beside her and inserted himself into her systems. He let his breath out in a rush as her systems responded to him. Her vitals were weak and he felt like crying in relief. He gently brushed aside the hair covering her wound, but there was only a deep bruise, surrounded by a rosette of tiny black specks—burnt out nanites. He cradled her head gently in his lap and stroked her forehead as he called her name softly.

"She's dead, you idiot," Gabriella sneered, but she quelled at the look Ryan gave her. Weaponless as she was, she wasn't a threat any more. While broken arms wouldn't have stopped anyone properly trained, it was more than enough to immobilize Gabriella. Despite her nanites, she was no longer a threat. He continued to minister to Nicole and after a few minutes his efforts were rewarded as she opened her eyes and looked at him weakly.

"Did it work?" she asked and Ryan nodded, unable to speak as tears filled his eyes. He ignored Gabriella's gasp as he leaned forward to hear Nicole better.

"I thought so. I'm pretty sure they don't have headaches like this in heaven."

"It's just the bruising. It will subside quickly."

Nicole just nodded and closed her eyes. After a moment she opened then again. "Gabriella?" she asked quietly and Ryan gestured with his chin in Gabriella's direction.

"Is she dead?"

Ryan smiled and chuckled. "Not yet, I had more important things to worry about."

"I'm fine. Leave me and take care of her. She's caused lifetimes of grief and it has to stop now."

Ryan nodded and looked around. Very gently he picked Nicole up and carried her over to Michael's headstone. He set her down again, propping her up gently against it so she could see what was going on, and then he turned to face Gabriella. He was surprised she had managed to crawl over to Justin's headstone, but whatever she had planned, it was too late.

"Game over," he said, but to his surprise she just smiled.

"Do you know that you and Nicole have been officially dead for almost half a day? Your death was highly publicized. I've been searching for any relevant press releases and so far I haven't seen anything about Justin's formula."

"So?"

"So I think he was bluffing. I don't think there really are two copies of the formula. I think that there's just this one here."

"Again so what? We only need the one and we've got it."

"Do you?" Gabriella asked and Ryan felt uneasy at the edge of confidence in her voice. "You know, in all the spy novels that I've ever read and movies I've seen, the evil villain always commits suicide at the end rather than face a life in prison."

Ryan just stared at her as he wondered where she was going with this.

"Does this mean that you're going to do us all a favor and kill yourself?" he asked sarcastically, but to his surprise she just nodded.

"That's right, I am. But I've always had a problem with the way those villains have killed themselves. Regardless of the method chosen, it almost always impacts only them. Seems like a waste to me."

Ryan tensed and prepared himself for her to produce another weapon from somewhere but to his surprise she just laughed.

"You're right, the game's over," she said, "but I still win." At the last minute Ryan figured out what she intended to do, and he turned and threw himself on top of Nicole as Gabriella vanished in the unmistakable plasma-grenade ball of light.

He felt the heat wash over him but he was outside the main blast radius and he knew he had survived with only second-degree burns. If it hadn't been for his nanites, it would have been a lot worse. He overrode the pain and levered himself upright to look at Nicole. Most of her nanites had been used up protecting herself from Gabriella's point-blank shot, which was why he threw himself over her. Without their protection, the blast could have killed her. Despite the pain, he smiled as she looked up at him, relieved to see that her skin was unmarred.

"I take it that we don't have to worry about Gabriella anymore?" she inquired with a weak smile and he nodded. With an effort, he turned to look at the spot where Gabriella had been standing. What he saw caused him to stop in shock.

"What, what is it?" Nicole asked and he gingerly edged off her, keeping the unburnt side of his body facing down. As soon as he had moved far enough for her to see what he had seen, he heard the same sharp inhalation. He closed his eyes, but the image of the molten remains of Justin's headstone stayed with him.

"So that's what she had in mind. I was wondering why she didn't try for us," Nicole said and Ryan nodded heavily. "I guess she did win after all," she said listlessly and Ryan looked at her sharply, his pain forgotten.

"She only won if you let her win," he said and Nicole looked at him in puzzlement.

"What do you mean?"

"I mean, all she managed to do was destroy the formula. She wanted to kill us too, but we're both still alive. Not only that, but we have each other. I don't know about you, but that means a great deal to me. As for the formula, maybe she was wrong about Justin bluffing. We haven't seen anything yet, but it could be on a time delay, like the program you wrote for him. And even if he was bluffing and the formula is destroyed, that doesn't mean that it's gone forever. I'm still here and I'm more than willing to provide all the blood samples necessary."

"But Stephanie and Gabriella tried that and it didn't work."

"True, but it was just the two of them. Now that the whole world knows about this, someone will figure out how to get it to work. After all, just knowing that something is possible is half the battle of accomplishing it."

Nicole smiled. "Whatever it takes, we'll work together to get it done."

"I'm sorry, but I don't think that's enough."

"What do you mean?" Nicole asked in puzzlement.

"I mean it's not enough for us to work together. I want more than that."

He tried to stand up but the effort triggered a fresh burst of pain. He closed his eyes and waited for the pain to subside before opening them again. Nicole was still lying there, but she was struggling to get up as well and he laughed. "What a pair we are. Half my body is on the well done side, almost all your nanites are gone, and yet we're both trying to get up."

Despite her exhaustion, Nicole laughed. "Don't blame me. I was just following your lead. What were you trying to do anyway?"

He hesitated. "I was trying to get up on one knee," he finally admitted sheepishly. Nicole gasped as she realized what he was saying. "Nicole Emily West, will you grant me the great pleasure of sharing the rest of our lives together?"

She stared at him for a moment and then shook her head gently. "I don't think that's very fair…" she began and Ryan interrupted.

"I didn't ask for fair, I asked you to marry me. I know that you think that it's not fair since I'll outlive, you but these last few months that we've had have been the best of my life. It's like a whole new life for me, one that we created together. Let's live it for as long as we have, for each moment we're together is worth more than a lifetime of being apart." He looked up at her lovingly and she smiled at him as the tears streamed down her face.

"When you put it that way, how can I say no?" she asked. She wiped her tears away and took a deep breath. "I accept," she said formally and Ryan grinned. "But why now, why not wait until later?"

"Well, the way I see it, this was the perfect opportunity. After all, it's not like we're going anywhere. I figured I'd be able to wear you down and eventually you'd say yes just to shut me up." He grinned again at the look on her face as she shook her fist at him gently.

"It's a good thing I can't move, otherwise I'd come over there and kick your ass, burns or no burns," she said with a goofy grin and despite everything, Ryan had never felt happier in his life.

Chapter Nineteen

Olivia groaned. She was getting tired of being woken by someone shaking her. Not only did it interrupt her much needed sleep, but lately it usually meant something had gone horribly wrong.

"What is it?" she rasped as she opened her eyes.

"It's Ryan and Nicole, they are on their way in to Medical," Mia said and Olivia gasped.

"You mean they survived the crash?" she asked.

"I don't know all the details yet, but apparently they weren't onboard the aircar when it was shot down. They called from a cemetery that Nicole owns. There was some sort of confrontation with Gabriella. She's dead, but Ryan and Nicole aren't in great shape either. He's got second-degree burns all down his back and the underside of his legs and arms, and Nicole is suffering from nanitic shock. Something happened that fried almost every nanite in her body."

"Jesus," she said involuntarily and Mia nodded in agreement.

"I have a flitter waiting to take us to Medical. We might be able to beat them there, if we hurry."

Olivia nodded as she sat up and hopped off the bed. She knew her appearance was less than presentable, but she didn't give it a second thought. Pausing only to wake up Brooke, the three of them hurried out to the flitter.

Despite their haste, Ryan and Nicole had arrived first and were already being treated. One of the doctors noticed their arrival and hurried out to meet them.

"How are they?" Olivia asked worriedly.

The doctor shook her head grimly. "It's not good. We've never had to deal with these kinds of injuries before. We're doing the best we can, but we lack the proper equipment for this kind of trauma. They would be better-off in a proper hospital, preferably one that's had some experience with enhanced individuals."

Olivia shook her head automatically. "You may be right, but their physical safety has to come first. At the moment things are too unsettled for them to leave the grounds. As for treating them, you let me know what we're missing and we'll get it—equipment, trauma specialists, whatever. I don't care what it costs. If we can't buy it, then we'll either borrow or steal what we need."

The doctor looked at her for a moment and then nodded. "I'll make a list."

"Good, give it to Mia. She'll take care of everything." Mia nodded in response. After a moment the doctor turned and reentered the operating room where Nicole and Ryan were, and could be heard barking orders.

Olivia was about to ask Mia and Brooke about holding another press conference when an earsplitting alarm suddenly sounded. She put her hands over her ears involuntarily as the high-pitched warbling continued. She turned to ask Mia what was going on, but the commander was already charging outside. Olivia followed her automatically, suddenly concerned. What she saw made her stop, stunned, at the entrance. Security flitters were converging on the Medical building and a group of field trained security staff formed a protective perimeter. She wondered what all the fuss was about when suddenly she saw something.

It was a dark smudge on the horizon, growing with incredible rapidity as it drew closer, until it was hovering in front of the Medical building. It was larger than anything airborne had a right to be and she suddenly felt uncomfortably claustrophobic. Sleek atmospheric sting ships darted around it, like lethal hummingbirds, and she could see more circling in the distance. She just stood with her mouth open, unable to fathom what was happening. Suddenly the bottom of the ship opened and close to a hundred armor clad figures leaped out. They plummeted like stones, falling so quickly they were hard to track. She watched in sick fascination, certain that something had gone wrong, but with a sudden gracefulness they landed gently on the ground. She blinked as even her untrained eye recognized a protective formation. Moments later another group of individuals, only four this time, plummeted from the ship, followed by large bundles of equipment, landing with the same sudden gracefulness in the dead center of the circle. The precision of the maneuvers took her breath away.

One of the armored figures approached her, but before she could react Mia and a couple of other guards had moved protectively in front of her. The gesture caught her off guard and suddenly she realized what she had been taking for granted all these years. The figure stopped a respectful distance away and the armored hood retracted. For some strange reason he reminded Olivia of Ryan. He looked nothing like Ryan, but there was a solidness to him that felt instantly familiar.

"Ms. Morgan, I'm Major Lloyd. The commander of Edwards Air Force Base sent me to assist you."

"I see," she replied more calmly than she felt. "And what form of assistance would that be?"

"I understand that you have two enhanced individuals here suffering

208

from SNDS." She raised an eyebrow questioningly and the major flushed as he elaborated. "Sorry, Ma'am, SNDS stands for Severe Nanitic Depletion Syndrome. It occurs when an enhanced individual loses more than seventy percent of their nanites. Thirty percent is the minimum required for nanites to be self-regulating. If the level drops lower than that, especially in trauma cases, the nanites lose their ability to self-regulate."

"Which means what exactly?" she asked impatiently.

"It means they start to eat their host," a new voice interjected as another armored figure approached. It was one of the individuals who had dropped to the middle of the circle and she noticed a caduceus displayed prominently on each sleeve. "I'm Dr. Shaw," he said introducing himself, "and early treatment of SNDS is critical. You may not have realized this, but biological nanites are just that—biological. They are specifically designed to replicate quickly. Normally they do this by piggy-backing off the body's digestive process, as well as scavenging body wastes, but without direction they'll turn to the nearest source of energy—their host."

Olivia paled as the implications hit her.

"Most civilian doctors are unaware of this condition," Dr Shaw continued, "which isn't all that surprising. While it is far from common in a civilian environment, it does occur frequently in battlefield conditions, and we're trained to handle it."

Olivia glanced at Mia and nodded. After a moment, the Delphi guards who were crouched protectively in front of the Medical building parted reluctantly. Dr. Shaw inclined his head in gratitude as he grabbed the equipment floating behind him and rushed into the building, followed by his colleagues. She saw Brooke trail after the four of them and she relaxed a little, knowing that she could trust Brooke to keep an eye on the newcomers as well as ensure there wasn't any resistance from the medical staff.

"My commander also authorized me to offer our assistance in supplementing or even relieving your security forces. With your permission, of course," he added. Olivia looked over at Mia who frowned.

"Of course we don't have to do either," he interjected.

Mia looked at him. "What? Oh, I was just considering how best to use them, not objecting to your offer. Part of the issue is our security system. Without nanitic bracelets, they will have limited access. I could issue some, but I'm hoping this is just a short-term measure, so I'd rather not do that if I don't have to. If it's all the same to you, I'd like each of your soldiers to pair up with one of our guards. It's not perfect but it will free up a large portion of my field-rated staff."

"Makes sense," he agreed with a small smile. "It's good to work with someone so professional."

Mia snorted. "You mean someone used to working with men, don't you?" She laughed at the look on his face and waved a hand at him. "I don't expect you to answer that by the way. I've had to deal with my share of bigots, so I know just what you mean. It might surprise you how many of my staff are men. It used to be that way for only the field-rated staff, but Ryan is more open to having men work at the senior levels than his predecessor was."

"Oh, we're well aware of her views on the matter," he chuckled. "If his predecessor was still in charge, then in all likelihood we would have made a more, ahem, forceful entry."

"Do you mind my asking how you knew that Ryan and Nicole were here, and how you knew what was wrong with them?" Mia asked.

"Not at all," he said with another smile. "After news about the formula broke, Ryan contacted us for some, shall we say, 'unofficial' help. During that time, he somehow came into possession of a military grade stealth field. You may not know this, but all military grade stealth fields link automatically with military satellites. This allows us to maintain communications through the stealth field. It also allows us to track the field. We started tracking it once Ryan began using it. After some hijinks designed to shake any physical surveillance, we tracked it to a private country estate just east of here, where it remained until this morning. Then it proceeded to a location not far from the cemetery where you found Ryan and Nicole. It stayed there only five minutes before taking off again and a short time after that it was shot down."

Olivia looked at Mia as the pieces clicked into place. "He must have been piloting it remotely," she said and Major Lloyd nodded.

"That's our thought as well. Since we were monitoring the stealth field, we were able to backtrack the missile to its launch site. It took a while to get the authorization for a forced entry, a bit too long unfortunately." He paused for a moment, frowning. "What we found there was very disturbing. Stephanie Lake had been brutally murdered. I've been a soldier for over thirty years and I've seen a lot of sick things in my time, but never anything as coldly psychotic as that. And that wasn't the worst of it. We searched the premises and found a hidden basement lab. I'm using the term lab loosely and only because of all the scientific equipment. The term torture chamber would work equally well, perhaps better. We found several dismembered bodies and one intact male in cryogenic storage." He shook his head slowly. "Once this is settled, my men and I are going to have to get counseling or it will haunt us for years."

There was a brief silence as he stared at something only he could see. Mia and Olivia exchanged a glance that said the same thing—we're better off not knowing.

"We had just started to revive the guy in cryogenic storage when we intercepted Nicole's message."

Mia looked puzzled. "So why didn't you just pick them up yourself? Why all the rigmarole?"

"I'm afraid you'll have to ask my commander about that." Something about the way he said it told Olivia he knew more than he was saying.

"You didn't want to get involved officially or at least not directly," Olivia said and he nodded cautiously. "I can understand that. This way they are under Delphi's protection, not the military's. It has the same net effect, but without getting the military involved directly. Given how high tensions are running that's a wise decision." He relaxed visibly and Olivia chuckled. "Really, Major Lloyd, you might want to start getting used to the fact that we are quite reasonable."

He colored as he responded. "Sorry about that, Ma'am, it's just that most of our interactions in situations like this are generally less positive. We've gotten used to being cautious, a strategy I've found to be well worth it. It's part of why we made the approach that we did. After all, we could have just as easily made a conventional landing and offloaded the medical team and the extra soldiers. The reason we didn't is to help keep us fresh and prepared for anything. And please, both of you, call me James."

"I can appreciate that, James" Mia said, "and I'm also grateful for the impromptu test of our response time, but in the future it might be a wise idea to touch base with us first. After all tensions are running high here right now."

He accepted the rebuke with a small nod, and Olivia knew that as far as Mia and James were concerned the issue was settled. That effectively settled it for her as well, not just because she relied on Mia, but because she'd had the same concerns about their unorthodox approach. Not that she was overly concerned. Of more importance to her was the positive PR that having the military on-site would generate in the male community. It neatly neutralized the possibility of rioters attacking Delphi, the second largest threat she had worried about, Gabriella and Stephanie being the largest. With those two threats taken care of, Delphi's security was more than enough to deal with anything else.

Movement caught her eye as the armored figures redeployed themselves to augment the guards fanned out around the Medical building. She realized that Mia and James had been quietly conferring about how best to work together and she smiled. It was an encouraging sign.

She turned and looked at the entrance, wondering how Ryan and Nicole were making out. The motion did not go unnoticed.

"Let's go see how they're doing in there, shall we?" James asked, glancing at Mia. Olivia nodded and they all headed into the Medical building.

Nobody noticed their entrance at first, and then Dr. Shaw straightened up as he saw them. He spoke quietly to one of his colleagues and then came over to greet them, Brooke trailing quietly behind him.

"How are they doing Rick?" James asked.

"Not great," he said tiredly, but then he must have sensed Olivia and Mia's sudden concern. "Oh, they'll be fine eventually," he said hurriedly, "it's just I wasn't expecting them to be in such bad shape. From a purely medical standpoint, Nicole is in better shape, but both of them had their nanitic systems hammered pretty hard. Nicole used her systems to block a point-blank shot to the neck, something that even I have a hard time believing. Her focus must have been incredibly tight, and there's no doubt that it was a civilian weapon, but it's still unbelievable. We have her stabilized and are rebuilding her nanite population. That will take a few days, since we can't add too many nanites at once without overwhelming the existing ones. If we do that, we'll lose control and have to start over. So, slow and steady is the mantra in her case." He paused and rubbed his eyes.

"As for Ryan, physically he's in bad shape, and although his nanites weren't as depleted as Nicole's, they're having to deal with more. There's the physical damage, of course, but there is also some neurological damage that they are struggling with. I think it's related to feedback from the aircar explosion—the damage matches previous cases I've dealt with. The same feedback also wiped out about half his nanites, which obviously doesn't help. We've got him stabilized, but we're going to have to keep him under for at least several days. We can't augment his nanites until they've finished repairing the neurological damage. We did manage to block his other injuries so his existing nanites can focus on the neural damage. Once that's done, we can bring his nanite population back up to normal at the same time we repair the physical damage."

"What happened to him?" Olivia asked.

Rick shook his head. "Sorry. He has second-degree burns covering about forty-eight percent of his body. The damage is consistent with the thermal bloom from a plasma grenade. He was at the outer range and, from the damage, he must have been lying down on something. That's good since it means we don't have to worry about facial reconstruction or optical damage. So like I said, they should be okay but it will take time."

"I'd like to issue a press release indicating that they are still alive and undergoing medical treatment. I'd also like to announce that, at our request, the military is providing medical treatment and additional security." She paused and looked around. "Does anyone have any suggestions or comments?"

"Don't forget about Gabriella and Stephanie."

Olivia shook her head. "Good point Brooke. Anything else anyone? Fine then. Brooke, I'd like you to help me draft the press release."

"Not to mention help with your wardrobe choices," Brooke said smiling.

Olivia laughed. "Please, I was trying to block that aspect of it. Mia, I'd like for you to ensure that our guests are provided for."

Mia laughed, too. "And just where should I put them? We're already having difficulty providing space for our own employees. Don't forget that we sealed the grounds early this morning."

"Right. I think we can unseal them, but let's wait until after the press conference. Assuming it goes the way I think it will, we can let everyone go home. That should free up more than enough space."

"Sounds good."

Everyone nodded and Olivia took a moment to appreciate her team. They made it look easy and she knew all too well just how much everyone was dealing with. She smiled proudly as they split up. No matter what happened Delphi had weathered the worst events in its history and had come through intact.

Chapter Twenty

Nicole looked around her office as she fidgeted in her seat, trying to get some relief from the itching without scratching. She had forgotten just how much new nanites made her skin itch. She knew it was just a temporary reaction as her body adjusted to them, though that didn't help much when every square centimeter of her skin itched. Scratching would just irritate the skin and that would attract more nanites to the area, making it itch more. Of course it could be worse—she could be dead. It had shocked her when she had woken up and found out how much time had passed.

She could still remember Ryan proposing to her and how happy they were, despite their injuries. She had felt her strength ebbing, but it hadn't seemed so bad. Because of their injuries, neither of them had been able to move. She remembered linking into the caretaker's shed and calling for help. That was the last clear memory she had.

Waking up had been the real nightmare. Learning how close they had both come to dying and discovering the extent of Ryan's injuries had come close to overwhelming her. It still upset her even now that he was under sedation for neural damage.

So despite the itching, she was grateful to be alive. And if being alive wasn't enough, her new nanites were more powerful and robust than her old set. Besides, her itching would be over by the time Ryan woke up, so she could tease him about the itching when he got his new set. She had a lot to be grateful for and a lot to look forward to, but at the moment all she could think about was just how damn itchy she was. She gritted her teeth and growled in frustration. She forced herself to relax and take a deep breath as she tried to ignore the itching by force of will alone.

She turned her focus to the overflowing inbox on the screen in front of her. Many of the messages were either 'get well soon' messages or questions about the formula. She quickly wrote a script to dump them in an off-line file for her to review later. That got rid of almost three quarters of them, and while the remaining number was high, it was still manageable. After that she turned her attention to the Urgent category. Fortunately, her staff had already dealt with most of those and they just needed final approval from her. Once she had finished those, she turned her attention to the remaining low and normal priority messages, working her way through them by name.

She was about halfway through when she suddenly stopped, frozen in shock. The message header that she was looking at said it was from Justin

Lake. She forced herself to breathe and move again. She couldn't bring herself to open it right away. She was too afraid that it was a cruel hoax.

First, she checked the employee database, but there was no record of any current employees with that name. Then she ran a trace on the message. It was conceivable that someone had spoofed the message header, although it should have been blocked if it was. The trace came back and she blinked. The originating message had come from HR. Digging further she found that it had been sent by the delayed distribution program. She checked the date on the original message with trembling fingers. The date was the day before Justin's death, and she felt tears well up in her eyes as she realized that this really was a message from Justin. She didn't know how it had happened, or why she was getting it now, but at the moment she didn't care. She tried to open the message and laughed as she found she couldn't see the screen, she was crying so hard. It took her almost a minute to calm down enough to be able to open it. The screen cleared and then darkened to reveal Justin, and Nicole forgot everything as she stared at his video image.

"Nicole, if you're receiving this message it means that Gabriella is dead. I only hope you've managed to survive her schemes alive and unscathed. I don't know how much you may have found out, but I'm going to tell you everything.

"I'm afraid that I lied to you. I've always known that I would be killed by Gabriella. The truth is I've counted on it. As much as I love you and want to be with you, I also love my sister. She was a good person once, and I want to give her a chance to redeem herself. I've taken anti-interrogation nanites, but I'm sure that Gabriella will push too hard and the suicide protocols will kick in. I hope that my death will shock Stephanie enough for her to begin thinking for herself again.

"In regards to the formula, I've put some precautions in place. One of them is designed to keep you alive. We've managed to keep our relationship secret so far, but I'm certain that once Gabriella starts digging into my activities, she'll find out about us. She has Stephanie's money and Christina's security connections to draw on, so the safe bet is to assume she will find out everything. There is a copy of the formula linked to your personnel file in HR. I know you won't leave Delphi until you have recovered the formula, at least not while you are alive. The formula will be released when your status is changed to deceased."

He paused and grinned. "If you don't already have the formula, all you have to do is kill yourself. I know that's not funny, not really, but right now I'm taking humor wherever I can find it.

"The other copy of the formula is the one that you know about, the one that you hid on the servers in the lab for me. As you know, it's not really the formula that is hidden but a clue to its location.

"Again, if you haven't found it already, it's hidden in my gravestone. By the way, I hope you didn't mind that I arranged to have a gravestone delivered to the family plot after my death." He laughed. "I guess you could say that I'm taking my secret to the grave with me. Sorry for the gallows humor."

He sobered and then continued.

"I know that you are wondering why I just don't release the formula right now. If I had the time to take all these precautions, I should have had the time to distribute the formula. It comes back to the people I love.

"Without the formula as a form of life insurance, Gabriella will kill you, if only out of spite. I also want to give Stephanie time to realize that the problems I've been talking about are real. I imagine you've wondered why I wanted the program on the servers in the lab hidden for forty years. I know that I explained it as the time needed for the men I treated to live long enough to eliminate any doubts that the formula really works, but that's only part of it.

"There is another reason. I've modeled, as best I can, the impact of the artificial embryogenesis machine on the current social issues. My best estimates indicate that the issues will start to strain our ability to deal with them anywhere from forty to fifty years from now. I picked forty years, hoping the problems would be visible enough for Stephanie to believe they are real. Unfortunately, I can't rely on her to do the right thing, as much as it pains me to admit that. I know that I can count on you, but all Gabriella has to do is kill all the men who received the formula to prevent you from retrieving my message.

"That is why there is a third copy, copies actually, that I've sent to media outlets and data storage companies. It's a time delayed press release, set for fifty years from now."

He looked at her soberly. "I'm not sure the third copy is all that wise. I've always had my doubts about Gabriella's sanity. She's not very stable and this kind of threat, looming over her like the sword of Damocles, might push her over the edge."

He sighed and then looked directly at her. Nicole felt her heart catch. It was the way he had always looked at her when they were alone, the look they didn't dare share in public.

"I will miss you and I'm sorry for what you are going to have to go through." He chuckled quietly. "I guess if you're viewing this then you've already gone through it all. I wish that it could be otherwise, but at the end of the day, the formula is more important to me than almost anything. I almost decided to abandon my research, and run off to live with you someplace where Stephanie and Gabriella couldn't find us, but if I did that, I wouldn't be the person you fell in love with. More importantly, I wouldn't be the person I want to be. And so, while I can't do anything for me, I've done what I can for you and Stephanie. God willing, everything will turn out okay."

The screen went black, but Nicole continued to stare at it as her thoughts raced. She suddenly realized that she had been just sitting there for almost half an hour, staring at the screen. She would never have anticipated him leaving her a message like this, but even if she had, she would still have been unprepared for it. This was more real and more personal than anything she could have imagined.

She played the message again, looking at him more than listening to the message itself, and she felt a pang of longing. Yet even as real as the message was, it didn't affect her as much as she would have expected and she felt a new, fresh, pang of grief as she realized she had moved on. The fact that he would have expected that, even anticipated it, still didn't mitigate the grief she felt at finally letting him go as she buried her face in her hands and sobbed.

* * *

Ryan smiled as Nicole came over and sat on his lap. It had taken longer than anyone anticipated for him to recover fully, and it had amazed him at what had transpired while he was unconscious. He had been stunned to hear about Justin's message and the fact that the formula had been readily available all these years. As Justin had joked, Nicole had Brooke change Nicole's status to deceased in the HR database and out popped the formula.

It was kind of sad that so much time had been lost but he knew that Justin had done what he felt was right. Certainly without the hope of getting their hands on the formula before anyone else, Stephanie and Gabriella would have killed them all years ago. Admittedly, the formula would have been released in another ten years, but he wasn't sure that Noram society would survive that long. Still, he was glad he didn't have to find out the hard way.

Records recovered at Stephanie's secret lab showed that she had been anonymously funding the more radical feminist groups. While none of it was illegal, support for those groups disappeared with remarkable haste once Stephanie's role became clear. He was sure the die-hard radicals would resurface elsewhere, but they were gone for now. That, combined with the news that the formula was available, pretty much stopped the rioting on both sides in its tracks. An uneasy truce had emerged, but every day it became easier as both sides realized just how much they had to gain from it, as well as how much they had to lose by breaking it.

That had been almost a month ago, and if he had marveled at what had happened while he was unconscious for a week, it paled in comparison to how much had happened since then. Although he was conscious for this part of it, somehow it felt more surreal than the changes he'd had to deal with when he had woken up.

Delphi had never been busier and the regular Saturday night dinners at Olivia's were almost the only time they were able to get the whole group together. The group was slightly larger now, as it included Mia. It was a relaxed casual atmosphere but it was where they made all the decisions. Well, almost all the decisions he thought, as he turned to Olivia.

"I can't believe how quickly the FDA moved to grant approval for Justin's formula. I'm sure we set some sort of record here."

"Yeah, thirty days is kind of miraculous," Olivia agreed, "but I think they realized that it was the only way to keep the riots from breaking out again. What surprises me more is the way they did it."

"What do you mean?" Ryan asked.

"There was never any doubt that they would approve Justend®"—Olivia paused and smiled at the official name that they had given to the formula in memory of Justin—"but they've combined it with a clinical trial approach. Normally, a drug of this type would need decades worth of clinical trial data before it could be approved."

"Decades?" echoed Mia incredulously.

"At least," Olivia explained. "After all, Justend® is a life altering drug and there could be several long-term side effects that at the moment we are unaware of. It's tempting to compare it to Menssation®, but even though the results are similar, the methodology is different. Menssation® regulates an existing biological process and needs to be taken on a regular basis. Justend® only needs to be administered once, since it alters men's DNA."

"But, Ryan took it forty years ago and he appears okay."

"True, and that's supported by every test we've been able to perform on him. But, Ryan is only one of a dozen men who Justin gave Justend® to. Not only that, he's one of only two surviving members, admittedly for good reasons. Even if everyone in the original group had survived it still wouldn't be statistically significant. In fact, it is statistically significant just how statistically insignificant the original group was."

Mia crossed her eyes and then shook her head in mock confusion and everyone laughed.

"So just what are they doing?" Mia asked curiously. "I'm afraid that I've been a little busy lately." She grinned as everyone laughed again. Given the role she played during the crisis, her strong performance in that role, and Ryan's incapacitation, he had promoted her to acting VP of Security. Getting up to speed on that would be more than enough for anyone to take on, but in addition, she was also assuming most of Ryan's responsibilities for the immediate future.

"Well like I've said, they've combined it with a clinical trial approach. They've made Justend® available to anyone who wants it, but with a catch. They have to sign up to have their medical status charted and tracked."

"What exactly does that entail?" Mia asked.

"Initially it means a full medical workup—DNA mapping, brain mapping, and a full blood work with a basic medical scan. They'll also have to provide a bone marrow sample as well as a semen sample. They have to repeat this every decade for the next ten decades with normal blood work and the basic medical scan annually."

"That sounds more complicated and expensive than necessary."

"It is complicated, but the FDA wouldn't budge on the level of testing. As for the costs of those tests, we've already factored that into the price. Basically they pay one price upfront, a price that covers all the costs including data analysis, plus a respectable profit margin which we've committed to reinvest into R&D. We'll even provide low interest loans to ensure that anyone who wants to receive Justend® will."

Mia nodded slowly. "Sounds fair to me, but I'm not a guy. How do you think it will fly with them?" She glanced sidelong at Ryan and Olivia, who appeared to defer to him for the answer. Of course his viewpoint on the subject was just a little biased given his extended lifetime. It was closer to a female viewpoint now than it was to any present-day male.

Ryan laughed. "We've had a waiting list of over a hundred million for weeks now. As soon as we got the official word from the FDA, we contacted everyone on the list to let them know of the FDA's terms. If they agreed then we would schedule them for all the necessary appointments."

"And?" Mia prompted, knowing there was more to this than he had said.

"And we've got positive responses from over eighty percent of them in the last two days. There's still five days left to the week that we gave them to respond so I expect we'll see closer to ninety or ninety-five at the end."

Mia whistled softly. "That's a lot of people."

Ryan shrugged again. "Yes and no. The current Noram population is a little over half a billion, of which seventy percent is male. About seventy percent of those are of legal age, which means that less than half of the available male population has indicated interest. My guess is that this is the first rush of people who just can't wait, likely some of the older men and those in a midlife crisis. The twenty to forty year olds don't need it yet, and so are willing to wait to see how it all pans out."

"Wait a minute, you said elderly men? Will the formula still work on them?" Mia looked at him and then at Olivia and they both shrugged expressively.

"We just don't know," Olivia replied. "That's why the FDA is insisting on these tests. Of course some men are grumbling that we women never had to go through this and they're right. We've learned by trial and error about what works and what doesn't. On the whole, I think I prefer this approach better. It's pretty open as far as trials go, but at least we'll be collecting lots of data."

"What about the other countries, will the same requirements apply to them?" Mia asked.

Olivia nodded. "Yes, even more so. There's always been a difference between North Americans and Europeans when it comes to genetic backgrounds, not to mention the Asian and African populations. Fortunately we shouldn't have to worry about that for a while yet. We're gearing up our manufacturing facilities, but the immediate future demand will likely outstrip supply by a significant margin. We've committed to satisfying local demand for the first few years, and then pro-Menssation® countries next. As Ryan and Nicole clear anti-Menssation® countries, we'll add them to the list. By the time that happens, we should have a little more data to work with, not to mention we'll have had time to have thoroughly studied Justin's formula."

Mia looked solemn. There had been a few countries, mostly European, who had petitioned Noram to either be brought under the auspices of the Noram government similar to Australia and New Zealand, or to be provided with Menssation®. That those countries had done so indicated their willingness to accept the societal benefits that it granted to women, and the resulting disadvantages to men. Given that these countries were run by both men and women, it indicated an open progressive attitude, where having both Menssation® and Justend® would result in balanced population growth.

There were other countries that weren't so progressive, countries where even if both drugs were made available, use of Menssation™ would be token only.

Mia shook her head as she considered it all.

"Boy, I don't envy you and Nicole," she said to Ryan. "You guys have your work cut out for you."

Ryan nodded but even though he agreed with her about the workload, it excited him. Convincing countries that were anti-Menssation®, either openly or covertly, was a challenge. And it was the kind of challenge that both Ryan and Nicole were uniquely suited for. Ryan, as the only living recipient of Justend®, was walking talking proof of its effectiveness. Nicole was an example of the benefits of longevity for women, being one of the oldest living recipients of Menssation®. The story of how the two of them had worked both separately and together over the last forty years to bring Justend® into existence, would show that the two genders and the two products could and did work well together.

All of that was true, but it was only part of the reason they were going. Together the two of them would decide which countries would be allowed to get access to Justend®. There was no one who would dispute their qualifications, or that they were entitled to make that decision. The fact that they were both representatives of Delphi, as well as being a gender-balanced team, ensured that a perception of fairness prevailed. Of course their absence left a void in the upper management levels of Delphi. Even though they would be accessible, the realities of business, and their jobs in particular, required immediate responses. That was why Mia was so busy. She was going to be the point person for security in Ryan's absence. Nicole's department would function well enough even in her absence that there wasn't a need for an immediate replacement for her, although she was working on it.

"So next week's your last week," Olivia said with a sigh. "Just when I get used to having you around Ryan, you go and disappear on me again."

"Don't worry, you'll see me again, I promise."

"Just don't make me wait another forty years," she grumbled good-naturedly and Ryan grinned and glanced at Nicole. She and Brooke had been relatively quiet during the discussion, although for different reasons. Nicole gave him a wan grin in return and nodded. Brooke was practically hopping up and down and Olivia looked at them suspiciously.

"What's going on?" Olivia asked slowly and Ryan shrugged.

"Nothing," he replied innocently. "I was just thinking that you'll only have to wait about eight months. We should be back by then and odds are we'll be staying here for a few years after that."

Olivia's jaw dropped as she looked at them and apparently put it all together. Nicole's quietness, Brooke's excitement and his artful innocence. "You're pregnant!" Olivia exclaimed and finally Brooke spoke up.

"I know, isn't it great, I've been dying to tell you, but they wouldn't let me. I couldn't trust myself not to blurt it out so I just decided not to speak."

"I was wondering why you were being so quiet," Olivia remarked dryly and Brooke just stuck her tongue out at her. "Mind you, I'm not sure how comfortable I am hearing that my head of HR is having trouble keeping employee information confidential," she teased and Brooke shook her head in a patiently exasperated manner as everyone laughed. She then whipped a bottle of Dom Perignon champagne from behind her on the sofa.

"I think this calls for a celebration," she declared and Olivia laughed as she went to fetch the glasses.

Olivia reappeared with a tray topped by Waterford crystal champagne flutes just as Brooke popped the cork. Ryan's hand shot out and caught the cork just before it knocked down all the flutes like they were bowling pins and Olivia glared at Brooke.

"That was a close one," Brooke said cheerfully, her enthusiasm undiminished by the close call. "You're a good guy to have around Ryan."

He and Olivia grinned. It was impossible to be annoyed with Brooke. Brooke quickly poured the champagne and offered a glass to everyone. She hesitated when she got to Nicole.

"How are you doing, are you up for a glass of champagne?" she asked solicitously and Nicole nodded.

"I've taken special nanites to aid the pregnancy and they are having a hard time cooperating with my existing systems, mainly because everything is still so new. The whole thing is making me nauseous, which is ironic because they're supposed to prevent morning sickness. On the positive side the effects should dissipate in a day or two. Meanwhile I'm hoping that a little alcohol will help speed the process of integration." She gratefully accepted a glass from Brooke. "Besides, I'm not going to let a little thing like nausea stop me from celebrating this moment."

"Here, here!" Mia cheered and everyone laughed.

"To Ryan and Nicole and their baby," Brooke said, raising her glass high, and everyone echoed her as the delicate tinkle of crystal rang through the room as they clinked their flutes.

"To the future," Ryan said firmly after that first sip as Nicole looked at him lovingly.

"To the future," she echoed softly and then everyone else chimed in.

"To the future!"

§§§